SAVAGE DAY

SAVAGE DAY

THOMAS WISEMAN

DELACORTE PRESS/NEW YORK

For my mother,
for my wife, Malou, and
for my son, Boris

Published by
Delacorte Press
1 Dag Hammarskjold Plaza
New York, N.Y. 10017

Manufactured in the United States of America
First printing

Designed by Jo Anne Bonnell

Library of Congress Cataloging in Publication Data

Wiseman, Thomas.
Savage day.

I. Title.
PR6073.I77S2   1981   823'.914   81-3273
    ISBN 0-440-09070-9   AACR2

AUTHOR'S NOTE

Because there are obvious historical counterparts for one or two of the characters in this book, it is not a mere formality to assert that this is a work of fiction. Because characters—in terms of their positions in the world, their roles in historical events, and even, perhaps, certain of their personal characteristics—sometimes may bear a resemblance to real-life personages does not mean that I intend to depict real people. I have used some of the mythology surrounding the historical figures, and some circumstantial detail, for the sake of fictional authenticity, and in order to make my story. But it is an imaginary story, even if at times it sticks close to certain known facts, and in the treatment of these facts I have permitted myself the usual author's license to embroider, to re-arrange events chronologically, to construct scientific theories that no scientist ever conceived, and to invent many, many things that did not occur at all.

T. W.

Had I been present at the creation,
I would have given some useful hints for
the better ordering of the universe.

Alfonso the Wise
(1221–1284)

The greatest minds are capable of
the greatest vices as well as of the
greatest virtues.

René Descartes

Discours de la méthode (1637)

ONE

A MATCH TO LIGHT THE SKY
NEW MEXICO,
JULY 1945

ONE

The first thing that struck Helen Bamberger about northern New Mexico was the sense of vast transparent space. She was told it was the dry air that created this deep clarity of vision. In the circular range of mountains that form a rim around the Valle Grande there were places from which you could see for a hundred miles. To the east lay the Sangre de Cristo mountains, and to the west and northwest the green Jemez hills. She learned that the area thus encircled was the site of a volcano ten million years ago, and these peaks and valleys, and long fingers of land reaching out like a hand, and weirdly sculptured rocks resembling human and animal shapes, were what was left when the earth finally had come to the end of its upheaval. She was suitably awed to be standing in the place where such primordial forces had spent themselves. All around was the detritus of that great convulsion—the entire basin was an extinct volcano. The ground on which she stood, the canyons and the cliffs, were volcanic ash, soft and easy to dig into, which was why the mountains were so full of caves. You could dig them out with a spoon, they said. Through the caldera, the saucerlike depression left by the exploding volcano, ran the Rio Grande. When there were storms above the mesas to the north where the soil is red, the river here, they told her, became as spectacularly red as the Sangre de Cristo mountains at sunset. It was very dramatic country.

As soon as one got away from the river valley, the earth became too dry for cultivation, was largely desert sparsely covered with low-growing scrub and cacti. This bare reddish-brown landscape seemed to go on forever. The deep cracks that you saw were arroyos. They became turbulent streams when there were storms and then dried up again. And those steaming holes in the ground were fumaroles—those vapors came from the inside of the earth. She was from New York, a city girl, had never been to New Mexico before and knew none of this. They told her all these things.

Above the valleys, the force of the constantly draining water flowing eastward had over the ages cut innumerable deep canyons out of the mountains in the form of a gigantic comb; the teeth of this comb were steep-sided mesas of varying width, some a mile or two wide, some less. They were densely covered with piñons and junipers and all kinds of scrub on their lower slopes, and on the upper levels with ponderosa pine, fir, spruce, oak, and aspen. The tall aspens were most striking in the fall, when they were a brilliant yellow and their leaves trembled in the slightest breeze.

It was to one of these mesas that Helen Bamberger had come in the early spring of 1943, a hidden, desolate, beautiful spot. David, her husband, was setting up a scientific research establishment there. It was just a few log buildings on a hill, with shacklike laboratories strung around and some extra government housing, the entire enclosure surrounded by high wire fences, patrolled and guarded, and everything painted green so it would disappear into the surrounding hills. Going up there for the first time, it had seemed to her like the edge of the world.

She mustn't ask questions, David had told her, mustn't mind the strangeness, the discomfort, the isolation, the limitations on her freedom of movement, the other irksome security regulations, or the break with the life she had known, because the project that he was getting under way was something that would win the war.

That was almost two and a half years ago, and now she was waiting in the dark for this fearful thing to happen. Though it was going to happen two hundred miles away, it would be seen from the vantage point of Sawyer Hill, they had hinted. Which was why she was here now in this unexpected rain, getting drenched.

4

She did not dare move in case she missed the Big Event. Until tonight it had been almost unbearably hot, and now this downpour! She could see some of the other wives, but they did not talk to each other. Nobody was supposed to know anything.

Helen Bamberger had a taste of fear in her mouth: a clean, harsh taste, not like ordinary fear; this was more like the sort of fear that, she imagined, must accompany the greatest discoveries and the greatest crimes. She wondered how David was feeling at this moment, now that it was about to happen. He'd be calm, she thought; oh yes, very, very calm, as always. But that did not answer the question about how he would be feeling. The answer was she didn't know. Did she know how he really felt about anything? Including her.

General Brown's group had arrived at Trinity base camp late on the fifteenth. The general was a dapper, bulky man, heavily jowled, smoothly moustached. He could be cajoling or bristly by turn. He had a full head of hair, with some white in it, though not much, and his nose was straight and his eyes were clear, and if you took away the excess poundage you could see the handsome college student, his clean-cut lines preserved in the aspic of a solid, if so far hardly action-packed, military career.

Back in '42 he had been pining for combat duty abroad when he was given what at first looked like another Washington desk job, a building project that presumably had come his way because, as deputy chief of construction of the Army Corps of Engineers, he was highly experienced in building camps, airfields, ordnance and chemical manufacturing plants, depots, port facilities. But the new job proved to be different from anything he had done before.

Upon arrival at Trinity he noted the swirling excitement at the base and decided he did not like it. It was, to him, suggestive of undisciplined modes of conduct. He went at once to find the controller, Bamberger. This entailed a certain amount of running around, since the controller was in the habit of being everywhere at once, and nobody seemed to quite know where he was right now. Such ubiquity did not accord with the general's way of doing

5

things. He believed that the man in charge should stay in one spot and let others come to him. Finally found, Bamberger came out of one of the huts, smiling woefully, in a manner that Brown associated with the Hebrew temperament, which, it seemed to him, could never allow a man to be truly happy when things were going well—for if things were going well, were they not bound to get worse? Jews, in the general's experience, were at their best in disasters, from which (by virtue of their historical experience) they could usually salvage *something*. But there was an aspect of their nature that made them pull back from triumph, question it, dissect it, turn it inside out. They had a way of making it taste bitter. General Brown had no time for such perverseness. He was, he prided himself, a straightforward, normal man; and like all straightforward, normal men, he wanted to win. He knew who he was and had no inclination to identify with those on the other side. Whereas Bamberger . . . There were things about Bamberger that troubled the general. But the general had a fatal weakness for the best man, and Bamberger *was* the best. No question. So now Brown saw his task as being to shield the controller from the excessive excitement building up around him.

"Everything seems in good shape," he said encouragingly.

Bamberger shook his head. "Trouble," he said. "Big trouble." And he raised his eyes upwards in what Brown at first took to be a remonstration to the Almighty, but then perceived was merely a reference to the rain, the light drizzle that was dampening their faces. "This rain is going to fuck us up, General," Bamberger said gloomily.

"Doctor, I have total confidence in your ability to solve any problem that might arise."

"Well, that's good to know," Bamberger said. "Unfortunately— though we are sometimes accused of playing God—we have not yet licked the problem of how to control the weather."

"Never mind about the weather," Brown counseled. "Let me worry about that side."

"Well, if you say so, General. Let's get going, then—you'll want to have a look around. Show you some things." And he was off, in that way he had of almost seeming to run when he was

6

walking, and looking over his shoulder—another characteristic posture of his—to see where the hell everybody was. The general was already two or three steps behind. As the controller led the way from one hut to another, pointing to this and that, giving a rapid rundown on everything that was going on, he seemed to be like a kind of modern-art mobile: never still, always turning and twisting and spinning. The most sophisticated of these constructions sometimes separate into parts that then spin off in different directions, and Bamberger displayed a versatility of this order as he coped with everybody's problems at once. When the mobile was made to stay still briefly, there was a sense of force about that, too; the suspended animation was willed and controlled . . . he was driving, not being driven, and could stop as well as spin. The exigencies of a situation did not dominate him; he held the reins firmly in his own hands, called every move. The pace was chosen, not imposed, and could be varied at any time. Suddenly he would slow down and have time for some absolute inconsequentiality . . . the words coming out deliberately unhurried, the gestures as rounded and full as if he were strolling in the quadrangles of Yale. He seemed to be saying: This is the way I do things, with style. He was a man who drove cars fast, too fast sometimes on wet roads, but he was a good driver and could control the skids. It was even suggested that he enjoyed the skids for the opportunity they gave him to demonstrate his control over them.

Tall and very thin and tightly built, with a nose like the beak of an exotic bird, and a curiously high-perched head, lightly carried, he had the kind of tautly constructed lightness that suggested something made to take to the air.

"I hope I'm not rushing you, General," he said, with sudden polite concern, over his shoulder.

"No, no," Brown said, trying to breathe less hard. "Very instructive. Now this here, Doctor?"

"Earth shock readings."

"And this?"

"It's to help us work out the interval between the firing of the detonators and the reception of the first gamma rays."

"Right."

7

"Bill here is going to be observing the effect of radiant heat. We expect some cases of spontaneous ignition at considerable distances from the explosion. Dry rotted wood bursting into flame, that sort of thing."

Brown nodded and, stooping slightly, followed Bamberger through a low doorway and into another hut.

"Have a look at these, General. We're using lots of different cameras. Going to have some running at ordinary speed, some at very fast speeds—up around eight thousand frames a second, to catch the beginning of the blast wave."

When they were out in the open again and heading for the next hut, Brown caught Bamberger's arm and halted him.

"How ready are you to go, Doctor?"

"We've got the gadget up at the top of a hundred-foot tower, ten miles from here. Detonators are connected to a dummy, to enable us to go on making tests right up till the last moment. From a technical standpoint, we just have got to connect up, turn on the taps, and we're ready to go."

"Sounds good."

"We're getting wet, General. Step in here with me and we'll get Joe Kersh to tell you about the snag."

"What snag?"

"The rain." They looked up together, taking the rain fully on their faces. "It's getting worse," Bamberger said. "For two months not a drop. And now it's a regular downpour. Let's go talk to Joe— he's gone into this whole problem."

Inside, he beckoned to Kersh. "Joe, got a moment? Tell the general our problem."

"The problem is fallout," Kersh said.

"Yes?"

"The explosion is going to suck up a lot of material from the ground and from the tower, and this material is going to be radio-active and in varying degrees dangerous to life."

"We have calculations on that, haven't we?" Brown asked.

"Yes, we have. But I have been looking into this aspect in more detail, and the fact is that rain will bring down the fallout in a concentrated form over a small area. Under optimal weather conditions we would expect the fallout to be widely distributed, and its harmfulness greatly dissipated. But rain alters the whole picture."

"What do you propose?"

"I would be in favor of postponing the test twenty-four hours, in the hope that the weather improves."

A soldier in lieutenant's uniform put his head in at the door and, spotting Bamberger, said, "Ah, there you are, Doctor. Been looking for you, sir. Air Force at Alamogordo been on the line. Say observation planes won't be able to take off if this weather continues."

"Okay, noted," Bamberger said.

Brown was looking around. He saw a man at a telephone board asleep in a sitting-up position. "Major!" he barked, and the abruptly awakened major blinked open his eyes. "How much sleep have you had recently, Major?"

"None of us have had too much," Bamberger said, "and Major Douglas in particular."

"I don't hold with men getting themselves so exhausted they can't function," Brown said. "Major, I'm ordering you to get a couple of hours' sleep. We'll get somebody to deputize for you. Captain Fredericks, see to that."

"Yes, sir."

"My fault, General," Bamberger said. "I've been pushing everybody to their limits."

"I can see that. How much rest have you had, Doctor?"

Bamberger grinned. "I'm like the heart," he said. "I rest between beats."

"Is that so? Well . . ."

The phone rang, and immediately, reflexively, Bamberger reached for it. As he did so, he closed his eyes by way of illustrating his method of resting. He listened intently, then opened one eye and said, "Me too. I'm sick of antelope steak, too. How about eggs? We have eggs? . . . Yeah, yeah. . . . Well, that's my conclusion, if you want to know. Eggs and hash." When he had put down the phone, Brown asked:

"Is it necessary for you to concern yourself with the menu?"

9

Bamberger shook his head reflectively.

"We must have slaughtered a herd of antelope. The guys go hunting them with submachine guns. Doesn't seem exactly sporting." The phone rang again, and again Bamberger's hand shot out.

"Might be an idea," Brown said, "to let somebody else deal with some of these calls. Take some of the unnecessary pressure off you, Doctor."

Bamberger considered the advice, but picked up the phone nonetheless, with an apologetic little grimace, as if to say, I can't help it, I'm hooked on this stuff.

"Yuh?" he shouted down the field telephone. "What? Lightning? There's lightning around the gadget? . . . Well, I can assure you, Lieutenant, there is no danger. No danger from lightning. The detonators are not connected and even a direct strike would not set off the gadget." He put down the phone and said in an undertone, "Anyway, that's our theory, and around here we do not admit the possibility of error—right, General?"

Over the next half hour, as he watched Bamberger in action, Brown came to the conclusion that the controller was too keyed up, too high on his own adrenaline, to be brought down safely. He would have to be allowed to go on flying high. He seemed almost to derive a kind of perverse satisfaction from the sheer weight of trouble falling on him, as if engaged in some competitive sporting event in which he was going to show he could take more than anybody else. There was a perpetual bustle around him wherever he went. Advice was offered, or demanded. Dire warnings were sounded. Overoptimistic claims were made. He kept smiling and moving, taking the strain, resting between heartbeats, or in odd moments of temporary lull when, whether seated or standing up, his eyes would close for a few moments of profound repose. His breathing became deep and gentle, and he seemed to almost go into a spell of meditation, right there in the thick of everything.

Brown had to admit that the controller had a lot of style, the way he coped with everything, never getting fazed, never letting the pressure show. His easy, almost offhand manner had a very calming effect as he went around with his constantly refilled coffee mug.

The next time the phone rang the general reached for it first and said, "Dr. Bamberger is not here. I'll pass you to one of his aides." He beckoned to a man at the next desk to deal with the call, and took Bamberger by the arm and led him outside.

The rain had let up very slightly. It was blustery and misty out. After the smoky atmosphere inside the hut, the freshness was reviving. Bamberger raised his face up like somebody taking a shower.

"I'm all yours, General."

"As a matter of interest, what made you use the code name Trinity for this place?"

"That what you wanted to talk to me about?"

"It's sort of blasphemous, wouldn't you say?"

"It seemed appropriate," Bamberger said, vaguely.

Brown accepted the explanation and looked at his watch.

"I'm opposed to a twenty-four-hour postponement," he said. "The men are exhausted, but they're keyed up to go, and that will carry them through the next few hours. But not twenty-four. If we postpone for twenty-four hours we have to postpone for longer, to give everybody a chance to rest. And that includes you, Doctor. Also, a postponement of that length of time increases our exposure to mishap. Sabotage, security breach, technical failure."

"Mishap," Bamberger said, smiling strangely.

"Why do you smile, Doctor? Why does the prospect of a mishap make you smile?"

Bamberger shook his head, indicating he was not inclined to go into that.

"One might almost get the notion," Brown said, "that a mishap would not be unwelcome to you."

"All I can say to you, General, is that if the Almighty does not want this thing to happen, he'd better speak up fast."

The general's jaw set into a rigid line. "Let's aim to go as planned."

"It's not in our hands, General," Bamberger said, looking up. "Depends on the weather."

11

Brown thought for a moment, and then said, "Okay, put it back a couple of hours." He looked at his watch. "Let's see what the weather is like at four forty-five."

"All right, General."

"I suggest you get some sleep. That's what I'm going to do."

"Good idea, General. Sweet dreams!"

After walking the general to his tent, Bamberger jumped into a jeep and drove out to S-10000, the control bunker.

It was a structure of heavy wooden beams and reinforced concrete, covered by deep layers of earth. A trelliswork of overhead wires streamed out from communications masts.

Ten thousand yards away, the gadget hung from the top of a hundred-foot tower. It was not lit up at this time and could not be seen.

As he came in, Bamberger immediately became aware of a commotion, and it did not surprise him to discover that Leo Hepler was at the center of it. Hepler had a tendency to create turbulences around himself. Dormant differences flared up when he arrived on the scene, situations threatened to get out of control, passions boiled over, tempers were lost. That was the effect he had on people. The excitable theoretician had a fatal capacity for exciting others to the extent that even the calmest sometimes lost their cool. And just as they were losing their tempers, he, with wicked one-upmanship, would regain his—thereby putting them in the wrong.

Bamberger saw that this was the present stage. Everybody looked annoyed except Hepler. Hepler was looking innocent.

"You've been making trouble, Leo," Bamberger said knowingly. "I can see it from your expression."

"*Me?*" Hepler said, mock-affronted.

"Yes, *you*, Leo. You're not supposed to be here. You're supposed to be at base camp explaining everything to the military in simple language."

"Simple language is what I leave to you, Bambi. You are so good at it. I do not have your gift for politics."

"For once you are too modest, Leo. I've seen you operate. I've seen you in Washington. Oh boy! Nobody can teach you anything

12

about handling those guys." He gave Hepler a little backhanded salute.

"Except, of course, you, Bambi. Don't forget, I have also seen you operate. Oh boy! You can say that again." He returned the mocking salute twice.

Bamberger went ahead with his quiet, easy consultations that an outsider might have taken for casual chat, all the time aware of Hepler's challenging presence, and of unresolved conflict. While he made his checks, he was deciding how to handle Hepler.

Handling men was something Bamberger was good at—he had a knack of inspiring loyalty and almost fanatical devotion even in the most difficult men. But Hepler was something else. Probably nobody but Bamberger could have handled him; many others wouldn't have tried. Sometimes he'd say to Hepler, "Tell me why I put up with a little shit like you, Leo?" And Hepler would reply, "Because where else are you going to find a little shit like me to do your sums and get them right?"

It was true. He was good; he was better than that—he had a most exceptional mind. Everybody else went around with slide rules, but he didn't need slide rules: He could do it all in his head. He was fond of showing off his remarkable abilities, always challenging people. How to place eight queens on a chessboard so they could not take each other? He did not need a chessboard to work it out. He could picture it and hold the picture in his head until the problem was solved. He had ferocious concentration.

"It is true we are postponing?" he now demanded, dangerously, and Bamberger realized what the tension in the room was about.

"We are waiting for the weather forecasts."

"I say fuck the weather forecasts, I say—"

"And fuck the fallout question, huh?"

"There is no danger, I have done the calculations. The risk factor is well within the parameters of acceptability."

"Whose parameters? Whose acceptability?" Bamberger queried lightly. "Yours, Leo?"

"Don't be such a nervous old hen, Bambi." Hepler began to rap the table and to become excited. "We didn't come this far to be put out by a little rain. You have no right, Bambi—"

13

"Take it easy, Leo," one of the other scientists suggested.

"Who you telling to take it easy? Don't tell me to take it easy. I will take it any way I like."

"We can all hear you," somebody else said. "You don't have to shout, Leo."

"If I want to shout I will shout. Who is this son-of-a-bitch college kid to tell me I mustn't shout?"

"Cool it, Leo," Bamberger said. "Everybody's under pressure."

"It is your pussyfooting around with postponements that is creating the pressure," Hepler continued to shout. "I tell you, Bambi, I dissociate myself from any such decision."

"Okay, I've noted your vote," Bamberger said quietly. But Hepler was not to be so readily appeased.

"Furthermore . . ." he began, "don't brush me off with your smoothy talk, Bambi . . . I warn you."

The phone rang, and Bamberger reached for it as a means of getting a moment's respite. He spun out the call long enough to let Hepler calm down a bit, but not so long that he would become furious at being kept waiting. It was a fine judgment to make. When Bamberger put the phone down, he said, "Looks like the weather is getting better. We may be able to go ahead as planned."

"When will you know this?"

"Soon, Leo."

"Soon? What does that mean?"

"Leo," Bamberger said very softly, "I know it's sort of out of character for you, but be a good guy for once and get out of my hair. My kid gloves are wearing thin."

"I would like to see it," Hepler said, his eyes glinting.

"Not today, baby," Bamberger said, smiling. "But one day."

The five men of the arming party sat in two covered jeeps in the dark, in the pouring rain, waiting. Occasionally, almost as a kind of nervous reflex, one or another of them turned his flashlight on the bomb tower, just to make sure nobody was interfering with the gadget. It had been hoisted to the top of the tower only a few hours earlier, and now it hung there in the dark, a round fat object inside a steel container. They'd called it the Fat Man.

14

Dr. Stanley Jones, peering through the rain, followed the beam of his flashlight as it mounted the high scaffolding. Made him think of a guillotine, with that thing hanging at the top. The rain was coming down hard. Didn't look as though it was going to let up. Were they going to have to postpone? If rainwater got into the electrical circuitry . . . if something short-circuited. Jones put such thoughts out of his mind. He had that ability.

He was a rather boyish-looking Englishman, lanky, with fair hair and a pleasant face. Easy to get on with, it was said. Not prone to panics. That was why he had been chosen for the ticklish job of heading the arming party. When the word was given, he was going to have to turn on the taps to make the bomb live. After that, the countdown would begin.

Brennan said, "Give you a penny for 'em, Jonesy."

"Oh . . . I was thinking of Joe Minerva's bar in San Antonio."

"Yuh, wouldn't mind a little nip of something myself."

"All those rows and rows of bottles," Jones said wistfully. "When this lot goes off, there won't be one of those bottles left. What a waste of good booze! Breaks my heart. I almost think we ought to risk the security breach and warn Joe."

On Compagna Hill, twenty miles from ground zero, the man known as Mr. Steele was standing alone, a green loden coat draped around his shoulders, a broad-brimmed black hat on his head. He looked rather like an old cardinal, with his long, lean face and high, noble brow and tight, ascetic mouth. A gray kind of luminosity came from him. Everybody referred to him as "the old man." He seemed to belong to an older generation. When his name—his real name—was mentioned, people linked it automatically with Max Born and Rutherford and Niels Bohr and Einstein. It was usually forgotten how young he had been when he first came into contact with these men.

Bill Stevens of *The New York Times* came up to Mr. Steele and introduced himself.

"Really!" the man called Mr. Steele said. "That is really who you are? How careless of Colonel Delacy to have a real science reporter, and such a well-known one, reporting upon our manifestation. Well, so you are privy to all our secrets. . . . Such devotion on the part of the United States government to the principle of public relations! However, I presume your story will not be appearing in tomorrow's edition."

"There is naturally a time embargo on anything I write. I wanted to ask you, sir—what goes through your mind at this moment? Could be said that this, today, is your baby."

"My baby? Hardly. I did no more than contribute to the background music while conception was taking place."

Stevens chuckled. "Both Dr. Bamberger and Dr. Hepler were your pupils."

"That is true. But you know, I also had a pupil called Zander, and he became an SS general—so you see, one must not be too quick to take credit for one's pupils."

Allison Dubinski was sitting by the window of her Sundt apartment. She checked the time. It should have happened by now. She looked up at the sky. Still raining. Must be the rain that was holding things up. She lit a Chesterfield as she walked up and down; by the open door of her son's bedroom she stopped and looked at his sleeping form. A night light cast a soft glow over his features. She listened carefully to his breathing, alert for any harshness, any wheezing. He had been such a healthy, happy boy. But since his father's death, one year ago, he sometimes got asthmatic attacks. Woke up during the night not able to breathe. The doctor said not to make too much fuss, distressing though it was to see. It was a nervous form of asthma, and it was important not to give him the impression that he was delicate or abnormal. With luck, he would get over the asthma when he got over his father's death.

Benjie had always been such a lively, outgoing boy before, but now he was often very quiet, locked deep inside himself. Wouldn't let himself be drawn out. Wouldn't say what he was thinking about.

Asleep, his face had that trustfulness that she had always found so touching about him. He had always been such a trusting child . . . which must have had to do with the way Jake had always

16

been so open with him, answering all his questions without evasion. But nowadays Benjie's waking expression was often one of suspicion.

This suspiciousness began after they told him his father had died as a result of an accident in the laboratory. From burns. Only his left hand had been burned, and the day it happened he was sitting up in bed looking quite well, joking. Twenty-six days later he died. Of a burned hand. Benjie knew that they were lying to him.

There were tears in Dr. Bamberger's eyes when he told Benjie about his father's death. Benjie knew that Dr. Bamberger and his father were close friends—but all the same, Dr. Bamberger was not telling the truth. People didn't die of a burned hand. They were hiding something from him—they had something to do with his father's death, and they were all covering up for each other, like one doctor hiding another doctor's mistake.

Allison wondered what Benjie would think when he finally found out exactly what had happened. In a few weeks he would know. She could not predict his reaction. Children were such moralists. Benjie often expressed his disapproval of her attempts to exterminate the insect population that sought to share their modest living space. What harm did ants do anyone? It was cruel to murder them. How would you like it if you were an ant? Maybe to God that was what we were: ants.

Very soon he was going to find out what his father had been working on when he died. He had always regarded his father as such a wonderful man. She wondered if he would still think so when he knew. . . . The child with his big, solemn, and so-hurtable eyes was like conscience itself; you couldn't slip anything past him.

Suddenly she was feeling weak and had to sit down. She felt the tears well up in her. Oh, Jake, she said to herself—oh, Jake, why aren't you here to explain it to your little boy, to explain why it had to be done, this terrible thing? You were always so good at explaining things to him, Jake. You would have been able to make him understand. I'm afraid I may not be able to, and that one day he'll condemn us for what we've done.

She was glad she was not outside with the other wives. All day

17

long she had felt the excitement building up. They were hysterical with anticipation, some of them. Not Helen—she was calm and controlled, as always. But some of the others. Though they were not supposed to know, they had put together bits and pieces of information, and they had a pretty good idea. But they did not really know; they did not know what Allison knew.

The other wives waiting on Sawyer Hill could not tell if Helen Bamberger was hiding something. You never could tell with Helen; she was always a little remote, a little distant—which presumably the controller's wife to some extent had to be, though some people said, controller's wife, baloney!—she was just stuck-up, superior, that's what it was. No, no, her defenders said; she was shy and probably obliged—by all those damned security rules—to be very careful about what she said. Probably she was lonely, and not permitted in her position to get too close to anyone. She could not allow herself the luxury of a heart-to-heart. (Even if Dr. Bamberger did keep strictly to the rules and told her nothing, she must have overheard plenty, and over two and a half years put two and two together. Several times over.)

So there were very mixed feelings about Helen. Some of the wives detested her, others said she was all right when you got to know her, as long as you could accept her as she was and did not ask of her what evidently she could not do: to let you into her confidence. The men mostly liked her, which was not surprising: She was a beautiful woman, in her mid-thirties, with natural honey-blond hair, a definite asset in that era of the blonde. She often seemed immersed in herself, and the sensual mouth, and a certain heaviness of the eyes, led some of the men to conclude that the thoughts that so occupied her must be of an erotic nature. Before coming to Los Alamos she had been a journalist, contributing to literary journals and political reviews articles of quite intimidating cleverness. But it was impossible for her to keep up this work from Los Alamos, since nobody was supposed to know where she was. She and Bamberger had simply disappeared, as far as anyone "outside" knew.

18

This was the climax, now, that everything had been building up to since the first day. She remembered what it was like then. This strange new place, so far away from everywhere, so alien: part boom town, part prison. She had felt imprisoned not only because of being cut off from friends and colleagues, and by the onerous restrictions imposed upon her, but just physically. The place felt like a prison. Oh, there were jukeboxes in the PX, and movies most nights, and a theatrical society and an anthropological society, and all sorts of social activities; but still, when you looked out, it was through high wire fences topped with barbed wire. There were guarded gates where you had to be checked in and out, and there were watchtowers, and at night the perimeter of the Technical Area was illumined by fifteen-hundred-watt floodlamps. Whenever you went outside the compound all chance meetings had to be reported to the Security Office and explained. You were not allowed to meet friends, unless you had been given permission. You were not allowed to make journeys, except under very special circumstances, and then only accompanied by a bodyguard, who, to Helen, was no different from a jailer. Your real name was a secret you were required not to divulge. You had to put up with the high altitude, the same faces day in, day out, the same food, the boredom.

The town that had sprung up had a ramshackle, temporary air—as if nobody expected it, or required it, to last very long. One building was put up in one place, and then another was stuck onto it (with a communicating first-storey covered bridge) as an afterthought. There was a five-bed hospital; when more beds were needed, the original single straight-line structure became an H structure. Whenever more accommodation was needed (and more accommodation was always needed), the Army added another of its expansible government caravans to the vast unsightly sprawl on the western outskirts of the compound.

She was one of the handful of privileged people who lived in the area they'd dubbed Bathtub Row because the houses there had bathtubs, whereas the newly put-up apartments had only showers. Her house was probably the best house in the whole of Los Alamos, a handsome, spacious log cabin that was part of the original

19

ranch school complex taken over by the government. But even living in this better area around Ashley Pond, where most of the laboratories were, too, you walked along unpaved roads that were always deep in mire summer and winter. In summer the rain dissolved the loose topsoil and produced a thick, gluey mud that adhered to the soles of your shoes, making your feet bloated and heavy. In winter soot belched from the forest of metal chimneys and turned the snow into black slush. McKeeville and Morganville, two of the less salubrious subsections, were full of low, dark doghouses called Pacific hutments; here lived the lower-grade technicians—their wives were always standing around with curlers under their turbans, and their trousers dragging in the mud, gossiping under the laundry lines.

Everywhere children played freely in the streets. It was a very protected community. Spies or saboteurs would have a job getting in, the way everybody was screened so thoroughly, including the cleaning women; and anyone not cleared by the intelligence section of the Security Office could come into the compound only under armed escort.

There was no need for the houses to have locks in such a protected community.

Helen Bamberger was glad it was all coming to an end now—this phase of her life. Whatever happened, if the gadget, as they called it, worked or didn't, it would all be over. David had promised her that.

———

At 4:05 the rain stopped.

Everybody sat tight waiting for the weather forecast. While it was coming through, Bamberger was on a hookup with his principal advisers.

"Winds aloft very light, variable to forty thousand surface calm . . ."

Even before the end, the import was clear.

"Well?" he asked formally. The "go" votes came in fast. "Okay, go," he announced. He got Jones on the radio telephone. "Jonesy, old boy, old son, get your finger out and let's go."

20

"Just when I was having a quiet little nap," Jones said, already on his feet. He made sure he had his checklist. "Sanders," he said, "I'm going to call out each move before I make it. In case anything goes sour, they'll know what not to do next time. You relay each step back to control, and give me the signal that it's been received and understood." Sanders appeared to have gone a bit green. "There's no danger," Jones said. "Just being extra careful."

Each man in the arming party had his task to perform. Jones had chosen for himself the job of climbing to the top of the tower and switching the detonating circuit from the dummy to the gadget. In the course of the hundred-foot climb his shoes once or twice slipped on the wet iron rungs of the ladder. When he got to the top, he seated himself under the dark belly of the Fat Man and lit a Craven "A." He couldn't stand the American fags. Filthy things. After a couple of puffs, he called down, "Righteeo, then. Just about to turn on the tap. If the bathwater runs over you'll know it's the third little bugger from the left, otherwise known as P3 . . . got that?" He saw Sanders speak into the telephone, and then give a sign. "Starting to switch on now," Jones called out and pressed P3. "Well, we're still here," he sang down. "So far so good." He got out his checklist. There were forty-seven items on it. They all had to be run through to make sure everything was functioning. He started to work down the list, announcing each move before he made it. He worked away concentratedly for fifteen minutes in this way. One more connection to be made. Squatting on an iron crossbar, he shone the flashlight over the round, darkly glinting object. "Up the Arsenal," he murmured, tossing away his cigarette end; he called out the last number and made the final connection. Then he scrambled down the ladder like a fireman called to a fire.

When he hit the ground, the others were already in the jeeps, engines running. He switched on the marker lights for the observation planes and the floodlights for the cameras, turning the bomb tower into a blazing beacon, and then he got into the jeep and Sanders put his foot down hard; showers of wet sand rose from the churning car wheels as they roared off.

"Hey, hey!" Jones cried. "Take it easy! What's the hurry? Twenty-five-miles-per-hour speed limit around here. Didn't you know?"

On Sawyer Hill Pam Jones was walking about stamping her feet. She was tired and cold and wet—bloody boots let in water. Shoddy American goods! What on earth was she doing here? Waiting for the Big Bang, like this was some kind of show. She wished she were back in England. Stan didn't seem to miss England, but she did. Her life was there. But he liked America. He was like all the Americans, gadget mad. The bang was late, and she was worried that something had gone wrong. She didn't know exactly what Stan's job was—something to do with turning on a tap, he had said. Suddenly she was afraid. A cold, tight hand was closing around her heart, and she thought, Oh my God, something terrible is going to happen, I know it; and a little panic flared up in her as she thought of her two children, Tony and Sarah.

At three minutes before zero, Leo Hepler, his face white with a kind of swooning voluptuousness, said to Bamberger:

"Nervous, Bambi?"

"Not a bit," Bamberger said, lifting a hand and making it shake. He took a look round. Everybody was pale and tense. Scarcely breathing, some of them. Fielder was swaying on his feet. Weissberger was holding on to something. General Childs looked like a man about to go over the top. Only Jones was unaffected. He was manning the stop switch that would have to be used to override the automatic timer if anything went wrong during the final forty-five seconds of countdown. His usual rosycheeked self. Thank God for Jones! Nothing seemed to shake him. But the others . . .

"Okay, you guys, place your bets," Bamberger called out. "I say it's gonna be a boy. And I say it's gonna ignite the atmosphere and blow up the world. Or maybe just New Mexico. Okay, what am I given?"

Hepler chirped up. "I back my calculations. A month's salary against ten bucks."

"You're on, Leo."

Suddenly half a dozen people in the room were calling out their

22

bets for or against the proposition that the world was going to be blown up in just under three minutes' time, or maybe just New Mexico.

"It's gonna be a boy and he's gonna weigh a hundred tons."

"Ten thousand."

"Fifty thousand."

"I bet it's a fart."

"*Rien ne va plus,*" Bamberger called out as the countdown went over to automatic.

The last seconds seemed to last forever. Bamberger was glad to see that most of the men looked better now. The gruesome betting had taken the edge off the tension, bringing the unspoken fears into the open.

Big Greg McClure sat by a field telephone next to the emergency exit of the control bunker. In addition to being Bamberger's bodyguard, he was head of personnel protection at Los Alamos. In the event of an emergency, it was his job to make sure that certain key people survived—the ones who were indispensable to the continuation of the project. McClure had the life raft list in his head.

Now he checked his gun and, sitting up very straight against the damp-feeling concrete wall, crossed himself inconspicuously.

Pam Jones was getting palpitations. It was all that waiting. Something had made her anxious. What she wouldn't give to be back in England, with a general election coming up, and a good chance of Labour getting in. She was missing her chance of a parliamentary seat because of being here with Stan. In this godforsaken place. Bloody America! Land of Coca-Cola and Betty Grable—oh God! She didn't want her children brought up in a country where everybody was gadget mad and money mad. It had affected Stan. There was some gadget in which he had a patent with four others. They stood to make two million dollars each, he said. That was why he wanted to stay on. But she wanted to go home. She had an awful feeling that if they didn't leave, something terrible was going to happen.

Jones, cigarette dangling from lip, was peering through a haze of smoke at the instruments that would indicate malfunction, his thumb poised over the red stop button. He was smiling to himself.

At zero minus eight seconds a sudden silence came over the room. It was so total, after the hubbub, that people thought that their heartbeats could be heard.

Bamberger said softly to Hepler, "Now I'm nervous."

"No need to be nervous, Bambi," the theoretician muttered through tightly clenched teeth. "I've worked it all out, and am I ever wrong?"

Lips were seen to move in prayer. On Compagna Hill the man known as Mr. Steele carefully finished spreading suntan oil over his face and lay face down on the ground, the last to do so, feet toward ground zero. General Brown, also face down, was thinking, What if it doesn't go off? What a fool I'll look!

At Potsdam President Harry S Truman turned to his secretary of war, Henry Stimson, and said, "Still no word?" and Stimson shook his head. The Jones children did not stir in their bunk bed, Sarah on the lower, Tony on the upper. Pam Jones, on Sawyer Hill, bit her lip, drawing blood, as the sudden vivid ghastly premonition flooded through her mind. Allison was thinking about her dead husband, Jake, and keeping his face before her. Helen Bamberger thought, It will end the war; it'll all be over. We'll be able to go home.

At minus one Jones called out, "Happy New Year!" and then the voice on the Tannoy said: "Now!"

To the wives on Sawyer Hill the light came with startling suddenness after the long wait. Helen Bamberger felt terror; it was no ordinary terror . . . it was a sense of having tampered with the basic order of the universe, and she had a vision of this fire in the sky going round and round the earth and never stopping. She saw the trees leap out of the darkness and become starkly, individually, defined, and she saw the other wives all looking up at the sky, which was lit by a light like no light any of them had ever seen. (It was so brilliant that two hundred miles from its source a blind girl demanded what the strange brightness was.)

In the control bunker Bamberger leapt to his feet, yelling "It's

24

a boy!" and ran out into the open, looking away from the flash. He saw the mountains lit up as in a vivid dream, every contour, every crevasse, etched sharp . . . a picture of overwhelming detail. He saw others, Hepler among them, follow him out and felt a sensation of heat on all the exposed parts of his body, as if he were standing under a very strong midday sun. A second later he turned to look toward the explosion, using the welder's goggles they had all been given to protect their eyes. He was pushing all feelings to one side, and concentrating on making precise mental notes. This was not a moment for triumph or foreboding, but for scientific observation. He noted a roughly spherical, highly luminous conglomeration of flames that he decided must be about twenty or thirty times brighter than the brightest sun at noon. These flames were swelling out into a great ball of fire, engulfing the surrounding air. He calculated that the fireball was rising at a rate of two thousand to three thousand feet per second. The silence—there was no sound yet—and the intense light, which made everybody look like a ghost, created a sense of time having been stopped. It went on for nearly forty seconds, this strange hiatus, during which everybody appeared to have become petrified; and then the air blast hit. It blew out Hepler's disorderly mass of hair as he stood with arms rigidly extended, like some kind of scarecrow; his fists opened, and scraps of paper fell out and were scattered by the shock of air. Then came the sound, which was as if the earth had been put in a nutcracker and cracked open.

The very intense white light, while it had seemed to go on for ages, actually had lasted only a couple of seconds and was over long before the blast hit or any sound was heard. Now the fast-growing fireball was becoming engorged with dust and sand and debris sucked up from the ground and climbing higher and higher into the sky, dragging its great black tail after it.

Shortly after the air blast hit, the fireball changed from brilliant white to dull purple, Bamberger noted. Continuing to rise, and at the same time spreading out, it broke through the clouds at fifteen thousand feet, and still it went up. Within a minute it was four miles high. By then, the elongated fireball had densened; become reddish brown, some said. Others said golden, violet, orange, gray, blue, mauve. Not everybody saw the same thing that day. But as a whitecap began to form over the long dark stalk and foamed and spread, everybody at the same time saw the resemblance to a mushroom.

"Well, I'll be damned," Bamberger said. "Well, I'll be damned." He kept repeating this over and over. Then he said, "I guess we're all sons of bitches now."

Hepler said, "Beautiful, beautiful . . ." A flush of sensuous exaltation brought the color back to his face. His wild hair flapped about in disheveled wings.

As the fireball slowly started to disperse, it left an unearthly violet-colored glow over the hills, suggesting some jiggery-pokery interference with nature. They were all outside the bunker now, watching the surging pillar of smoke and the whitecap spilling over like some poisonous cornucopia. For a while the dense smoke retained its mushroom shape—then, like writing in the sky, it began to fade and blur.

———

People outside the project who saw the light in the sky had no idea what it was. But it was of an intensity and awesomeness to make some pray. There were those who thought it signaled the Second Coming, and others that it presaged the end of the world.

In some areas of the Rio Grande Valley there was talk of a witches' sabbath, for the fireball is the traditional mode of transport of witches, and never had anyone seen such a big one. There must have been thousands of witches on the move, people concluded. One old man had seen a yucca plant suddenly burst into flame, which was witches' doing for sure, and someone else had felt a sensation of heat all over his body, followed by cold, a certain indication of the passing of witches.

———

On Sawyer Hill, as the light died out, Pam Jones told herself she had been getting very jumpy lately. All those morbid thoughts. Well, it was done now. The thing was done. She hurried home

26

to the children and found them sound asleep. The flash had not even waked them up.

But it had waked Benjie Dubinski; and seeing his expression of distress, Allison rushed to him, fearing he might be about to have an asthma attack.

"It's nothing, it's nothing," she reassured him. "Go back to sleep."

"There was a terrific flash of light," he said. "It woke me."

"You were dreaming," she said. "Or maybe it was a flash of lightning. Go back to sleep, sweetie pie. Go back to sleep, honey. It was nothing, nothing." And she showered kisses all over him and hugged him to her; her eyes had tears in them.

"Is it what Dad was working on when he—? The secret weapon?" Benjie asked.

"Go to sleep, baby, go to sleep," Allison urged. "It was nothing at all."

"Then why are you dressed, and all excited?" he asked. "Why are you shaking, Ma?"

"I couldn't go to sleep," she said. "It was so close and heavy. I wanted to get a breath of air. I just was going to see the sun come up."

He considered this explanation carefully, with his serious, pained eyes seeming to demand: Why does everybody tell me lies all the time? Why? Why?

"Go and have your walk, Ma," he told her. "Go see the sunrise. You don't have to watch over me. I'm all right."

———

On Compagna Hill, as the scientists and distinguished guests scrambled to their feet, there was a moment's applause, which tailed off abruptly amid sheepish expressions. The man called Mr. Steele was standing very still, watching the light die, and shaking his head slightly. He shivered and drew the loden coat more closely around himself.

"Surprisingly chilly," he said, to *The New York Times* science correspondent eagerly awaiting a quote.

The sun rose, and it was another day, and Bamberger told himself: Well, we're still here. It's happened, and the ground didn't open up. It's just a bigger bang, for Christ's sake. When dynamite was invented, they said that was going to blow up the world. The cannon was the ultimate weapon once. Now it was all over, and the brief elation had gone; he was feeling enormously tired—more tired than he had ever felt in his life. He felt squeezed empty, with all the juice of life sucked out of him. But there were things still to be done.

The sky was becoming lighter all the time; soon it would be day. The first day of the Fat Man.

He said to McClure, "I want to get back to base camp."

"Sure thing, Doctor."

"Coming back with me, Leo? Give you a lift," Bamberger offered.

"I accept," Hepler said. "I want to go out to ground zero as soon as possible. To get samples of the soil."

"When Entry Permission say it's safe to go, not before."

"Entry Permission can go fuck themselves. What do they know?"

"Leo," Bamberger said wearily, as they walked to the jeep, "have you got to buck every system?"

"It is because you make such boring systems."

"You'll wait, Leo," Bamberger said.

"I will wait until nine thirty," Hepler announced. "My calculations show that by then it will be perfectly safe to go in."

"All I can say, Leo, is it's fortunate they didn't commission us into the Army, or by now you would have been shot about seventeen times for insubordination."

"You are full of shit, Bambi. I am very reasonable. If the Army cooperates with me, I cooperate with the Army. Ask General Brown if I am not cooperative."

At exactly nine thirty, without bothering to check with Entry Permission, Hepler climbed aboard the lead-lined tank and commanded the crew to go to ground zero. There he opened a trap door and took samples of soil. He saw that an area of about four hundred yards in radius had become covered with a green glasslike surface where the sand had melted and then solidified again.

"Well, there's one thing can be said for Leo," Bamberger remarked. "He has faith in his own calculations."

"As I predicted," Hepler said when he got back. "Just as I predicted . . . I was right."

"Somebody remind me to buy that man a drink," Bamberger said. He gave a little exhausted giggle. "Or kill him."

As the morning wore on, many of the scientists began to leave base camp. They saw no reason to stay. By early afternoon General Brown had come to the conclusion that fallout did not constitute a problem, and he left, too. But Bamberger stayed on and between other tasks continued to check the radioactivity readings coming in.

In some areas there were isolated "hot spots" where the radioactivity was substantially higher than in the immediate surroundings. Must be due to special combinations of meteorological, atmospheric, and ground conditions, he concluded. It was disquieting. It meant that special conditions could lead to unpredictable fallout patterns. You were at the mercy of winds and air currents and barometric pressure and weather.

As he drank endless cups of coffee and studied the figures, he began to see, with the force of actuality that no theoretical prognosis could have spelled out in the same way, what was in store.

All the fallout would not settle in any one area. Some of it would be carried around the world. And with every single explosion of an atomic device there would be this worldwide fallout. The ultimate consequences were only dimly conceivable. The stuff would hang in the air like some sword of Damocles. It would be brought down by gravity, and rain and snow and hail. Prevailing wind patterns would carry it rapidly eastward, take it in a complete circuit of the globe. In four to seven weeks there would be hoops of it girdling the earth.

That was the dismal vision. His tiredness was making him see the blackest side. It probably was not going to be as bad as that, he told himself. His apprehensions were likely to be exaggerated at a time like this. He decided to go back to Los Alamos. He wanted to be with Helen. He wanted to get some sleep.

He called Greg McClure and said they were going. Stepping out of the hut and walking toward the car, the blood suddenly left his brain, like a camera shutter closing to a pinpoint. When he recovered consciousness, Greg was carrying him. He was like a baby in the big Secret Service man's arms.

"Just a little faint, Doctor," McClure said. He put him down on the car seat, took his pulse. "Pulse is back nice and strong now," he said.

"Yuh, I'm okay," Bamberger said. "Just tiredness, I guess. You better drive, Greg."

Greg grinned. It was very unusual for Bamberger to let anyone drive him. The chauffeur-bodyguard usually had to sit in the passenger seat next to the controller.

"Yes, I think I better drive this time, Doctor," Greg said, getting behind the wheel. "Take a shot of this, Doctor." He offered him a pewter hip flask.

Bamberger drank deeply—grateful for the quick infusion of energy that the brandy gave him. It steadied his mind, too—before, it had seemed to be floating away from him.

"Why don't you try to get some sleep, Doctor," Greg said, starting the car. "I'll drive the jalopy gentle as I can."

"I'll try," Bamberger promised. He took another long gulp of brandy from the flask. But he did not sleep. He stayed with his head pressed against the cool glass of the car window, looking out into the Jornada del Muerto. It had been given this name, which meant Journey of Death, because there was no human habitation for ninety miles around, and in the old days of the Spanish wagon trains anybody who got stuck there was just left to die. Now there was a new and better reason for the name.

He had eaten so little the past few days, and slept so little, that the brandy affected him strangely. It did not make him drunk, but it knocked out the part of his mind that was exhausted and near to some edge and rigid with the controls that he imposed upon himself. That part of his mind was blotted out by the brandy. But another part came to a sharp focus.

30

Ever since dawn the sky had been strangely colored. There was an amber stain spreading out from the horizon, which was not at all the color the sky ought to have been, and now he was seeing vague shapes moving through the distant dustiness, those ancient beasts, and the pale horse, and the one with many heads. The desert, of course, was famous for inducing visions. He was seeing things, he realized that. In the peculiar mental state he was in (with the tired part of his mind knocked out, but another part brilliantly clear and sharp) he was finally allowing himself to see certain things. Consequences. Actions had consequences—events in the real world were not reversible. It was not just the flaming skies and flattened cities that he saw—he had faced up to all that before, of course, and had accepted it. What he now allowed himself to see was the next stage, and the next. He did not normally indulge in "what if" speculation. That mode of thought was unscientific, futile, morbid. But in his present state of mind, under this unnaturally colored desert sky, brandy on an empty stomach blotting out normal constraints, he could not help asking:

What if the chain of nature were to be broken?

What if a series of explosions of the kind they had just set off were to send enough small particles into the atmosphere to deflect just 10 percent of the sun's rays? The photosynthetic process of life would die out in places, the soil would erode, continents would vanish into the sand, as Mesopotamia had vanished.

What if the debris floating in the sky lowered the earth's temperature? How much sunlight would need to be lost to produce a new ice age? He had a vision of much of Europe frozen over. And when the temperatures rose again and the glaciers melted, there would be great floods, and plague and pestilence would follow.

There came to him, then, a phrase from the *Bhagavad-Gita:* "I am become Death, the destroyer of worlds."

TWO

Lieutenant Colonel Jack Delacy crossed the ankles of his highly polished brown riding boots on a pile of geodetic survey maps and tilted back the swivel desk chair; despite the almost horizontal attitude thus achieved, the position did not appear to be restful, to judge from his expression. The colonel's impatient, achieving nature did not allow anyone much rest, least of all himself. He passed his movie-tycoon cigar wetly from one side of his mouth to the other. He was working through a pile of problems. Jerking upright in the tilt chair, with such force that it seemed he might be catapulted across the room, he said, pointing his cigar at Richter, "You know there are holes in the fence? Rode around the perimeter this morning. Saw them myself."

"It's quite true," Captain Richter conceded. He was an older man, somewhat worn-looking, and by no means military in his bearing. He had a large, sensitive face and an untidy graying beard which he scratched from time to time.

"I don't see the point of having a double wire fence, with sophisticated alarm systems, and then permitting people to slip in and out through holes."

"It is a bit Irish, I agree," Richter said, his face breaking into an inappropriate smile.

"Explain the rationale of permitting it," Colonel Delacy said with the air of a man ready to be broadminded. "Explain it to me, Richter."

Richter lit his pipe, making a lot of smoke. "I don't know that there *is* a rationale exactly," he said finally.

Colonel Delacy was eagerly awaiting further elucidation. Richter, he knew, was inclined to be mysterious sometimes.

"Then what . . . ?"

"The controller believes that any closed system needs to have some loopholes in it to make it tolerable. I think there's something in that. I don't think those holes do any harm—oh, I know they're *untidy*. But I don't think they represent a real security risk. We do watch them. They're used by some of our more hell-raising types, and kids. Mostly kids."

"God!" Delacy said of the pipe smoke, seeking to disperse some of it with a fanning hand movement. "Why don't you have one of these?" He offered a fat movie-tycoon cigar as a substitute for the foul pipe.

"I prefer the pipe, if it doesn't annoy you, Colonel," Richter said, blowing out more of the strong fumes.

"Well, Richter, you know I don't believe in interfering too much with the man on the spot. But seems peculiar to me. The holes in the fence."

"It is peculiar, I agree," Richter said. He gave a sudden hee-heeing laugh. "The whole business of security is pretty peculiar."

"Yes, yes—you're right there," Colonel Delacy said, frowning. It was to be gathered that he did not think security quite so funny. He got up and started to pace. He went to the window and looked out.

"No major problems today?"

"No—surprisingly, the press was quite willing to accept the explanation that an ammunition dump had blown up at the air base."

Colonel Delacy swung round and looked pityingly at Richter.

"My God, you should have been there, Richter. It was like being present at the Creation, when the Lord said 'Let there be light.' It was awesome, awesome. . . ."

"It must have been," Richter agreed, a faint quizzicality in his eyes. "Some of the Indians thought there had been two sunrises. Sun came up, didn't like what it saw, went right back in. Then

33

the Mother of the Universe, whose lover the sun is, practiced her feminine wiles and got him to come out again."

Colonel Delacy nodded vaguely. Richter had his ear to the ground, all right, but he sometimes heard things not exactly relevant to the job.

"No lax talk?" Delacy demanded.

"On the whole, people appear to have been careful."

"I cannot emphasize to you enough," Delacy said, "how important it is that there be no relaxation in security during the next two or three weeks, and after. *And after.*"

Richter nodded understandingly. "Oh, yes."

"I would say that security is the number-one consideration now. We have got to pull out every stop to get the show *securely* on the road."

Richter was acquainted with the colonel's driving, galvanic nature. At the end of last year Richter had received orders to get out to Allied headquarters in France, where he had found Delacy chomping on a fat cigar and outlining his plan for "going in." The colonel was always very eager to go in. On this occasion the scheme was for a group of ALSOS people, led by Delacy, to parachute behind the enemy lines and kidnap the physicist Werner Heisenberg, who was believed to be in a picturesque little village called Haigerloch, near Hechingen, making a German atomic bomb. By kidnapping the scientist, Delacy had asserted, they would be able to (a) find out how far the Germans were with their bomb and (b) set them back substantially, however far they were. Richter was necessary to the project because he was both a trained intelligence officer and a physicist and would know what questions to ask Werner Heisenberg. At the same time, he was not a physicist from whom the Germans would be able to extract much useful information if he were captured; nor would it be so enormous a loss to the Allied cause if he were killed. Thus he was a perfect choice for the mission. Richter was a man eternally tempted by the unexpected byways of life; and faced with the prospect of making use of his one lesson in parachuting, he had been game to go in. As it happened, the mission was canceled at the last moment, on the grounds that it might give away more than it gleaned. But Richter spent ten days at close quarters with the colonel, and in that time he learned something about Delacy's way of thinking. Colonel Delacy was a man who believed in bringing matters to a head. Something left in the air was anathema to him; he felt perpetually challenged to bring it down. And so when the parachute jump was called off, the colonel did not sit around twiddling his thumbs. He formed a T-force and, with two or three armored vehicles and some thirty men, raced ahead of the French army, captured Hechingen and Haigerloch and Werner Heisenberg and a lot of other German physicists, and bundled them all off to Farm Hall, England, for interrogation. He was a man who got things done.

Now Richter could see that his questing mind was zeroing in on a new primary target.

"After today," Delacy said, "things here are going to be different. We need to strike out in new directions. In short, to bring things to a conclusion."

"What had you in mind, particularly?"

"The leak," Delacy said. "We need to finally and once and for all—*pin down the leak.*"

The image of pinning down a leak seemed to entertain Richter; in a way it summed up the whole arcane nature of security work.

"Yes," he agreed, "it would certainly be useful if we could."

"Concentrate on Bamberger," Delacy said. "He's the key. He has run this project all the time as he saw fit, and he never saw fit to cooperate fully in matters of security. That was something we had to put up with in the past. I personally always thought that we should have gotten rid of the doctor a long time ago. But I was overruled by General Brown, as I think you know. There were considerations of winning the war to be taken into account. But after today, there is no longer any necessity to go easy on him. You should make it clear to him, Richter, that from now on he is required to cooperate with us fully."

"If he hasn't done so in the past, what's to make him do it now?"

35

Colonel Delacy slowly collapsed into the swivel chair and tilted back so far that there was some danger of him overbalancing. He looked up at the ceiling in deep thought.

"The doctor wants his place in history. Well, that's all right by me—he can have it," Delacy said with an air of bountifulness. "No skin off my nose. Provided . . ." Up swung the chair again, with force. It was rather like having a conversation with a jack-in-the-box, Richter reflected. "Provided he comes clean."

"What are you referring to, sir?"

"The doctor is hiding something. I know it, and he knows that I know it."

Richter said, "Might be helpful if I knew too."

"There is no need for you to know, Richter. At this stage. When you need to know, you'll be told."

"Difficult working in the dark like that."

"Oh, not at all," Delacy assured him. "You just put the screws on the doctor. He knows what it's about. Make it clear to him that we can destroy him if we want to. When he indicates a readiness to cooperate, let me know."

When Colonel Delacy had left, Richter thought about this task that he had been given. He had, of course, learned all about the need-to-know principle in intelligence work: It had been drummed into him, together with Ju-jitsu, and Surveillance, and Codes, during his six weeks at the FBI training school in Washington. Colonel Delacy had been to the same school, had found his vocation there. Surveillance, Interrogation, Interception, Extrapolation, Assignations, Assassinations, One-Time Pads, Safe Houses, Drops—Delacy had shone in all these fields.

Richter put away his papers and went out. The green camouflage paint was peeling from the low, shedlike laboratory buildings around Ashley Pond, had been peeling for as long as Richter could remember. It was a town that had gone shabby even as it was being built. He picked his way around huge puddles. The sun was going down rapidly behind the Jemez Mountains, and Richter paused to watch the familiar but invariably impressive spectacle. Tonight the sunset was strange. Not the proper color. An unnatural amber hue. Something was not right.

36

He walked on slowly, heading vaguely in the direction of the east gate, reflecting that just as Delacy was eminently suited for this work, he, Richter, was not. Considering that he had not been very brilliant at the FBI training school, it was surprising that he had been chosen for the Los Alamos job. Eventually he learned why he had been chosen. There was always a great deal of tension between the military and the civilians. Security regulations were resented; some were openly flouted. The security officers were often treated with contempt by the scientists, who enjoyed baiting them. It was thought that Richter, being a scientist himself, might manage better than someone whose background was limited to security. At least they would not be able to blind him with science.

It was a new field for him. Before the war he had earned his living as a writer for popular science publications. He explained what made seas blue and sunsets red, how a wireless receiver worked, and about magnetic fields, and the principle of the suspension bridge, and how motion pictures created the illusion of continuous movement, and what made lightning strike, and he wrote about the digestive systems of dinosaurs, and about the stars and the tides, and voodoo and hypnotism. If he did not know something, he usually knew where to look it up.

At one time he had hoped to be a real scientist, the kind who made discoveries about the mysteries of existence; he had studied in Germany when the new physics was opening up those astonishing—mind-boggling—visions of the universe. But it had all proved too boggling for his mind. He thought he had understood Einstein's relativity theories, but apparently only about twelve people in the world understood them. The rest didn't even understand what it was they didn't understand. This was the point at which he began to suspect that he might not be cut out to be a physicist. Others seemed at ease with the new concepts. But he felt uncomfortable with them. He belonged to that old-fashioned school of thought which wanted the music of the spheres to have a melody. Instead of accepting the uncertainties of the Uncertainty Principle, he foolishly wished to resolve them, which was not at all the right way to proceed.

He had been ready to accept the internal structure of the atom as resembling a miniature planetary system (even the concept of particles traveling at the speed of light through infinitesimal space); but when it turned out that this was merely a picture of something that could not be pictured, he felt adrift. He could not follow the physicists where they were going. He was not sufficiently single-minded to make himself at ease in their abstract worlds, and was too inclined to be sidetracked.

He realized that one reason why so many of his brilliant contemporaries made such good time along their single track was because they were pursued. That was the secret. He saw it in their eyes. It was only the pursued who could make that kind of time. And Richter, though he had his hangups like everybody else, evidently wasn't pursued enough. He was always ready to stop and wander off into some intriguing byway, could not resist stopping to look at a wild orchid unexpectedly growing in a field of buttercups, or at butterflies of unusual coloring, or to tease spiders from their lairs by delicately strumming the strands of their webs.

If, as a result of his discursive nature, he had not really got anywhere, he had picked up a great deal of interesting information about this and that. Irrelevant, perhaps. But irrelevant to what? A career? That he had rather obviously failed to make—at any rate, no career of any note. Yes, while he had been chasing butterflies, and discovering orchids in the most unlikely places, the world of success had passed him by. *Tant pis.* He no longer minded that too much.

He was always coming out with peculiar information. The fact that *Omitermes meridionalis*, the compass termite, builds its termitarium with the axis invariably along the north-south line. That people bleed more readily at full moon. That *Argyroneta aquatica*—the water spider—constructs its web underwater, and a bubble of air in the web serves it as a diving bell. One of his jobs before the war had been to compile a "Would You Believe It?" column for a popular science magazine, and so he had literally thousands of these strange bits and pieces of information in his head.

He had faced up to the fact that he was not a real scientist. He was an amateur; but if so, he was, he liked to think, an amateur in the sense in which the French used the term, meaning devotee, lover, enthusiast. He was all of those. But he was not a professional man of science.

Bamberger! Now there was a man of science, an all-rounder, as well as being a specialist in his own field. Richter had arrived in Göttingen two years after Bamberger left, and had heard all about his brilliant fellow countryman, who had been in such a hurry to get on that he had taken his exams a year ahead of time, and passed them all with distinction. It was said that as soon as Bamberger had got what there was to be got out of a person or a place, he was anxious to be off.

Normally, students were not permitted to graduate ahead of time; but Bamberger had pleaded economic circumstances. If he were not allowed to take his exams early, he would be forced to leave without his doctorate. A blatant trick—for his family was wealthy. By the time Richter arrived at Göttingen this story was already part of the Bamberger legend. There were other stories, all contributing to a picture of dash and daring and intellectual glamour. How he had faulted his teacher, the great mathematician Hofmannsthal, on a calculation. How he had managed to get himself asked to tea by Einstein, and told him what was the one flaw in the general theory of relativity. Not merely to understand the theory, but to be able to criticize it! The story went that Einstein had found the criticism "very interesting."

To Richter all this was heady stuff. The romance of science. He lapped it up, the way as a child he had lapped up the stories of Galileo and Louis Pasteur and Madame Curie. The fact that he was being taught by some of the teachers who had taught Bamberger fostered a spirit of identification with the older student—older, but only by a couple of years. Richter was not the only one to be so affected. A whole later generation of students saw in Bamberger their ideal of the scientist: brainy and worldly. Deeply involved in the world *as it was*.

It was this last quality that was so striking. Everything that was said about him, and later written, pointed to the fact that he was not one for the ivory tower: He partook of life fully, on all its levels, chased after girls like any young man-about-town, took up vigorous political positions, was healthily interested in money, lived well, went to good restaurants and to nightclubs, played Mozart on the violin and jazz on the clarinet. And at the same time had this extraordinary grasp of the imponderable forces of the universe.

Long before he ever met him, Richter had the feeling of knowing Bamberger—not, of course, intimately, but in the way that one feels one knows an author whose work one has assiduously followed and admired.

It was in measuring himself in relation to Bamberger that Richter finally had come to the conclusion that he was never going to be a real scientist himself. He did not have the originality or the obsessiveness, or the sheer far-reaching imagination. At best he could be a popularizer of other people's ideas. That was how he had drifted into scientific journalism.

Throughout those years when he was compiling his "Would You Believe It?" columns and his popular mechanics articles, he kept up with what Bamberger was doing. In part it was a professional obligation, for he was often called upon to explain in eight hundred words of simple language the latest startling scientific finding. But he had also kept up with Bamberger for more personal reasons, seeing in his successes an indication of what he, Richter, might have been—if only he had been cleverer, or smarter, or luckier . . . or something. He'd had a phase of being envious of Bamberger, but in the end the envy had given way to admiration.

It was very shocking to him, therefore, to be told now that he must tighten the screws on Bamberger, let him know that there was something known about him that could destroy him.

What could it be?

Bamberger had shown not just brilliance but almost superhuman dedication in molding a group of people of many different nationalities, vastly different temperaments and political persuasions, and sometimes violent antagonisms—a group of people described by General Brown as "the biggest bunch of crackpots ever assembled in one place"—into a team, as of today a winning team. This was his moment of triumph. And Colonel Delacy was saying to tighten the screws, to let him know they could destroy him.

It was just not to be believed.

As he walked unhappily on, Richter was passing groups of returning scientists. Their faces had been baked by the desert sun and beaten by the wind, and they looked haggard and deeply tired. But there was something exultant in their eyes, too, as they bear-hugged colleagues, and gave the thumbs-up sign, and said, "It's a boy, a big bouncing boy." He asked several of these men if they had seen Bamberger, and they said he was around somewhere. But where, nobody seemed to know.

Richter went by the controller's house; it was in darkness. He did not want to wake Bamberger if he was already asleep. He was not going to start carrying out his instructions right now. Let the man have his day of triumph. Everybody else was celebrating. Although it was not supposed to be known what had taken place at Alamogordo, the pulse of the town had unquestionably speeded up.

Richter wandered on, looking about. There was an overspill of servicemen and WACs outside the PX; smoochy bursts of music came from the jukebox every time the swinging doors opened. He walked through the unlit streets and suddenly did not know where he was. Even after being here more than a year, one could easily get lost among all these identical dwellings. The streets had no names. The only big landmark was the water tower, and he now looked around for that, and once he had found it was able to reorient himself. He was making his way back to what was sometimes laughingly referred to as the honky-tonk district, or the Strip, when he suddenly spotted Bamberger, all by himself, standing in the dark. It seemed almost as if he were hiding. He was behind a line of parked automobiles, lighting a cigarette. He was pale to the point of transparency. His toughness of mind and his energy when he was fully charged made him seem stronger than he was. With the current off, he appeared terribly fragile. Right now he looked on his last legs. He was weaving a little, and shaking himself, and trying to hold on to the wall, and Richter was about to go to his aid when he saw Mrs. Bamberger approaching.

41

Bamberger saw her before she saw him; he called out to show where he was, and she squeezed between the fenders and joined him behind the cars. Richter saw them embrace. It was the sort of embrace you saw at a railway station when someone has returned from a long and hazardous journey. He held her very close, his face against the side of her neck, and appeared to draw strength from her. When they finally drew a little apart, he had miraculously revived. What a remarkable woman! What an effect for anyone to have! Richter was feeling pretty shabby about spying on such a private moment. Now he saw them look intimately into each other's eyes; something passed between them, something wordless, and Bamberger pressed her hand very tight, and then, hand in hand, they came out from behind the cars, looking about them a little guiltily, like a couple of youngsters who have been kissing in the dark. Already Bamberger was different: The current was flowing again, his step was firm, and, though he still looked wretchedly weary, there was a tight forcefulness in his bearing that was much more like the controller everybody knew.

Richter had not done very well in Surveillance at FBI training school, but fortunately the Bambergers were quite oblivious of anybody else as they walked like a pair of young lovers toward Fuller Lodge. Richter came several steps behind, as if he just happened to be going that way, too. Well, why not? There were quite a number of people going to the lodge to celebrate.

As he arrived, Bamberger received a round of applause from half a dozen colleagues at the bar. He responded by clasping his hands above his head in the manner of a victorious boxer. The attitude combined the triumphal and the ironic. Some good-natured banter followed. Richter watched from a little way off. If the men looked completely drained, Mrs. B. was positively blooming. Never had Richter seen her look so gorgeous, giving off such sexual glitter. The tired scientists felt it, too, and were bucking up fast. She was in a dark box-jacket outfit, the oval line of the waistcoat scrupulously following the anatomy of her bust. Her long neck was both hidden and emphasized by a white silk foulard. How the men looked at her! She was giving them all her very special smile. It was a very inward smile, as if she were smiling to herself, savoring some absolutely exquisite private joke that nobody but she—and one or two other rare spirits—would be able to get. It was not possible to be sure that this joke was not at your expense. You had to wonder, because it was so private to herself. Yet, seeing this doubt in your eyes, she briefly shared the joke with you *a little*—a concession on her part—without actually telling you what it was, just made you privy to it in an honorary kind of way. Because you were there. You were in, said this smile; you were in, you lucky fellow. At this point most of the men smiled, too. Richter also smiled, feeling himelf included in her smile, which was both very general and at the same time personal to each man.

Richter felt the extraordinary allure of this woman whose smile was so mysteriously flattering as to be able to reanimate such very tired men.

Like others, Richter had wondered about Mrs. Bamberger, about her smile and what it meant. Did it mean what it sometimes seemed to mean? The signs people gave out always meant something; not necessarily what you first supposed, but something. Richter, seeking to penetrate the mystery of Mrs. Bamberger's smile, made up an aphorism on the subject: A scintillating woman is never entirely innocent. That being so . . .

Through the general hubbub of talk, Leo Hepler's voice made itself heard. He was raising his glass and proposing a toast.

"To the baby. Our baby. And to the proud papa." He lifted his glass to Bamberger. "The putative papa, at any rate." Some of the laughter produced by this quip sounded strained.

"And here's to you, kiddo," Bamberger responded. "The truly *terrible enfant.*"

It may have been simply exhaustion that made Bamberger's face seem to be lacking in true jocularity at this moment.

"One thing I will say," Hepler remarked, "it certainly helps having such a wise old papa to check our sums. How did I do, Papa?"

"Oh, you did okay, son. You do your sums pretty good. Usually."

"An overprotective papa," Hepler said, his eyes glinting. "Spent all day correcting my homework, didn't you, Papa?"

Hepler seemed to be stimulating himself by means of these veiled provocations, overcoming his tiredness in this way. Wearily Bamberger heeded the taunts. From long experience he knew not to conduct such an exchange on the level of badinage, but to deal with the underlying complaint seriously.

He said, "I was correlating all the readings as they came in. I don't think we reached any real danger levels anywhere."

"As I predicted."

"As you predicted. Right. Right."

"You know what today's yield was?"

"We haven't got those figures yet."

"I will tell you. Between seventeen and twenty thousand tons."

"It's a reasonable bet," Bamberger said.

"Not a bet, Bambi. A calculation. I have worked it out."

"Without the instrument readings? You worked it out without instrument readings?"

"Without instruments, yes. In the moment when the blast wave hit you may have noticed I dropped some bits of paper. I measured their displacement. On the basis of that, it was comparatively simple arithmetic to work out the approximate yield."

"Well, your advance calculations were pretty close, I am ready to believe."

"Only pretty close?"

"You worked it out as well as anyone could have done in advance of the event."

"You are suggesting in some respects I was disproved?"

"As far as we know, so far, Leo, you got it right. As far as we know."

"Oh, what a quibbling old rabbi you are, Papa. On the one hand I appear to have been 100 percent right. On the other hand—who knows, I may still turn out to have been wrong."

"I *am* a quibbling old rabbi, didn't you know?"

"You owe me ten bucks, rabbi."

Bamberger, remembering the bet, grinned and said, "Cheap at the price." He reached in his trouser pocket, fumbled, and came up with no more than a couple of dollars. "I'll have to owe you, Leo."

44

"Don't forget," Hepler said, "I'm plar
bucks framed. Want to make another bet,

"No, no—I can see you're on a winnin;
. . ." He hesitated, debating with himself
in such a discussion right now. ". . . I (
ued, "we ought to be too cocky. Just beca
up this time. My point is that the earth i
and water, and that the atmosphere is ign
is found. Thank God we hadn't found the right match this
time."

"There's more risk you fall off that bar stool and break your
neck," Hepler said.

"That may be true," Bamberger said. He was swaying a little.
"And that risk factor is mounting by the minute. So . . . I'm
going to leave you guys."

"Listen, Bambi," Hepler said in all earnestness now, brow fur-
rowing, eyes intense. "Coming back from the desert, I had some
thoughts . . ."

"So did I," Bamberger said.

Hepler's eyes gleamed with their excessive brilliancy.

"You know what today opens up. . . ."

"I want to stop you right there," Bamberger said. "This place is
not private, and we should be careful about what we say."

"I do not mean that," Hepler said impatiently, with his customary indifference for considerations of security. "*That* is nothing to
do with us now. That is a delivery job."

"A delivery job, yuh."

"I made some calculations, Bambi." His voice became lower,
which was surprising for him, since he hardly ever lowered his
voice for any reason, whether of politeness or of discretion. But
his voice now had become so soft that Richter, on the fringe of
the group, could barely hear what he was saying. "The temperature today in our Big Bang must have been pretty close to temperatures reached in the interior of the sun. . . . I calculate ten to
twenty million degrees."

Bamberger seemed to be highly uncomfortable about the trend
of the conversation, and Richter, too, was becoming worried. He

45

und. The only people within earshot were scientists who
en part in the test. But even so . . .

eo," Bamberger said, "this is not to be talked about here.
. . Captain Richter over there is looking very disapproving. He
will have us all thrown in the clinker."

Hepler, however, refused to be stopped. When he was animated
by some idea (or by any strong impulse), he found it hard to contain himself. Coming very close to Bamberger, he continued to
develop his thoughts. Richter could not hear what he was saying.
Probably only Bamberger and Mrs. Bamberger could hear. He
spoke for a couple of minutes in a low voice. Then the conversation became audible again. Bamberger was saying, "Leo, don't
you think we have done enough already?"

"If it can be done, somebody will do it. It might as well be us,"
Hepler said. "Why not?"

"Because that might be the match."

"You and your fucking matches."

"Leo," Bamberger said firmly, "I'm not debating this with you
tonight. Frankly, I'm not up to taking you on. Save it, huh? We'll
go into it another time. Okay?" With that, he slid off the bar stool,
took his wife's arm, gave a jocular salute, and left.

From the door he called, "See you tomorrow, Leo."

Richter left soon after. The scientists had a name for the security people: creeps. Richter felt he had done enough creeping for
one day. He felt the need of more humanizing activity. Like eating. He was hungry.

In the kitchen of his small Sundt apartment, he looked in the
icebox and considered what to make. Cooking was one of those
sidelines by which he had become distracted when he should have
been concentrating on more important things. He enjoyed cooking, and he enjoyed eating. Rather too much! He was somewhat
overweight. But, then, he told himself, he did not have the nature
of a lean man. It was perhaps true that he cared too much about
food. People had different forms of greed. Some were greedy for
money, others for fame, or women. He wondered what Bamberger's greed was. Not food—there was a lean man for you. His

46

place in history—was that what Bamberger was greedy for? Well, each to his own greed.

He was musing in this way while considering what to cook. The Santa Fe chili had a character all its own. It was different from the kind you got in the East, or even in San Antonio or Phoenix. Santa Fe chili was especially hot. He began to prepare the mature red pods of the chili peppers.

A pity there was not some pretty woman to share his meal. He had been married once, briefly, but it had not worked out, and since then he had lived by himself most of the time. He was used to it now. He liked women, but was not what you would call a womanizer. He tended to leave such things to chance; but chance had lately been remiss in this respect, and tonight he was feeling lonely. Something to do with the sense of occasion in the air. It was not a time to be alone.

The walls and floors of Sundt apartments were thin, and he could always tell what was the mood of his neighbors. Tonight it was celebratory. The heavy sounds coming through the ceiling, like furniture being moved, meant that the Weissbergers were dancing. From the apartment on his left came the sound of the Andrews Sisters in a rendering of "Bei Mir Bist Du Schoen"; somewhere else a Harry James trumpet solo was being played.

Later, as he ate his solitary meal, Richter thought of Mrs. Dubinski, the young widow whose husband had died so tragically in a laboratory accident. A very attractive young woman, and the little boy, Benjie, was a nice kid. Richter was fond of children, though he had none of his own. He liked to talk to children. Was it Wittgenstein who had said that one must talk to children? Had abandoned philosophy and gone back to schoolteaching. There was a period when Richter had been a schoolmaster, and it was a profession he occasionally considered going back to. Yes, one had to talk to children.

He would have liked to get to know Mrs. Dubinski. She had shown great strength at the time of her husband's death, and he liked strong, self-reliant women. She was a scientist herself. She

47

was also a dish. He had taken quite a fancy to her . . . perhaps, on this occasion, he would not leave it all to chance.

He went to the window and looked out. People were converging from all around, making their way along the dim streets toward the center. Some of the girls were wearing galoshes, carrying their shoes. Oh, there was going to be dancing tonight.

He lit his pipe and frowned as his mind returned to the conversation with Colonel Delacy.

He tried to think what Delacy might have on Bamberger that could destroy him, but was distracted by the mounting sound of people determined to have a good time. The whole town was beginning to jump. Well, perhaps he would go down and join them. Have a drink at the Services Club. See what was going on. It was his job to keep an eye on things.

TWO

TEMPTING FATE THE EVENTS OF EASTER, 1946 (I)

THREE

The Lenten season can be very cold in northern New Mexico, and at the altitude of Los Alamos there are often snowstorms and barbed winds; Easter, 1946—the first Easter of peace—arrived cold and windy, with snow clouds gathering above the Rio Grande Valley.

Leo Hepler wore his fleece-collared lumber jacket, and gloves, inside the car. It was a prewar Ford station wagon that rattled like a rag-and-bones cart, and the heating system wasn't working.

Down State 4 to White Rock, rattle, rattle, rattle. On rising ground the cones of the piñon trees were glistening white globules. There was frost on the ground, and higher up the volcanic cliff face, densely spotted with black cave openings, there was snow.

Hepler had his photographic equipment in the back.

As he drove, he chain-smoked, lighting a fresh cigarette from the stub of the previous one. His fingers were nicotine-stained. His hair spread out in frizzy clumps from the side of his head. He drove fast, leaning forward in the driver's seat with the kind of violent attentiveness that he brought to every task he performed.

Four miles past the junction with U.S. 285 on the road to Cundiyo, he was supposed to take a right turn. He was watching out for it intently. Jones had said you could easily miss it. But Hepler saw it in time and made the turn at speed, car wheels slithering in icy loose gravel. It was a bumpy ride down. Jones had said it would be. In places the dirt road just fell away a foot or so in the middle, and there was nothing to do but make the descent in a series of jolting drops. The old car shuddered and rolled with the punishment. Twenty minutes of this rough ride and he was in a wilderness that could have been a thousand miles from civilization. Hepler no longer could see the modern asphalt highway above. He was on a two-rut trail that bored down into the earth in a series of corkscrews; the canyon walls were getting closer together and almost perpendicular. The sense of isolation was complete.

Hepler hung on tight, wondering if the old car was going to fall apart under this kind of treatment. At each jolt he gave a sort of snarling smile. This was really rough going. Now the ground leveled, and the trail ran alongside a fast-flowing stream that twisted like a shimmering snake, keeping to no fixed path. The trail was becoming narrower and narrower. He saw there was nowhere along here to turn around, if that necessity should arise. He would have to reverse all the way back up. It seemed unlikely that the car could make that. Going down was with the help of gravity; but up . . . Jones had said to keep on; a car could pass all the way through. Ahead appeared a kind of needle's eye in the mass of rock. He approached it with fierce attention . . . you could get through, according to Jones. Provided you didn't mind scarring your car. It was a tight squeeze, and there was a moment when he became stuck like a cork in a bottle, and got through only with a screech of tearing metal. On the other side the gorge opened out and he saw the dark huddle of pueblo ruins ahead. This was Xoaté. He would have liked to photograph it, but did not want to stop for that today. His sharp eye took in everything. Soon he was passing the ruins. The timbers of these adobe structures had crumbled long ago, and the earth roofs were in many places open to the sky. The walls of the pueblos were poorly bonded. The early architects had not appreciated sufficiently the advantages of using large stones at corners, or for jambs. In many instances, protruding contiguous poles were all that remained of the roofs; their mud substance had literally dissolved away. Looked as if they had been in this condition for a great many years. Further on, he passed recent ruins, sprawling, messy structures. They were clearly of more than one storey, but exactly how many levels existed it was difficult to say, because of the almost organic way in which these weird and beautiful mud habitations had spread and grown. Some bore signs of having been lived in not that long ago. Thick clumps of weeds sprouted from their roofs, but the basic structures here looked more or less intact, and they had wooden doors and shutters, and window openings in some of the upper storeys had been fitted with slabs of dimly translucent selenite. Repairs had been effected by filling up holes with rags and sticks bonded together with mud plaster. On the terraces there were long ladders reaching to higher levels. Most of these pueblos, he thought, must be unoccupied. They had the fetid desolateness of abandoned places. Everywhere walls were deeply cracked; the process of falling apart, where it had not yet begun, was imminent. The whole village was in varying stages of decay and dissolution. But as he passed it, he sensed a faint pulse of life coming from the central plaza, though he saw nobody. There were wisps of smoke rising from one or two iron pot chimneys, and here and there in the dim interiors of the pueblo the shifting darkness indicated people moving about.

Jones had said to go past Xoaté and carry on for another ten miles, through alfalfa and corn fields, and then to leave the car in a small copse of junipers, and from there continue on foot.

He clocked the distance on the mileage gauge, found the copse, and left the car. He slung the cameras and lenses over his shoulders and the binoculars around his neck, put his sandwiches and Thermos and reading material in a rucksack, which he hoisted onto his back, and set off. He kept climbing until he was high enough from the floor of the valley to have a clear view of the winding approach to the church. Cruciform in shape, with a dome at the crossing, it had no windows in its softly undulating adobe walls. Only the wooden superstructure of the belfry had openings for light and air.

Before doing anything else he prepared his cameras. He set up one on a tripod, focused it, and took numerous shots of the church, using slow exposures. Then he prepared his other camera, attaching a telephoto lens and focusing it, and made a series of readings with a light meter. Satisfied, he put down the meter and seated himself behind a large rock, which afforded protection against the wind, and ate his sandwiches and drank coffee. When he had eaten, he occupied himself with his thoughts. The agility of his own mind was a continual source of pleasure to him. He loved to work out things in his head. He could daydream in numbers. The things he could postulate . . . the unthinkable!

In this way he passed the time quite agreeably. There was little sound, except for birds and the movements of trees bending to the wind. Once he saw a coyote. It appeared suddenly a few dozen yards away, on a rock. It was not a creature that was customarily loved, and he knew it was dangerous, but he found it splendid. Its unwholesome reputation thrilled him. How it sniffed the air, scenting prey and danger! Beautiful! In Indian legend it was honored as a trickster. It was magnificent. All the same, he felt in the pocket of his rucksack and took out a small army revolver, in case the splendid animal should decide to attack him.

He was setting himself a new mathematical conundrum when the stillness was broken by a faint but continuous sound that made him prick up his ears. He listened intently, eyes brimming with excitement. Oh, he was in luck! Yes, yes—the plaintive, distant wail was becoming stronger. He placed himself by the rock and began to search the surrounding countryside through his binoculars. He saw nothing, only rocks and shrubs and trees. But the sound was continuing, and it was being made by human beings. Now he could make out the notes of a flute, and presently the wailing became more definite. The sound was approaching. He waited expectantly. In a little while he began to hear more clearly the regular chanting of male voices. The chanting grew louder, swelling into a fierce and somber hymn. An *alabado*. He could distinguish occasional Spanish words. The chanting was accompanied, and overlaid, by wailing. Must be a large number of people to produce such a massive sound.

At last he saw them. The brothers, most of them dressed only in white cotton shorts, were walking at a steady pace, singing and wailing, and as they walked some of them whipped themselves with plaited yucca whips. There was a fixed pattern. They took three steps forward, then brought the *disciplina* sharply round over the left shoulder; another three steps, and then the right shoulder.

Blood flowed profusely down their bare backs, staining their white shorts and running down their legs.

Excitedly, Hepler sighted through his cameras, focusing the telephoto lens of the Leica. Oh, this was splendid! He began to click away, going from one camera to the other. The self-punishment was not just symbolic; some of the brothers looked on their last legs, were staggering and gasping, and needed to be supported by their attendants. What primitivism, what savagery! Hepler was ecstatic as he focused and clicked, focused and clicked. Some of them carried crosses and were masked, others wore only cowls and their faces could be seen. Then he saw the one toward the rear, staggering under the weight of an enormous wooden cross and wearing a crown of thorns. Hepler took many shots of him. Once he fell, and Hepler photographed him sprawled on the ground and being helped up by the other brothers.

The light was beginning to go; soon it would be too dark to get more than blurs, but he continued to photograph the procession as it slowly mounted to a knoll. The chanting and wailing was rising to a frenzy of woe. The brothers were tightly bunched together—something was happening out of sight; it went on for some minutes while the cries and wails became increasingly anguished. Then the throng parted and Hepler saw several brothers pulling on ropes, and slowly, slowly the large cross was raised up; to it was bound a man in the attitude of crucifixion. The lamentations reached a peak as the cross became upright.

The procession then began to move again, going down from the knoll and then along a curving path toward the church.

The regular monotonous wailing was becoming oppressive, almost hypnotic. He could see that there were casualties among the brothers. Some had collapsed from loss of blood. Others were writhing and shaking uncontrollably, as if undergoing epileptic fits. One or two attendants stayed to watch over them, but the main procession continued without even any change in their steps and the rhythm of the self-flagellation. In single file the procession entered the church, until all were inside except the casualties and the figure on the cross and the various attendants.

It was getting dark, and all the forms on the distant rise were blurring and becoming increasingly improbable as they faded into the landscape.

Night fell suddenly. The moon made a strong yellow light. The church spire, and the cross with the man tied to it, cast long moon shadows over the hills. The sound of hymn singing from inside the church was swelling to a great furor. A single light came through the circle of window openings in the tower below the Gothic belfry. As the sound of praying and psalm singing mounted toward an ecstatic, anguished climax, this light began to dim in stages, like the light of heaven going out, and finally the church was dark. For a moment there was silence, and then a great swelling pandemonium broke out. The sound seemed to burst through the walls; there were screams, bestial yells, inhuman bellowings, accompanied by a rattling of wooden ratchets, the clattering of chains, and over all of this the fervent-voiced singing of the *alabado* continued, the singing voices pitted against the screaming, and the former gradually were drowned out. Presently the singing stopped and the tumult prevailed.

"Yes, these really are good," Jones said, studying the photographs spread out before him; he placed several, one after another, under the lens of an enlarger, and adjusted the height to vary the magnification. "I would crop along here," he advised in the case of one photo, drawing an imaginary square around a cowled face. "Bring this up. It'll enlarge beautifully. Look." He moved the enlarger up to demonstrate his point, and the cowled face leapt out of the dim mass with an expression of ferocious ecstasy.

"I would say you've got a good chance with these for the Camera Club prize," he said.

"You really think so?"

"I do, Leo, I do. Mind you, Annie Danzinger's insect studies are awfully good too. Totally different type of work. She was working from close, you from far. Just as well, I may tell you. Those blighters don't like being watched, let alone photographed, and some of them tote a gun. They've been known to take potshots at outsiders spying on their manifestations."

56

"I never saw anything so weird," Hepler said. The long finger of ash in his mouth suddenly broke and spilled all over his polka-dot bow tie. He blinked rapidly through the thick, stinging cigarette smoke that hung over the piles of photographs like a mist. The dining table was a platform of seething figures, faces, forms: blood, crosses, hoods, masks, whips.

"It's really a little piece of the Dark Ages," Hepler said, one hand moving rapidly through the piles of photos, shuffling the faces. "Now just look at this one here."

The face was placed under the enlarger and brought up large, too large for an instant, so that it became all white empty space; an appropriate reduction in size made it once more recognizably human.

"Isn't that a face out of the Dark Ages?" Hepler demanded. "The primitive passion, the fanaticism, the ignorance. That face is a throwback of four hundred years. Look at the eyes. It's as if science had never existed. That man is still living on a flat platform in the air, with the sun moving around him."

"And God in His heaven," Jones said. "A just and jealous God. Mine is the vengeance, saith the Lord. Oh, yes, you can see it. You've caught it beautifully. What good pictures what are! Well done!" He smiled his broad, blond English smile, and poured another measure of Gordon's gin into his teacup, stirred with a spoon, and winked at Hepler as he drank.

From the kitchen came the sound of Pam Jones's voice.

"Another cup of tea, Stanny?"

"Not for me, thanks, love," Jones said.

"What about Dr. Hepler?"

"You mustn't call me Dr. Hepler," he said. "It's Leo."

"Leo?" She put her head in.

"Yes, thanks," he said. He brushed ash from the glistening white nylon shirt that stuck to his body in places, and lit a fresh cigarette from the burning ember between his lips. "It got dark, and I couldn't see anymore, and then there was all that uproar, the noise was indescribable . . . indescribable."

"*Las Tinieblas,*" Jones said. "It's something, isn't it? Reenacts the darkness and confusion following the death of Christ."

"And what happens to Christ?"

"Well, the ropes cut off circulation and he loses consciousness. Usually he is cut down before death occurs. Usually, but not invariably. Depends how far it is felt symbolism should be carried. There are different sects, and they all have somewhat different attitudes to this. Some don't practice crucifixion. Others use nails instead of ropes."

Jones was continuing to shuffle through the photos. He appeared genuinely enthusiastic, and Hepler was pleased. "I think you could sell some of these to the magazines," Jones said. "You should try *Life*."

"You consider them sufficiently professional for *Life?*"

"I don't think that matters. What matters is that you have got a unique record. *Life* used my Hiroshima pictures last year."

"Your pictures were newsworthy."

"So are these, Leo. There have been some items in the local press about a new wave of activity among the Penitentes. Of course, in the past . . ." He sipped gin from his teacup and scratched his head. "In the past, resurgences of this sort of thing usually have occurred in times of plague and pestilence and great disasters." He shrugged, and gestured toward the photos. "But there's your evidence, isn't it? There *is* a resurgence of this activity. You've got the proof."

"The other side also makes itself felt, I have heard," Hepler said, eyes glittering.

"You mean the witches. Oh yes. Oh, they are very much part of the tradition around here." He chuckled. "Go hand in hand, so to speak—the penitents and the witches. Do you know, when I first came here—did I ever tell you my witch story?"

"No."

"Well, you must hear this, Hepler. A salutary warning to the rational mind." He paused, looked over his shoulder to see if Pam was coming, and quickly splashed more gin into his teacup. "When I first came here, I got a young lad from the University of Albuquerque to show me around. Son of some academic friends of ours. The boy knew the area well. One day we were near the place you passed today, Xoaté. Suddenly he stopped and said he did not think it was wise to go any further. I asked why, supposing it was something to do with the difficulty of the terrain. Looks passable, I said to him. But he was very uncomfortable, and didn't want to go on. I was sort of playfully bullying him to continue, and at last he just stopped and blurted out, 'Dr. Jones, sir, it is not wise to go to Xoaté. Xoaté is a bad place. Some time ago they executed witches there who made very bad spells on everyone.' 'Well,' I said, trying to make light of his evident distress, 'as long as they've been executed . . .' I tell you this story, Hepler, to show the kind of hold these superstitions have still—even on an intelligent, trained mind. This boy was a physics student at the university, exceptionally gifted. His parents were distinguished academics. And there he was, absolutely petrified of going into Xoaté, because the witches might put devils into him. Well, what I did was, I told him to stay outside and I would go in by myself and take a quick look round—since we were so near, it seemed a pity not to. I spent ten minutes there, not much longer. There is not a lot to see. It is a very rundown place, mostly abandoned. Largely old sick people. Well, the old and sick tend to look rather witchlike to the young, and in that setting I could see how the story could have started. When I got out again, you know he had gone? Left me the car and walked all the way back up to the road—gone. The rational mind in full panic-stricken flight before the forces of superstition and ignorance. When I saw him the next day—naturally I went to see him to find out that he was all right—he said he had not been feeling well, something to do with his stomach, and had had to leave."

Pam Jones came in and gave Hepler his cup of tea.

"A biscuit, Dr. Hep—Leo?" she corrected herself quickly. "What you Americans call a cookie."

"I am flattered to be taken for an American," Hepler said in his unmistakable Viennese accent. "I know I speak like an American, but I thought perhaps some little nuance gave away that I am not a native son. I must tell you, Pamela, I was born in Vienna, believe it or not. Vienna, Austria—not Virginia. There is also a Vienna in Virginia, where I was not born."

Pamela Jones looked unsure of herself. She was never entirely comfortable with Hepler; his jokes were sometimes obscure, and she was not certain when to laugh.

Now she smiled and, for lack of anything else to say, said, "Do you miss Vienna, Leo?"

"I detest Vienna," Hepler said. "I refer to Vienna, Austria. I have nothing against Vienna, Virginia—having never been there. But as far as the former capital of the Austro-Hungarian Empire is concerned—you can keep it."

"Oh!" Pamela Jones said, dismayed. She was flustered. Was she being kidded? Was she meant to take this seriously? "I always thought Vienna was such . . . such a . . . wonderful city."

"No—it is a dreadful place. Good only for *Hochstaplers* and psychoanalysts."

"Music, surely," Pam Jones said. "Isn't it a great musical city? Oh, I am sure that you are kidding me about Vienna. I am sure it must have given you *something.*"

"Yes," he said, "it taught me the pleasures of *Schadenfreude.*"

She frowned uncomprehendingly. "My German is not—"

"It means," Jones said, "taking pleasure in the misfortunes of others."

Hepler sat there white and glittering with wickedness through all his cigarette smoke, utterly delighted with himself.

Pamela Jones's face had reddened, and she smiled uncertainly. Her face had a tendency to redness. When she went out she applied face powder liberally to nose and cheek and brow, but now her flushed face was quite nakedly red. She looked at Hepler to ascertain if he was kidding her.

"Oh, you're having me on," she protested.

"Pamela, my dear, I am not having you in any kind of way," he said.

"Really," she said crossly, "you make yourself appear to be a lot wickeder that you are, I am sure."

"Don't be sure, Pamela. Do not be sure."

"Schadenfreude?"

"Of course, not in England. The English do not have such disgusting feelings. But in Vienna, yes. You do not laugh in England when somebody slips on a banana skin?"

"We do not have a special word for that kind of cruel pleasure."

"You have so many words, and you do not have a word for that?" He shook his head. "But *hypocrisy—that* is in the English language. So perhaps it is not necessary to have *Schadenfreude* if you have *hypocrisy*—hmm? Also, you have the saying 'Vengeance is sweet,' which is not quite the same as *Schadenfreude*, but is related to it."

"Then it's vengeance, is it, Leo? You're getting your own back? On the world? Or just Vienna?"

"Ah! Ah! Ah!" he exclaimed in mock consternation. "I have been found out by Lady Freud here. Well, well, well, well. Oh, you will be happy back in England. A country without *Schadenfreude*. Bravo!"

"Yes, I am very happy to be going back to England," she said steadfastly, refusing to let herself be intimidated.

"It's time to go back," Jones said, stirring his empty teacup.

Pamela Jones got up abruptly and went to open the window. "God, how the smell of stale booze hangs around." She breathed in gulps of cold fresh air with evident need. Jones shivered.

"Shut the bloody window, Pam," he protested.

She fanned the air vigorously with her hand.

"It is my cigarettes?" Hepler asked without apologizing.

"How many of them do you smoke?" she demanded, coughing.

"Three packs a day."

She closed the window with a bang.

"Not good for you," she scolded lightly.

"I know. But I have been smoking since I was eight. . . . I am hooked."

"What *haven't* you been doing since you were eight!"

"Now you have found me out."

"You can see," Jones said, "what a dazzling career lies ahead of our Pam. A born politician! Knows what's best for everyone."

"Well, you think I don't know what's best for us? *For us,*" she said hotly, turning on Jones. "All right, you can mock me, you two, but if people love somebody, are they supposed to just stand by and watch while he drinks himself to death, pretend it isn't happening? Let that person just go right ahead, and say nothing?" She moved her head sharply toward the teacup. "I do the bloody washing up, Stan. Don't you think I know what a cup that's had tea in it smells like? I can tell the difference between tea and gin." She turned with a little sob of desperation toward Hepler. "Stan always drank a bit. But never like this . . . never."

"You are right. You will be better off in England," Hepler said.

"I'm sorry about the outburst," Pamela said.

"They no longer trust us—the British," Jones said, standing up and, now openly, getting the bottle of Gordon's from behind a sideboard and splashing gin into his teacup. "They have cut us off from access to any new material."

"So I have heard," Hepler said. "Now, of course, if you were an American, like me, you would not have that problem."

"I thought about it," Jones said. "But Pam doesn't care to stay in America."

"She is right. For her, she is right. When will you go?"

"We go in the summer. First we'll take a trip to Mexico. We've never been. Pam thinks the kids ought to see it. God knows when we'll be back here again . . . if ever."

"You should see Mexico, definitely," Hepler said.

"Mind you," Jones said, "for myself, I can take it or leave it. Frankly, I've had the wide open spaces. Give me city life. Crowds. Traffic. Packed trains and buses. Queues. Stinking humanity. I want to live in the middle of Piccadilly Circus. I don't like all this quiet—all this peace. Peace! Too much space. What's all this about open space? Who needs it! Don't need to breathe that much air. Pack 'em in tight, I say. Stew in their own juice, yes. The human stew."

"I want the children to see Mexico," Pamela said firmly.

"That's right," Jones said, "and they will, they will. We'll probably go with the Peirelses," he told Hepler. "They are going to go. Fuchs is going with them. We will make it a party. Okay, Pam? Okay?"

"Why are you so angry with me always?" she said, turning still redder.

He sat silently for a while, sloshing gin around his teacup.

"It's true," he said eventually. "Pam is right. America is not good for me. Something about it. Don't know why. It's a recent thing. Used to like it a lot. Suddenly went sour on me—suppose like Vienna went sour on you, Leo, huh?" He shifted in his chair. "Pam and I used to get on very well. Now we bite at each other."

"That may not be to do with America. You know, Wilhelm Reich says the natural life of any marriage is four years. I tend to think that is giving it rather long, but . . . ."

"You're an old Viennese reprobate and cynic, Leo," Jones said. "We dull normal people . . . well, Pam and I have always been very close, you know. I'd never do anything to hurt Pam. Or the kids. Doesn't mean I don't have my restless moments. . . . But that's not our problem. We understand each other that way. It's something else. . . . Pam still believes in the possibility of justice and equality . . . whereas, frankly, I don't. Okay, let's look at it scientifically. In a given physical system, consisting of indistinguishable particles (that's us, mates), all possible arrangements of particles have equal probability. Right? Thence to extrapolate to the human condition. There is no just line in nature, since all possible arrangements have equal probability. There can, therefore, be no justice. No ideal. Just the fact of its being so. The way it is. Whichever way that is."

"Exactly," Hepler said. "Or put another way: Who can you complain to?"

"There you are, Pam," Jones said, turning to her. "He agrees with me. Mozart of the numbers agrees with me."

"It is always gratifying," Hepler said, "to have somebody quote back to you something you have told him yourself."

"Ah, good old Leo," Jones said, "he thought of it first. Naturally. He's thought of everything first."

"It sounds like his sort of philosophy," Pamela said, fixing Hepler with a look of quiet, contained hatred. "A system of thought that enshrines injustice as inevitable and normal must give some people a lot of *Schadenfreude*."

Hepler stood up to leave.

"What's the programme for tomorrow?" Jones asked him. "We

continue with the CUNT?" Pamela's eyes flickered. "Stands for Counted Units of Numbers Tests," Jones explained. "Been giving us a lot of trouble."

"What an apt choice of name. It's the cunts that give the trouble, is it?" Pamela said.

"This one," Jones said, "is a regular *vagina dentata*." He faced Hepler. "Seriously, Leo . . ."

"Never fear," Hepler said. "We shall draw the serpent's tooth."

"Leo," Jones said severely, shaking his head, "I want to talk to you about the safety aspect."

"We'll talk about it," Hepler said.

"When? When, Leo?"

"Ask Allison. Ask her to schedule a meeting for that purpose. Very soon. Next week."

"Next week!" Jones said, shaking his head.

"Whenever Allison can find a slot to fit it in," Hepler said. He bowed to Pamela, from the neck, and said, *"Ich küsse Ihre Hand, Madame,"* without actually attempting to do so.

FOUR

Allison Dubinski was a pretty woman of thirty-four, with a neat, capable, down-to-earth look about her. She wore her hair in a chignon, and was often to be seen in a loose white coat, worn over skirt and blouse, top pocket full of pencils. With her upswept hair, her fine exposed neck gave a sense of surprising vulnerability to that competent body.

After the death of her husband, Allison had wanted to leave, but they told her that she couldn't, that she was needed. In fact, she was indispensable, they said. She was the group's technical secretary, and the only one who could correlate what everybody was doing. Without her it would be chaos. Besides, she would be a security risk in the outside world. In her anguish she might give away the circumstances of her husband's death, and then it would be easy to deduce what he had been working on.

They knew when they came to the hill that they had signed on for the duration—husbands, wives, children, bodyguards, the lot. Nobody would be allowed to leave. If a marriage broke up, tough luck! For the rest of the war they'd just have to put up with each other.

For a while she had felt very resentful about being kept there against her will, but they managed to make it seem like a protective measure for her own good. Someone in her position—a widow, alone—would be exposed to various dangers if it were found out what she had been involved in. Words like *kidnapping* were used, and *blackmail*. The security services could not adequately protect her and her child in New York, because if it were found out that she was getting protection it would tell an enemy agent a great deal.

She didn't argue too much, because, in any case, where could she go, what could she do, with a small child to look after? On the hill she had a life; limited though it was, it was clearly the only kind of life she could have for the time being. She would have to make the best of it. Which she had done.

She had loved Jake deeply, and his death came close to destroying her. At one time she thought she was going out of her mind. But somehow she managed to hold on, finding a source of strength in her child's need of her. She did not think that she would ever get over her grief completely, but eventually she found that grief and some degree of pleasure could exist side by side.

She had once been with Jake to a funeral feast in a Tuscan village, and she remembered how the young widow's somber expression had been overcome bit by bit during the course of the evening as the relatives sat eating and drinking and singing bawdy songs and telling risqué jokes. In the end, one of the jokes had made the widow laugh. She couldn't help it. Allison had thought it unseemly, but Jake had said, No, no, it was possible to be in great pain and laugh, and it was also possible to be in great pain and make love. Perhaps that was when you most needed to.

She remembered this when Jake was killed. At first she had thought that all capacity for pleasure was dead in her forever; but she quickly found that this was not so. Life went on. One still had to eat and drink and breathe, and exercise the mind and body, and finally, after much resistance, she was forced to accept that she also needed to make love.

If that's how it is, that's how it is, she decided practically. She became involved with Joe Davidson, a technical sergeant from one of the machine shops. Security found out and immediately came on like a heavy father. My God, with Jake dead just a few weeks! What did she know about this guy? She must surely realize how fraught with dangers such liaisons were, considering how much she knew, what she might unwittingly reveal in an unguarded moment. Joe worked on site, but he didn't have a white badge; he didn't have top-level clearance. Didn't she realize that? If she had to do that sort of thing (and they managed to make it sound pretty depraved that she should have to), couldn't she choose someone with a white badge? She had pointed out that the people with white badges were a closeknit circle, and practically everybody in that circle was either married or attached, and she wasn't going to go around busting up her friends' marriages because she needed an occasional lay. It was not an argument that much impressed Security. It had to end, they said, the affair with Joe Davidson had to end. She said, hotly, that nobody was going to tell her whom she could or could not go to bed with, not even the United States Army. When she refused to give the guy up, they threatened to have him posted to the Pacific. He was in the Army, they could send him where they liked; rather than have him sent to his death, like Jake, she gave him up.

After that episode, Security was always coming round to question her about her love life. To get her own back on them she invented outrageous stories about guys she picked up on the road. And they went chasing off to try and find them. And came back saying the person in question could not be found, and was she sure . . . ?

She had hoped this obsessional interest in her private life would subside when the war was over. But not at all. On the contrary, now they were even more worried about her. Anybody could be a secret Commie agent. How they wished she would meet some nice guy, with maximum security clearance, and settle down, and stop giving them worries.

In the light of all this, it had been a bit of a joke that Jerry Richter should suddenly have gotten so interested in her. "It's not that you want my body," she accused the first time they went to bed together. "You just want to stop anybody else getting their hands on my secrets." And later she said, "If I ever marry you, it'll be for Security."

When he told her that he loved her, she said she loved him, too, but, mind you, Security hadn't given her much choice. There were only three people in the whole place who were not married, attached, or homosexual and had also got maximum security clearance. "One is Leo Hepler, and he is a plain wolf. The other is Hofmannsthal, and he is sixty-six, and a priest of science. And the third is you. So it had to be you, as the song says."

"I'm glad I've got all that going for me," he said.

"You're also sweet," she intimated. "And very good with Benjie, which is very important to me. Love me, love my child."

"I do. He's a terrific kid."

Despite all the joking, she had soon found herself very involved with Jerry Richter. He was someone who would not blow away in the next strong wind. She had known men who would make the most total commitments to you one night, and a week later they'd changed their minds. And then back again. All the time vacillating between one extreme and another. Jake had been a bit like that. It was either all love or all hate, nothing in between. With Jerry, things were less . . . less extreme, less violent. The ups were less high, maybe, but then the downs were not nearly so down as with Jake, and she felt, at the age of thirty-four, that she was willing to settle for a calmer kind of happiness. She was sick of all the Sturm und Drang. And the other thing was that she could talk to Jerry—their minds were more or less on a par— whereas with Jake, and with most of the men of his group, she had been decidedly on a lower level. Of course, it was thrilling to be in with a bunch of geniuses, but it was also wearing.

For the first time since Jake's death she had been able to think about some kind of future life. Up till then she had just been living from day to day. She could trust Jerry Richter, she felt, not only in relation to herself, but also in relation to Benjie. Throughout all her changes of feelings over the past years, the ones constant in her life had been her complete and utter devotion to Benjie—whatever the cost to her, the child must be spared further shocks. She would have given up any man instantly if she had felt unsure of him in relation to Benjie, if she thought he might be a bad influence, or an improper model. Even now, she thought she would be able to give up Jerry if he and Benjie didn't hit it off together. But fortunately they did. That was her great luck, she told herself. She thought she probably had fallen in love with Jerry, seeing him with the child; the way he showed Benjie things, insects, plants, trees, birds—explained to him about nature, the stars, the oceans, space; told him stories. He was a man who had time. Which Jake never had. Jake was a genius, and he could express the most extraordinary concepts in equations of great elegance and simplicity, but he didn't know about spiders, or orchids, and he couldn't cook. She would tell the story of how, on a drive into the country once, Jake had suddenly spotted an almond tree and cried, "My God! Food! Food growing on trees!" He was an urban man.

That day after the Easter break, she had lunch with Jerry and then went to find Hepler to check the program for the afternoon. Hepler was quite capable of completely changing his plans in the course of lunch. If he suddenly got a new idea, he could easily abandon what he had begun (in which case it was her job to tidy it all up as neatly as possible, so that it could be returned to, if need be) and embark on something quite different. It was always necessary to check with Hepler. Sometimes he went home, if he did not feel in the mood to work.

Hepler had told her that he was going to have lunch with the controller at the lodge, in the small private dining room. So, after leaving Jerry, she drove from the cafeteria up to Ashley Pond, along Dubinski Drive. They had named a road after Jake—unpaved and muddy, like all the rest. One day they were going to put up a museum of physical science bearing his name—one day. There were lots of grand plans. Cozy new villas to be put up in the western area, after the slum of expansible trailers had been cleared, and some day the fences would come down (they had already done away with the unreliable prowler alarm) and the ugly sprawl of technical buildings around the pond would be moved, and that whole area around the lodge would be laid out with lawns and flower beds, and there would be statues of all the Los Alamos greats, and fountains. It was not going to remain a closed town always. One day it would be open to visitors. Bamberger had been heard to say that they would make it such a goddamned beautiful place people would come there to retire, like they went to Florida to retire. There were going to be tree-lined boulevards on the hill, and in the new modern labs research would be done into the peaceful applications of atomic energy. They'd find out how to heat homes with it, how to drive automobiles with it. They'd look into all the related possibilities. How to use the sun's energy as a source of clean, inexhaustible power. They'd find ways of extracting thermal energy from rocks. From ocean waves. From winds. There'd be a health research laboratory. They would develop fabulous electronic computers that would be able to calculate just about anything. That was Bamberger's dream. He was going to show that splitting the atom need not be looked upon as an evil hour in mankind's history. To which Jones said, "Methinks Bambi doth protest too much." Jones thought that was all camouflage, that the real purpose would be to build bigger and better bombs. And Allison remembered Jake saying to her, "It'll be done, because when something is technically very sweet, as this thing is— I mean, just the sheer mathematical beauty of the whole thing, the way it all *works*—then there is a tremendous impulse to go ahead and do it, and think about the moral implications afterwards. That's why I know it will be done, whatever is possible, because that's human nature. Nobody is going to say, 'I just rather would not do that, if you don't mind.' That's something nobody knows how to say."

After she had got the afternoon's schedule from Hepler, she went to pick up Hofmannsthal. There had been something between Bamberger and Hepler, some extra tension. She had the impression of having interrupted a heated argument. Well, it was not unusual for Hepler to get heated, but it was unusual for Bamberger to rise to it.

She did not know why Bamberger put up with Hepler—why didn't he fire him? Of course, they had known each other a long time, and once had been very close, but nowadays they were often in conflict. And then, you couldn't just fire a man like Hepler. He was too important, had too much influence in Washington. She had to admit that the way Bamberger handled all these scientific prima donnas was just beautiful. Allison thought that Bamberger was just beautiful. He was such a gentleman. He had such style. She had known him a long time; he and Jake had been very close friends.

There was no scandal about Bambi; though, as far as she was concerned, he was the most attractive man in the whole scientific establishment, there was no whisper of him ever having cheated on Helen. When some gal made an obvious play for him, and it happened all the time, he just got a sort of faraway look in his eyes, as if he hadn't noticed.

If he liked someone a lot, and was attracted to that person, he would look at you with a wistful, vaguely sorrowful expression, which seemed to be saying, "What a good time we might have had together, if things had been different."

If things had been different.

There was no doubt that he and Helen had a terrific thing going for them. It was a marriage for all seasons, that. Beautiful Helen. Allison had seen the whole beginning of that romance. Bambi used to bring different girls round all the time—oh, she remembered a whole stream of them, all gorgeous, after his first marriage broke up. Then Helen came on the scene, and that was that. He had to have Helen. She was the great prize, and he had to have her. If Bambi wanted something enough, he usually got it. Whatever it was. Defeat was inconceivable to him. Everything had been going his way for so long that he took for granted that this was the way it would continue.

Theoretical Building Y-3, where Allison worked, was in the southeastern corner of the Technical Area, close to the perimeter fence and the canyon rim. The patrol road, along which the mounted guards rode at regular intervals, was just behind. Like most of the hurriedly thrown-up wartime structures on the hill, it looked rather like a large garden shed. It was a theoretical building and did not contain much equipment. There were some simple pieces of electrical apparatus of the kind that you could have found in any physics classroom of a small-town school. There were wall blackboards and desks and filing cabinets, and that was about all.

Like everything else on the hill, Y-3 gave the impression of temporariness. You felt about the whole place that its wooden sections could be dismantled and folded away anytime. The haphazard sprawl had the feeling of a fairground that might be gone tomorrow. Only the original ranch school buildings around Ashley Pond gave any impression of permanence. The strange little town had fulfilled its role in history, and now it could just fold up and disappear.

Professor Hofmannsthal did not have a car; he got about on a bicycle. You often saw him riding through the town with his shopping or laundry in the saddlebag, fiercely tinkling his bell, giving his peremptory hand signals. He was a familiar sight in his broad-brimmed black velour hat and long yellow scarf, and there was sufficient authority in his bearing to make even those who did not know who he was give him right of way. At any rate, he made the assumption that other traffic would stop for him, and usually it did. Allison used to warn him, "Professor, you're going to get yourself run over." To which he would reply jokingly, "But surely they know who I am!"

"The truck drivers don't know who you are, Professor."

Nearly everybody else, of course, did—now that he had been able to drop his nom de guerre of "Mr. Steele."

When the group engaged in experimental work in the canyon, Allison usually chauffeured the professor back and forth, since the road out was very muddy and in places too steep for a bicycle.

She had become very fond of the old boy, though it was not exactly easy to get close to him—there was a kind of kingly distance that he maintained. The only relationship you could have with him was of a master/pupil sort. That suited Allison. Though you could not really discuss things with him, you could ask questions.

A handsome old man, with his fine high brow and his severe gray eyes and priestly air. Always correctly dressed. Summer and winter he wore a three-piece suit, a gold watch chain dangling across the vest, and always a tie. The informality of open-neck shirts was not for him.

It was said that he was working on a new theory of time, based on information derived from the fact that subatomic particles travel around their infinitesimal space at the speed of light, and thus were subject to the time distortions postulated in the theory of relativity. Anyway, he often looked as though he were thinking about something like that. He was otherworldly. What this world could offer, he had had long ago. A Nobel prize at age thirty-two, for work done eight years previously. At thirty-five, with the publication of the Hofmannsthal principle, he had been recognized as one of the giants of modern physics. The principle established a mathematical relationship between incalculable quantities, binding together, in the form of equations, the infinite and the infinitesimal, forever and never. Whereof one may not speak, thereof had he made mathematical equations, mathematical philosophy, some people called it, or numbers mysticism. He had made numbers God. There was no end to numbers. Allison was fascinated by Hofmannsthal's indifference to worldly rewards, by the simple way he lived. He wasn't after anything. But if so, why choose to stay on the hill? Any of a dozen great universities would have been glad to have him. But he had decided to stay on at Los Alamos. When she asked him about this, he replied, "Oh, one place is much like another. People dash about the world believing they will find somewhere else. But they don't, you know. It's all much· the same. Van Gogh writes in one of his letters to his brother that everything there is to be found he found in Arles."

"And you find everything here on the hill?"

"Everything I need."

"That's so amazing. The rest of us all complain what a dump this place is!"

"You and I are looking for different things," he said with his faint smile, which placed such a distance between himself and ordinary human appetites and desires.

She loved to ask him questions. It was a bit like consulting an oracle.

"What is the purpose of life, Professor?"

"To see what happens, of course."

In his dry, remote sort of way, Hofmannsthal seemed to be fond of Allison. Seemed to enjoy her asking him questions. If ever anyone needed something of him, Allison was sent.

Now, as she came breezing into his little office, she called,

"Hi, Professor, we're off. All ready?" She pulled up—for he seemed far away, peering out through the perimeter fence to canyons and river valleys, mountain forests, great black mesas with steep cliff sides, and, enclosing this side of the caldera, the distant Sangre de Cristo mountains. Perhaps he was peering with his far vision into time itself.

"Sorry to interrupt your train of thought, Professor. But we're resuming. You had lunch?"

"Oh, yes."

"A sandwich, I bet. Egg and cucumber?"

"I have forgotten. Something like that."

"Yes, I am sure. And not even a drink?"

"I have my Thermos of coffee."

"Well, we better get going, Professor."

"Yes, yes."

He got up very fast from behind his desk, and she was conscious again of the fact that, although everybody referred to him as "the old man," he was not that old, only sixty-six, and very lithe. Some of the bodyguards assigned to him used to come back exhausted from his Sunday walks.

They drove out to the canyon along a road that got progressively worse. It was raining again. Raining all the time. And the most violent thunderstorms. Special shelters had been built to which workers handling dangerous materials could go during storms. When you were working with high explosives, lightning was no joke. The way they treated that stuff—just banging away at it with rubber mallets. Or sawing it like it was wood. Playing a jet of water on the saw was the only precaution anyone took. Safety was not exactly given priority. Recently a safety program had been initiated, but by and large things were still being done in the same rough and ready way as always. Before Jake's death she hadn't thought about the safety angle any more than anybody else did. Heavens, radioactive materials were handled with something that looked like long coal tongs! There was a guy who always went around with his mouth wide open, and one day he was chipping away at a sheet of high explosive when a bit flew off and he swallowed it. Didn't seem to do him any harm. They had all become rather blasé about the dangers. Like people who live in an earth-quake zone on top of a major fault.

But since Jake's death Allison had not found it so easy to put certain thoughts out of her mind. In her position, she knew exactly what could happen. Some things did not bear thinking about. You just had to say to yourself it was not going to happen. Most of the time she more or less convinced herself of this, like everybody else. She had to, or she couldn't have gone on. But coming to the canyon always made her nervous. You were obliged to use one of the outlying labs for experiments that were considered potentially dangerous. The lab was at the bottom of a hollow, and there were sand-filled barricades around it, but such safety measures were pretty laughable when you considered what they were working with. It wasn't as if what they were handling were just gunpowder.

The scary visions forced themselves into her mind. Nowadays she allowed the images. It was a trick of hers. If she thought about it, then it wouldn't happen, because it would be too much of a coincidence for something to happen that she had just thought was going to happen. That was why she had to think of it. To be safe. Let the calamities take place inside her head; then they couldn't happen in reality. When Jake's accident occurred, she hadn't yet discovered this trick of handling fate. She never used to indulge in morbid forebodings then. Didn't think about anything like that. And that must have been her mistake; that was how life had tricked her. Because those sorts of things always happened when you were least expecting them. Nobody ever said "Now I am going to be hit by a car" and then was hit by a car. The chances against its happening in that way were a million to one. So—therefore—by saying it to yourself, by keeping the image of disaster firmly in her mind, she could prevent it. When it had happened to Jake she had been unready, had even been taken in by his casualness on the phone. "Darling, I've had an accident." He had sounded a bit shaken, nothing more. Basically calm. How bad an accident could it have been, if he was telling her about it so calmly? "I'm phoning so you won't hear about it from some-body else and get worried. I'm going to go over to the hospital."

75

"What sort of accident, Jake? Oh, Jake, are you all right, darling?"

"Nothing, I got a bit of radiation. Just my hand. They want to do a blood count." That was how she heard about it.

Now she stopped the car at the top of the hollow, and she and Hofmannsthal got out. And he saw how pale and tense she was.

"You are worried about the experiment?" he asked kindly.

"To be honest, yes, I am."

"Yes," he agreed, "the procedure is a little . . . risky, I agree."

"If you think so, too," Allison said, "why don't you stop it? You could insist."

"Insist with Hepler? You know what he is like. He would simply excuse us fainthearts and get others to assist him. He is such an impatient fellow. Hates to be slowed down by anything. The only way to stop it would be to cancel the experiments altogether, and only the controller could do that."

"Why don't you speak to Bambi, Professor? Bambi would listen to you."

"I have already done so. He is considering the matter. But he says, and I can believe it, that it is politically very difficult to stop Hepler doing anything. Dr. Hepler is very popular with the Pentagon, since he promises them always bigger and better bangs."

"It seems crazy that we should feel this way, and not be able to do anything."

"Let us not look too much on the black side," Hofmannsthal said with his wintry smile. "Dr. Hepler is a good scientist. On the whole he does not make mistakes. And we are there, too. We must ensure nothing goes wrong."

"Well, hope you are right, Professor."

There was a wire fence around the hut at the bottom of the hollow. Three of the other scientists, Anton Wexler, Victor Greenson, and Stanley Jones, had arrived and were waiting. Allison used her key to let them into the laboratory.

Hepler arrived a few minutes later.

"Good, good," he declared. "So—we proceed?"

He immediately fell into an attitude of deep thought.

On a workbench stood two hemispheres, two feet apart, connected by a metal bar that passed through their middles. The hemispheres were made up of detachable segments, so that it was possible to vary their respective masses. Wires ran from the hemispheres to a panel of instruments. Hepler studied the apparatus. By it there was a pile of dog-eared papers covered with calculations. The blackboards in the room also were covered with calculations, and these were being studied by the other scientists. They were all as silently contemplative as men around a chessboard.

"Supposing," Hepler finally proposed, "that on the left-hand side segment three is removed . . ." He looked up toward the others. Hofmannsthal was studying a diagram of the apparatus on one of the blackboards. He nodded.

"Yes, three . . ."

"Remove three," Hepler said, "replace it with seven, and on the right-hand side replace twelve by five, and we then move the left-hand hemisphere six point five millimeters towards center."

Hofmannsthal made these changes in the diagram and then proceeded to calculate the effect, covering the blackboard with a long string of numbers. Meanwhile, Hepler, using a different mathematical method, was also working fast, covering a sheet of paper with his calculations. Anton Wexler was looking over his shoulder, checking every line of the calculations, nodding steadily. Greenson checked Hofmannsthal's calculations, and Jones worked on a third set of calculations in a corner. After about ten minutes of intense work, Hofmannsthal reached a final figure, which he underlined. He put down the piece of chalk and looked toward Greenson, who finished his checking and nodded agreement. Almost at the same time, Hepler came to his final figure and read it out. It was the same as Hofmannsthal's. Finally, Jones read out his figure, which was also the same.

"No bloody good," Jones muttered. Everybody in the room studied the apparatus and the diagram once more. While the scientists were engaged in rethinking the problem, Allison copied down the calculations on the blackboard. They would be filed as one of the possibilities that had been considered and discarded.

For the next hour and a half, the work proceeded in this way, with one or another of the scientists proposing a variant, which they all then translated into figures. The twelfth variant of the afternoon, proposed by Hofmannsthal, produced final figures that everybody seemed to think were interesting.

"We try it out," Hepler said.

The others nodded.

Hofmannsthal looked up and said quietly, "As a small concession to our new safety program, I suggest Mrs. Dubinski stay outside while the experiment is being conducted. There is no need for her to be in here with us. She can watch through one of the portholes."

"Yes, yes," Hepler agreed offhandedly.

"I will keep her company," Jones said, with a grin.

Both went outside, and Allison shut the heavy lead-lined lab door with the safety handle. She took the left porthole, Jones the right. An intercom system enabled them to speak with those inside the experimental chamber.

Allison got out her notebook, wrote down the date and the time, the proposed variant, and the supporting calculations from the blackboard.

Her stomach felt tight with nerves. Although there was a measure of protection in being outside the room, the fact remained that some ten feet away they were going to move two hemispheres of uranium 258 along a ratcheted bar, and see at what point the configuration approached the supercritical state. In other words, she reminded herself, in accordance with the trick she had developed of telling herself the worst so that it would not happen, they were playing with two halves of an atom bomb, and if the parts came too close together, due to either a slip of the hand or a miscalculation, then an uncontrollable chain reaction might be initiated and the bomb set off.

She'd be all right once it got under way. She always was. They had done dozens of these experiments, hadn't they? And nothing had gone wrong. The job of keeping a precise log of the course of each experiment would occupy her fully. But she dreaded that preoccupation, too, because it meant that, briefly, she might not be able to keep the possibility of disaster in the forefront of her mind, and then it could creep up on her in its sly way.

78

The others were all quite unruffled, and she scolded herself for her nerves. Hepler had a cigarette dangling from his lip, and from his manner you might have supposed it was a chess game he was about to embark on. Hofmannsthal, as always, was supremely calm. It was all of interest to the natural scientist, wasn't it? since the whole purpose of life was to find out what happens. Wexler and Greenson also looked unconcerned. The denial of danger. They could shut it out. Useful ability to have. She had had it once. But she had lost it.

Jones, on her right, seemed cheerful enough at his porthole. What had made him come out? Had he got scared, too? Unlike him. The guy who turned on the taps at the Trinity test. Though lately . . . She saw him reach in his back pocket and take out a small shiny flask and put it to his lips. So that was the reason. To have a drink. She had heard about his drinking.

4:46:12, she wrote in her notebook, *Calculated Units of Numbers Test No. 34*—or CUNT 34.

Left-hand hemisphere. 8, 6 & 12 removed. 7 added.

Right-hand hemisphere. 9 & 3 removed.

4:48:50. *Left-hand side safety catch screws loosened. Three turns.*

LH moves left-hand hemisphere, she wrote.

"How much?" she asked over the intercom. Hepler took the reading on the calibrated bar.

"Three point five millimeters."

Wexler, at the neutron counter, said, "Levels normal."

Jones could see the whole range of instrument panels from his observation porthole.

4:50:10.

"Twelve millimeters," Hepler called out, moving the left-hand hemisphere closer to the right-hand one.

Allison recorded this in her notebook. But for the substances involved, the procedure was not unlike sliding weights along the bar of a pharmacy weighing machine. Hepler had found that the best position for him was sitting on the floor, with the device in his lap. The only tool he used was a brass screwdriver for loosening and tightening the screws of the safety catches.

He was nudging the left hemisphere a fractional amount closer to center when he looked up, straight into her eyes. Something about her expression must have affected him, for he continued to look at her. She wanted to scream: "Don't look at me! Don't look at me, for God's sake! Keep your eyes on the device!"

But she said nothing. She realized that she must look terrified. But she said nothing. Mysteriously mesmerized, she held his look. And still he did not look away. Perhaps her fear excited him. She was conscious of the fact that his eyes were extraordinarily bright. Their expression was exultant and mocking. Oh my good God! His eyes were saying to her, "See what risks I take, see!" A mad dare. Doing it deliberately. To scare her? It was a way of flirting with her by flirting with death. Risking all their lives. Her heart was pounding wildly; her whole chest cavity was filled with this pounding. She felt at the same time the strong sexual pull of this crazy pass. Violent images flashed through her head: tangled metal and flesh, open flesh. He could read it in her face, this voluptuous terror, and was savoring it cruelly.

On another level to this, she was still functioning professionally, noting everything down; the panic utilized only one channel of her being. She was noting the steady click-click of the neutron counter, like billiard balls colliding at precise intervals.

Without taking his eyes off her—how many seconds had this look gone on?—Hepler was touching the rounded metal which was no longer shiny silver, as in its natural state, but a kind of tarnished black silver from oxidization.

The others all had their eyes on dials as they monitored readings, and she continued to note them down as they were called out. She was conscious of the fact that these readings were mounting toward the critical. The billiard ball click-click-click was becoming faster, but her heart was going faster still, racing the clicking of the neutron counter; the two rhythms—the one so mechanical and cold and ghastly, the other hot and frightened and inside herself—seemed painfully linked, interdependent, and she began to feel this mechanical dead heartbeat pulsing through her, a hollow alternative to her own. And then she saw Hepler's hand slip.

Vision slowed as the inanimate beat of the atoms went crazy, and her own heartbeat with it; both went beyond being countable by human senses, and the entire laboratory filled with a dazzling bluish glare, and she saw the two hemispheres come together, and her mind screamed, *"Disaster*—DISASTER.*"* Through the panic the thought intruded that there would be absolutely nothing left of any of them. At Trinity the iron scaffolding and thousands of tons of rock had simply became vaporized. She saw shocked disbelief on the faces of Greenson and Wexler; saw Hofmannsthal quietly, observantly, take leave of his life; saw Jones blinking rapidly, his reactions slowed by gin. Saw the two hemispheres sliding toward each other, come together and then saw Hepler prize them apart again. The bluish glare told what had happened.

She heard Hepler's voice on the intercom: "Allison, initiate grade one alarm."

She did so automatically.

The incident had occurred so quickly and unexpectedly that nobody had even ducked. They were all standing frozen, and Hepler's eyes went rapidly around the room, fixing each man's position precisely in his mind, measuring his distance from the device and his angle of exposure.

After the initial shocked silence, there came an outcry of voices. Hepler cut through what was being said.

"There is no need to panic—but everybody should leave the room quickly."

She had initiated the alarm; there was nothing else for her to do now, and with Jones she left the hut and climbed up to the top of the canyon, where she stood shivering slightly, a sickly horror rising from her stomach, her bones aching with the awareness that she had known this was going to happen. She had known. Known. Known.

Soon the others joined them at the top. Hepler seemed preoccupied. Everybody was looking at him with unspoken questions. Finally he said, "Exposure was less than half a second. According to my calculations none of you can have received more than twelve roentgens. The device was on the floor and the lab bench protected you from direct exposure. Most of the radiation must have gone over your heads."

Greenson and Wexler looked questioningly at each other—was this believable?

Hofmannsthal said, "I think he is right."

"I am sure," Hepler said, "that neither Allison nor Jones were exposed to any danger."

"I agree with that," Hofmannsthal said.

"What do we do?" Greenson asked.

"Wait for the safety crew to arrive, and then go to the hospital and have blood counts," Hepler said.

He took Allison by the arm and led her a few steps away from the others. For the first time since she had known him, he appeared somewhat at a loss for words. He kept nodding his head, as if in agreement with unspoken thoughts. Then, at last, he said to her, "It is very unfortunate—a bad mistake. Still, I do not think you will come to any harm. My calculations clearly show—"

"And you, Leo?" she interrupted him.

"For me . . ." He gave his Viennese shrug followed by a pale, bold kind of smile. "For me there is no chance at all. That is obvious. I was in the direct path of the radiation."

It was ten minutes before the safety crew arrived. They were wearing heavy water-repellent suits tied at ankles and wrists, work gloves, tight-fitting caps, goggles, and filter masks. They were armed with water sprays, fire extinguishers, long tongs, and organizational dosimeters.

The scientists remained at the top while the safety crew went in, approaching the hut as if it were an enemy pillbox, reading their dosimeters every few steps.

There was no sign of the ambulance that had been called.

"It will be quicker to drive to the infirmary," Hepler said. "Those who were in the room with me should go to have your blood checked. I will stay here."

"I think we should do that," Hofmannsthal said. "If I may go in your automobile, Greenson."

"I will also make my way back," Jones said.

Allison offered to stay with Hepler.

She thought: It doesn't work, the trick doesn't work; somebody has gotten smart to it. It is all going to happen, all the worst things I can think of are going to happen, I've been picked out for them.

No, she told herself, that's paranoia. Like my thinking that Jake's death was not an accident, that he had been picked out for it. She had needed forty-eight hours of deep-sleep treatment to get over that crazy notion. And even so, she continued—to this day—to have those dreams, in which she had opened the door to Death, Death wearing the smiling, erotic mask of a seducer.

For weeks she had been coming to the canyon for these experiments, all the time feeling in her bones that something would go wrong, that something like this was going to happen, and letting the dreadful thoughts fill her mind so that she would not be taken by surprise. And now it *had* happened. Almost on cue. The CUNT had blown up on them. Who had dubbed it that? Jones. Jones was the one to contrive all these waggish initials. He had dubbed the computer experiments INSANE—Instant Numerological Sampling Answering and Naming Experiment.

Allison was feeling very unwell—she thought she was going to faint. She wished somebody would come, somebody in authority, so that she would not have to think about what had happened, could pass that burden to someone else. She wished Bambi would come.

It was Jerry Richter who arrived.

"I don't feel good, Jerry," she told him.

He said, "I've seen Hofmannsthal, and he confirms what Hepler says, that you and Jones are in no danger. He assures me of that."

"I don't think I can stand up. . . . I think I'm going to pass out." She caught hold of him for support. The solid Richter. Someone to hang on to. She was glad he had got there. "I'm afraid, Jerry," she said. "I'm terribly afraid. See, I've got this crazy idea in my head again—I don't feel it was an accident. It's the same feeling I had after what happened to Jake. It's a feeling that it's been ordained. That we're all marked down."

"Come on, Alli," Richter said, "you're a scientist. I won't let you give way to these irrational feelings."

"I feel awful, Jerry. I feel I can't breathe."

"You can breathe. You're breathing beautifully."

"I feel I'm dying, Jerry. I feel we're all dying."

"Pull yourself together, Alli. I'm going to ask you some questions."

"Questions?"

"Yes. I want to know how it happened. How does it work? How does the device work? I want to know how Hepler came to let it slip."

She looked away, shaking her head. He forced her to face him.

"This is official now, Alli. Answer the questions. How does it work?"

"There's a bar . . . a bar . . . a metal rod. The hemispheres slide along this rod. Their distance from each other can be controlled. Apart, they are in subcritical state. But as they come closer together, they approach a critical configuration."

"There's nothing holding them, these hemispheres?"

"The bar is ratcheted. There is a spring catch on each hemisphere which clips into the ratchets, holding the hemisphere in place. The catches each have a little screw in them. When the screw is tight, the hemispheres won't move. But if the screw is loosened, you can press the catch so that it clears the ratchets. So the hemispheres can be slid along."

"The catch is disengaged when it's pressed?"

"Yes."

"And when the finger is taken off the catch?"

"It engages again."

"Dead-man's brake principle . . . take your foot off and the train stops."

"Yes."

"Then why did the hemispheres slide away out of his hands? Why didn't the catches engage?"

She looked at him in perplexity. "I don't know."

"Think, Alli. How could it happen? Give me a theory."

"Well, if he kept his finger pressed down on the catch . . ."

"As he felt the hemisphere slide away from him? The instinct would be to take his finger off the catch, wouldn't it?"

"Unless he did the opposite by mistake. Like pressing on the accelerator instead of the brake, which people sometimes do when they're trying to stop in an emergency, when they are confused."

Hepler came out of the hut with one of the members of the safety crew.

"I think we should get you to the hospital," Richter said.

"Very well, we go to the hospital," he consented with a little helpless shrug.

"We'll take my car," Richter said. Hepler had begun to look very fatigued, and he was breathing hard, as if he had just climbed a mountain instead of a slight rise.

They drove to the hospital.

"Have always hated hospitals," Hepler said as they went in. He lifted his hands. They were beginning to swell. "The swelling is the first symptom," he said. They stood waiting in the corridor for somebody to come out and attend to the injured scientist, but nobody came. Hepler began to fume. He was never good at waiting, and to have to wait when he was clearly an emergency case was intolerable. When a young doctor put his head out of a door, Hepler pointed a fat finger at him and called, "You, you jerk—how long do I have to be kept waiting while you assholes make up your mind what to do with me, hey?"

"Take it easy, Doctor. Take it easy. We're reorganizing things to get you a room to yourself. Save your strength."

"What for? Are the nurses good-looking?"

"Sensational."

"In which case, I take your advice." He sat down, and Richter sat next to him.

"How'd it happen?"

"How? How? A temporary lapse of attention. An aberration. Must have been. Like driving on the wrong side of the road. My hand must have slipped."

85

"Are you assuming that? Or do you recall it happening?"

Another young doctor came out and said, "We are fixing for you to get a private room. That's the delay."

Richter repeated his question. "It slipped out of your hand?"

"Like a wet fish."

"Can you explain it to me—the technicalities? As I understand it, each hemisphere is fitted with a safety catch."

"Yes."

"Dead-man's-brake principle . . . only when the catch is pressed down is the hemisphere free to move."

"Yes."

The fatigue was beginning to take its toll of Hepler. Simply to pay attention cost him a great deal.

"When are these assholes going to get me a room?" he demanded with feeble anger. "That is how they treat you when you are at a disadvantage, the bastards—keep you hanging around. . . . I will not put up—"

"Dr. Hepler," Richter said, "could I get the exact sequence of what happened? According to Mrs. Dubinski, you were moving the left-hand hemisphere towards center. Therefore you must have had the safety catch on the left-hand side depressed."

"Yes."

"How is that done? Can you press the catch and move the hemisphere with the same hand?"

"No, it is awkward with one hand. You do not have sufficient control. I press the catch with one hand, and move the hemisphere along with the other."

"Let me see if I have got the picture. You are sitting on the floor. The device is on your lap, securely wedged between your upright knees and your stomach. You are depressing the left-hand side safety catch with one hand and with your other hand sliding the left hemisphere along the ratcheted bar."

"Yes, that was the procedure," Hepler agreed, struggling against the exhaustion.

"My understanding is that the two hemispheres came together."

"Yes, that is so."

"So, somehow, they *both* slipped out of your hand?"

"Yes."

"I can understand the left one slipping out of your hand . . . but the right-hand one? Why wasn't the safety catch holding it?"

Hepler thought about this, his eyelids pushing up against the great weight of his brow.

"My mind is not clear on that point," he finally conceded. "You must realize . . . this . . . this tiredness . . ."

"Dr. Hepler," Richter insisted, "if the two hemispheres slid towards each other, then you must have been depressing both safety catches."

"No, no." He shook his head firmly.

"Then maybe only the one hemisphere moved."

"No—both. Both. They both were sliding towards each other. When I separate them, I pull both apart . . . like so." He showed the clawing-apart hand movement.

"I don't see how that could have happened," Richter said. "If all the other details you have given me are correct . . . one hemisphere would have been unmovable at that stage."

There was a lengthy silence. Hepler was white and still in a deep daze, breathing painfully. But he suddenly roused himself, and it became apparent that he had been working things out in his head.

"The only explanation that I can think of—of how it happened—is that somehow the screws were loosened—too much, and so—"

A senior doctor and a medical orderly came out to them. "We've got you your private room, Dr. Hepler." They helped him to his feet. The doctor took in Hepler's condition and said to Richter, "I think enough questions for the moment, Captain."

———

From the hospital Richter went directly to Y-3 on the other side of Ashley Pond. He wanted to see Allison, to make sure she was all right, and to ask her some additional questions.

She was alone in her small office, smoking a cigarette and staring out of the window. There were no papers on her desk; had she been sitting like that for the past hour?

"All right?" he asked her.

She nodded somberly.

"I need your help," he said. "Get out your log." She did so. "Turn back to just before lunch."

She found the place and said, "Yes?"

"When you left for lunch—by the way, what time was that?"

"Twelve forty-three," she said, reading from her book.

"Any indication of how the apparatus was left?"

"What do you mean?"

"Just tell me what you've got written down. For the last minutes."

She began to read out her notes. Richter stopped her.

"No, later. I want to know the last thing Hepler did before leaving."

She looked at Richter, puzzled.

"Just read it out."

" 'LH tightens left-hand screw three turns. LH tightens right-hand screw three turns,' " she read.

"So he did do that?"

"It's always done at the end."

"Means that even if you depressed the catches, the hemispheres wouldn't move."

"Right."

"So when he came back after lunch, he had to loosen the screws to resume?"

"Yes."

"Read that to me."

She turned the pages of her notebook and read out, " 'LH loosens left-hand screw three turns.' "

"Three turns," Richter said. "You are sure it wasn't more?"

"It's always three turns. If you turn it more, it becomes too loose."

"Explain that to me."

"Well, you simply unscrew the safety catch completely. It's done to slide off the hemispheres and dismantle the device."

"So it was always three turns of the screw to tighten, three to untighten."

"Yes."

"Is it possible that you assumed he made three turns, because that's what he always did, when in fact he gave a few more turns?"

"I am sure I saw him give three turns. It's three complete turns of the wrist. It's a detail, but I am there to record details."

"Still, it is just conceivable, with an action that has been repeated many times, that you *assume* that what was done was what was always done."

"All right, it's conceivable. But I don't think so."

"I am just raising that possibility, because I cannot see what other explanation there could be. Hepler maintains he had both his hands on the left-hand side hemisphere when the mishap occurred. He is also sure the hemispheres slid towards each other— that *both* moved, which wouldn't have been possible unless both safety catches were depressed at the same time."

She considered this for a moment.

"Can you think of any explanation other than the one we are both thinking of?"

She said, "No, I can't."

"All right, let's say it openly. Somebody loosened the screws. Deliberately?"

"Might not have been deliberate . . . might have been by some kind of a . . ."

"A what?"

". . . some kind of mistake."

"All right . . . by mistake or deliberate intent, we are saying, those screws were loosened."

"It looks like that," she agreed dully.

"Who locked up?"

"I did."

"You were the last to leave?"

"Yes. Me and Hofmannsthal. I was driving him back in my car."

"Were either of you alone in the lab at any time?"

She thought, and then said, "Yes. He was. While I went to the john."

"And you?"

"No."

"Then you had lunch with me," Richter said. "And after lunch you went to see Hepler to get instructions for the afternoon. And you got to the canyon lab at what time?"

"It was around two forty-five."

"With Hofmannsthal again?"

"Yes, with Hofmannsthal."

"Was anybody there?"

"Yes. Greenson, Wexler, and Jones. They were waiting outside. I let them in."

"When did Hepler arrive?"

"About five minutes later."

"During this time, prior to Hepler's arrival, was anyone at any time alone in the lab with the device?"

"No, we were all in the same room."

"That means somebody must have got to the device between twelve forty-five, when you all left, and two forty-five, when you returned."

"Looks like it."

"Apart from you, who had a key?"

"Hepler."

"Anyone else?"

"There are keys to all the labs in the controller's office. And you have got a set in the Security Office."

Richter nodded. "None of the others in group Y-3 had a key?"

"They could have got one easily enough. They only had to ask me, or go to the controller's office."

"But if they had done that, they could not have just taken it. They would have had to ask. There would be some notation of this."

"Yes."

"Presumably the controller's office keeps all keys, as we do in Security, in a locked key safe."

"They do, yes."

"Who has the key to the key safe? I know I have one to ours."

"I guess Bambi has one to theirs."

90

In the evening Richter returned to the hospital. All the scientists who had been in the experimental room at the time of the mishap were being kept overnight for observation, but so far only Hepler had developed symptoms associated with severe radiation exposure: bodily swelling, severe fatigue, nausea, vomiting, and diarrhea. Hofmannsthal, Greenson, and Wexler were not suffering from any such symptoms. Their lymphocyte counts showed no appreciable fall, suggesting that their exposure to radiation had been minimal, since even minor radiation exposure could affect the level of lymphocytes produced in lymph nodes and spleen. By contrast, Hepler's lymphocyte count was drastically down. The other blood tests, including a white blood cell count, a platelet count, a red blood cell count, and a neutrophiles count, were more ambiguous, but broadly consistent with the provisional supposition about levels of exposure.

The doctor in charge, Schneidermann, seemed optimistic about Hofmannsthal, Wexler, and Greenson.

"And Hepler?" Richter asked.

"It is too early to say. His symptoms are consistent with a substantial dose, but we are not yet in a position to come to any accurate estimate of how high. If his own calculation of a dose of between three hundred and five hundred roentgens is correct, that would place him in the 'survival possible' category. If it was higher, over seven hundred roentgens, we would say survival is improbable."

"When will you know?"

"It is a picture that emerges gradually. The most reliable indicator to the level of radiation comes from the platelet count, where the degree of depression from the normal is roughly proportional to the dose. The problem there, however, is that significant decreases in the platelet count do not appear until some time after exposure. We must wait and take all the indicators together."

"How is he now?"

"Quite comfortable. We have been able to do something to alleviate the nausea. The treatment is the classic treatment. We have given a blood transfusion. We give liver extract and vitamins, especially B_1. And if infection develops, which is often the case, we give penicillin."

"You are not too pessimistic, then?"

"As I have said, if the dose was under five hundred, survival is possible. I would not think it was a much greater dose, or by now we would have seen signs of hyperexcitability, ataxia, respiratory distress, and intermittent stupor—however, these symptoms could still develop."

"Can I go in and see him?"

Schneidermann hesitated only for a moment, and then said, "Yes. He is not at death's door. In fact, you will see he appears to be much better. That is also usual. After the first few hours, during which the initial symptoms appear, there often is a latent period of apparent well-being. It can go on for a week or more."

Hepler was sitting up in bed and smoking when Richter went in.

"You're looking better," Richter said. He approached the bed and pulled up a chair. "Anything I can get you? Anything you need?"

"Cigarettes. Sobranies. Pencil and paper. The other things I would need I do not think you are in a position to get me, *mon capitaine.*"

"How's it going?"

"They subject me to a variety of humiliating procedures, such as changing my blood. . . . But never mind that. What I want to tell you, Richter, is that I have been thinking—the loosened screws. Somebody has done that. No doubt. Which means that you are dealing with an attempt at mass murder. You realize that, Richter?"

"It is something that had occurred to me."

"What are you doing about it?"

"I've been checking who had access to the device. If anyone got at it, it must have been during the lunch period."

"Yes."

"You had lunch with Dr. Bamberger at the lodge. When did that finish?"

"Just before two."

"So quite early. But you didn't get to the canyon until almost three. Why was that?"

"I went back to my apartment to change."

"To change? Why was that necessary?"

"Bambi had spilled ketchup all over me."

"How clumsy of him. He is not usually so clumsy."

"You are correct. The reason is, he was angry with me."

"That also is unusual. Doesn't usually lose his cool."

"This time he did."

"What was it about?"

Hepler became vague. "Oh, the usual differences that we have, he and I."

"So you left before two o'clock, to change your trousers. And Dr. Bamberger?"

"He also—I don't think he was in a mood for dessert. He is not a big eater. A man frugal in all things of the flesh."

"Did he go back to his office?"

"I have no idea. That is for you to find out, Richter. I hope you are a good detective, because this is going to need brains, you know. You realize, whoever has done this is likely to be exceptionally brainy. I will help you while I can—I do not have much else to do while I lie here. So I will think about your problem. Perhaps we can solve it together. A man solving his own murder—would be a turnup for the book, hmm? . . . There is something you should see. Pass me my jacket."

Richter did so, and Hepler took out his wallet and extracted from one of the sections a folded piece of blue-lined paper, evidently torn from a school exercise book.

"It may just be a coincidence, but some nut sent me this in the post a few days ago."

Richter took the sheet of paper, unfolded it. In bold red print of plain upright lettering was written:

SUCH AS ARE FOR DEATH, TO DEATH
Jeremiah 15: 2.

93

Richter said, "Have you ever received anything like this before?"

"No."

"You have the envelope?"

"I threw it away—I didn't attach any importance to this. One is accustomed to this kind of sermon."

"Did you notice the postmark?"

"It was Santa Fe."

"And the writing on the envelope was also in print, and red?"

"Yes."

"Well, I don't know if this means anything. Probably not. But I would like to hold on to it, if I may."

He nodded abstractedly. "Keep it, yes."

"I will come and see you again, Dr. Hepler. Get better, Doctor."

"That is a tall order. But I will do my best."

When Colonel Delacy learned of what had happened, he immediately announced his intention of flying in.

"Of course, Richter," he had said on the line from Washington, "I have total faith in the way you are handling this. All the same . . ."

Richter had started to explain, but Delacy cut him short. "I'm coming in," he said. "Tomorrow. Let's have Tom Borneschaft and Greg McClure in on this. Set that up."

Greg McClure, in addition to being Bamberger's personal bodyguard and driver (when needed in that role, which was less often than before), was also head of the Los Alamos personnel protection service and as such concerned with overall safety measures. The newly formed safety crews came under his direction.

He was an ex–White House Secret Service man, big, with a bony, calm face and a measured manner. There was something very reassuring to the people he was assigned to protect in knowing that he was trained to place his considerable bulk between them and any assailant. He was in his middle forties now, but still very fit.

His greatest asset, it was said, was his ability to get on with people, and to make himself disappear into the woodwork when not needed. "A good protection agent has got to become unnoticeable to the person he is protecting," McClure always used to say. "The subject has got to be able to forget you're there. He has got to be able to take a shit in front of you and not feel self-conscious. Yeah, a bodyguard has got to take a lot of shit. That's the nature of the job."

McClure nowadays didn't do too much personnel protection himself; he was more concerned with organizing others. But he did still look after one or two of his "old customers," like Bamberger and Hofmannsthal, who were used to him, and when they needed personal protection preferred him to anybody else. He would drive Hofmannsthal wherever Hofmannsthal wanted to go, even if there was no need for a bodyguard. And Bamberger often found it useful to have Greg around. McClure was a great looker-after, would get you theater tickets, book your flight, carry your bags, tip the bellboy, answer the phone, scramble eggs, go out for a bottle of whiskey, play poker with you—or chess. And, it was said, fix you up with anything else you might need. "It's a job that shows you human nature in the raw," he would say, grinning.

Richter's office was not large. With Greg McClure, Tom Borneschaft, the FBI man, and Colonel Delacy also in the room, it was really overfull.

Borneschaft had the kind of shoulders that seemed made for breaking down doors. His chunky face was getting very crisscrossed with little strands of red, especially on the nose and the cheekbones and the jowls. He often gave the impression of peering at you through a mist, and at times this mist could be impenetrable. At this moment he was slurping black coffee and focusing hard. No matter how much drink he had put away, it was said, he could pull himself out of it when required, and it was evident that he was making a maximum effort of concentration now. He was an expert on the Red menace, and it was claimed that he had read *Das Kapital* and was familiar with the revolutionary writings of

Lenin and Trotsky. But basically, what he relied on, where Communists were concerned, was his sense of smell. "I can smell 'em like a water diviner smells water," he maintained.

"I'm not saying it's the fault of Safety," Delacy was saying. "I don't see what they could have done. I think it's the controller's fault for permitting such hazardous experiments without suitable safeguards. Endangering our entire capability, not to mention the manpower. Jesus Christ, supposing that thing had gone off! I am going to have to do a lot of explaining in Washington. I tell you, the mood they are in—they are going to want somebody's head." He looked around as if searching for a suitable one. "Well, Richter? What do you say?"

"It may be worse than that," Richter said.

"What?"

"We have been referring to what happened as an accident. That may not be the case."

Tom Borneschaft's face was all screwed up from the effort of getting his eyes focused right. His eyelids trembled, wiping away at the blurriness.

"I don't want to start any scares," Richter continued, "but Hepler now insists that what caused the mishap was not simply a slip of the hand, but the fact that screws had been loosened."

"Sabotage?" Delacy said.

"That would be one inference."

"What are the others?"

"Another scientist meddling . . . checking. Perhaps not too familiar with the experiment and making a mistake. Not tightening the screws sufficiently."

"Who would this other scientist be?" Delacy asked. "Who had access?"

Richter stated what he had established so far about everybody's movements.

"From what you say," Delacy said, "it would appear that Hofmannsthal was alone in the lab for a couple of minutes before lunch, while Mrs. Dubinski was in the toilet."

"Yes."

"Then after lunch, Jones arrived first at the lab, at around two twenty, and waited around outside—he being ten minutes early—until the others came: Wexler at two-thirty, Greenson a couple of minutes later, Hofmannsthal and Mrs. Dubinski at a quarter to three, and, last, Hepler, five minutes later."

Richter nodded that this was correct.

"So Jones, arriving early, was alone outside the lab for about ten minutes."

"But had no key," Richter said.

"Could he have got hold of a key?"

"Mrs. Dubinski had a key, and so did Hepler. There are duplicates in the controller's office and in the Security Office. Neither office has any record of their keys being given out that day."

"I guess," Borneschaft said, "any one of them could have borrowed the key at some time in the past and had a copy made, couldn't they?"

"It's a special key," Richter pointed out, "and only a locksmith could have copied it, and there is stamped on the key a warning that it is government property and no copies are to be made without official authorization."

"The Party apparat has got its own locksmiths," Borneschaft said.

"I agree," Richter said, "that if Jones were working for the Communist underground he could have got a key made."

"So Jones, and Hofmannsthal, in theory had access. Greenson and Wexler did not—unless all three are in a conspiracy together."

"Also," Richter said, "they were inside the lab at the time of the mishap. And so was Hofmannsthal. Whereas Jones was outside."

"And that was unusual," Borneschaft pointed out.

"It was the first time any of them stayed outside," Richter said.

"So it was also unusual for Mrs. Dubinski to be outside, and she had a key?"

"Yes. But Mrs. Dubinski was having lunch with me."

"Where were Wexler and Greenson during lunch?"

"They were having lunch in the cafeteria. That checks out. They didn't leave."

"And Bamberger was having lunch with Hepler?"

97

"Yes," Richter said, and hesitated.

"Yes?" Delacy said.

"The lunch finished early. Apparently Bamberger spilled ketch-up over Hepler—there had been some tension between them—and they didn't stay for dessert."

"What time did it finish?"

"Just before two. Hardly gave Bamberger time to go back to his office, pick up a key, go to the canyon lab, and be out again before Jones got there at two-twenty," Richter said.

"Unless Bamberger had the key with him at lunch and drove straight out to the canyon," Delacy said.

"It's just about possible," Richter said.

"All right," Delacy said. "So far we have established that Hof-mannsthal, Jones, and Bamberger in theory had access. Mrs. Du-binski had a key, but not the opportunity, since she was having lunch with Captain Richter. What time did your lunch finish? If she saw Bamberger and Hepler at the end of their lunch, she must have been at the lodge before two."

"Yes, we had a quick lunch. I had to get back."

"What did she do after seeing Hepler?"

"She collected Hofmannsthal from Y-3, spent a few minutes with him, and then drove to the canyon. I have checked that out. Thirty-five minutes to get from the lodge to Y-3, pick up Hof-mannsthal, and get out to the canyon is about right. There is certainly no way she could have fitted in an extra trip to the can-yon between two and two-twenty."

"I take it," Delacy said, "that you've checked nobody got a key from the controller's office during lunch."

"Nobody."

"That just leaves one other possibility," Delacy said. "Mrs. Du-binski was having lunch with you, and so she couldn't have gone out to the canyon. But she could have given her key to somebody. You have no proof she had it with her during lunch."

"She let the others in at two forty-five with her key," Richter pointed out.

"Whoever got it from her could have gotten it back to her in time for that. We're theorizing."

"All right, Colonel."

"So we have to add to the list Mrs. Dubinski and some unknown person."

"And me, too," McClure said, speaking up for the first time.

"Why you, McClure?" Delacy asked.

"Me and all the safety crews," McClure said. "Any of us could have come into the Security Office and gotten the key. So could Captain Richter."

"Or, for that matter, Tom Borneschaft," Richter said. "But the point is that to deliberately loosen the screws of the catch would call for a familiarity with that experiment, and with procedure, that only those in Y-3 group, and maybe someone like the controller, who was seeing the reports, would have. I would say that rules out nonscientists."

"So we come back to the list I just gave," Delacy said.

"They all sound very unlikely," Richter said.

"What are the other possibilities?" Borneschaft asked. He had finally got rid of the mist, and was fully alert.

"The other possibility is that . . . Hepler is mistaken about what happened. That the screws were not loose at all," Richter said. "That he got himself into this all by himself."

"How could that be? You say Mrs. Dubinski's log confirms all the moves that Hepler says he made," Delacy said.

"It would seem to," Richter said.

When the other two men had left, Colonel Delacy sat silently pressing the palms of his hands together in regular rhythms, as if playing some new kind of musical instrument. Finally he said:

"Richter, my advice to you is: Get after Bamberger. I have felt all along that the doctor is holding out on us. I told you that after Trinity. Now I am more sure of it than ever. Something happened between Hepler and him. There was a time they had a kind of mental love affair going, those two; they took off together. . . . Now I am not suggesting anything, you understand—I am speaking strictly of a *mental* love affair. But the fact is that now they're like two scorpions in a bottle. Why'd they fall out? Why did the doctor let Hepler take those kinds of risks? You'd almost think he wanted Hepler to blow himself up." He shook his head vigorously. "I tell you, it's not only differing political positions. There is a whole complicated subtext between those two, which is what you have got to tease out, I am convinced, Richter, if you're going to discover what the hell's been going on around here."

He took some thoughtful puffs of his cigar. "You know what you do, Richter? You go and see Hofmannsthal. That's it. He was their teacher. Get him to talk to you about the two of them—get him to open up. There may be a clue in something in their past, why they hate each other now. That's right. Go see Hofmannsthal. Work on old Hofy—I bet he knows something. And then—my advice to you is go after Bamberger with everything you've got, crack that brain of his open, and I'll bet you dollars to doughnuts you'll find something rotten inside."

Richter said, "Colonel, after the Trinity test, you told me you have something on Bamberger that could destroy him. Don't you think you should tell me now what that is?"

"I am not able to," Delacy said. "If and when it is thought necessary for you to have that information, Richter, you will be given it."

FIVE

The rain was continuous. It had not stopped for three days, and there still was no sign of its abating as Richter drove across to Theoretical Building Y-3 on the other side of the hill. Black clouds formed a low ceiling over the mesa, shutting out the piercing New Mexican light. When he got out of the car, he stepped into a stream of swirling water where there had been a path before. Twisting veins of electricity patterned the cloud as he ducked under the roof overhang of Y-3. The inside of the building smelled of wood and wet. He took off his raincoat and hung it on a hook, and went down the corridor and knocked on Hofmannsthal's door.

"Hope I'm not disturbing you," he said, putting his head in.

"Come in, Captain. A cup of coffee?"

"Well, that's most kind of you . . . if you are."

"I always bring a Thermos," Hofmannsthal said. He unscrewed the plastic cup and then the stopper and poured out coffee for both of them.

"What rain!" He sipped black coffee and stared out. "One feels put in one's place by the rain—one's human place. Whereas the sun makes one dream of immortality." He gave his dry laugh. "And other foolishness. How is Dr. Hepler?"

"Slightly more comfortable than he was at the beginning."

"There has been some improvement in his condition?"

"He has had a remission of symptoms—they think it is the latent period."

"What is the prognosis?"

"They will not know for another week or so. There seems to be a chance."

"I am happy to hear it."

Hofmannsthal sat up very straight, head high and curiously immobile, as if sitting for his bust. He had an air of quiet greatness about him. His gauntly magnificent head, with its touches of white, seemed to tower like a mountain peak above all the surrounding human flux. He was above everything: appetites, desires, wishes, longings, vanities. . . . He had mastered so much, gone so far ahead of the common herd. He had read everything, known everyone, participated in the most momentous discoveries of his time, and now he sat alone in a damp-smelling wooden shack on this remote hill.

"Well, Captain, in what way can I be of assistance to you?"

"May I ask how you are, Professor?"

"Oh, I am quite well. The rest of us have all been given a clean bill of health. As usual, Hepler was right in his calculations. We absorbed very little radiation." He paused. "It is most kind of you to ask after my health, but I take it that is not the sole purpose of your visit."

"There is going to have to be an inquiry . . . into the accident."

"Yes. Naturally. Dr. Bamberger, I believe, has appointed Dr. Fuchs to conduct it."

"Apart from the internal scientific inquiry, the congressional committee on atomic energy will want a full report from us—that is, from the Security Office—explaining how this thing happened. On that report will depend whether they decide to open a more intensive inquiry of their own."

"Yes?"

"It would be a help to me if you could give me your views of how it happened."

"How it happened?" There was a note of impatience in his voice. "It is perfectly obvious how it happened. Dr. Hepler's hand slipped."

102

"Why didn't the safety catches work?"

"Safety catches! When did Hepler have time for safety catches? Danger excites him—that is his makeup. He released the safety catches and then juggled with the contraption on his thighs. You have heard of youngsters riding their bicycles 'no hands'? It was something like that. He was delicately balancing the two hemispheres. Nudging them this way or that by raising and lowering one or the other thigh very slightly. He must have made an excessive movement, and so, naturally, the hemisphere on one side began to slide towards the other."

"You mean he did things like that all the time, and you put up with it? You allowed him to expose all of you to such dangers?"

"My dear Captain, as your President Truman has put it with his characteristic vividness, if you do not like the heat, you must stay out of the kitchen. Dr. Hepler appeared to be capable of controlling the device in this way."

"You must have had some misgiving, since you sent Mrs. Dubinski out of the 'kitchen.' "

He folded his hands before him and thought carefully. "Yes," he said, "that is quite true. Lately, I was becoming uneasy. I felt that Hepler had been tempting fate too long . . . too persistently, and that one day . . . Well, you must understand, I have known him a long time—he was one of my pupils, and so I am fully aware of his penchant for risky situations. I also have observed, in the course of my life, that fate, like the rest of us, if tempted too much will finally succumb. I was becoming worried, yes."

"And precisely on the day that your fearfulness expressed itself in suggesting that Mrs. Dubinski should stay outside, the mishap occurred."

"Yes, it is strange. If one were not a scientist and a rationalist one might almost think that fate sends us advance warnings of its intentions."

"Professor, can you say with certainty that both safety catches were being held in the off position by Hepler that day?"

"If they were not, the hemispheres would not have budged."

"Did you actually see the catches pressed down?"

"It was not possible to see his fingers from where I stood; they were hidden by the device. But there is no other explanation."

"Dr. Hepler has given another explanation. He says somebody must have loosened the screws."

"Ah—that is Hepler for you, always prefers a conspiracy to a simple explanation. Who would do such a thing? The lab is kept locked. Only a handful of us had access."

Richter waited a moment until Hofmannsthal had begun to grasp the full implication of Hepler's accusation. "I realize it sounds improbable . . ."

"Improbable!" Hofmannsthal gave his ironic laugh. "It would postulate a kamikaze assassin—prepared to take half of Los Alamos with him. Do any of us in Y-3 give you the impression of being suicide pilots, Captain?"

"The fact remains that Dr. Hepler has made this charge, and therefore—"

"It is very characteristic—he never can resist to make trouble. Even after his death he would wish to make trouble. I know him. The pathology is one for which there is no single English word. *Schadenfreude,* it is called in German. He is going to make sure that if he dies, it will be very bad for all of us."

"Professor, to make the committee accept your explanation— that Hepler brought it upon himself—that there was no outside interference—well, that is going to be hard to sell. Congress also is fond of conspiracy theories. It's going to be hard to make the House committee swallow your *Schadenfreude* theory. Frankly, it's hard for me to accept. I—"

"That is because you do not know Hepler."

"I think I know him a little."

"You do not know him, Captain. Take my word for it. You do not begin to know such a man. You are too . . ." He hesitated between various epithets. ". . . too much of a humanitarian to understand someone like Hepler. It is not, I would think, in your nature to *enjoy* to be cruel. But it is in his."

"You are telling me, Professor, that you think Dr. Hepler is quite deliberately falsifying what happened, for the pleasure of

104

making people suffer—a pleasure that he may not be able to savor for very long?"

"He has no compunction about making people suffer."

This was said with such an air of personal knowledge that Richter did not feel entitled to question it. Through the steamy rain a distant mesa top rose up like the tip of an iceberg. Everybody's life was a mystery. Who could say what anyone was, or was not, capable of? Richter could imagine, in theory at least, circumstances in which he would be obliged to put aside humanitarian feelings. There were times when one had no choice. In defense of one's nearest and dearest, or of one's country against an invader. Yes, yes—of course terrible things sometimes had to be done. But to take pleasure in them! Hofmannsthal was right; he could not conceive of that. But it was something that interested him.

"Surely, as a scientist, he must have some regard for the truth," Richter said.

"Ah, the truth! The truth is what it suits him to believe. He is always very sure of the truth. He believes it has been granted to him to see it better than other men. A gift of chance, but one to which he holds as determinedly as the Plantagenets held to the divine right of kings. And since he is very attached to sinister conspiracies, he manages to see them everywhere."

"You make him sound pretty paranoid. How can someone like that make valuable scientific discoveries?"

"My dear man, my dear good fellow, you must not think that science is *sane*. What a misconception!" He gave a dry Olympian laugh. "Science, contrary to what they teach you at high school— I mean the greatest science—is not a matter of following logical trains of thought to their inevitable destination. No—it is a matter of leaps in the dark, and not knowing where you will land. Terrible leaps. Don't think of the emotion of discovery as being the joy of illumination. Think rather of terror. It's the shiver of terror down your back that announces you are on the right track. Hepler is a good scientist because he is on the most intimate terms with that terror."

Richter pondered this for a while. Finally he said, "It's interesting—fascinating—as an idea. At any rate, I'm interested in that kind of speculation. But it is going to sound pretty fanciful to a congressional committee."

Hofmannsthal shrugged. "If I may say so, Captain Richter, that is your problem."

"I was sort of hoping you might help me with it, sir."

"I'm trying to be helpful."

"Yes, I realize. But it's just not . . . not very convincing—the idea that Hepler got himself in this accident because of some kind of metaphysical dare, and then turns round and claims somebody else was trying to kill him. Motivationally, it isn't right. What's his motive?"

"May I ask you, Captain, if you have ever been kicked in the shins by a naughty child? What is his motive? He just loves to do it. Have you never seen the pleasure children get from destroying? They enjoy to break things, let us face it. And Hepler is the same."

Richter thought about this while gently feeling the bristly beard of his neck.

"Professor, it might lend plausibility to your version of the mishap if you would give me a statement."

"About Hepler?"

"About him and Bamberger. Anything that would cast some light on this concept of yours of Hepler as a man who . . . who tempts fate."

"What does this have to do with Bamberger?"

"He's the controller. Finally, he has to take the rap. If Hepler was tempting fate, why was the controller allowing it? These are the questions the committee will want answered."

"What exactly do you want from me, Captain Richter?"

"You were their teacher, Professor, and you've known them both a long while. If you could give me some background to work with, about the two of them. Because the impression I have from you is that this mishap has to do with something between those two. Am I right? If Hepler is making up his story as a kind of revenge, what's he revenging himself against?"

"You ask very big questions, Captain."

"Better me than the House committee. No?"

"You wish me to talk of their past relationship—when they were my pupils at Göttingen?" He sounded vaguely relieved, Richter thought.

"Yes, why not? Let's start with that. It may cast some light."

"You must understand I would not wish to be questioned. You will have to simply listen to me—I will tell you what I feel at liberty to tell you, no more. It is to cast some light, that is all. I will not be questioned, you understand"—and he wagged his finger at Richter with a kind of jocular severity.

"That's fine by me."

"When would you wish to do this?"

"How about right now?"

Hofmannsthal nodded. "Yes, we might as well get it over with." He looked out of the window at the rain and took a cigarette from a packet of ten English cigarettes, Churchmans A1. As he drew in the smoke, he coughed a little. Richter lit his pipe.

Hofmannsthal spoke first of himself, pointing out that the identity of the narrator was to be taken into account in assessing any narrative. At first Richter prompted him gently, with a questioning look or a nod or terse query, in this way getting the flow going. But as his memories were stirred, Hofmannsthal needed no further prompting; he began to speak with a passion that suggested a need to come to grips, for his own reasons, with the difficult, disparate natures of these two brilliant pupils of his.

Richter did not interrupt, even if Hofmannsthal sometimes wandered from the immediate point.

HOFMANNSTHAL'S NARRATIVE

There are a few things that perhaps you should know about me, Captain, before I turn to Bamberger and Hepler. I am sixty-six years old, a widower, and though I presently live here in the United States, and indeed am in the process of becoming an American citizen, I think of Germany as my home—yes, even after all that has happened. The place of one's birth does, in the end, exact certain sentimental commitments. That is by the way.

107

I was born in Hamburg, a beautiful city in those days. My father was wealthy; he owned properties—what the English term a landowner. But the running of his business affairs did not really interest him. His life was devoted to the sciences, which he supported in various ways, with grants and foundations, and he was a man of science himself. He studied mathematics, astronomy, zoology, botany, physics, chemistry, and pharmacology. He spoke six languages, including Russian. He was a most remarkable man. My mother—was his wife.

First I studied in Munich, and later in Göttingen, where I graduated in 1906 from the Mathematical Institute. In 1920 I became a professor there. I had decided not to follow my father in the running of the family concerns, but to leave all that to my two younger brothers. The Hofmannsthal estates afforded me with an income more than adequate for my needs. So I have not had to earn my living, but was able to pursue my own interests irrespective of their profitability. My father wished it to be thus. When he perceived that I had a talent for science, he urged me to not let myself be distracted by business affairs, as he had been. I followed his advice— no, not merely advice, his passionate urging—and devoted myself exclusively to science. Consequently I am to this day a bit of a duffer about business. All this is due to my father. He taught me that one must be ready to say: I am not certain that this is the right course, but I believe it to be, and I am ready to back my belief with my life. He insisted that on the one hand one must not allow one's passionate beliefs to be confused with verifiable truth; conversely, one must not allow the fact that something is not provable—or not at present provable—to destroy a deeply felt belief. He felt—believed, you see—that there was a complementary relationship between science and belief. Certain forms of belief, he thought, must be a codified form of inherited knowledge, deriving originally from experience. He was fond of repeating the story of Einstein saying to him, "I am ready to believe anything that *sounds* right to me." Father thought that the knowledge

108

arrived at by our sense of rightness might be just as scientific, or even more so, as knowledge obtained by the most ingenious apparatus; it might be, he thought, that human consciousness embodies a scientific instrument of such a marvelous nature that we have not yet discovered how it works. I say all this to explain how I came to my own position. My father believed that this *sense* of what is right should be the guiding principle of one's life, and I, too, believe that. From this position it follows that a man is required to act in accordance with his principles—his sense of the rightness of things, which is made up partly of verifiable facts and partly of mysteriously—in the sense that we do not fully understand the mechanisms involved—acquired beliefs. But whatever the rationale of his actions, a man must act. He cannot refuse to act. Because to refuse is also an action, though a much less precise one. To act is at least to aim the arrow; not to act—that is, to let events force one's hand—is to fire blindly.

That is surely enough about myself. I have tried to respond to your question about the sort of ideas that I was communicating to my students, and I have sought to paraphrase in a few words a general attitude that I was expressing during my years in Göttingen. I cannot, of course, say what effect such ideas may have had. That remains to be seen. I will get on.

In the winter semester of 1926 two very remarkable young men joined my class, and it was a class by no means short in remarkable young men. Curious!—the sudden burst of genius that occurred in the physical sciences in the early part of this century; it is almost as if it takes a certain length of time for new ideas to ripen, and then suddenly there they are, ready to be picked. It is as if the genius lay in the times, and we, the physicists, were the lucky beneficiaries of a great windfall. Be that as it may, there was great intellectual excitement in our field, and it drew the very best brains. It was in Germany that this ferment was at its height, and we received many brilliant young men from America, speeded in our direction by the largesses of the Rockefellers. We received them gladly, not only because they were clever boys, but also because we badly needed the dollars. The most notable of these young Americans in my class was Bamberger. At the same time there arrived from Paris a young Austrian, a very excitable youth, with wild eyes and shameless arrogance, and not a penny. This was Leo Hepler. He was as off-putting as Bamberger was engaging, and though they were totally different types they soon became great friends. Or perhaps I should say "intimate acquaintances," for who can say about friendship? At any rate, they were—to state the matter scientifically and objectively—much in each other's company. They boarded at the same lodgings in the Friedlanderweg, and were always arguing. If it was not about the nature of physical matter, or Darwin's theory of natural selection, it was about electricity, or gravity, or women—in other words, the great mysteries. I must tell you there was, despite their frequent disagreements, a great complementarity in their thought processes—their minds took off together, and soared. And because they were, in many respects, far ahead of others, they used a kind of shorthand that left out everybody else. Others could not follow them. Were not permitted to. Only those who met their highest and most exacting tests were admitted to the private club of their special knowledge. They were an arrogant pair, bound to each other by their arrogance, their superiority, their unwillingness to talk to those less bright than themselves. That unwillingness often amounted to downright contempt for anyone who could not see what they so clearly saw. They were very cocksure, and not only in the sciences; all the problems of the world over which their dazzling minds ranged (just for mental exercise, for the sheer exuberant joy of flexing their intellectual muscles) were quickly defined, related to their new scientific precepts, resolved. They lit up in each other's company with their secret understandings. They played mathematical games: Hepler would start with some concept, stated in the form of a formula, write it on the blackboard; Bamberger would add something, continuing the proposition; Hepler would go on from there, each one deriving a new step from the preceding proposition—a kind of intellectual tick-tack-toe. The object was not to get into a dead end from which no new concept was deducible.

The female sex was never a part of their intellectual world . . . not clever enough! They were considered useful for one purpose only—or perhaps two, if you include domestic service. Women were either bodies to be enjoyed or questions to be debated. There was the Woman Question . . . like the Jewish Question or the Scientific Question or the Language Question. But the theoretical Woman Question was never allowed to interfere with more practical matters. Their empirical discoveries all showed that women existed to be the warrior's rest; that was their function, and as such they were highly prized: for their softness, their sensuality, their warmth, and their ability to comfort, and to dress wounds of all kinds. But they detested brainy women—they demanded that women embody the hot, mysterious beat of mysterious, unclassifiable forces. They did not want them to be rational physical creatures; they wanted them to be great games of chance.

Göttingen, of course, was a very special place then. Those of us who were privileged to be there had little doubt that we were at the very center of the great new discoveries. We felt ourselves to be inheritors of the tradition of Gauss, who had taught there in the nineteenth century, and the students were endlessly debating his enigmatic verities, and seeking to add to his hundred and forty-five pronouncements a few of their own. This tradition led to a taste for pronunciamentos. Everywhere, in the small streets and coffeehouses as well as in the more formal context of the university halls, statements large and small were propounded. And Bamberger and Hepler made themselves felt. Their heads were bursting with ideas. And since everybody was in love with ideas (good, bad, and indifferent), Bamberger and Hepler were always at the center of attention. It was not a time or place to be withdrawn. You had to make your pronouncements to make yourself felt. It did not much matter if they were true as long as they sounded good. A splendid paradox was almost as admired as a true insight, and could often pass for it. It is normal that it should be so. It is in the nature of youth to overflow with ideas—to let them pour out of its ears. The working-through of those ideas is a much longer, slower, and more painful process, by means of which many are finally rejected: the thankless labor of middle age. But at first, all that glitters *is* gold.

The intellectual climate was of course conducive to the most thrilling flights. Einstein had shown us that matter was a kind of solidified form of energy, and that opened up whole new worlds. There was room for great differences of opinion—nothing was certain now. Rutherford, you know, thought it was hogwash, as he put it, to believe that the energy of the atom would ever be utilizable, and it did very much look in the beginning as if he must be right. How were we to conceive of the center of the atom being breached when nature in her wisdom had surrounded the nucleus with a protective shield capable of withstanding millions of volts? The penetration of that core was surely contrary to God's wishes, or he would not have erected such formidable obstacles. This argument, I recall, was one that Hepler particularly enjoyed rebutting, since he was always very keen to pit himself against God and could not accept that his own ingenuity might be of a lesser order than the Almighty's. Having said this, I must add that he did at an early date perceive the basic principle of how the atomic nucleus could be penetrated, despite the defensive walls. "Perhaps," I remember him saying, "we should not look to a frontal assault to succeed. Perhaps we need to remember the principle of the Trojan horse." An example of his capacity for solving a problem by restating it, for so it turned out, of course, with Chadwick's discovery of the neutron in 'thirty-two. Since the neutron is electrically neutral, it would not be repelled by all those millions of volts. . . . Trojan horse indeed! Hepler has the kind of mind that could conceive of such a solution, prior to the discovery of the key element—in this case, the neutron—that makes the solution feasible. It is what I call the leapfrog method. First

112

the solution is found by some imaginative leap, and then you go back and look for a principle that could lead to such a solution.

This is the kind of mind that Hepler has. He is not concerned with pedantic step-by-step progressions. He takes leaps into the dark. It is a method that is likely to fail often; but if the practitioner happens to be blessed with genius it will sometimes succeed astonishingly. There is no doubt that Hepler was sure he was so blessed, and he had some reason to think this. His entire record up till that time was one of astonishing his elders and betters with his precocious brilliance. He drank up what each of his teachers could give him, and then went on to the next and the next. By the time he got to Göttingen he was a repository! And then he would shake up all this conventional knowledge into a kaleidoscope pattern of his own eccentric contrivance.

By contrast, Bamberger was much less wild. His mind was as good as Hepler's but not so freewheeling; he worked within the strict constraints of logic and mathematical proof. He was capable of doing a great deal of the sort of boring, detailed work for which Hepler had no time—for when Hepler has mastered something, he wants to get on to something new.

I can remember often seeing them standing in the street by the astronomical observatory where Gauss had worked, arguing at the tops of their voices, Hepler always sure, always audacious, always tremendously daring—to the point of folly. It was a daring that delights in outrageousness for its own sake, and in turning existing notions on their head. Many then-existing notions no doubt deserved to be turned on their heads, but it was not as infallible a way of arriving at the truth as he appeared to think. On the other hand, since a lot of current ideas usually are wrong, by asserting the opposite one stands a reasonably good chance of being proved right some of the time. In this way, Hepler often turned out to have been right.

I will come to a particular discussion, because I can still recall it vividly and it is relevant to the sort of man Hepler is.

I was then, and still am, fond of walking, and often these discussions took place in the course of long cross-country hikes. I would invite two or three of my students to accompany me, and we would talk and walk for hours.

On this occasion it was in the Hain mountains that we walked, through some of the most splendid scenery in all of Germany. I will try to reduce our discussion to its essence. I maintained then, as I do now, that the way the human mind functions is evidence of some central order in the universe and that because we ourselves are part of this universal order we are able to understand a little part of it. There is much to support such an argument. One perceives the most intricate numerological patterns in the structure of the elements, indicating—to my mind—that numerology is a method known both to nature and to man's mind. The fact that precisely two atoms of hydrogen and one of oxygen are needed to make water, and that no other amounts will do, indicates to me that nature is part of a strict numerical system. Likewise, the fact that the speed of light is always the same, always one hundred and eighty-six thousand miles a second, and that it is the maximum speed of the universe and cannot be exceeded, to me reflects an order based on numbers. I went on to conclude from this that man, in understanding a little about numbers, had learned some of nature's secrets and therefore was approaching the mystery of the central order. But Hepler would not swallow any of this numbers theism, as he called it. He asserted that everything we perceive in nature is simply a mirror image of things in our mind; that we invent solutions on the basis of the sort of beings we are, and then impose these solutions on nature as if they were hers. Having constructed a method of explaining things to ourselves by the use of numbers, we then say that nature works in this way. Having invented the concept of atoms for ourselves, we say that matter consists of atoms, and make our sciences accordingly. He was not saying, if I understood him rightly, that such constructions were necessarily wrong; merely that they reflected our method of thinking more than the method of nature.

And now came the audacious, and to my mind diabolical, leap: It was a fallacy to imagine that man derives peace and contentment by being in harmony with nature. Harmony is something created—or not—in his own mind and being, unto himself alone, and once it is in existence is imposed upon nature as upon a mirror. What we then take as being the rules of nature are merely reflections of our own inventions seen in Madame Chaos's great hall of mirrors. And Madame Chaos is supremely impartial, will reflect whatever is put before her. We peer into her depths, and see numbers and logic, and say, "See how orderly she is," and only when she shatters into a million disorderly pieces do we realize we have been seeing ourselves, and that we may be either orderly or not, according to how we invent ourselves.

I said, when he had finished his exposition, that what he was outlining was the perfect delusional system, which like all delusional systems is of course self-proving within its own chosen context. I argued that any scientific statement must be capable of being tested against some known external reality. But he was contemptuous of my "known external reality," saying that it is only that reality which my mind has chosen to see.

We talked ourselves hoarse, and I cannot tell you all of it, but it seemed to me that I was seeing in Hepler a deep-seated *wishful* belief in disorder, in chaos and chance and the arbitrariness of all laws.

I remember the ensuing scene very well, because of the sudden intervention of nature in dramatizing our discussion. When we had set out into the Hain mountains it was a fine day, but while we were busily talking, a change occurred, and now we heard the thunder and saw that one part of the sky was completely black. It was a blackness of quite ominous intensity; and yet the part of the sky under which we stood at that moment was still very bright. It began to rain heavily a hundred yards away from us, yet we kept dry. Now we became the spectators of a great performance by nature; thunder and lightning raged before us. Affected by the strange division of the sky into light and dark—and by, I suppose, the atavistic sense of terror that a violent storm will produce in all animals—I spoke rather melodramatically to Hepler.

"You are nothing less than a diabolist," I said to him. "Under the pretext of using the scientific method, of objectively weighing facts and arriving at decisions according to the evidence, you are expressing your deepest wishes: for chaos and disorder and world calamity."

He laughed while the lightning flashed around us like in the opera *Faust*. He had a very mocking laugh—he has it still. I was not usually put out by my students' opinions of me, but on this occasion I felt profoundly shaken.

"You, Herr Professor," he threw back at me, "are nostalgic for the discredited God of your childhood, God the protector of good little children who say their prayers and brush their teeth."

The storm was moving toward us in thick black layers of cloud, and the lightning was drawing closer; and I suppose we were in some danger on that exposed mountainside under the tall trees. I recall the exhilaration in Hepler's eyes as he watched the approaching storm: terror and sensuality fused into a kind of romantic ecstasy. He was like Macbeth on the blasted heath having his future predicted by the witches. He looked so young. Ridiculously young. He looked like a schoolboy. He was twenty, I suppose, but he had the face of a precocious fourteen-year-old. This is something he has retained—the look of the *enfant terrible*. I remember the thunder was very noisy. The earth shook. There is always a sense, during such storms, of the great primitive forces all around. Hepler was elated, triumphant, as if this great storm had proved his point in some way.

"I know you're always happy amid the louder manifestations of nature," I shouted between ear-shattering thunderclaps, "but perhaps it would be sensible for us to head back."

But he was excited and did not want to leave. He was very keen on explosions of every kind.

"Do you realize, Professor," he shouted above the storm, "that in less than a hundred years the greatest problem with which we will be faced on earth will not be war but overpopulation? And that wars could be the only means of saving mankind? Not by attaining any of the ostensible objectives of the protagonists, but simply by reducing population. Only war will be able to reduce the world's population sufficiently to enable some part of the human race to continue. If it does or not is of no concern to nature, of course; but it is to us, because in the course of our self-invention we have given ourselves dreams of immortality, and therefore of the limited options open to us at any given moment, we will tend to choose those that give us the likeliest chance of continuing. And if that means great wars of population reduction, we will raise such wars to the highest levels of human achievement. . . . Or else chance, indifferent to your central order, may intervene at any moment in the form of a supernova, and our earth would be vaporized."

He was becoming more and more excited by his thesis. "If some large object one kilometer in size struck this planet— and there are larger objects zooming around in space quite near to us—then there would be global earthquakes, and tidal waves on such a scale as to devastate all land in the vicinity of oceans. Have you considered, Herr Professor, what would happen if the magnetic field outside the earth's atmosphere were to change—this field which at present protects us against much of the sun's most lethal radioactivity? Change the field and you will produce on earth incredible genetic mutations, a pandemic of cancers, and completely alter the weather— and you can see how unpredictable that is already," he added, shuddering and flinching with fear and delight at another great burst of thunder. "Supposing, supposing," Hepler cried hoarsely, rain streaming down him, drenching his hair and clothing, "supposing the asteroid Eros were to hit this earth—it comes to within fourteen million miles of earth, and earth affects its orbit; it could be drawn into collision. What do you think will be left, then, of your central order, Professor? Or if any of a hundred other acts of chance were to happen?"

At this point Bamberger made the only contribution to the discussion that I can remember. He turned to Hepler, and in that composed way that he had—and still has—remarked with studied casualness, underplaying the storm and the excitement:

"Well, our friend Hepler has a faith, too, and its doctrine says, 'There is no God but the God of chaos and chance, and I am His prophet.' "

We all laughed; Bamberger had the gift of easing tense situations, a gift he has retained to this day. That is how he manages to keep a bunch of crackpots like us productively occupied instead of killing each other. Scientists do not take matter-of-factly the dismissal of their cherished concepts. If you think there is no fury like a woman scorned, you have never seen a scientist disproved in his theories. That is by way of saying how difficult we are to handle, and how well Bamberger does it.

Did I go too far in accusing Hepler, that day, of being a diabolist? He always loved explosions. Explosions of every kind. The verbal variety—he was given to great outbursts of rage or enthusiasm, seeing no reason to contain his feelings. The sexual kind—he had to always be exploding inside women. And the explosions contrived by men to kill each other—those, too, fascinated him. And yet this schoolboyish zest for letting off bangs of one sort or another went side by side with a mind of superb quickness, capable of pursuing abstract concepts into the most labyrinthine tunnels of possibility.

But I suppose the question of whether his powers were diabolically or otherwise inspired may not seem very relevant to you in your present task. So I will get on, yes. Yes. Get on with the story. Hepler and Bamberger.

As I have said, Bamberger always kept his temper; however

wild Hepler became in his assertions or acts, Bamberger, with humor and patience, and without sacrifice of his own point of view, kept their relationship going, avoiding the violent breach that was always in the offing. Amazingly, despite the foul and insulting language that Hepler so often used, they never came to blows: Already then Bamberger possessed great diplomacy. In a peculiar kind of way, I believe that Hepler may have needed Bamberger to keep him within certain limits—Bamberger was how far he could go and no further, and he welcomed that sort of boundary line. Later he got it from certain disciplines imposed by university life. He has always needed such constraints, however loose. In full spate, raging and insulting, on the verge of coming to blows with somebody, he could be pulled up by Bamberger saying, "Leo, cut it out. You've gone too far," and he would immediately stop, like a brutally punishing boxer stopped by the bell . . . until the next round.

I don't know what there was between them, if there was any genuine liking for each other. Bamberger always had girls hanging around him, because of his striking good looks and charm; and Hepler enjoyed the ambience of adoring females, and cashed in on it shamelessly, becoming for such purposes Bamberger's sidekick and the eager recipient of his castoffs. Sometimes not castoffs, either. He was a woman-thief without compunction. Bamberger was not serious about any of the girls, and he did not seem to mind. The other thing that Hepler greatly appreciated about Bamberger was the latter's readiness to pick up the bill. Hepler hadn't a penny; his clothes were literally falling apart, and sometimes he did not eat. Bamberger would often take him out for meals, which Hepler accepted without as much as a thank-you. He also accepted loans, and was in no hurry to pay them back. He considered everything that came his way as no more than his due.

His bad behavior with women was famous. He was shameless. And viciously mischievous. Once he wrote a letter to a girl purporting to have come from her fiancé, tearfully calling

119

off their engagement, on the grounds that he had picked up a syphilitic infection in circumstances that he went on to describe with much relish. The confession, though exaggerated, was basically true: The fiancé had allowed himself to be led astray by Hepler, and then Hepler had faked the confession as a wicked joke and sent it to the girl—a very low trick, the kind that Hepler relished. Moreover, in the style of this kind of self-accusation, he left out no detail of their debauchery, the villain/hero of which, naturally, was Hepler himself, whose indefatigable sexual prowess was described in terms of professed horror. There may even have been an element of self-interest on Hepler's part. "Oh, if you had seen his monstrous great organ . . ." Hepler wrote in the forged letter, according to legend, ". . . the horrifying size of it. The enormity of it was such that I was sure he would kill the wretched woman. Indeed, it is rumored that he has killed one girl by rupturing her womb by his violence and insatiability. It is said that she died ecstatically." The contents of the letter were widely quoted by Hepler himself. He was delighted by his own mischief.

The fiancé, when he discovered the low trick, responded by beating up Hepler, which included landing a number of hefty kicks in the area of the horrifying organ. Hepler did not defend himself. He was always inviting physical assault, and when it was finally provoked, he would submit to it with an air of enormous intellectual superiority.

Hepler had a capacity for attracting violence—it seemed to draw him; if there was a dispute going on, whether personal or political, he could not keep out of it, and with his intervention that dispute invariably became more heated, inexcusable things were said, animosities flared up, and finally violence, verbal or physical, ensued. He was someone who stirred things up. When the situation had exploded, he was the first to regain his calm; soon he had completely forgotten what the dispute was about. I don't think any of the arguments that aroused such passion really touched him deeply— he argued for the sake of arguing, and winning. He did not have any consistent attitude or position—this, he said, was because he was objective, but the truth was he had no commitments, and what drew him to one side rather than another was the opportunity for striking a pose. When he wished to strike a different pose, his attitude changed. He had no binding loyalties, but neither did he have long-standing grudges. He enjoyed standing things on their heads, doing the opposite, being perverse, and if that involved defending somebody he had recently attacked, he would do so with élan and without any sense of contradiction.

I say that he did not cherish grudges, but there was one thing for which he never forgave Bamberger—that he contrived to take his doctorate a year early, and so put himself a year ahead of Hepler, a year he put to good use in establishing himself on the scientific ladder—where, ever since, he has always been a few rungs higher up than Hepler. Hepler could have taken his exams at the same time as Bamberger and also passed with distinction, but it was something he hadn't thought of.

When both of them had gone, things were noticeably quieter, and I will say this: Hepler was missed, the way the noise and commotion of an unruly, troublesome child is missed when he has left home, and the house has become unnaturally quiet. Göttingen was not the same place without him.

This quietness that settled over us was marked by a kind of dull yearning. It was a period of profound ennui, of undecidedness and indirection. The new generation of students did not know what they wanted. They seemed to be falling into a sleep of boredom in the stuffy halls of liberalism; and Hepler's strident mockeries, and his invitations to violence, his vicious escapades, his disgusting behavior, his outrageous utterances, were endlessly recounted with fascinated horror.

Not long after Hepler had left, the Nazi brownshirts made their first appearance in Göttingen, and some of us then saw Hepler, in retrospect, as the storm petrel of their coming. His whole being had predicted this . . . the romantic intoxication with violence, the cutting of the bonds of decency, the standing of all values on their heads. There were often fights in the streets of Göttingen now, and voices raised incitingly, and it was all a kind of vulgar proof that, as usual, Hepler had been right. He had prophesied this, hadn't he? He had known it would happen. Not that he was in any sense a Nazi; his intelligence was much too fine for him to have tolerated their coarse stupidities, their *unthinking* violence. They were just moronic louts—and he could not have regard for such people. But they were also a force, and he was a respecter of force; they were even, perhaps, the inevitable force that his provocative spirit had been seeking.

We were soon so deeply involved in real and savage offenses that everything that Hepler had done seemed no more than nasty child's play. The obscene and foolish acts of the new order when it came to power—the anti-Semitism, the humiliation of the Jewish professors, leading to their departure or expulsion—all of this naturally perturbed me greatly. Nonetheless I felt obliged to remain, while my own position permitted. In times of national excess, if all the exponents of reason and moderation leave, it means that the country is abandoned to the barbarians. I enjoyed a certain status in Germany, and I felt that I could not turn my back on my fellow countrymen in their moment of agony. And so I stayed, despite the calls of many friends from all over the world to join them. I saw clearly that my country was descending into the pit of horror, but I felt I had to stay. I felt it to be my duty.

SIX

At this point in his statement, Hofmannsthal abruptly stopped and said, "That is all I am able to tell you about Hepler, and my past relationship with him. Now I must ask you to excuse me—I have work to do."

He appeared to have become suddenly tired, and weary of memories, although up to this point he had taken some relish in them.

As Richter stood up Hofmannsthal said, "I do not know what impression I have given you—I have spoken very freely of certain matters. Perhaps too freely. You will have gathered that I do not approve of Hepler. He is not an admirable person. However, I must add that I do not dislike him. That may seem strange to you; it seems strange to me. But it is a simple statement of fact. There you are. One's likes and dislikes are not governed by moral rules."

He stood up.

At the door Richter said, "Just one final thing, Professor . . ."

"More questions?" Hofmannsthal spoke sharpishly now. "I have surely said more than enough already. I fear you have led me into indiscretions."

"I just wanted to ask you what you were all working on when the mishap occurred."

"Cross-sections," Hofmannsthal said.

"What is the purpose?"

"To establish optimum size and shape."

"To what end?"

"End, end?" He seemed irritated and old. "It is to do with the effect of design changes on heat levels."

"Well, thank you, sir," Richter said. "I appreciate your help."

"Good-bye, Captain."

On his way out, passing Hepler's room, Richter tried the door and, finding it open, went in. The room was bare and impersonal. There were no papers out. It was Allison's job to make sure that nothing was left lying around, and she had seen to that. The wall blackboard had been wiped clean . . . almost. In one corner he could make out part of an equation. It touched some memory of his own days in Göttingen, and he jotted down the bit of the equation that was legible:

$$^2_1H + ^2_1H = ^3_1H +$$

———

Bamberger's house was unquestionably the best in Los Alamos. It was a handsome, low log-and-stone structure, with small pane windows, forming part of the original ranch school complex. It was called the Master House and looked it.

Richter had not been there before. In the past he had always seen the controller in his office, but this time the secretary had said to go to the house. He had found the front door open, as most front doors were on the hill, and after a couple of knocks to announce himself, he went right in.

In the living room there was a stone fireplace faced by a long, low leather sofa. The carpeting was off-white and wall-to-wall. There were tinwork masks—some quite grotesque in their expressions—and Indian blankets and Indian paintings on the walls, and also a tiny Klee, a Klimt, an Egon Schiele, and . . . He didn't have time to identify the others. Mrs. Bamberger was coming toward him, with that smile of hers which had made him compose the aphorism about a scintillating woman. How she scintillated! She was outstanding, and so was her home.

124

"I brought out one or two things from our New York apartment," Mrs. Bamberger explained, apologizing gracefully for the unusual degree of chic, "since we are obliged to do a certain amount of official entertaining—members of Congress come here to investigate us, as you know." She laughed lightly. "We like to make those investigating congressmen comfortable."

"I think you have done a great job with this place, Mrs. Bamberger. You obviously have a gift for interior decorating."

"Oh, do you think so? How sweet of you to say that, Captain. Do you want to see what I've done with Bambi's study?"

"Yes, love to."

She opened padded leather doors leading from the main room. A fringed rectangular block of light fell on a billiard table as lushly green and fresh as an English lawn. Bronze desk lamps switched on from the door, and cast a matching green light on the green-and-gold leather top of a partner's desk. A brown leather wing armchair faced the desk. In glass cases along the walls there were books, a violin, hunting rifles. Richter went to take a look at the violin.

"It's a Stradivarius?" he said.

"Yes," she admitted. "Bambi plays a little. Oh, not very well. It's a hobby, something he enjoys. And he always wanted to have a Strad. Finally he bought himself one. He enjoys having it. I must tell you it doesn't make his playing any greater."

"Hunts as well?" Richter said, indicating the rifles.

"No—just shoots at tin cans. Bambi doesn't approve of killing for sport. But he likes rifles—as ornaments."

"Rides too, I see. Quite the westerner."

Richter was looking at framed photographs of Bamberger in a Stetson, on a horse.

"We have a ranch in Arizona. We both do some riding there. Bambi needs some change from all that cerebral activity. . . . Oh, I think I hear him."

They went out again into the main living room. "I was just showing Captain Richter what I've done with your study, darling," she said, as Bamberger came striding across the room toward them, wearing a fresh white shirt open at the neck, looking shaved

125

and showered and pink. "I'll leave you, then," she said to them both. "Sandwiches on the table."

Bamberger planted himself on the sofa and examined the sandwiches.

"This looks like smoked salmon," he said. "And this is crab. And ham . . . chicken. What appeals to you, Captain?"

"I think—oh, maybe crab."

"Well, help yourself. What about a drink? You want a Coke? Or something stronger?"

Richter had an impression of someone who never has quite enough time. He was reminded of Bamberger's famous line on the phone, when asked if he had a minute: "Sure, if you can say it in thirty seconds."

Now he stretched out his long legs and began to bite into his sandwich with an air of needing to get through it fast.

"What's the problem?" he asked with mouth full.

"There's a lot of concern in Washington about safety here. . . ."

"Yes, I know." He flashed a quick, bright smile. "Those assholes imagine you can build an atom bomb, in less than two and a half years, starting from scratch, without cutting a few corners." He shook his head. "They should try it. . . . What do they want? I have appointed a scientific investigation team and the whole thing will be gone into very thoroughly."

"I have to go into it, too—from the nonscientific standpoint. The security angle," Richter explained.

"Do what you have to do, Captain. If you need to talk to me, I'll try to find the time."

"That's very good of you."

"I don't usually take more than twenty minutes out for lunch, so . . ."

"The obvious first question is why such an experiment was permitted, without more safeguards."

"Because," Bamberger said, "when you use a man like Hepler, there is risk involved, and nothing you can do about that. He does what he wants. You just have to accept that as one of your un-

126

known variables, calculate the odds as best you can, and take a deep breath and hope for the best."

"Couldn't you have insisted on certain precautions being taken?"

"With the benefit of hindsight, yes. But you know, we have taken a thousand risks here and it's one too many, but you don't know which one in a thousand is going to be the one too many. If we had worked on the basis of making every procedure a hundred percent safe before trying it, the atom bomb would still be three years away."

"That's a good answer," Richter said, "during a war, but we've got the atom bomb now and the war's over."

"I guess we got in the habit of hurrying."

"It's a worry."

"Okay. I accept that. Point noted. What else?"

"Dr. Hepler has made a statement that is . . . bothersome. He says the screws holding the safety catches on the apparatus had been loosened, and that this is what caused the mishap."

"He says that? He's nuts."

"It's what he says."

"You mean . . . he is saying somebody tried to bump him off? Is that it? Well, that's Leo. He has a melodramatic mind. And never can resist an opportunity of making trouble for others. Doesn't just want to go down in history as a famous scientist. Now wants to be a famous murder case. Whom does he accuse of wanting him out of the way? Me, I bet."

"What makes you say that, Doctor?"

"A good deal of his more evil mischief has been directed against me."

"I wonder why?"

"It's because we're old friends." He laughed.

"Yes, I know you used to be friends, close friends. You were at Göttingen together, weren't you? But there has been a falling out between you lately?"

"In a manner of speaking."

"It's rather well known."

"Leo is not a person to hide his feelings. I suppose he says things about me."

"Might I ask you why you put up with it—as a matter of interest? Surely you have the remedy in your hands. You're the boss here."

"Fire Leo? Easier said than done. Leo wouldn't let himself be fired, and he has a lot of pull. Besides, I never thought it right to do that. He may have a lousy character, but he also is sort of a genius, and God help us, we needed him. I thought I could handle him—hell's bells, I did handle him. Up till now. What has happened was always in the cards—it was a piece of bad luck."

"If that's what it was."

"Of course, that's what it was. I thought I could steer him away from the edge. But Leo is a man who loves the edge, gets some kind of kick out of it. It stimulates him. He needs the extra adrenaline to make that big heavy brain of his turn over. If he's saying somebody tried to kill him, that's not unusual. According to him, somebody's always trying to kill him. The world is full of his enemies. You want to speculate why that is?"

"I get your drift, Doctor. But the fact remains that he may die . . . which does lend credibility to his charge this time."

"I know, I know."

"I am obliged to take seriously his insistence that the screws were loosened."

"All right. Who could have done a thing like that? Have you established who had access?"

"Provisionally, yes. Professor Hofmannsthal, Jones, Mrs. Dubinski—if she had somebody in with her—and possibly yourself. If you had the key to the lab with you yesterday at lunch."

"I didn't."

"Doctor, yesterday at lunch, you and Dr. Hepler had a quarrel, as a result of which you spilled ketchup all over him."

"Yes, clumsy of me. But it wasn't as a result of the argument. I didn't deliberately open the bottle and pour the stuff over him. It fell over and he got in the way."

"What was the quarrel about?"

"Leo and I have had so many quarrels, it's difficult to remember

128

what any particular one is ever about. In any case, I never know. He just likes to quarrel with me. It's his nature."

"You cannot recall what it was on this occasion?"

"Just the usual stuff. . . . We have different views."

"You don't feel you can be more helpful than that?"

"I find it difficult to be helpful in a matter that I do not believe in. I do not believe that anybody loosened any screws except Leo. Therefore I cannot come up with any brain waves for you."

"In that case, I guess that's all. For now. Thanks for the sandwich."

On his way out his eyes ran over a row of books.

"You're interested in yoga?" he asked.

"Why do you ask?"

"I thought maybe that was the secret of how you keep your legendary cool under all sorts of pressures."

"Oh, that! I have to tell you, Captain, my legendary cool is somewhat apocryphal."

"I'll bear that in mind."

SEVEN

"Oh, Benjie's having such a good time," Allison said, taking Richter's hand and pressing it. The boy was running excitedly ahead, following a trail that twisted between the steep white walls of the Frijole canyon. The soft volcanic rock was pierced by hundreds of cave openings of all sizes and shapes, from narrow cracks just wide enough to admit one thin person to broad openings large enough for a family and their animals. All around was wilderness, with deep, savage gorges slashed out of the tuff by running water from high up.

"You know, I never came here with Jake," Allison said. "Nature was not his thing. Oh, he understood all about how it worked, understood the science of it, but he didn't care to go out in it—it was liable to be wet and uncomfortable. I'm so glad, Jerry, you've got Benjie interested in the countryside, and animals and birds—it's wonderful. They were all so turned inwards, that whole group around Bambi—only interested in the things in their own heads. At times it was really sick. I thought Benjie was going to go that way, too, the way he'd become so withdrawn, but you got him out of that, Jerry, you got him out into the open air, and I'm really grateful."

"He's a terrific kid, interested in everything. If you make an effort towards him, he responds. I think he's going to make his way. He's bright."

"Quick, quick—you've got to come," Benjie was calling to

them from the top of a ladder going up to one of the caves.

"What have you found?" Richter called back to him.

"Come see."

They hurried to where he was and climbed the ladder into the cave.

"Guess," Benjie urged.

"Oh, I don't know."

"No, please, guess! Oh, Jerry! Ma—guess!"

"I know. You've found the hole—it's called a sipapu."

"A what?"

"A sipapu. Through which the first people arrived from the underworld. Back at the beginning. It's around here somewhere." He grinned.

"Noooo!" Benjie protested. "This is real . . . it's a cave drawing."

"Yes, there are some in these caves."

All three examined the faded but still clearly discernible design at the back of the cave. Richter studied it, with his glasses up on his forehead.

"Beautiful thing," he said. "Amazing, isn't it! With all the problems they must have had of sheer survival, that they found the time and inclination for decoration."

"What is it meant to be?" Benjie asked.

It was a stepped shape rising to a peak.

"Like a setback skyscraper, isn't it? A silhouette of Radio City Music Hall? Come look at this here, Benjie."

"What is it?"

"It's a petroglyph. A bit different from a cave drawing. Petroglyphs are figures cut into the rocks, usually representing animals or birds or some other meaningful object."

"This one," Benjie said, "looks like a dinosaur. You think that's what it is?"

"No, no—it wouldn't be that. All the dinosaurs had died out by the time the first man appeared."

"Oh yes, sure, sure I knew that—of course." Benjie was annoyed with himself for having made such a silly slip. He was a boy who hated to be caught out in a mistake.

"As a matter of fact," Richter said quickly, to pass over the area of sensitivity, "this whole mountain range—because all this is part of the Rocky Mountains here—came into existence round about the time of the last of the dinosaurs. About sixty-five million years ago. Though the part we are in now was created only about one million years ago, out of the Jemez volcano."

Benjie was looking frowningly at the petroglyph that resembled a dinosaur.

"How can anyone be sure," he asked, "that there were no dinosaurs at the same time as man?"

"No dinosaur bones have been found after the end of the Mesozoic Era," Richter explained. "In the lower layers of rock you find very large numbers of such bones, and then suddenly there comes a layer many feet thick without any. It's a dead layer of rock, generally. After that comes a layer containing the bones of early mammals—the ancestors of the camel, the bison, the elephant. But nobody has been able to explain the dead layer in between, representing millions of years. What was going on in that age? Why was the earth so dead? Or what was it that existed and died out without leaving any trace of itself behind? It's a fascinating problem."

"What do you think happened, Jerry?"

"Oh, there are a number of theories. That some change occurred in the earth's temperature, and the dinosaurs couldn't adapt to it because they lacked the temperature-regulating mechanisms of mammals. Or that their small brains were not adequate for dealing with some other circumstance that arose. Or there may have been some catastrophic change in plant life that affected their food supply—it's purely speculative, but if for some reason the photosynthetic process were to have been impeded—that is, the effect of sunlight on plant life—then the whole chain of nature could have been broken and halted until it found a new start somewhere else. There's also the possibility that the dinosaurs simply came to the end of their time. They'd been around for a hundred and thirty-five million years—and maybe everything has a preallotted span and at the end of it has got to go. The one thing it does tell you, though, is that no form of life has been given any guarantees by anybody about going on forever, and that it's possible to make a foul-up of things."

On their way back they stopped at the Tynonyi ruins. Benjie walked slowly around the circular remains of the fourteenth-to-fifteenth-century pueblo, looking carefully at the ground plan revealed by the remaining stones.

"Look!" Richter said. "He's picturing it—working it out. What it must have been like six hundred years ago."

Benjie suddenly came haring toward them, calling out excitedly, "Hey, Jerry! Jerry! I saw a snake, a big one, with a diamond pattern all down its back. Those are the ones that are dangerous, huh?"

"Yes."

"What should you do if you get bitten by one, Jerry?"

"Well, if you haven't got any snake serum, best thing to do is make a little cut in the bite to get the blood to flow, get rid of the venom."

"I don't know if I could do that."

"Best thing is not to get bitten. Usually snakes don't attack you—they get out of your way if they know you're coming. So in an area where there are snakes, you beat the path ahead of you with a stick. Though once, I tell you, I was standing in a stream looking at a crimson finch acting very aggressive towards a hen zebra finch, watching them through my binoculars, when, what do you know, a snake winds itself around my calf. Must have taken me for a rock, I was so still."

"Oh my Gawd! What happened, Jerry?"

"I just stood perfectly still until it went away."

"Gawd! How long?"

"Oh, about fifteen minutes."

"I'd have died! I couldn't have done that."

"Well, if I'd tried to pull him off, that's when he would have bitten."

"Gee! I couldn't do it—I'd panic."

"No you wouldn't. Just remember, Benjie, if I ever see a snake curled around your leg and I call to you, 'Freeze,' you just

133

freeze." He ruffled the boy's hair fondly, and Benjie ran back to study the ruins some more.

Allison said, "He loves you, Jerry. And speaking of that . . . that makes two of us."

He did not reply, and she said quickly, "Did I say something I shouldn't have?"

"Why?"

"I saw a shadow pass across your brow."

"Yes," he said.

"Well, what?"

"You're leaving," he said. "How can you say what you just said and be leaving?"

"How do you know I'm leaving, Jerry?"

"I have to know things like that. You gave in your notice immediately after the accident."

"I had given it in before, and then I took it back . . . because of you. You were the only reason I stayed on."

"And I'm no longer a reason?"

She looked unhappy. "Both of us have said we're not going to stay on here. Come, too. Let's go to New York. I've had this place—it scares me. First Jake, now Leo. It's given me the willies. I keep feeling something else is going to happen. I'm afraid. I'm afraid for Benjie. For all of us. I think there's a jinx on this place—I know I shouldn't say that, as a rational human being and a scientist, but I have got that feeling, and it gives me the willies and I want to get out. And quick."

"Next week. That *is* quick."

"Listen," she said, suddenly flaring up, "people are always holding me here—especially you security people. One way or another. First I couldn't leave because I was Jake's wife, and then when he was dead I was needed—and, besides, I knew too much, and there was a war on, and it wasn't safe for me to leave. Well, I don't feel safe staying. That's the truth. I want to get out. I have a small child, that's all I have, and I get funny feelings."

"I understand," Richter said. "I certainly understand. But leaving like that—you didn't even discuss it with me. It feels like you're running out on me, and also—"

"I didn't want to discuss it with you because I knew you'd try to talk me out of it. So I thought, I'll do it first, give in my notice, and tell you after. Then it'd be done. Why don't you come with me, Jerry? Let's go together—right away. We'll be happy in New York. This is no kind of life here. This place gives me the creeps."

"Allison, it's understandable for you to feel this way after what you have been through. But I can't leave. You forget—I'm in the Army. You are not just allowed to leave when you like, or do what you like."

"You could apply for a discharge, or transfer."

"They are not going to give me that in one week. Besides, I want to finish what I'm doing, I want to clear up this whole business . . . the accident."

"All right—-then you join me when you can," she said, in a flat, steely voice.

"What does that mean, Allison? *When I can.* Could be months."

She said, "I can't stay here, Jerry." Her face was set and firm with a grim kind of resoluteness. "I've made up my mind. I'm frightened. For Benjie. Do you realize what might have happened, if Hepler hadn't separated those hemispheres in time?"

"That's why it's so serious, and the reason I have to stay on, and find out who loosened the screws, and why."

"There were no loosened screws—except in Hepler's head," she said, flaring up violently. "His hand slipped. I saw it. I saw it all happen. He's sending you off on a wicked wild goose chase with his stories. All that is baloney, believe me."

"What makes you so certain?"

"Because I know, Jerry. I know because—" She stopped herself, and then, with a little what-the-hell shrug, went on defiantly, "I know because when it happened, he was looking at me."

"Looking at you? What do you mean?"

"Instead of looking at the device. Making eyes at me, if you want to know. That way he has of looking at women, which says exactly what's on his mind."

"He must have had plenty of opportunity to express what's on his mind where you are concerned. Why choose a time like that?"

"Deliberately. That's Leo all over. It excited him. Don't you see? A dare—a perverse dare. Showing off. Taking his eyes off that contraption—taking his eyes off it even for a moment—was insane, the way he had it sitting on his lap, balanced like that. But that was the whole point, the insanity of it. Making a crazy pass."

"Were you leading him on?"

"No, no, how could I have been? I was terrified."

"Then what made him choose that moment? Why then?"

"I think he saw I was terrified, and that excited him in some way. My fear excited him. Have you never heard of that? Getting me more and more afraid . . . like some kid driving a car on the wrong side of the road, deliberately, while he fools around with you. You never heard of adolescent games like that?"

"Why didn't you go away from the window? If he'd had no audience to show off to . . ."

"I couldn't. That's the whole point. He'd gotten me mesmerized with fear, or whatever. I couldn't budge to save my life. That's right—to save my life I couldn't. Besides which, I was supposed to be there. That was my job. It is true that I should have looked away, or done something—put my tongue out at him, something to have broken the spell. The point is, I didn't because I couldn't."

"You were excited, too?"

She didn't answer at first, just looked unhappy, and kept wringing her hands in agitation. Finally, she forced herself to speak, after first looking around to make sure that Benjie was occupied and far enough away not to hear.

"It was like in a dream when you have no willpower to control what is going to happen—and the fact that it was so perverse, so dreadful, that he should be handling that machine of death and at the same time making this terrific pass at me. . . . It connected with something in me—well, evidently—because, as I say, I couldn't look away. It was like we were in some crazy suicide pact—I just was compelled to go along with him.

"It seemed like the realization of a dream that I've kept having ever since Jake's accident. In this dream I'm with this man who is—well, let's say everything you are not, Jerry: cruel, totally selfish, using me solely for his pleasure, brutish. And there are things he does . . . Well, anyway, the thing is, I'm tremendously excited by this guy in the dream, I'm frankly flipping, and—and . . . well, you know. And that's when he peels off his face, which is a mask, and it's Death, that's who it is. Yes, *himself.* Old skull-and-crossbones with the scythe. I am terrified. I try to wake up, because I know it's a dream, but I can't, I've gotten trapped in my own dream and can't get out, and I am so terrified because I have let Death into my house, have let him seduce me with his lecherous ploys . . . and I'm scared for Benjie. That's the dream. And it was exactly that kind of feeling I had with Hepler, of being trapped in a terrible dream and not able to get out—and suddenly there it all was in reality, happening to me."

She was trembling. "Give me a cigarette, Jerry." He did so and lit it for her.

"Calm down," he said.

"Anyway, I'm glad I told you. It was eating me up."

"I'm glad you told me, too."

"Benjie! Benjie!" she called. "We're going home."

He turned to her and said, "Even with all that, I'm going to ask you to stay. I'm going to ask you to stay because I love you and I don't want you to go. It'll be all right, Allison—I promise you."

She said nothing.

EIGHT

"What about a little drinkee?" Jones said. " 'Fraid there's only gin." Richter declined; he took out his pipe.

Jones went to his briefcase, unlocked it, and produced a bottle of Gordon's wrapped in brown paper. He poured gin into a tumbler and took a long gulp.

"You can drink that without ice, or orange juice or anything . . . ?"

"Orange juice!" Jones said disgustedly. "What has orange juice got to do with it? You don't imagine I drink this for my health, do you?"

"Why *do* you drink, Dr. Jones?" Richter asked with gentle directness.

"I drink, you fool," Jones said, "to ease the pain of living—why the fucking hell else do you suppose anyone drinks? And to piss at the moon, that's why." He let out a long sigh of relief, shook his head like a wet dog, and said, "That's better." He poured more gin into the tumbler. "Sorry if I was rude," he said with a grin, combing his fingers through his lank blond hair. "I needed that drink. Better now."

"I brought Benjie," Richter said. "He wanted to see Tony and Sarah—you mind?"

"No, no—good idea, as a matter of fact. They can go and play—otherwise they listen. They hear everything. Every bloody thing. Can't keep anything from kids." He called: "Tony! Sarah!

Benjie's here. Run down and play. Go on, buzz off. . . ." He aimed a jocular kick in their direction as they came running through the living room, two tall, thin, blond copies of their father.

Sarah Jones, aged nine, said, "Do you know Mr. McClure, Captain Richter?"

"Yes."

"He says he used to be Mr. Roosevelt's bodyguard. Is that true?"

"Yes."

"He says that if somebody tries to shoot the President, the bodyguard has got to protect him with his own body. Is that true, Captain Richter?"

"They are trained to do that, as a last recourse."

"Wheeeew!" Sarah said. "I wouldn't like a job like that."

"They wear bulletproof vests, stupid," Tony told her. "Don't they, Captain Richter?"

"You can still get shot in the head," Richter said.

"McClure says he's so tough his skin is bulletproof," Tony said with a sneer. "That's what he claims."

"That may be exaggerating a bit," Richter said. "But it is true he is very tough."

"Okay, men," Jones said, addressing the children, "skedaddle . . . disappear."

"Where's Benjie?" Tony asked.

"Just outside." Richter gave a little awkward cough. "Allison— Mrs. Dubinski—doesn't want him to leave the compound . . . so you play around here, okay?"

"There's no harm in them going out," Jones said. "You can't keep children caged up . . . they're not like scientists."

"I would prefer if you stayed around here," Richter said. "I was asked to say that, so if you wouldn't mind, Tony . . . ?"

"Okay, Captain. We won't go far."

"Thank you."

When the children had gone, Richter said to Jones: "So you'll be leaving quite soon, I gather."

"Yes," Jones said vaguely. "I expect so."

"Staying on here is definitely out, then?"

"There's no point, is there? Since your lot don't trust us."

"What makes you say that?"

"Come on, Captain. Don't try and pull the wool over my eyes: there's a wall been put up between us—the British, that is—and any really important stuff."

"You feel that?"

"I know that."

"Well, perhaps it is felt that since you are leaving, and will no longer be responsible to anyone here. . . . I'm guessing."

"No, this wall started going up before it was known we were leaving. I felt it. Even Hepler—when he talks to me—is careful not to let on too much."

"Careful about what?"

"Don't you know, Captain?"

Richter relit his pipe. "Careful?" he prompted.

"You don't trap me like that," Jones said. "If you don't know, I don't know. How is Hepler?"

"Not so good."

"He's going to die," Jones said. "He's got that look."

"You saw him?"

"Yes, I went to see him. Want him to leave me his telephone numbers in his will." He gave a laugh. "Don't know how he does it . . . funny little runt of a man. All those women. Of course, women are fascinated by his sort."

"What do you mean by 'his sort'?"

"Shits."

"You don't seem to like him."

"He's not the most endearing fellow in the world, is he?"

"How did it happen, do you think? The accident?"

"Things like that always happen to Leo. He's fated."

"Is that why you went outside the lab that day?"

"Yes, I thought you were going to ask about that. Well, the answer is I don't know why I did it. I was not aware of having any special reason. Perhaps I had an *unconscious* premonition. Something telling me, stay outside. But I didn't consciously work it out that something was going to happen. It was just—a feeling."

140

The children came bursting into the room, and Tony demanded heatedly, "Dad, isn't it true that the atom bomb is condemned as a war crime by the Geneva Convention? Benjie says it isn't."

"What the Geneva Convention says," Benjie replied, "is that cruel methods of warfare are prohibited."

"Well," Tony Jones said triumphantly, "isn't the atom bomb *cruel*? What could be crueler?"

"All methods of warfare are cruel," Benjie said. "The atom bomb is no crueler than—"

"Then what's the point of condemning any of it," Tony Jones insisted, "if it's all the same? Then what are we doing putting the Nazis on trial at Nuremberg?"

"There's a difference," Benjie maintained.

"What's the difference?" Tony Jones demanded. "Come on, you tell me! What's the difference between what the Nazis did and us dropping the atom bomb on the Japs? Go on, you tell me."

Benjie looked to Richter to help him, but Richter was saying nothing.

"Well," Benjie began, "it's difficult to explain exactly. . . ."

Tony Jones did his superior sneer. His little sister giggled. "Because you can't explain it," he said.

"Oh yes I can," Benjie said. "It's like . . . people under the Nazis were in their power. . . ." He began to flounder a bit. "And the Nazis killed those people. . . ."

"Go on, then, *explain* it," Tony Jones said.

"Well . . . if somebody is in your power and you kill them it's different. The Japs could defend themselves . . . or they could have surrendered. . . . But the Jews couldn't."

When the children had been packed off again, Jones said thoughtfully, "Going to be a smart Jewish lawyer, that Benjie. Jews are very good at splitting hairs—the Talmudic tradition. That's the way Bambi does it. The speed of the thought deceives the mind."

"That's a bit harsh, isn't it?"

"Yes, it is. I agree. As a matter of fact, I think it's rather loyal

141

of Benjie to stick up for his father—unlike my lot, only too ready to condemn me as a Nazi war criminal. Though they're probably right."

He laughed, poured himself more gin.

"Marriage is a wonderful institution," he said, drinking, "but like the man said, who wants to live in an institution? Oh, Pam is a fine woman, and what's more, is going to make it a better world. Why does that make me want to puke?"

"Perhaps you don't want it to be a better world . . . perhaps you like it as it is."

"Hepler's world, yes. Use and be used. That's his rule of life. None of this sentimental twaddle about women and children first, hey? The law of nature is *me, me, me.* The rest are *Unmenschen.* We're all *Unmenschen* to Leo, movable objects in his universe, governed by the rule of force and nothing else. Superior force, that's all that counts. And women love it . . . women love being *Unmenschen,* you see. Thrills their little masochistic *Unmenschen* souls. You know something, Captain? I wish I had the courage of that little shit. I'll tell you something shocking—I can't stand Pam anymore. Can't stand my wife, you see. Not a unique problem. I don't know why I should be able to stand her, since I can't stand myself either. In fact, if anything, I can stand her slightly more than myself."

———

The muslin screen at the end of the small isolation ward did not extend across the entire opening, and Richter could see beyond it and inside. This room was even more shedlike than others on the hill, and it had a strong smell of Dettol. A tall, angular nurse was rubbing lotion on Hepler's body. He was on his stomach. "Here we go," she said, and flipped him over on his back again. "Oh, you can come in, Captain," she called out, spotting Richter behind the screen. "Dr. Hepler is almost all through now."

As Richter came toward the bed, he saw that Hepler's face was shiny with fever and swollen. His glistening eyes moved within their puffed-up sockets like marbles rolling to and fro on cushions.

142

He was watching his nurse intently, passionately, as she moved around the bed tending to him. He watched her every movement. She was a plain girl, and it must have been a rare experience for her to arouse so much interest in a man. As she moved around the bed, Hepler kept seeking to touch her, and she kept dancing clear of his fumbling hands, with a continuous "Now, now, Doctor, now then . . . none of that, you know." He was muttering things to her as she placed his pillows and puffed them out, holding him easily forward; suddenly he pushed a bundle of dollar bills into her hand, and she turned away, exhaling wearily, without giving him an answer. "He's all yours, Cap'n," she said over her shoulder, and then she motioned to Richter and took him just out of earshot.

"He's got over a hundred and five," she said. "Delirious."

She opened her hand to show the bunch of crumpled, moist dollar bills. "Seems to think this place is some kind of cathouse— keeps forcing money on all the girls. Wants us to do things that are not part of a nurse's duties." With a sour expression, she riffled the sticky bills and then put them into a large brown envelope already bulging with money. "Can you imagine?" she said with a short, raw laugh. "Me? I'm not exactly Rita Hayworth." She laughed again incredulously. "He's delirious," she snapped. "That's what it is."

Richter approached the bed.

"How you doing, Doctor?"

"You want to know? I am covered in blisters, which become infected because my white blood cells are so low. My hair begins to fall out. I have other problems with other parts. My body is slowly putrefying, Richter. Also, I am bored. Dying is a very boring business. You know what you could do for me, Captain, if you wanted to do me a favor?" He looked around furtively, and then beckoned Richter closer. "You have a gun—hmm? A military man. Bring me a gun, Richter." He grabbed at Richter's sleeve. "Will you? *Will you?*"

Richter said nothing. Hepler let go of his sleeve and made a disgusted motion of his hand. "If you won't bring me a gun, at least give me a cigarette, you shit-faced baboon."

143

Richter took out a packet of Chesterfields and offered them to Hepler.

"You don't have Sobranies, of course . . ." He took the pack nonetheless, fumbling to extract a cigarette from the tightly packed bunch. His fingers were as swollen as the fingers of New Year's balloons. Richter took out a cigarette and put it in Hepler's mouth. He lit the cigarette for him, and Hepler drew in smoke with relief. "You know the story," Hepler said, "of the great man who was dying and he was asked if he would like a lying-in-state after he was dead? The great man said no, he would feel too self-conscious. I can tell you, Richter, I feel in sympathy with that man. They all come in here to look at me, and I can see in their heads, What, not dead yet? How long is he going to mess about like this, hanging around on the edge? . . . I tell you, the gun would be the best solution."

"I talked to Dr. Schneidermann. He says there is some improvement in your platelet count. He thought that was an encouraging sign."

"Bullshit," Hepler murmured. "Dr. Schneidermann is a great bullshitter. . . . Well, Richter, what do you want? You have found my murderer? That is one present you could bring me that I would appreciate."

"Dr. Hepler, nobody I've talked to is willing to believe that anyone loosened any screws, apart from yourself."

"Naturally they would say that."

"You might expect one person to say that—the one who had loosened the screws. But all of them say it."

"Are you suggesting *I* am lying? What interests do I have? Of course they all pooh-pooh the idea. . . . It is less trouble to make me out crazy than to have to prove they are innocent. In any case, they are not so innocent. . . . You have established who had access?"

Richter nodded.

"Well, who was it?"

"It looks as though it's limited to Hofmannsthal, Jones, maybe Mrs. Dubinski—*if* she had an unknown accomplice—maybe Dr. Bamberger . . . *if*—"

144

"Ah, yes, Bambi, of course . . . after he spilled the ketchup over me. Perhaps that was why he did it, to give him the opportunity. . . . He could have gone to the lab?"

"In theory. If he had the key with him during his lunch with you."

"Yes, this is interesting. . . ."

"Are you seriously suggesting . . . that Dr. Bamberger . . . ?"

"No, I make jokes. Because this is such a funny situation I am in. . . . My Viennese sense of humor, you think?"

He sank back in the pillows, his white features merging into the surrounding whiteness, breathing hard. When he could manage to speak again, he said:

"He is a man of conscience, Bambi. Always examining his conscience. How does it look today? It is parted on the right side. Does it suit me? Do I look good wearing it like this, or might I look better wearing it like that? More to the left. . . . He is a lefty, of course, you know . . . but how far left, that is another matter. He is also a pragmatist . . . he can part his hair in the middle, too. Of course, you know that he has always had chauffeurs and butlers and maids. People to wash and iron his shirts. He changes his shirt three times a day. Did you know? To maintain that air of unperspiring cool. He travels everywhere first class. He goes only to the best restaurants. But all the same he is a lefty . . . not out of true conviction, not out of logic, not even out of sympathy with the workers. When has he ever spent five minutes with a worker? He does not know what a worker is as a person, only as a statistic. No, he is a lefty of the worst sort—out of guilt. That whole bunch around him were the same—Jake, Allison. . . . Yes, Captain, Allison. She is another. They were quite a little cell at one time. Did you know about Allison's first husband? Oh, you did not even know she *had* a first husband. Yes, briefly, very briefly. Victor Clement. Oh, a real Red. They were married the day before he left to fight for the Republicans in Spain. It was very romantic. Jake was best man. When Victor was killed, a few weeks later, it was Jake who brought the news to Allison in Paris, and then she promptly took up with Jake. Oh, she's a real Red lover, our Allison."

"Are you saying Allison is also a Communist?"

"Let me put it this way: Communist men are her type. Are you also a Red, Captain?"

"People say you like to make trouble," Richter observed.

"What a thing to say to a dying man! Have you no respect for the dying, Captain?"

"You are sticking by your statement—that somebody attempted to kill you?"

"Attempted? Captain, what do you mean 'attempted'? Succeeded. It is only a matter of time now. In a few days' time you will be handling a famous murder case. Are you up to it?"

He gave an exhausted mocking laugh.

NINE

Richter's head was whirling when he left the hospital. What to believe?

He needed fresh air. Was Hepler really dying? He seemed very sure of it, and he was never wrong. Dr. Schneidermann had said the illness was taking its expected course; there had been the usual latent period, followed by the onset of severe symptoms, but the prognosis remained the same as at the beginning: survival possible. Dr. Schneidermann said he saw no reason to alter that opinion. It was only relative to the latent period that Dr. Hepler would appear to have taken a turn for the worse. In fact, his illness was progressing normally.

Richter drew the fresh night air deeply into his lungs, and looked up at the stars. Mysteries; one was surrounded by mysteries.

If Hepler was telling the truth, one of his distinguished scientific colleagues had tried to kill him—and God knows how many others. It was inconceivable, wasn't it? Hepler had said, "In any case, they are not so innocent." What did he mean by that? Did he mean, because they had made the bomb? Or was he referring to something else?

Questions, questions, questions.

Nothing was clear.

There was no one about. It was not a night place. Lights and music were coming from the Services Club, and from the lodge, but the unlit streets were empty. One did not walk around after dark. The patrols would stop you and ask what you were doing. Only around the hole in the fence (beyond the area of expansible government trailers) was anything going on: people slipping in and out. The guards knew their hell raisers and turned a blind eye to it. The Technical Area was brilliantly illuminated, like an empty stage all lit up.

The same characters spun round and round in Richter's head. Hofmannsthal, Allison, some supposed accomplice of Allison's, Jones, Bamberger. The same cast. Always the same.

He could not believe that any of these people could have done such a thing. He was a man who believed that people could not help giving themselves away, if only one knew what to look for. People told you who they were. Richter had studied body language. He had read Confucius, and Confucius said, "Observe the manner of men's behavior, observe the motives of their actions, examine those things in which they find pleasure. How can anyone conceal himself!" This was surely true. Except that spies and murderers did successfully conceal themselves. Sometimes.

Hofmannsthal had said, "Do any of us strike you as suicide pilots?" A good point.

Allison and Jones had been outside the lab at the moment of the mishap. On the assumption that the chain reaction would be halted, anyone outside the lab could have reasonably expected to survive. But it was a big assumption. No; anyone doing such a thing would have to be crazy. Or—a suicide pilot.

Which of them gave signs of being that? Jones?

Jones was outside the lab at the time of the mishap. He had gone out on his own initiative.

Jones, so unflappable at one time, had become a drunk. Detested himself. Detested his wife. Detested Hepler. Jones thought of himself as a war criminal. Also, he had arrived at the canyon lab early—enough time to go in, loosen the screws, come out again, and be waiting outside when the others arrived. He would have had to have a duplicate key. Could have had one made on some previous occasion when he had borrowed the key.

Was Jones the suicide pilot? Tanked up with gin?

What about Allison? She was the other one outside the lab at

the time. She had the key. She could have given it to someone—
who?—and he could have used it to get in during the lunch hour.
Plenty of time.

Allison, as Hepler had pointed out, was very involved with
Communists—even if only on a romantic level. Her first husband
was a Communist who died fighting against Franco. That could
have made Allison more than ever committed to the Communist
cause. (And it was worth bearing in mind that General Brown had
fought on the other side in the Spanish Civil War—*for* Franco.)
Allison's second husband, Jake Dubinski, if not an open Communist, was certainly a pinko, and a supporter of front organiza-
tions. He, too, had died. There was good reason for thinking
that—on some level—Allison held the scientific research establishment and the U.S. government responsible for Jake's death, and
that she thought there was something behind it, that Jake had in
some way been picked out.

There was no question, Allison was scared. What made her so
scared?

What did she know that had scared her into wanting to leave
immediately?

Or did she want to leave because she was afraid that certain
things about her might be found out?

What things?

Supposing she had given someone the key to the canyon lab.
Out of a sense of grievance. Or out of some kind of romantic
loyalty to the beliefs of two dead husbands fallen for the cause.
So—she gives the key to someone, thinking he is going to sketch
the apparatus, or photograph it. She doesn't know he is going to
fiddle with the screws, but she is nervous, and her nervousness is
perceived by Hofmannsthal, who sends her out. Not impossible.

Against this he had to place his instinctive human feelings about
Allison. He thought: I trust her. That wasn't a very scientific approach, and it wasn't in accordance with the teachings of the FBI
training college in Washington. But it was in accordance with
Confucius—how can anyone conceal himself? How could Allison
conceal herself from him to such an extent? It defied all credibility. One surely knew a person one was that close to. And there

was Benjie. Did a woman who loved her child as she loved Benjie go in for such terrible and dangerous things?

No . . . not unless she was a split personality, two completely different people, with *one* of whom he was involved, while the other . . . But no, he could not believe that.

Who, then?

Bamberger? Hofmannsthal? Hofmannsthal was in the lab at the time of the mishap, so in his case the suicide pilot theory would have to be invoked. Hofmannsthal, the noble-minded Hofmannsthal, capable of mass murder? Well, who was?

Was Bamberger? Bamberger had not been in the lab at the time of the mishap. Bamberger had a running quarrel with Hepler, and something evidently had flared up between them that day. Bamberger had a key. He could have gotten to the canyon lab between two and two twenty, if he'd had the key with him at lunch. Had he deliberately spilled ketchup over Hepler in order to terminate the lunch early and give himself time to get out to the canyon lab before the other scientists?

There were other worrisome things about Bamberger.

Delacy had said he had something on Bamberger that could destroy him.

Richter did not know what that something was, but there were some other things that he now knew about Bamberger.

There was, first of all, Bamberger's past involvement with communism. This was known at the time of his appointment, but at that time the assessment had been that it did not represent an insuperable obstacle. The Russians were allies, and anyway, Bamberger had long ago ceased to believe in communism. So he said. But was this true?

There was the incident in 1943—the Jenny Latham incident.

In December 1943 Bamberger had visited a former girl friend, Jenny Latham, at her apartment in Washington. After giving his bodyguard the slip, he had taken deliberate evasive action to throw off any tails. Changing taxis twice, he had arrived at Jenny Latham's flat just before midnight. And he had stayed the night. When he left in the morning, he did not get a taxi in the vicinity of her apartment, but walked for twenty minutes before picking one up. Were these the actions of a man trying to keep secret an act of infidelity? Or were they excessive for that? It had to be borne in mind that Jenny Latham was a girl friend from Bamberger's Communist period. In fact, she was part of the New York circle that included Jake and Allison and other Communist sympathizers.

There was a rule that even the most casual encounter with anyone outside the project must be reported and accounted for. And here was the controller himself spending the night with a former girl friend, who had once been a Communist and perhaps still was, and not reporting it. Indeed, he had gone to some lengths to conceal it. If it was simply a visit to an old flame, why hadn't he let someone know, discreetly, so there would be no question mark hanging over the episode? But he obviously thought he had gotten away with it, and that nobody knew.

Then there was the intercepted note. Unsigned, printed in capitals on school exercise-book paper, it had said, simply: *Don't get in touch with me. Some time very soon when I judge the moment right I will join you on your morning walk.*

What did this mean? Was this another illicit affair?

It all had to be considered in the context that there was known to be a leak in Los Alamos. The Gouzenko material indicated it. And with the arrest of Dr. Allen Nunn May it had been corroborated.

Allen Nunn May had confessed—arrogantly, self-justifyingly, making out a moral argument for his treason.

In May 1944 Allen Nunn May had attended a scientific conference in Chicago. It had also been attended by Bamberger, among others—among many others, true. But it remained a fact that Bamberger had been in contact with Nunn May. Had had the opportunity to pass information to him. And it now was established that somebody had passed on to the Russians, early in 1945, the secret of the plutonium bomb, and the means of detonating it by the implosion method. Nunn May's work in Canada had not given him access to this very specialized material. Only somebody in Los Alamos, very close to everything that was going on, would have been able to pass on the precise details of how the plutonium bomb was triggered. The plutonium bomb had presented various special problems. The gun method of detonating the uranium bomb involved shooting a wedge of uranium into a slightly subcritical mass and thereby making it critical and initiating a chain reaction. But this method could not be used in the case of the plutonium bomb; it was too slow, because of the tendency of plutonium of mass number Pu-240 to spontaneous fission. Assembly in the case of the plutonium bomb had to be extra-fast. Los Alamos scientists and technicians had found a way of achieving this—it was something entirely original, and only a very limited number of people knew about it; and this secret, there was now proof, had been passed on to the Russians.

Supposing, despite all his denials, Bamberger was still in his heart a Communist, a believer in the cause. Ready to do anything. That did not fit with his known condemnation of the Nazi-Soviet pact, or with his passionate denunciation of the Stalinist purges of the thirties. But supposing all that talk was a cover, to make everyone believe he had changed his views, whereas in reality he had convinced himself of the historical necessity of these ruthless acts. Supposing he had gone underground. Because his views were known, he would have had to cover himself by affecting a change of heart. He would have had to say those things about the Nazi-Soviet pact (while giving himself the argument that it had been necessary to gain time); he would have had to publicly condemn the purges (while saying to himself that they were necessary to protect the purity of the revolution against the forces of reaction).

Such a scenario involved the supposition that he had deliberately set out to deceive everyone—all his friends, all his colleagues and associates. Was that feasible? And what about Helen—where did she fit in? Did she know? Or was she also one of those to have been deceived? Scintillating Helen, with the mysterious smile. Why did she scintillate so much? She already had a man. The way he had taken her into his arms, after Trinity, and become restored . . . was that a man who had betrayed his country's biggest secrets? Suppose she was in the plot with him. That would involve the supposition that she, too, was a believer in the Communist cause.

If so, she had kept it remarkably secret all her life.

It did not make sense that Bamberger, with his three clean shirts a day, and his Stradivarius, and his Schieles and Klees and Klimts, and his whole smart rich radical life, a man who had been heaped with honors, and was obviously eager for more, would have sacrificed everything for the cause of communism.

On the other hand there *were* surprising sides to Bamberger's nature. For all his civilized, cultured airs, and his style under pressure, he was the man who had categorically opposed an initial demonstration use of the atom bomb. "I don't think the Japs are going to be very impressed by us letting off some firecrackers in the sky," he had said.

Delacy said he had something on Bamberger that could destroy him. Delacy thought there was something rotten in Bamberger.

This was very difficult for Richter to entertain. He had long admired Bamberger, seen in him the ideal of the scientist. How could he now turn him, even hypothetically, into this monster of duplicity and treachery and murderousness?

Pieces of the puzzle fitted together, made a picture—up to a point; and then he added another piece and the picture suddenly buckled . . . broke apart.

He thought of Allison's fears—Jones, too, had talked of an unconscious premonition. Hofmannsthal had evidently felt it and sent Allison out of the lab. And Benjie, even now that he knew what his father had been working on, still suspected, deep down, you could see, that he had been lied to in some way.

Allison wanted to leave. She was quite panicky with fear. Was there any real basis for that? He and Greg McClure had gone through all the accident records, going back to the beginning of the project. There had been twenty-five fatalities: seven from construction accidents; six from traffic accidents; two from falls; one from drowning; one—Jake—from radiation exposure; two from accidental shootings; one from a smudge-pot explosion; two from self-administered poison; three from accidentally drinking ethylene glycol—*three*. In addition, deaths from natural causes were higher than you would expect in a town of its size. But, of course, general statistics could not be applied to a place like Los Alamos. There

153

was no comparable community. So many brilliant minds. So many people of widely different origins thrown together, shut up in the same place—it was a pressure cooker. It had immediately been noted that the level of psychosomatic illness was higher than in other places. The nature of the work—the making of the bomb—must also have exacted some psychological price at one level or another. What did it mean, then, if there were more heart attacks in Los Alamos than in other communities of its size, and more accidents?

He was walking around the pond; its slightly ruffled surface was alive with faintly flickering moonlight and other reflections. Richter thought how different his life might have been had he chosen to go into medicine or biology or law instead of physics. In these other fields he might have done rather well. It was the science of physics that had eluded his grasp, with its vast, esoteric visions. The new physics appeared to contradict the evidence of the senses, and of the heart; it set man adrift in an abstract universe. . . . Tonight he could feel the terror of that loneliness.

Security files were the literature of half-truth. Half-truths had constituted much of his reading lately.

What to believe?

They said that Bamberger had half hoped that the Trinity test would turn out a dud—he would have taken that as a sign from God that it should not be. For an atheist, Bamberger talked a lot about God.

It was the sort of night to give one cosmic dreams and cosmic anxieties. Richter thought: I have browsed my life away. I am a browser; I dip into this, I dip into that. How many books have I started in the middle and never finished; how many subjects—how many? I was once terribly interested in Gurdjieff. Now all I can remember about his ideas is that he thought our cosmic role was to pass on hydrogen . . . sort of passing the buck around the universe. Did we need bodies and sexuality and brains just to pass the buck?

Lately, his browsing had been largely confined to security files—bits and pieces of information floated through his mind. Snippets of biography. Odd facts . . .

154

Hofmannsthal, the high-principled Hofmannsthal, was, it seemed, a difficult man to live with. At any rate his late wife had found him so. According to her letters—some of which, in the way that these things happened, had found their way into the security files. Also, a letter from him to a colleague at the time of his wife's death, a letter dealing mostly with other matters. He came to his wife's death in the third paragraph of the second page.

Poor Anna finally died yesterday—a merciful deliverance, but I feel lost without my life mate of so many years. Cannot deal efficiently with minor household tasks that I am no longer accustomed to performing. I was so used to her taking care of all such things. Will have to, at my age, re-educate myself in these matters. Poor Anna. I miss her vague hovering presence. But, contrary to the poet, I cannot say that anybody's death (least of all my own) truly diminishes me—that is the brutal truth of the matter. I confess it to you, my dear old friend, but not a word to anyone else, lest I be considered a heartless monster. People disappear from one's life, even people who have been very close to one, and soon their empty space is filled with some other vague shadow . . . it is all a shadow play. Life is a brutal affair, necessarily so, I fear, and one is too sentimental about death . . . children should be taught death at school, the subject should be de-mystified. But we have made it the one great repository of all our terrors, and so, of course, we must dread it, and appease it with sacrifice. . . . I want no one to mourn me when I go . . . I want my empty space quickly filled, my flitting shadow replaced by another. . . .

Remembering this letter now, Richter thought about Hofmannsthal and his remark "Do any of us strike you as suicide pilots?"

A man who could love the human race en masse, but had difficulty loving any single representative of it.

From the other side of the pond came the sound of raised voices. In the still night air, voices carried easily. As he drew closer to the clamor he realized that it was coming from the Master House, and presently he recognized Bamberger's voice. So it was true. His perennial cool *was* apocryphal. The controller could lose his temper like anybody else.

He was screaming at her.

What a commotion! Richter did not like to listen to their private quarrel, but told himself this was hardly a time for such squeamishness, with so many mysteries remaining unsolved.

The words being used by Bamberger were harsh, very harsh. Richter could scarcely credit that Bamberger was saying these things to his wife.

He listened, taking careful note of what was being said.

There was a rising curve of emotion to the row . . . it was all the time building and swelling toward some unforeseeable climax.

"This is the end, this is the end!" Bamberger was shouting. "I swear it!" And then, in a profoundly bitter voice: "God, *how* I would like to put an end to it all—to both of us. Both of us, Helen. You hear me. Biggest favor anyone could do me is put a bullet through both our fucking brains. . . ." Helen was sobbing and pleading; he was hard and abrasive-tongued, with a great churning violence in his voice, and Richter grew fearful. There were guns in the house. He did not want another tragic shooting accident. From the sounds of panting and movement he had the impression that the two of them were engaged in a physical struggle.

He decided that he could not simply walk by. He went to the door and knocked on it hard. No answer. Their shouting voices drowned out everything. The shouting was coming to a strained, gasping pitch. He tried the door and, finding it open, went in.

As he came into the main living room the struggling figures separated. Blood was running down Helen Bamberger's face, and she was breathless from emotion. Bamberger seemed not himself. But he was first to regain a measure of self-possession.

"What the fuck . . . ?" he began, turning on Richter.

Richter raised a placatory hand and said, "None of my business, I know, I know. But I heard a lot of noise and it was sort of worrying and I couldn't just walk by. . . . Mrs. Bamberger, I see you are bleeding a little. Could I help?"

"Thank you, Captain," Bamberger, under control, said icily. "I can manage." He was very white; his head was almost skeletal, and there was a circle of dried white spittle around his lips.

Richter hesitated; he noticed papers smoldering in the fireplace, papers scattered all over the floor. With a quick, gingerly movement he extracted a thick bunch of pages from the grate before the flame could catch.

Turning round, brushing ash from his hands, Richter said, a trifle apologetically, "Guess I just hate seeing books—or manuscripts—burned." He watched the fury gathering around Bamberger's tight, white-ringed mouth. "I know, I know—none of my business," he added quickly, smilingly.

"All right, Captain," Bamberger said, "I apologize for the noise and disturbance and I appreciate your neighborly concern. Things are all under control now . . . thank you. And good night."

Ignoring the clear instruction to leave, Richter said, turning to Mrs. Bamberger, "What could we do about that cut?" He went closer and examined it. It was an abrasion above the left cheekbone such as might have been caused by a fist blow. "You have a styptic pencil?" he asked generally.

Bamberger said nothing.

"I guess in the bathroom," Richter said, making his way toward it. He came out after a little while with the stypic pencil, cotton wool, and mercurochrome; and, gently leading Mrs. Bamberger to a light, he proceeded to work on the cut.

"I think I indicated for you to get the fuck out of here, Captain," Bamberger said through dry white lips.

Richter continued to work on Mrs. Bamberger's cut; he was managing to diminish the bleeding with the styptic pencil, and dabbing mercurochrome on the abrasion. He said, "I couldn't find a Band-Aid—do you know where they are, Mrs. Bamberger?" Her breathing was becoming controlled, but she still was not trusting her voice. She made a negative gesture of the head. "Oh, I think this is going to fix it," Richter said. He was aware that Bamberger

157

had gone back to the fireplace. Quietly he said, "It'd be a mistake, Doctor—burning anything." He examined his work on the cut.

"Captain, I don't want to be impolite . . . but I suggest that you take yourself out of here, and stop poking your nose into my private affairs."

Richter made another placatory sign—like a gentle traffic cop signaling to a fast-approaching vehicle to slow down, slow down. Stooping casually, he picked up some of the scattered pages from the floor, and with a passing glance—which took in small, neat handwriting and a word here and there—he put them on a table neatly, next to other pages covered with the same handwriting.

"Now before we find ourselves becoming really impolite to each other, Captain . . ." Bamberger said.

Richter stood by the table, looking down at the sheets of paper, reading a phrase here and there. Bamberger turned again toward the fireplace.

Richter said quietly, "At this stage of things, *anyone* burning papers, whatever they are, is asking to expose his action to misunderstanding."

"I have made a note of your point of view," Bamberger said.

Richter seemed unable to think of any other ways of delaying his departure. He started slowly toward the door. As he was about to go out, he turned around again, shaking his head.

"It does sort of worry me," he said slowly.

"What?" Bamberger said in a controlled snarl.

"That you might note my point of view, as you put it, and do something else—like burn these papers."

"I think that is something that can be left to me to decide."

"That's what I'm afraid of."

"Well, tough shit, Captain."

"I am beginning to think, Doctor, that it might be best all round if I took charge of these papers until we have sorted out what's what."

"I don't think you have the slightest idea of what you are blundering into."

"I am willing to be told."

"This is entirely a private matter," Bamberger said. "You have to take my word for that. What I decide to do with my own property . . ."

"Well, first of all, Doctor, I think we would have to say that it was not your property—it seems to be Mrs. Bamberger's property; anyway, it's her handwriting. Secondly—well, secondly, this is not any ordinary time or ordinary situation. If Dr. Hepler dies, we are possibly going to be involved in a murder investigation. Apart from any intelligence investigation already in process. Therefore anything that may have any bearing . . ."

"This has no bearing, Captain. This is completely private."

"It's a diary, isn't it? You've kept a diary, Mrs. Bamberger? I wonder if you realize, Mrs. Bamberger, that it is contrary to regulations for anyone to keep a diary here. I don't want to be officious; it may be no more than a technical breach . . . but it is contrary to security regulations. Without making too much of an issue of this, I think maybe what we should do is for me to take charge of this material, check it through—and if it is, as you say, purely private and of no relevance to anything else, I'll return it to you tomorrow and nobody else need know about it."

"It really is very personal and private," Mrs. Bamberger said, finding her voice now. "It was not meant for *anybody else's* eyes." She looked up briefly at her husband and then looked away again.

"I do understand," Richter said. "All I can say is—think of me as a doctor or a priest. I realize that thoughts confided in a diary are not meant to be read by others."

"It is out of the question for you to take this material away," Bamberger said. "I have no intention of allowing it. This is something that concerns only my wife and myself."

"I sympathize with that point of view. Under normal circumstances . . . yes, you would be right. But in these very special circumstances . . . ."

"Captain," Bamberger said, "you are not taking anything out of here, except yourself, and I am going to suggest you do that fast, before I lose any more of my legendary fucking cool."

Richter said slowly, "I'm sorry, but I can't accept that."

159

"Are you refusing to leave? Do I understand you are—"

"Yes, Doctor, with respect, I *am* refusing to leave . . . until I have ensured that nothing in this room is going to be destroyed."

"How about if I *throw* you out?"

"I think that is going to involve both of us in losing our cool."

"Nonetheless, it looks like the only way, if you refuse my polite request."

"I hate to get into this situation with you, Doctor," Richter said tautly, "but, again with the greatest respect, you compel me to be formal about it. Under section eighty, title eighteen of the United States code, it is a felony for anyone to knowingly falsify or conceal a material fact in any matter within the jurisdiction of an agency of the United States. I think burning something pretty effectively conceals it, and I am an agency of the United States, namely the United States Army, Intelligence section, and I believe this material comes within my jurisdiction by virtue of the fact that we are inquiring into various matters here, including a grave accident, that has implications . . . of possible sabotage." He stopped.

Bamberger was grim, and the skin of his face had become drum tight, showing all his bones.

"I find it appalling . . . appalling," he said, "that you push in here, like some secret policeman of the Gestapo, and treating us like common criminals demand to take away private papers of my wife's. It's an outrage."

"Doctor," Richter said gently, "sit down, have a cigarette, relax. It's probably just a formality, but we are obliged to go through it, if only to be able to say we have done so, when questions are asked in the future." He stooped to pick up more of the scattered sheets and placed them neatly next to the others on the table.

"My wife," Bamberger said, lighting a cigarette and drawing in the smoke deeply, "not being aware that such formalities would have to be gone through, permitted herself to . . . to put down things . . . things not meant for anybody else's eyes."

"I understand," Richter said. "I don't know what to say. I suppose you would be entitled to ask for this material to be impounded and sealed, and read by someone nominated by you, as long as he was also acceptable to us. Somebody else in Security."

"No, let him read it," Mrs. Bamberger said. She looked directly at her husband, with defiance in her eyes. "My husband makes it sound very appalling, and you may agree with him. If so—well, that's too bad. There it is." Her eyes lit up with their secret, sharp amusement, which Richter suddenly saw was at her own expense, not anybody else's.

THREE

PAGES FROM THE PAST HELEN BAMBERGER'S DIARIES (MARCH 1943– DECEMBER 1945)

TEN

March 20, 1943

What a strange place! It's like living on the edge of the world. I feel I have been transported to another time. This narrow shelf of the mountain was once occupied by Pueblo Indians—you walk over their pottery shards; in places it literally paves the ground. They used to farm in the valley for squash and beans and corn, and then retreat at night to caves dug out of the soft pumice cliffs. In the forests they hunted deer, bear, elk, and turkey, all of which abound still. There are pueblo ruins in many areas around here. Some have the strangest stories. Witchcraft is part of the "local color," and so is the most sensational kind of religious practice. There are sects here that practice mock crucifixions, and self-flagellation.

I feel completely divorced from the kind of world I have known. All that could not be further away from me now if I were at the North Pole. David is my one tenuous lifeline, and since we have been here I have hardly seen him, he is so busy. They are setting up some kind of secret war project. The wives are not allowed to know what it is. We have been told not to talk to anyone in Santa Fe, and if circumstances should force us to, we must say we are from Washington, D.C., and that our husbands are engineers—we must not say they are physicists. Some of the scientists who are well known have been given false names. I am Mrs. Bergman. I keep forgetting about this, and get told off by the security people, who seem to be everywhere and watch us all the time. Always creeping about and listening. Inevitably, we have called them "the creeps." We have bets on who the creeps are. I bet that the barman at the La Fonda Hotel in Santa Fe is one. So now we all watch him to see if he is watching us. He is quite put out by this. Of course, if he isn't a creep and has no idea who we are or what we are doing here, and why we watch him, he must think us a real bunch of weirdos.

March 23

Snow. Very cold. Biting wind. Streets impossible. No snow-clearing equipment. Food grim. Half the time we are opening cans. Tuna fish, sardines, and beans in tomato sauce. Difficult to get a decent piece of fresh meat because of the logistics of our situation—the long drive in to Santa Fe, the lousy roads, the lousy automobiles assigned to us, which are always breaking down and getting stuck on the lousy roads.

March 24

There is a sense of not just being cut off—but of having ceased to exist. For most of our friends that is literally what has happened. We were not allowed to say to them where we were going. We have no address here, only a post office box number in Santa Fe. Our outgoing mail has to be handed in with flaps not stuck down, so it can be censored without the recipients knowing it has been censored. Had a letter of mine returned to me by the censor-creep because I had described some landscape here. It is an extraordinarily beautiful part of the world in which we have been buried. The creep said I must not describe the landscapes, because this place might be identifiable from such descriptions. Adding to the sense of isolation up here is the fact that our only communication with the outside world is by means of a Forestry Service phone line to Santa Fe. One line. Only possible to have brief shouted exchanges, and only on essential topics. No chance of having a

166

chat. In any case chatting is verboten. Furthermore, there is nobody to chat with.

March 25

More snow. I have never seen so much snow. I am not supposed to be keeping this diary. Another rule that the creeps have made. The necessity of keeping these entries secret from everyone (including David, who is a stickler for the rules) has in a way freed me. It's like talking to myself—which, no doubt, I would soon start to do, if I didn't have this. The men seem to be less affected by the isolation—they have their work.

Civilization around here means Santa Fe—that's an 80-mile round trip. It is not a journey to undertake casually. The shortest route is by State Highway 4 through Espanola. As far as Pojoaque it's a twisty dirt track, strewn with boulders, and in heavy rain it's often closed by flooding. The Rio Grande (which is not very Grande here) is crossed by a 250-ft-long suspension bridge. It's a single lane, and if a truck has tried to make the 90° turn from the narrow sidehill cut on the eastern side and failed, then the bridge becomes blocked, and if the truck can't be shifted you just have to turn around and go back and take the long route (ten miles longer) by way of State 5. The third road that links us, tenuously, to civilization is from the west, via the Valle Grande, but this one is even rougher than the others and is often closed by snow in the winter. David chose this location—or suggested it; and the Army went along. David is responsible to a general in Washington for the scientific and technical aspects, but there is an Army commandant responsible for our living conditions and the overall running of this place. Seems they miscalculated the number of people who would be needed. At first they were thinking in terms of about 30 scientists for whom the 27 houses of the ranch school complex would have been fine. But now it looks like we are going to be at least 300, and that means in the initial phase hundreds of construction workers as well to put up the extra housing that is needed. The bulldozers are everywhere. They are throwing up shacks like somebody struck gold around here. We are lucky to be

167

living in the Master House (a handsome log cabin) instead of in one of those hastily built new Sundt apartments. The whole place has a ramshackle temporary air, as if nobody expects it to be there more than a few days before we all pack up and move off again like a gypsy caravan. We have caravans too. They are called expansible government trailers and are dumped anywhere they're needed, which seems to be all around. There are also structures with corrugated iron roofs, low dark doghouses called Pacific hutments, with black soot belching from their tin pot chimneys. Every day you walk down the road and the town has grown, it's spreading out in all directions in a totally haphazard way. They put up a structure and they find it's not big enough for its purpose and so they add a corridor in the middle and put another structure alongside, making an H. Or else they put an overhead bridge to provide a connection between a building on one side of a road and one on the other side. Everything is painted green, so we'll blend into the hills.

What makes all this temporary living worse is the knowledge that it's not so temporary, that David has signed up for the duration. I am going to be living here like this as long as the war lasts. Nobody is allowed to leave. Traveling further than a hundred miles is only permitted under very special circumstances, and even the most casual encounter with anyone "outside" has got to be reported and accounted for to Security. Means we are thrown upon each other's company like snowed-in characters in an Agatha Christie story.

March 28

In Santa Fe and around, a variety of rumors circulate about what goes on "up there." Of course, they know it's some kind of Army base because they see all the Army vehicles and the construction workers going up, and Indian women from the pueblos work as domestic help, so naturally stories get out. One story is that a new kind of submarine is being developed here. The fact that we are so far from navigable waters does not seem to scotch the story. Another story has it that we are breeding man-devouring combat dogs to be used against the Japs. Another story is that enemy scientists are interned here, which accounts for all the foreign accents and the foreign-looking people and that we live inside a barbed wire compound.

March 29

Dr. S prescribed sleeping pills for me. Seconal. Said it's the altitude. A lot of people here suffer from it, he said. Need time to acclimatize.

April 1

Didn't put my nose out. Listened to Jack Benny. David had a colloquium. Allison went but I couldn't because I don't have a white badge and am not supposed to know anything.

April 5

Dinner in Santa Fe. Good. I had a Chalupa Plate—corn tortilla with pinto beans, cheese, beef, sour cream, paprika, guacamole, pozole, and Spanish rice. David had Pollo Adovo, which I tasted. Deboned chicken breast baked in adovado sauce, with green peppers, sour cream, pozole. Excellent.

April 6

I have found out what they are making here. It's some new kind of bomb.

April 8

The Jemez hills seem to rise out of a steamy bath. As the mist clears some areas suddenly become illumined by strong sunlight pouring through innumerable small gaps in the clouds—the effect is of light streaming through cathedral windows. The mist clears and you look out across a great unmoving stillness, upon a supine

169

universe: silent, unreacting, stark, calm, beautiful. It becomes one of those incredibly clear New Mexico days, a day of the most lucid light. One of our code names for this place (since we are not supposed to refer to Los Alamos) is Shangri La. (In terms of remoteness, isolation, and unreality, it is fitting.) Another one is: the Asshole of the World. Also apt. More neutral names for it are Project Y, the Project, or just the hill.

April 9

Now, Voyager. I didn't see it when it came out last year. The title is from Whitman. "Now voyager, sail thou forth to seek and find." Bette Davis, uglified for her art, in pebble glasses and spinster hairdo, blossoms out unrecognizably (with the love of Paul Henreid). Kitsch, but compelling, and it made me cry. The blossoming-out scene in Rio is, of course, skated over delicately.

April 10

The vulture, standing on a rock. Looking like a banker from *Citizen Kane*. Head sunk into its wings. Wings massive when spread. Yellowish hooked beak, purple below jaw—too much red meat. Incredibly wrinkled scrawny neck. Back of head like much wrinkled skull cap. Thought of *Volpone:* a kind of somber greed, an old man's greed. It seemed like a very old bird. One of death's attendants.

April 12

Dr. S says that the fear of sudden death is an aspect of neurasthenia. Naturally, he does not believe in premonition, though he concedes that there are things that can be sensed—like somebody else's state of mind. Says not to exceed 300 milligrams of Seconal in any 24-hour period.

April 14

David's bodyguard, Greg McClure. He has the most amazing ability with automobiles. Can tell from sound of engine exactly what's wrong with it. Very highly trained, ex–Secret Service. At crossroads watches out for the shadow that a car coming from a side road will throw ahead. Something like that can make the difference between ambush and escape. Can whip car round in 180° turn in seconds. Most of time drives very sedately, though.

April 25

To the Dubinskis for dinner. Since Allison works on the Project, I always feel a bit left out on these evenings. They all talk to each other in an allusive way about things that I do not remotely understand. But I like Jake and Allison—she is the person I have gotten to be closest to here. At the beginning I thought it would be awkward between us, because they, the Dubinskis, have known David from way back—in his bachelor period, when he was always bringing girls around to their apartment, and afterwards discussed them. He must have discussed me, too, when he first knew me, since I was one of those girls he brought around—to be assessed and approved. In those days, I had the impression that Allison was in love with David. That maybe they'd had an affair once; if so, it would have been Allison's doing, because David loves Jake and would not do something like that to Jake, except in a moment of weakness. But David is not weak, and he has always had plenty of girls, so perhaps I am wrong in thinking there was ever anything like that between him and Allison. I just sense that there was *something* between them at one time.

Anyway, whatever it was, Allison couldn't be nicer or warmer, and she knows everything that's going on, so if I want to know anything I ask her. I asked her what the men are working on, and she said it was something very big and very secret, and that they were all under tremendous pressure because the Germans are also working on the same thing, and whoever gets there first is going to win the war. It's the first time anyone has told me it's something as big as that.

171

Allison has rather taken me under her wing—perhaps David asked her to see I was all right. She is highly competent and a trained scientist, whereas I am a fly-by-night litterateur, so naturally David would suppose I need looking after. More to the point, I have endless spare time on my hands, since I don't work on the Project, and so have to find ways of filling my day. There are plenty of other wives in the same position—Allison is one of the very few to have sufficient scientific training to work on the Project. I teach English at the school for three hours a day, but it isn't enough to occupy me fully, especially as David works a 15-hour day, and sometimes more. They are organizing lots of activities for us underemployed wives and (as the controller's wife) it actually is one of my main tasks to see that the other wives are O.K. and kept out of mischief. But I do that kind of thing with a quarter of my mind. It is not so much that I can't find tasks for myself, it is that none of them really interests me. . . . I am organizing a Dramatic Club, an Arts and Crafts Club, I'm involved with the Victory Garden Group, I am doing some fencing and have taken up shooting—we have got a Rifle and Pistol Club. I play tennis. But none of it really interests me profoundly. This is not my scene. Allison says I must try to get back to my own line of work. How? I hardly am in a position to write articles from here—she says I have to give myself some project, work on a book, or something. How she imagines I can work on a book here, where I am not allowed to know what is going on, mustn't even ask, and at the same time am not free to move about outside to gather any other material . . . It would have to be a novel.

April 26

Since yesterday I have been thinking more and more about the idea of a project for myself. At the very least, I feel I should take notes, keep some kind of record. The trouble is that all the momentous things that are going on I know nothing about, all I ever hear about are what vegetables we should grow, and what the Christmas pageant should be, and everybody's emotional problems. I see David less than Allison does. She and Jake work very

172

closely with him. Perhaps I can pump her for more information. She is much less obsessed about security than David.

May 3

Continual tension between us and the military. Sometimes, the way they act, you would think they were here not so much to safeguard the Project as to keep us locked in. The simplest requests have to go through Army red tape. They are so goddamned officious. There is a lot of hostility towards us—the scientists are referred to by the enlisted men as "the phonies" or the "Technical Area jerks" or "the longhairs." Of course, most of these young soldiers don't want to be here and have no idea why they are here. While scientific staff are able to live with their families, enlisted men and junior officers live in barracks, and wives are not allowed to live nearer than 100 miles from the compound, which means Albuquerque, not Santa Fe. One sees the enlisted men through the fence that divides the military from the civilian sections of the main site Post Headquarters, and they look miserably bored. Evenings they hang around in a desultory way with nothing to do. A lot of entertainment is laid on for them; that isn't what is lacking. The trouble is, there are hardly any women here on their side of the fence, only seven WACs; and the Military Police Detachment alone consists of 200 men, and the Provisional Engineer Detachment has another couple of hundred.

A big cause of resentment is the fence inside the main site. This fence separates us—the scientists and technicians—from the Military Police and the Provisional Engineer detachments and the construction workers. There are two gates in the fence and during the day it is possible for anyone to pass freely between these two areas. But after six one of the gates is closed and the other is controlled by a military policeman. While we from the general civilian area are permitted to pass through this gate without question—for example to go to a cinema on the other side—the soldiers and construction workers are not allowed to enter our area unless they have been specifically invited by someone here. They have to have a pass from one of us to get in. This is felt to be segregation, which of course it is, and bitterly resented. So is the fact that our Post Exchange is receiving better equipment and supplies than theirs. They even have brought in special foods for us that are normally not authorized by Army Regulations. They have done this on the grounds of needing to keep us civilians happy. Another cause for resentment of the civilians is that there are more women on our side of the fence—though this will change when the new contingents of WACs come in. But for the moment our side of the fence seems to have all the women and that is seen as something else to keep the longhairs happy. Whereas the soldiers have got to do without, mostly. At night they loll against their side of the fence and look you over, which often degenerates into ribald tomfoolery if there are several of them. There are wolf whistles and hands describing hourglass figures as they lounge around drinking beers and smoking, and they come padding after you in imitation of Groucho Marx, throwing out obscene invitations with wildly jerking eyebrows. Presumably they sometimes have some success or they wouldn't keep trying so persistently. One wonders what kind of women would go in for that kind of thing, and *where*, since the men live in barracks. I had heard about some place behind the parking lots. I asked Allison and she said, "Up against the huts behind the Services Club, or back of the filling station. Knee tremblers . . ." I said, "What sort of girls will do that?" And Allison said, "Oh, you'd be surprised. A lot of the wives here are very frustrated and with all those horny guys hanging around, and the fact is it's a pretty anonymous tumble in the dark—I mean they don't run much danger of getting involved with those guys." I asked her how she knew all this, the underlying meaning of my question being pretty obvious, and she took me up on that quite openly and said, "No, I haven't. Jake and I are O.K. in that way. But I know somebody who has." "It must be awfully uncomfortable," I said, and she said, grinning, "My friend says you don't notice."

174

May 6

I realize from the way Allison talks to me (and not only Allison) that it is assumed I am totally superior to such goings-on. I am often told I have a superior, off-putting sort of smile. There was that Dickson boy I was seeing at Cape Cod the summer of '34 who was always saying, "You seem to be laughing at everyone. You put everyone down with your exclusive smile. You make a fellow think he isn't good enough for you." I said to him, which was awful but he was asking for it, "Maybe that's because you aren't." I laughed, of course, and said it was a joke, but it wasn't. I realized it was the God's truth, and then I thought: In that case, who *is* good enough for me, if B. B. Dickson ("Beebee"—what was his real name? Bernard? Bruno?) isn't, and he clearly wasn't? He was a rich creep, that was all. Though most of the girls I used to know then thought Beebee the cat's whiskers. I suppose I am an odd mixture: Dad a Viennese adventurer, Mother his Boston adventure which came home to roost. The fact is I spent the first seven years of my life in Vienna, and though I have never felt Viennese, I haven't felt exactly Bostonian either. Vienna and Boston. Some melange. I felt at home in New York, because everybody there is just as much of a melange. David, for instance. Whose father came from Russia and whose mother is French. What mixtures we all are.

David never minded my smile or my supposed superiority. Anything that David wanted had to be superior. If I hadn't been so superior he wouldn't have been interested in me. Well, he was such a superior guy himself. Not just a scientist, but a poet as well, for Christ's sake, and a musician, with his violin playing and his clarinet playing. And he painted, would you believe it? And spoke five languages, and skied, and wrote the funniest clerihews about everybody he knew, and he knew everybody, and what was more had studied Eastern philosophy and Yoga, had been in analysis, had been married and divorced, was the father of a terrific boy, whom he adored, and was still only 34. He just had done everything faster than anyone else. In and out of communism before anybody else had gotten to chapter two of *Das Kapital*, which takes some getting to, admittedly, though not for David. He has this enormous concentration when something interests him, and that was how he concentrated on me: single tracked. One time it was Karl Marx, another time it was me. In each case, something difficult to be mastered, and he mastered us, like he masters everything he sets his mind to. Sometimes, in those days, I thought of him as an enormously skillful conjurer perpetually keeping a dozen things up in the air, revolving around him, without letting a single one drop. He never became fazed by anything, seemed to *like* the pressure, it drew something out of him. It is when nothing is "happening"—a very rare state of affairs—that he gets nervous. Even then, his nervousness is the kind of "nerveux" that the French apply admiringly to a high-powered and highly tuned automobile.

When I met him David had been divorced for three years, and out of analysis two years, and out of communism five years. You had the feeling that he had been through all the phases. Now he was ready. Marriage was right for him now, because now he knew what marriage was, he'd had the other; and politically he was becoming more mature too, and dismissive of "quick solutions" or "politics that ignore the science of human nature"; it was his Zen phase, acceptance of reality, good-bye to boyish idealism and quixotry and fucking around.

In 1936 I was 27. We met at the Wollheims, I was bowled over by him. He said, "You know, you are the most beautiful thing I have ever seen," and I said with, I suppose, my superior smile, "What do you mean 'thing,' sir?" and he said, recovering brilliantly, "I say 'thing' because I am not just speaking of women, I'm comparing you with all the manifestations of nature." Later, he told me his great character failing. He was a perfectionist, and a perfectionist in a hurry, what's more. He had to have the best and he had to have it now. Currently that meant me, and it was made clear he was not going to wait around. He gave some large hints that if he was not successful after two dates he forgets about you—he was also good at cutting his losses. On our second date I felt the deadline looming up. What the hell, I thought, how many times do you make it with young Einstein? I could always change my mind *after*. That was the way. So it was after we'd been to bed on our second date that I started playing hard to get. Now he couldn't threaten me, as he had done at first, saying: "Failure makes me lose interest." Now he had to really pursue me, and he did. I said I didn't know if I wanted to marry Einstein and he said better than Isaac Newton, Isaac Newton was a real cold fish. . . .

At this time I was sort of half engaged to Grant Wendover, and David would say, "What do you want with that deep-frozen lump of Americana? Marry me." And he said, "You never had such a good offer in all your life, belle Hélène, so I would grab it if I were you." And he said, "If I've got you, I'm made, and if I haven't, I'm done for. The truth is—you may have heard this said before—I can't live without you." He idolized me so, I thought, I am bound to disappoint him eventually. I said, "How about what Freud says about the overvaluation of the love object?" "Never mind Freud," he said, "I'm finished with Freud, I'm on to you now, don't confuse the issue." I didn't know. I really didn't know— he was breathtaking, but he was also daunting. He was more than a bit overwhelming. I did not know if I could keep up with him. I didn't know if I could stand the pace. I didn't know if I could have any identity of my own married to him. One day, making love, he wept in my arms, this dazzling polymath wept in my arms, out of a sheer overflow of feelings, out of desire and sadness and thinking he might lose me, and that was when I said Yes, that was when I fell in love with him, with this needy boy who had everything. It changed after that; almost as soon as he had got me, could be sure of me, his mind turned to something else that he had to have. I became simply one of the many objects whirling around his busy head. His attention returned to me just often enough to keep me, too, aloft, and spinning fast enough not to wind down. . . .

May 10

Strident music coming from the Services Club. Sounds lively. Our part of town is dead. I walked by and got the usual looks and

177

remarks. Turned around and went back. Listened to the Fred Allen show.

May 11

Lubitsch's *Heaven Can Wait*. Laird Cregar.

May 12

Inside, the soldiers stood around looking at the girls, whom they outnumbered about five to one, and the girls, WACs mostly, but also some civilians, flirting by with their powdered faces and lipsticked lips and their flashy curvy bodies, and the guys laughing among themselves, making hourglass figures with their hands, giving wolf whistles. The way they look a girl over leaves no doubt about what is on their minds. They go through a whole pantomime of wincing sexual torment when some especially cute piece goes by. One of these jokers was writhing on the ground, rapturously looking up skirts and describing what he saw in frenetic sign language to his pals.

June 3

What they are making here is a new kind of bomb. One such bomb will be able to wipe out an entire city, tens of thousands of people will be incinerated by a heat so intense it will vaporize rock, the blast will flatten a city center, people twenty miles away may find their clothes bursting into flame, and those that are not killed in any other way will be contaminated by a deadly radiation, a seeping, invisible, insensible emanation which enters the body and destroys the structure of its cells. They are using for this bomb the element uranium, but a form of uranium that differs from the naturally occurring element so it can be more readily split. It is in this splitting of the atom of uranium that the enormous explosive energy is released. It seems that what they are doing is breaking into the basic unit, the basic building block of the universe, and splitting the force that holds everything together. An energy not unlike magnetism or gravity. Inside the atom there is a kind of solar system—a nucleus which forms a central mass, and whirling around this, like planets around the sun, are tiny particles called electrons. Except that it is not really like this. This is merely the imagery that our mind can grasp. It seems that the planetary metaphor is not, strictly speaking, true, for in another sense these planets are not planets at all but a kind of mist of energy. And all of it is happening unseen inside atoms that are too small to be measured singly. They can only be measured in their millions, from which what happens in any individual atom is deduced. Anyway, they have discovered a way of making this unseeable atom break up and release its energy, and each atom that breaks up releases neutrons, which make the atom next to it break up, and in this way a chain reaction occurs through all the atoms, and they all give up their energy. It all happens in a millionth of a second. The basic method they use for creating this explosion is as follows. Uranium 235, being unstable, will, when it reaches a certain mass, which they call "critical," spontaneously give off neutrons—and thus chain-react. The technique of the bomb consists of making the mass "critical" at the precise moment you want it to explode. They have developed a way of doing this which they call "the gun method." It consists of having a subcritical mass of uranium inside a bomb casing, and a device for firing a bullet of uranium into it, and this bullet by increasing the mass renders it "critical" and therefore makes it chain-react and explode. This is one of the processes they are now perfecting.

All this I have gathered in the course of the past two or three weeks by assiduously listening to such scraps of their conversation as I can. A sentence here and there when I bring them coffee and biscuits. Usually they all stop talking when I come in, but it is not instantaneous—I make sure that I come in quietly. They assume that anything I hear would be gibberish to me anyway, since I am known for my ignorance of science. I let them continue to believe this, though I have now taken some steps to inform myself of elementary principles. In a surprisingly short while it became possible for me to understand what they were talking about. And since I have begun to understand, I listen. I listen all the time now.

179

June 4

Summer storms. Three nights in a row. The rain comes down with such force you think everything is going to be washed away. The lightning is like a regular slow pulse. Before a storm, I can sense the accumulation of electrical tension in the air. There appears to be less air to breathe. A small amount of alcohol can sometimes make me quite drunk. I am still not entirely used to the altitude. I feel conscious of the violent forces all around me.

The sunsets are most dramatic after a storm, when the sky has cleared. D. H. Lawrence wrote that the skyline seen from Taos is the most extraordinary in the world. I must go again to Taos, and to San Ildefonso. And Xoaté (to which I have never been), where the witches were supposed to have lived, witches that ate little children, according to the story.

June 6

Hofmannsthal came to dinner, a rare enough honor. I made him chicken fried in bread crumbs and sweet and sour cabbage and a potato salad. He was most appreciative. He is remote—Olympian, in some ways—but will come down to your level to talk of ordinary things, too. He has the grace to express appreciation when one has made a special effort for his sake. Unlike Hepler, who is utterly oblivious of you. Hardly ever talks to me. The impression I get is that nothing I might say could be of any conceivable interest to him. He is always eating at our house. He often has scientific matters to discuss with David and they sit and talk and talk, and if their talk runs into dinner time he stays on and eats with us. I have served him countless dinners, and never has he brought as much as a bunch of flowers to express thanks. His attitude is that women are there for that. In particular, wives; he has other uses for other kinds of women, but wives and mothers are there to cook and clear away. He eats, looks at his watch, and goes. I think he makes after-dinner dates. Saves him having to talk to the girl all through dinner. David says Hepler is very successful with women. Difficult to imagine why. He is small, a couple of inches

shorter than me, and not what you would call physically handsome—
though he does have great intensity, and enormous concentration.
Untidy, with cigarette ash all over him. Always wears a bow tie.
Quite jaunty in some ways. At first smokes his cigarette through a
little white ivory holder, but puts it away when he starts to seriously chain-smoke. There is a sort of great insolence about everything he does and says. His mouth turns down easily to show contempt and derision. His entire personality is jagged—I can see no
gentleness in him anywhere. Yet he who respects no one and
nothing, is respectful towards Hofmannsthal.

David, of course, adores the old man. He played an important
role in David's intellectual development and David is very attached to all the people who have furthered his education: his
mother (his father he lost when very young and scarcely remembers); a young rabbi who officiated at his Bar Mitzvah and became
the first of a line of spiritual counselors in his life; a science teacher
at high school, who was also a musician; Hofmannsthal at
Göttingen; his psychoanalyst; his yoga master; General Brown.
. . . (One never hears of the person who recruited him to communism. That person must have fallen out of David's graces.)

Yes, even though he and Brown are miles apart as men, I sense
that his relationship with the general falls into the same category
as his relationships with his other mentors. Brown, whatever anyone says against him, chose David for this job, and stands by him
staunchly, and David attaches enormous importance to personal
loyalties.

He is loyal and in return he expects loyalty from others. And if
they fail to give it, they are excommunicated with a severity that
less close friends would not incur. A person towards whom he has
shown friendship or love who rats on him becomes an enemy, and
there have been many such fallings-out in his life. Once it was
touch and go with his son, with his greatly adored son, before the
boy, by means of a sweet spontaneous gesture, succeeded in re-
deeming himself. When a breach seems imminent, David will
make every effort to avoid it. When it has occurred, he will strive
to repair it. He gives people second and third and fourth chances.
But there finally comes a point when he says quite suddenly,

"O.K., let it go." And then that person is gone and damned, and usually there is no returning once this point has been reached. Perhaps because he is so tenacious and even long-suffering in holding on to a friendship, through thick and thin, when the big break does finally occur it is violent. Lately, I have felt that this could happen anytime with Hepler.

June 7

I find myself thinking about Hepler. Has he ever loved anyone, is he capable of that emotion? Sometimes when he smiles you think, well, he is human after all. He has moments of charm. He is disagreeable because he gets excited, and then he sweeps everyone out of his way in his determination to prove himself right. I have watched him and David argue. Hepler goes on like some demagogue haranguing a crowd and David just listens with his half-smile. When Hepler has gotten to the essence of his irrefutable conclusion, David will say something mild and neat that sometimes brings Hepler down like a bird shot in flight. "Yes, yes," Hepler will acknowledge when David is clearly right about something, "as you say, it is impossible." Then comes the insolent smile. "But why so afraid of the impossible? The solution is a good one, you agree? So we will *make* it work." He is like that. David's mind seems to move in a strict sequential way, from one point to the next, until he comes to an obstacle. He then tries to get round it. If he cannot, he goes back to the beginning and tries some different approach. By contrast, Hepler's mind simply flies over the obstacle, and he gets on to the solution. Obstacles are only things in the mind, you can ignore them if you so choose. Once the solution has been found, he will go back and eliminate the obstacle, or simply leave it there, as an inexplicable inconsistency. If the solution works, he says, one should not be put off because it is impossible. The difference between David and Hepler is that Hepler takes leaps in the dark, whereas David must see where he is going. Hofmannsthal called them his wunderkinder last night. He is fond of David, you can see, and not so fond of Hepler, but

182

he approves of Hepler's approach to science. He believes that science should be an act of the imagination, a fantasy almost.

June 8

Everywhere the burnt primitive landscape, the volcanic cliffs, the steaming fumaroles, the cracks in the earth. The earth is so cracked and split here, you have a very real sense that everything we call civilization is just a thin veneer, and that beneath there remains the savage interior.

June 9

The strong way the sun falls. It makes the scenery black-and-white: black shadows printed on the sun-whitened square.

June 10

They argue all the time about the rights and wrongs of what they are doing. It could not be said that it is something they don't think about. They think about it endlessly, in all its aspects. I listen and make notes. For my novel—that I will one day write, which I cannot begin to write yet because I do not know how it will all end. And the ending changes everything. The whole way of looking at everything. So I wait to see what will happen, and make notes. Making notes is a way of holding on to myself; sometimes I think it's all that keeps me from going mad. When I hear all those things that I hear. And have to contain them, because I'm not supposed to know. I contain them here.

Anyway, they have their discussions, and it's all very intellectual à la Bernard Shaw. A sort of ethical conundrum. Last night Jones started them off by saying that in the Soviet Union Kapita is under house arrest for refusing to work on the bomb. To which David replied, "O.K., that's his decision, and I respect it. But we weighed it up and we made a different decision."

Then they all came in on it.

JAKE: We have no choice. If the Germans get there first, they will rule the world. We are doing it to defeat Nazism. Kapita is wrong not to work on the bomb—it's moral cowardice. He's undermining his own country, and bringing Nazi domination of the world closer by his action.

JONES: And if America gets there first, America will dominate the world.

DAVID: Well, rather America—with the English, of course, Jonesy—than Germany. No?

JONES: The history of the world shows that whenever men get too much power it makes them feel godlike and when men feel godlike they act like pigs.

DAVID: I agree we have to watch ourselves. But at least in a democracy there are checks and counterchecks to human hubris.

JAKE: Fat chance! We love success too much. And you know what hubris invariably leads to—nemesis.

HEPLER: So what? Frankly, you all make me sick with your perpetual agonizing. Rise and fall, birth and death, tumescence and detumescence, that's the pattern of life. You want to know why we do it? We do it because we can.

DAVID: You're just a natural fascist, Leo. How does what you have just said differ from Might Is Right?

HEPLER: I don't talk about right. You talk about right, and try to justify yourself. I talk of superior force. That is what works. In the world, in the universe. How can we as scientists deny that? It is the most elementary form of Newtonian physics. A given force acting on a given mass. . . . *Ach*, you are a bunch of Canutes telling the tide to go back.

DAVID: Whereas you would be quite happy for it to come in and drown us.

HEPLER: My feelings do not come into it, if that is the tide's course.

DAVID: Your feelings don't come into anything, that's your trouble, Leo.

HEPLER: Ah, you think you have a monopoly of the finer feelings. You are a pompous ass, Bambi. It is useless to talk to you. What I am saying is that, whether we like it or not, what must always win is a superior force deployed in a superior way. It can be mental force. But the decisive factor is superiority. The meek do not inherit the earth, contrary to the propaganda of one J.C.

It is not a discussion in the true sense, because there is no tempering of one point of view in the light of the other. They all have their fixed positions, and when they talk they are really talking about themselves, about who they are. Each expression of opinion is a kind of capsule autobiographical statement. They believe what they believe because they must, because their whole lives have brought them to that point. So there is no chance of their opinions converging, except insofar as their lives meet—have to meet— here. To that extent—since they are now in this together and have no choice—they accommodate each other's viewpoints in order to go on. David is the one who has to steer them through this treacherous sea of disagreement, and keep the crew from mutinying.

June 12

David in Washington.

To San Ildefonso and Xoaté with the Joneses. They have made themselves the experts on the local scene. They are the leading lights of the Anthropological Society. Want me to join. But I have already got the Pistol and Rifle Club, the Dramatic Club (we are doing *Miss Julie* by Strindberg), the Sketching Club (we are doing the Male Nude), and, for my sins, the Victory Garden Club.

Pam is very keen on the black pottery of Maria Martinez.

Leaving San Ildefonso, there is a sudden moment when the horizons open up and you have the sense of a vast stillness. The air trembles faintly. The wind and weather have formed bizarre sculptures out of volcanic ash. The great massed pure-white clouds are like in a painting. The air is so clear, and you can see so far all around, you have a perception of the earth's curvature. You feel yourself to be a heavy object in curved space.

San Ildefonso is a thriving community of artists and craftsmen

185

where the pueblo style of adobe building is wonderfully preserved: it continues to be a viable village, with its unique life-style. There is a central kiva, with a circular staircase leading up to the rim. One cannot go in, since this is the holy of holies for the Indians.

Xoaté is such a contrast; a bleak and dying place, and virtually inaccessible because the road is so poor. The part which is still partially inhabited we were not able to enter. Jones says he went in there once and got a very unfriendly reception. Only a handful of families remain. A mixed group. There are the descendants of the original villagers, plus down-and-outs of various sorts, who have taken up squatter's residence in the ruins. They say that the church, which is kept in good repair, and the adjoining quarters are the morada of a sect of Los Penitentes. This is difficult to establish for certain because these sects are like a secret society and do not let outsiders find out too much about them. On those occasions when the morada was in use, Jones explained, guards would be posted to make sure that outsiders did not get in. Nobody can be sure of what really goes on there.

We were able to look around the part of the pueblo (the greater part) that is no longer occupied. It is in very bad condition. Jones says the traditional way of repairing an adobe roof is to pour on another few buckets of mud wherever it leaks. Such practices, over the years, increase the load that has to be borne and cause the structure to cave in, a process that is further promoted by the rotting of the timbers. The sun-dried adobe walls (consisting of clay and sand) are subject to erosion and need to be frequently reinforced at the ground line in order to preserve the structure. When this kind of upkeep is neglected, slow deterioration sets in, and the shambles that we saw are the result.

In the case of Xoaté there was also, according to Jones, a progressive moral decay that preceded the falling apart of the village, and perhaps this more than anything else was the root cause of the physical rot.

He was rather mysterious about the cause of the moral decline. He said there was a gruesome story connected with the village, but he would not tell it.

Finally Jones told me the Xoaté story.

Back in the 17th century there arrived a fanatical new priest, sent out from Spain to minister to the village. He was determined to stamp out all traces of paganism. All pueblo rituals were prohibited—they were nothing but witchcraft, the priest declared. Soon after he had put an end to some of the secret curing ceremonies (by means of which villagers were cured of nervousness or insanity) the priest began to suffer stabbing pains in the back while saying Mass. He became convinced that the village head priest, the cacique, had put a spell on him. So he called in the Spanish soldiers from Santa Fe and sent them into the kiva and had all the sacred objects removed and burned in the square. The cacique was denounced as a witch and arrested. When he denied that he had bewitched anyone, he was put to the torture. They suspended him by the thumbs. He eventually confessed he had stolen holy water from the church and had attempted to work magic with it. He was hanged. Some years later the Spanish friar was found dead in the village square, his thumbs twisted, and his pockets filled with chili seeds, dirt, and corn.

Thirty years after the death of this priest another Spanish priest in Xoaté went mad. A young boy called Gaspar Quintana was arrested and charged with having maddened the priest, and he admitted it. He said he had obtained a handful of the priest's hair and mixed it with feathers and cotton and excrement. He, too, was executed as a witch.

From this time on there was a continuing struggle in Xoaté between the Church and the forces of darkness. Many witch trials were held. The witches were said to have caused villagers to cough and spit blood, and others to choke to death on their food; to cause evil winds and bad rains; and were responsible for villagers dying of drinking the water that the witches had poisoned by flying in the clouds and filling them up with poison.

The trials of witches went on into the 20th century. One case concerned two male witches accused of being child-eaters. It was said that the bones of dead children had been seen coming out of the witches' mouths and noses and ears. An order was made by the head of the pueblo authorizing the "fiscals"—the constables—to execute the child-eaters, and this was done. Soon after, the headman and the four executioners were arrested by the U.S. civil authorities in Santa Fe and brought to trial. The headman told the court that the execution of the witches had been carried out on his authority, following a vote of the entire village. Every single person in the village had voted for the death sentence, and it had been the duty of the constables to implement the verdict.

Faced with the prospect of putting an entire village on trial, the judge had limited himself to imposing a nominal fine, equivalent to the court costs.

June 20

The debate continues.

JAKE: We ought to have a say. We are making the fucking thing, and so we should be consulted about how and when and where and for what reason it's going to be used. For my part, the reason I'm doing this is to defeat Nazi Germany. For no other. What I am asserting, Bambi, is the fundamental right of the inventor over his own invention.

DAVID: The point is, it's not your invention, and if you pulled out—much as that might hurt us—you could be replaced, so could I. We are servants of the state.

JAKE: Maybe. But I'm not prepared to give the state carte blanche with the product of my brain. Even if you are right in saying that none of us, individually, is indispensable, all of us together *are*. And so it is together that we should make our demands.

HOFMANNSTHAL: No state ever willingly surrenders one shred of its power.

DAVID: The state is a cold monster. It has to be.

HOFMANNSTHAL: Yes, it is the nature of the beast.

JAKE: We do not have to accept that.

HOFMANNSTHAL: My dear Dubinski, what can any of us do about it? Do you have any concrete proposals? If you have, I would be interested to hear them. But all this expressing of views—committees to advise the President, writing of letters—even if you get an answer—is the ponderous mechanism of impotence. If we all press for it, of course the government will make some token concessions to us, will ask us to form advisory committees, write reports. But in the end Mr. Roosevelt will thank us for our valued advice, and do exactly as he pleases.

JAKE: If our advice were rejected, we would be entitled to act.

HOFMANNSTHAL: Act, act? In what way act?

JAKE: We are not entirely helpless.

DAVID: I don't think it's our role to interfere in the decision-making process. I don't think we're qualified for that.

JAKE: Who is qualified?

DAVID: It is the role of our elected representatives.

JAKE: Because they are wiser, nobler than us? Cleverer?

DAVID: No, because they've been elected. I happen to believe in the system of democracy under which we live, and that means allowing it to operate according to its rules and principles. We can't say democracy is O.K. most of the time, but sometimes, when it suits us, we'd rather have an oligarchy made up of us.

JAKE: Let me ask you something, Bambi—in a democracy, the individual has freedom of choice?

DAVID: Up to a point.

JAKE: Can anyone compel me to invent something I do not wish to invent?

DAVID: Scientists can't *not* invent. It's in our natures to want to find out.

JAKE: We could, if necessary, restrain ourselves a little, no?

DAVID: It's too late for that, Jake. You can choose not to bring children into the world, but once they're in it they are their own masters.

189

HOFMANNSTHAL: Supposing it is a matter of bringing a monster into the world.
DAVID: It's too late to stop it now.

June 21

Pistol and Rifle Club.

June 24

Pistol and Rifle Club.

June 28

Heavy gray masses overhang the mountains, suppurating balloons of gray mist. . . . Pistol and Rifle Club.

June 29

Dull dense sensation in head. Sudden tiredness.

June 30

The sun illuminating, bathing in light, the russet browny gold trees—the bare-branched trees, making them glow. As if the light is coming from within them and they are pulsating with this light. Van Gogh trees. Pistol and Rifle Club. I am getting to be quite a good shot.

July 1

Low. Death thoughts.

July 3

Good days, bad days . . . mostly boring days. Sudden moments when my energy level drops, it's a kind of causeless faint. Fear? Fear of what?

July 4

At the Sketching Club our subject is the Male Nude. Only four others in the group, all women. Our Male Nude is a young Indian boy of about 18. Good physique. We are concentrating on the rear view for the moment.

July 10

Burning needle sensation in the back of my head. Death thoughts. Hofmannsthal said the other night that one was only entitled to complain about mortality if one could think of a better arrangement.

July 10

Dr. Franks says my blood pressure is O.K. and that I should not worry about the burning needle sensation in my head. He says it's the altitude. The altitude is also the cause of the dull dense feeling in my head that I sometimes get. Why do I not believe the voice of reassurance? Why do I think that something terrible is going to happen to me?

July 14

It was funny really. We had moved to the frontal view of our Male Nude, and suddenly he had an erection, and everybody pretended it hadn't happened, and they all went on drawing his penis in the limp position. Only I drew it erect.

July 15

I often think about how long I am going to live. I sometimes think it will not be much longer. Why do I think this? What puts such gloomy thoughts in my head?

July 18

In the case of the P bomb, critical mass is 35.2 lb. for pure Pu-239. Can be reduced further . . . to 22 lb. by surrounding with nonfissionable U-238, which reflects neutrons back. Wedge-shaped pieces of P which together make up sphere arranged at equal intervals around a neutron source. Explosive charge behind each wedge. Wedges shot inwards by means of specially designed explosive lenses, which focus the explosive force. Wedges all touch at same moment: assembly: critical mass: chain reaction: explosion. (Compression of mass in the implosive method is a factor in producing critical mass for less weight. . . .)

July 19

I spend three mornings a week teaching. We are doing *David Copperfield*. Twice a week, Mondays and Fridays, the Women's Liaison Committee meets. We put forward our requests to Army Special Services on matters relating to our various needs. We discuss night-school arrangements, religious observance arrangements, dances, bingo games; we complain about the nonavailability of certain items in the Trading Post stores. We complain about the lack of beds at the hospital, with so many women pregnant. The hospital was enlarged to take nineteen beds, but 24 have been crowded in, and are fully occupied most of the time. The military infirmary was designed for three beds, but ten have been crowded in. One fifth of married women now in some stages of pregnancy.

We are urging that communicable diseases should have to be reported through military channels to Oak Ridge. VD is what we are mostly worried about. One half the population is military, two thirds male and one third female. In this kind of situation there are inevitably some busy gals making the rounds. We have said that rubber preventatives should be more easily available to the men; suggest vending machines in toilets . . . but the Army says the men do not like them, and also, it seems, there often isn't time . . . the way these things tend to happen. Around the back of the Services Club, or out in the fields, things happen fast, and

192

as Captain Petersen put it in his customary direct way, the guys feel they have to strike while the iron is hot . . . preventatives slow down the action.

After the committee meetings, my afternoons are usually free. I am often tired—or rather, weary. Weariness is the most common female ailment here. And it ain't the altitude.

July 24

Allison says that the Germans are two years ahead of us in their research. One has to take care not to cause panic, but there is a real fear now that they may have a usable weapon ahead of us—she does not say what this weapon is, refers to it in general terms as a very powerful new weapon. I sense her fear. She obviously thinks she is concealing it, and that in any case I don't know what sort of weapon she is talking about. She says that Jake thinks we should be working in closer cooperation with the Russians on this weapon; by pooling our resources we might beat the Germans to it.

July 25

We seem to have a much higher ratio of illness to population than the rest of the country. There are more miscarriages and stillbirths than you would expect, and respiratory illnesses with associated heart problems, and other illnesses of a mysterious nature that the doctors dismiss as psychosomatic or due to altitude. The military tell us that, with the large percentage of "intellectuals" we have here, we are, as a community, more prone to "mild medical ailments" and more likely to "require and seek medical care," by which they are saying we are a bunch of hypochondriacs. Hypochondriacs and crackpots. But the fact remains that just in the past few weeks Don Rafferty died, of a heart attack, aged 51; Siegi Peretzman died, aged 57, of a lung embolism; Henry Lewis, one of our vets, died of hydrophobia after being bitten by a guard dog he was treating. I don't know how normal this is related to national statistics, but the indisputable fact remains that our hospital resources are strained to utmost and dangerously inadequate. In the case of an epidemic we would be unable to cope, and the security requirements mean that there is great reluctance to use outside medical services or even to consult outsiders. So, often, we do not have recourse to the additional medical opinion that in certain cases would perhaps be desirable.

Apropos the deaths, Dr. Franks said I was beginning to reach an age when I noticed that people really do die.

July 27

The method works by having explosives of different velocities and appropriate shape so that when detonated at a particular point they would produce a converging detonation wave. The lenses are not what is conventionally understood by that word—they are of steel and tooled to focus the explosion inwards, to produce the implosive force that will instantly assemble the plutonium wedges into a sphere. In the machine shops they are experimenting with many differently shaped lenses to get the ones that will be exactly right.

July 28

The Indian view of life is that man is part of a delicately balanced system in which all the thousands of individual parts have a definite role to play, and interact with each other, and that all these life forms and natural elements are of equal importance to the overall harmony of nature, and that man is only one of the many elements; his unique position lies in the fact that only he, of all the elements, is capable of upsetting the overall balance.

July 28

When the fruit of the giant saguaro has ripened the Papagos hold wine festivals. The saguaro provides them with fresh fruit and syrup. From its seeds they make a cake. The syrup-making process has as by-product a juice which is then kept for a number of days in "the rain house" under the eye of a Keeper of the Smoke, who is the village headman and ceremonial leader. While the liquid ferments, rain songs are sung and men and women dance at night. Sexual license is permitted at this time as part of the ceremonial fertility rites. When the liquid in the "rain house" has fermented it is made into wine and poured into wine baskets over which long poems are recited.

July 29

Not enough blood in my head. The altitude? A low pulse—under fifty. I improve with a glass of wine in the morning. It seems to move the blood to my head.

August 28

For the first time last night David talked at some length about Hofmannsthal, and how he came to America. In the beginning he steadfastly refused to leave Germany—that is to say, from 1933 onwards, when it was becoming plain to many others the way things were going. He had invitations from all the leading universities of the world, and he was traveling widely to lecture, but he kept telling his friends in other countries that he could not abandon his "gute Burschen." His place was in Germany. He argued that if all decent civilized people leave a country that is succumbing to barbarism, it made barbarism that much more inevitable. Perhaps it already was inevitable, he admitted, but even so, while there was a chance to exercise the smallest moderating influence, it was his duty to remain. This was said in strictest confidence to people like David and to Hepler and Jake Dubinski and others who were urging him to come to America. Publicly, he remained on good terms with the Nazis. His friends around the world were appalled by the way he allowed his name and prestige to be used.

David says that by '38–'39 he, too, was very worried about the course his old teacher was taking. They met at a scientific congress in Bâle and David expressed his feelings frankly. Apparently, Hofmannsthal succeeded in reassuring David, explaining that while he maintained good relations with the Nazis he was able to intercede on behalf of colleagues and friends. Zander, the head of the Reich Science Office, was a former pupil of his, and Hofmannsthal also had some connection with Himmler. Himmler, he told David, lent himself to a certain amount of horse trading. "I do what I can," he told David at Bâle. David was convinced. More—he thought that Hofmannsthal was playing a brilliant subtle game with the Nazis. A most dangerous game, of course. David says that once he understood what Hofmannsthal was up to, he admired him more than ever.

The way it worked out was that Hofmannsthal was at first left alone, and permitted some influence behind the scenes, but then, as part of the normal mutual blackmail that was standard procedure in the upper echelons of the Nazi hierarchy, some opponent of Zander's dug up a trace of Jewish blood in Hofmannsthal's past . . . a great-grandfather. It was a weapon to be used against Zander. At first, Zander decried the validity of the evidence, with Himmler's concurrence. But it became apparent to Hofmannsthal that it was only a matter of time before the political necessity would arise to have him exposed, and so he made his plans. He would have to act before falling out of favor, and while his movements were still unrestricted. For the time being, Zander, as part of his repudiation of the skeleton in the cupboard, had to let everything continue as before, and so Hofmannsthal was permitted to pay a visit to Niels Bohr in Copenhagen for a scientific exchange of views, and at the end of three days of meetings his plan was put in operation. A stratagem had been devised for eluding the tails, and first Niels Bohr, and then an hour later Hofmannsthal (not all the great eggs in one basket), were ferried by night across the Sound to neutral Sweden. From there they went, separately again, by boat to a secret British bomber base in the Shetlands. The whole thing had been beautifully organized by British Intelligence, which also took the precaution, on the next stage of the journey, to seat the scientists over the bomb hatch in their separate planes, so they could be instantly dropped out into the North Sea in the event of the planes being forced down—this eventuality entailing the risk of the scientists' recapture by a suddenly surfacing U-boat.

Hofmannsthal said that the thought of himself and Niels Bohr hurtling earthward like bombs struck him as somehow appropriate.

September 18

The feeling of not enough blood in my head. David has suggested yoga exercises: standing on my head, for one. I have tried it, and I feel better for a while, but soon the sensation returns, this drifting headiness. The altitude, they say. Sometimes it feels to me as if I am not here in this time and place, not here at all—whatever I mean by that. I feel I do not have enough blood. I would like my blood pressure to be stronger, not to have this numb dullness in my head. The wine makes me feel better. Am I on my way to becoming a dipso? I start with two or three glasses at noon, holding off until then, at any rate on those mornings when I teach. Don't want my pupils to go around saying I have a winey breath. When I am not teaching the first glass is sometimes earlier, sometimes as early as nine or ten. The wine does not make me sleepy or blurry: it stimulates me, it clears my head, and it makes my heart beat fast . . . too fast. Then I have to lie down and rest until my pulse has returned to a more normal rate.

I seem to be afraid of something.

Sometimes, at night, when the moon is out I can see the glistening paths of water below, and feel the rushing water going over the gravel . . . it gives me gooseflesh, as if somebody is walking over my grave.

October 3

Oh God! I see I have come full circle. Whereof one may not speak . . . oh shit! Only I drew that boy's penis erect, the others—lying fishwives!—drew it limp. Hah!

October 4

Bought a Navajo blanket, with a stylized thunderbird motif. It's a lovely thing which I am going to hang in David's den.

The trader Ortego talked fascinatingly about Navajo mythology. Before this Present World there were Previous Worlds underground where there was no light. The First People made their way into the Present World by means of a hollow reed in a badger hole in southeast Colorado. One of the main forces is Ever-Changing Woman who married Sun and Water and gave birth to twin boys, Monster-Slayer and Born-of-Water. Changing Woman lives on an island in the Western Sea where she is visited by her husband, Sun. There is no supreme deity, and all deities are capable of both good and evil. But some are more habitually helpful (or not) than others.

October 10

Hepler believes that if the Germans have got a working atomic pile, which he thinks they must have by now, they could make enough radioactive material to lay down a chain of radioactivity across Europe, an invisible Siegfried Line, forming an impenetrable barrier against our armies.

October 12

They talk of something they call fallout. It is a kind of poisonous afterwind that will traverse the earth. They speculate about the genetic effect on unborn generations.

October 13

Allison is so capable, they way she looks after that bunch of geniuses at Y-3. She keeps it all going. When there's a problem, they say, "Ask Allison." She's good. Next to her I feel so useless here where I have no function. In New York I also had "my work," and the gratification of knowing that what I do is wanted, is paid for. Partly because she has this image for me of cool efficiency—of having it all organized—I loved her story about the French movie star. Oh boy! Had me in hysterics. And she told it unblushingly, with that directness that she has. It was François

198

Lautier—whom we all daydreamed about in our youth. Ze Great French Lover, no less. Only she got him in the flesh—well, up to a point. She was a young kid at the time, and he was making personal appearances around the country for one of his films, and at some summer resort where he was being mobbed he caught her eye over the heads of the screaming fans, and with a very French sort of gesture invited her to stay. Well, she thought, what had she got to lose? Since that was something she had already lost when she was eighteen. As soon as he'd disentangled himself from the bobby-soxers he came over and asked her to sit with him in his auto. He had a bar in the back and he offered her a green Chartreuse in a Spanish goblet, which struck her as très très film starry. Golly, I'm having cocktails with François Lautier, she thought. In his automobile! The auto was one of those gangster-style Buicks with running board and wood-spoke wheels. He explained he'd been making these personal appearances all over the country, and he hadn't had a woman in three weeks, and by God, he was a Frenchman. Would she like to do him a favor and come around to his hotel later on? And they would drink a cocktail or two.

And he would show her what Frenchmen are made of. She said O.K., why not? What had she got to lose?

When she got to his hotel room later that night she was a bit surprised to find herself received by him not in his famous white dinner jacket, in which he habitually received Joan Crawford and Irene Dunne, but in a short white toweling robe. She thought maybe they were going out and he was just changing, but no, they weren't going out, judging from his condition—which was very flattering, but she'd hardly even gotten through the door yet, and she was about to tell him this was all very sudden, when he seized hold of her and at the same time began to shake. A sudden whoosh and it was all over, and all over her. She literally didn't know what had hit her. He was full of apologies. An accident. It was because she was—how shall he say?—such a lovely fresh vision of youth. Sometimes it work like a clock, and sometimes ze clock she is a little fast. But to come back tomorrow, for breakfast, and everything will be made up for. It is a promise, and when a Frenchman promise something . . . et cetera. So she thought, what had she got to lose—except her illusions—and turned up for breakfast at 10:30 A.M. as she'd been told to. Once again he was in toweling robe, which was really much too small for him, and it was evident, not to say conspicuous, that the clock was re-wound. Well, she thought, you have to say this for him: He's ready. This time, half suspecting that things might move fast again, she wasn't wearing anything underneath, and since the pre-liminaries had sort of been disposed of the previous night she just lay back on the bed blissfully, dress up around her waist, eyes closed, thinking that this was what millions of women dreamed of, when—oh no! here we go again, she thought, ze darn clock she is fast again. And abruptly sitting up, chin on hand, she says she looked like someone expecting a custard pie in her face. In a manner of speaking.

October 14

In a way, it was quite unexpected, that story, coming from Allison. Of course, she was a kid at the time, but it has made me think: She is someone who has adventures with men. Easily, I should think. It makes me wonder again about her and David.

The only time Mother and I ever talked of such things was at Thanksgiving, 1940. We were all a little tipsy, and Mother had a flushed happy look, and out of the high spirits of the moment I said, "Daddy and you, you still have a high old time of it, eh?" And Mother immediately got that disdainful look on her face that some people say I, too, have got at times, and she said in her cutting Boston tone, "As infrequently as possible, my dear." I wanted to jolly her out of this aloof mood, and so I said, "Come on, Mother. You've had four children," and she said with a kind of perverse tipsy pride, "One has to put up with that kind of thing from men—they expect it. But I have tried as far as possible to confine it to holidays and your father's birthdays." Before I could dissolve into disbelieving laughter, the thought hit me: My birth-day is almost nine months to the day after Daddy's. Jamie's date of birth? I calculated. Nine months after Thanksgiving. And Nora's? Nine months, give or take a few days, after Christmas.

And William's? January 27. That meant the end of April, beginning of May. No holidays then. Not even Mother's own birthday. That was in October. Had Mother for once relaxed her stern rule? Had something come over her on that day in May? A little spring fever? Had she drunk too much, or been stirred by music? Or had Daddy insisted? It was not like him to insist on anything. He was too polite. In a spirit of teasing, I said, "But Mother, what about William?" And I saw her redden, and thought: Is it possible that Mother had a lover, that . . . ? Oh no.

October 15

The whitewashed houses, sculptural, undulating, curvilinear architecture. In the distance, beyond the mesa, the blue-mauve mountains, like ocean waves . . .

October 16

JAKE: The whole concept of its being *our* secret is artificial. Self-serving sophistry. Denmark and Great Britain probably have made greater contributions to the theory.

DAVID: I agree. We *are* sharing with Britain. Denmark is under German occupation, so it doesn't arise.

JAKE: If we share with Britain, why not with the Soviet Union? Who are also our allies.

DAVID: That's a political decision. There are arguments for sharing with the Russians, and there are arguments against. I personally feel like you do—that probably we should be sharing with the Russians. But it's not for us to decide that.

JAKE: Isn't it? Isn't it?

DAVID: On what basis. . . ?

JAKE: God damn it, because we know best. We do.

DAVID: Isn't there a danger of moral arrogance in that attitude?

JAKE: There is always a danger of something. Isn't there a danger of passing the moral buck in your attitude?

201

I keep everything in separate compartments: my life with David; my social life with the other wives; my schoolteaching; my glasses of wine; my most private thoughts . . . watertight compartments. One has to be able to split oneself up so that one can fulfill all the roles one is expected to play.

October 17

DAVID: If you really want to know, the reason we are doing it is because it's an organic necessity. A scientist wants to know what lies underneath, that's what being a scientist is about, and it's something you cannot stop because it's getting you into dangerous waters. Can't say: Let's not discover that. Because if something is technically very sweet, as this thing is, the way it's working, there is a great drive to go on and do it.

JAKE: Would you feel obliged to discover bubonic plague if it didn't exist—just because you'd gotten some germ culture that was technically very sweet?

October 18

DAVID: The reason all of us here have sort of been opposed, emotionally, to the security provisions is because the secrecy which is imposed on us strikes at the very basis of what science is. Learning cannot be secret: it has to be disseminated. Likewise, I do not believe in a secret science, saying: this is for us only and not for them. To say that strikes at the very basis of science, which is to publish our discoveries, to share them with others, to communicate. Thus what we are doing here, in secret, is a kind of perversion of science. It is a mockery of the scientific spirit. But it is something that is forced on us by necessity, by war. Wartime considerations force this condition of secrecy upon us, and we accept it because we have to. But it is something we cannot approve of. If there is a contradiction in what I am saying, it is an inevi-

202

table contradiction, an unavoidable contradiction. Because we accept it for the moment does not mean it is something we should be willing to institutionalize on behalf of government, so they can forever after hold us to this secrecy for their own ends. There must be a point when this secrecy is no longer beneficial, and then it has got to cease. I don't know that this is a decision that can be left to government, because in this respect the governmental interest will always be diametrically opposed to the scientific interest; governments want to keep things to themselves, scientists want to communicate their findings. When the time comes, we will have to act.

October 19

A very tense evening. Hofmannsthal, Jonesy, Allison, Greenson, Jake. I have never seen Jake so emotional, so carried away. He said that the Russians were bearing the brunt of the fighting, were spilling the lifeblood of their nation, their soldiers were dying in the tens of thousands, in the hundreds of thousands. They were our allies. It was a crime, nothing short of a crime, to deny them any scientific knowledge that might help them win the war. Furthermore, for us to have the weapon and not them would sow perpetual suspicion and distrust and destroy any possibility of postwar cooperation between us. They would be bound to take the view, and rightly so, that we had not shared the secret with them because we were going to use it to threaten them. "Isn't that the real reason why we won't share the secret? We want to keep it to ourselves so that we can rule the world. I happen to believe that any nation with that kind of superiority is doomed. Hubris/nemesis. Doomed, Bambi." David asked, "What do you propose?" Jake said, "If necessary, we scientists have got to act." "In what way?"

At this point I thought it time to break up the conversation, which seemed to be getting into very deep and murky waters. David said, "We'll talk about this later, Jake." I started making drinks. There was no ice, and David said he'd go and get some. After about five minutes, when he hadn't come back, I went to

203

the kitchen myself. I could hear the discussion was still going on—naturally, he'd forgotten about the ice. I was going to go in when something in David's tone of voice made me stop: a wariness, a picking of his words.

David was saying, "I think Joe Davidson has got to be told that getting that sort of information to somebody he knows in the Soviet legation is not the kind of thing I would ever lend myself to. When I said that I was in sympathy with the principle of sharing our secrets with Russia, what I meant—and I think I made that perfectly clear—was that I was in favor of the President, as commander in chief, saying: This is what we're going to do. But I would never dream of doing such a thing by way of the back door. Joe has got to be made to understand that very clearly." At this point I broke in on them, saying, "Darling, you forgot about the ice," and David turned on me, in a way I have never seen him before, and yelled: "The ice! Jesus Christ, Helen, I'm not the fucking iceman."

Joe Davidson. I have never heard that name mentioned before. He's not one of our circle.

October 25

Joe Davidson is a technical sergeant who works in one of the machine shops. On the explosive lenses. Very active union man. In FAECT. Which is said to be very Red-riddled. David knows him presumably through his union activities.

204

ELEVEN

March 18, 1944

A year that we have been here. Seems longer; it seems like forever. The day-by-day reality of this place and what is being done here overrides all other realities, all previous realities. Our New York life already seems so remote. I think: A year ago I was living in New York, I was walking in Central Park; doesn't seem real. I have become a Los Alamos wife. I teach English, take part in community activities, organize functions and entertainments, serve on this committee and that, drink my secret glasses of wine. I go for walks. Or drives. Sometimes I go to Sante Fe or Taos and buy blankets or pottery. I watch the sunsets.

July 19

The sun lays a glaze of heat on the ground.

Slab of heat falling like a weight out of the sky.

One's eyes dazzled by the intensity of the light. Coming into a dim room from sun-whitened square, one is blind for some moments.

The way they make their colors for the blankets and rugs. Peach leaves for yellow green; apple bark for reddish yellow; iron nails soaked in urine for black; wild plum roots for rust red. These colors don't fade, but change.

July 20

There has been an accident in one of the labs. Jake was hurt. Fortunately not too seriously—he got his hand burned.

July 22

The injury to Jake's hand is more serious than it first seemed to be. The radiation absorbed by him has affected his blood. I see Benjie at school, and he seems to have no idea how seriously ill his father is. He thinks it is just a burn. I feel awful, knowing what I know. I don't think they should mislead the boy into thinking it is something trivial, because it's going to be touch and go. They are so concerned about security, they don't want to say more than they have to. Always tightlipped, the creeps. My heart aches for the boy. He loves and admires his father so much. I pray for Jake, yes, I pray. In moments like this you refind your belief in God.

July 28

Allison is sturdy as steel. She has extraordinary resources. I don't know from where she gets such strength. She is a very valorous lady—she must know the worst by now. Jake looked frightful when I saw him today; I don't know if he does not realize how ill he is, or merely pretends not to in order to make things easier for his visitors. His blisters have become infected and do not heal—his white blood cell count is very low. He has high fever, and his hair is beginning to fall out. I had had only one glass of wine before seeing him; when I got home I finished the bottle.

August 13

Jake died this morning. The first victim.

David in Washington. It was not expected to happen yet, it was thought he would hang on another few days, at least. Nobody suspected it was so close. Of course, Allison saw him every day, but I had not been for almost a week. I wish David were here. I am no good alone at such times. I need something—to make the blood flow in me again, there is not enough of it in my head . . . I sit here swigging vin rouge and trying to ward off the horrors. I have had them all day. They will not go away. I keep seeing Jake's face as it was a week ago; suddenly he was gasping desperately for breath and I pretended not to see that he was dying. If only I could have said to him, "Oh, Jake, oh Jake, I know, I know," and cried, perhaps he could have shared his death with me and that would have made it easier for him, but I simply denied it was happening, and he did too, and so we abandon people.

It does not seem like an ordinary death. It seems unnatural.

August 14

Seeing Allison and Benjie—oh that child, it was just heartbreaking—I wished she would have broken down, I could have helped more. . . . Afterwards, I just walked around. I did not know where to go or what to do, with David away. I'd had a few glasses of wine. If I went home I would just sit there drinking until I was drunk. I did not want it to be night. I did not want to be by myself in the house in the dark. But I did not want to see friends either. We would just sit there talking about Jake, and it would all be gone over endlessly, how he had looked at the end, and all the medical details, which I did not want to know. . . .

I tried to make myself cry, because I could feel the need in my chest and throat, and I thought if only I could cry it would relieve something in me, but I couldn't. And that also made me feel guilty. That I could not weep for Jake. What a lousy friend. But I couldn't. The tears stuck in my throat . . . and would not come out.

I was wandering about aimlessly, and I went through the gate into the military side of the main area. There were more people on that side, more lights, it was livelier, with the soldiers as usual standing around and wolf-whistling. There was something comfortingly normal about their lecherous looks. The crude directness of their interest was reassuring. I kept walking until I came to a part of the site they call Morganville, an eyesore of expansible

207

government trailers and laundry lines. Some buried bit of knowledge must have been guiding me, because without any conscious plan I began to duck under the hanging laundry and make my way to the perimeter fence, and there it was, as I knew it would be: the escape hole. The woven wire had been cut, and by lifting a section of it and stooping a little it was easy enough to get out. I could have gone by the main gate as easily, but for some reason I preferred this way. Outside the fence I found myself on the boundary road that is patrolled by the mounted guards. I crossed the road and walked at a strolling pace into an area of scrub and bushes. The ground sloped gently downwards. I saw the beginning of a well-trodden path and started along it. Within a few minutes I realized I had wandered into a lovers' lane. I saw couples embracing amid the trees and others lying on the soft ground, and the air was filled with secret soft sounds. Oh my goodness, I thought, laughing, what have I wandered into! I had gone perhaps a hundred yards before realizing where I was. I started back and now I could not help seeing lovers everywhere, against trees, or in the bushes, and on the ground in the open. It was rapidly getting dark and they were becoming bolder all the time. I could make out regular movements, and deep long slow kissing. I passed a couple against a tree kissing in this way—I must have passed them going out, without noticing. They were very still, still as statues. I saw them look in each other's eyes, and I thought, oh my! there is going to be some fun here tonight, as soon as it is dark enough. I felt a wave of sensuality sweep over me like a warm moist wind. As I walked back I saw a couple on the ground who had not been ready to wait until it was dark. The guy was lying on top of the girl and they were partially covered by his tunic, beneath which he rose up in regular humping movements; the girl's nylon-stockinged feet were far apart and I heard some gaspy cries come from her. In a minute it was going to be like that all over.

When I got back to the hole in the fence I still had the problem of not wanting to go back to an empty dark house. Not just yet. It was still early. There was the whole long evening to kill. And so I carried on, taking an ascending path that I knew from my daytime walks. There was a moon, which gave enough light for me to see. I could not explain what I was feeling. The pall that had been hanging over me all day was lifting. The fact that I had slipped out secretly through the escape hole (like the soldiers and their girls) excited me strangely, it was like having gotten away with something. Well, it is true: A closed system is only tolerable by virtue of its loopholes, and now I had crept out through one of those loopholes. Clever me! I was getting up among the enormously tall aspens that grow at that level. There were sycamores and elms and maples too, and slender soft-barked trees. I was thinking of all those girls getting laid down there, and it made me smile to myself and feel very amorous. I thought of the wolf-whistling soldiers by the fence and of the wives who reputedly let themselves be taken behind the Services Club for a knee-trembler up against the storehouse wall. It was not something I could have done. My upbringing (Vienna and Boston) did not permit of such coarse pleasures—I cannot let myself go, to that extent. Though at university I got up to one or two things. But that was different: the experimental stage of growing up. One is allowed to be exploratory in adolescence. But the controller's wife isn't. My head was full of pictures of soldiers and their girls humping in the dark. I'd caught glimpses of some of the preliminaries, walking back. Skirts rumpled up; a flash of white thigh against the dark of the trees; the hot urgency of it all. All those gaspy little strangled cries. I thought of Allison's philosophy in these matters—"what have I got to lose?"— and that released something in me: my normal inhibitions. I stopped and leaned against a tree—I was feeling quite feverish, not myself—and touched myself there where the ache was, and was amazed by the heavy warm wetness that my fingers found, and by the coarseness of my sexual cry. It did not sound like me, not like me at all. My eyes closed, my head rolled from side to side, and my hips moved with slow regularity. I was in a half-faint of mounting sensations. In a moment I would come—oh, I would have to stop this, some madness had got into me, evidently. But I thought: One is always stopped by something—by fathers and husbands and duties and children, by this and by that, by pride, by fear, by a sense of propriety. Well, fuck propriety, my wood demons were urging me, and I was ready to comply. What had I got to lose?—anyway, I really was not myself at all, it was not me pulling my clothes off crazily but some wild crazy forest nymph, and the realization of what I was doing made me shake with laughter, and the way I was going on you would have thought I was drunk, to say the least. All the same I was doing this: cavorting about totally naked under the huge sky, and the warm and incredibly soft night air on my open flesh was almost making me come as I wriggled and twisted about like some savage. I was going from tree to tree with the lewdest of intentions, until finally I found one that suited me: a slender silky-barked tree. Which I embraced. And then, in my crazy passion, sought to climb. Oh, it was my tree of life—and as I felt the sticky sweet sap on my fingers I began to topple over into that beautiful fall.

August 15

A curious dream last night. I was back in New York, on Lexington Avenue waiting for a bus. I wanted a bus going to the Public Library, where I was doing some research for an article. There were two men on the bus line with me, and each wanted me to go with him somewhere else. One was going to the Village, to an arts festival, and the other was going to some disreputable joint on 42nd Street. I had a great deal of luggage—I don't know why I had so much luggage to go to the Public Library. Both men were helping me on the bus with my heavy luggage. When I was on, I asked the driver, "Are you going to the Public Library?" and he shrugged indifferently and said, "I can't tell you where I'm going, you'll just have to wait and see, lady."

"But I want to go to the Public Library," I said.

The bus had already started and the driver was shaking his head and exchanging looks with the two men who had gotten on with me, as if to say: "Women! Always want to know where they're going. . . ."

August 16

The dictionary definition of incubus: an evil spirit that descends upon women in their sleep and seeks to have carnal intercourse with them. ("Belial the dissolutest Spirit that fell, The Sensuallest, and after Asmodai, The fleshliest incubus."—Milton, *Paradise Regained.*)

September 5

It's just over three weeks since Jake died. And already it is accepted, the new reality is that he is no longer among us, and we have adjusted to it. In physics when something that they call a dislocation occurs, matter is under tremendous pressure to rectify the imbalance, to restore the previous wholeness. I feel we are under this pressure, to make up for the loss of Jake and restore the integrity of our circle. Allison is the loose-flying particle that has to be stabilized. How? Since everybody's married. She is pretty and vital and men like her, and as I know from her she cannot be alone for long. It has disturbed all sorts of things, Jake's death.

September 10

As I was leaving I spotted Allison dancing with an Army sergeant. They were dancing very smoochily. It seems soon—too soon. One month that Jake has been gone . . .

September 13

Allison was in the PX with this guy, the same one. He has the stripes of a technical sergeant. They were standing together, smoking, looking into each other's eyes. I asked somebody who he was, and was told, "That's Joe Davidson—'Red' Davidson."
    From where do I know that name?

September 13 (later)

Suddenly came to me—Joe Davidson. I looked back through my diary entries, and sure enough. Joe Davidson was the one they were talking about last fall, when Jake was arguing that we ought to share our secrets with the Russians, and there was that conver-

211

sation in the kitchen about Joe Davidson knowing somebody in the Russian Legation. . . . I hope Allison is not getting herself into something she'll have cause to regret. She acts at the behest of her emotions. A man touches her in a certain way and she is completely in his power. Of course, she and Jake were always very pro-Russian.

September 20

Allison was fuming, said the Security people insist that she stop seeing "some guy"—she didn't mention him by name—because he hasn't got a white badge. Says she told them her private life was her own business, and she wasn't going to let anybody tell her whom she could or could not see. I said for her not to do anything foolish. Pointed out that there's a lot of nervousness on the Security side and that, considering what she knows, it's maybe understandable. She said, "Oh, Jesus Christ, what do they think? That I'm going to blurt out the Secret Formula?—that's not my conversation in the sack. To hell with those bastards, I am not taking that."

September 28

Allison doesn't see Joe Davidson anymore. Seems they got to her, the Security people, and she gave him up. I wonder how they managed to get her to do that. She was very determined not to knuckle under. I'm glad she's given him up. He wasn't her style, a burly guy with thick lips and a Don Juan moustache. What's more, with a wife in Albuquerque. She can do better.

September 29

Late heat spell.

In the clubhouse some were jiving, others dancing close. The heavy dimness, the cheap powder smells, the cheap perfume, and the sexual tension between the men and those cute cute chicks. It's a very erotic ambience. I had not meant to stay long, but the music and the heavily charged dimness held me. It was so lively, and where we are it's dead at night. I was lingering with, I suppose, my superior smile, which in the past had protected me, distinguishing me from the fair game. My smile made it clear that I was just looking. Not interested. All the same, I was being closely examined by one of the guys. He was lounging against a wall, knee drawn up, surrounded in cigarette smoke. Not bad-looking. Italian appearance—a lean and hungry look. It was obvious what he was hungry for right now. I couldn't help noticing that he had an erection. The way he was sprawling against the wall drew the material of his pants tight over his groin. I must have looked a second too long, because he took it for encouragement and came over and asked me to dance. I had never danced with any of the men before, had always said, "No thank you." But I was feeling lonely tonight and sorry for myself—David was away on one of his trips—and a little flirtation with a randy young soldier might lift me out of my low mood. Why not? What had I got to lose? It was only a dance. He held me close, and I could feel his erection jigging up against me. I told him my name was Alice. He said his name was Jim. He was trying to place me.

"Seen you before, haven't I?"

"Could be."

"Nurse—I bet you're a nurse."

"You guessed it, Jim."

He gave a little seductive laugh.

"Is that right what they say about nurses—eh?"

"What d'you mean?"

"Oh, nurses have got quite a reputation around here."

"That so?"

"Hot-blooded, they say—nurses."

"I wonder why—I mean, why nurses?"

"It's their job does it, I'd say."

"Yes?"

"What would you say, Alice?"

"I don't know."

"I bet you're hot-blooded, Alice."

"You would?"

"Yeah."

"What would make you bet that?"

"You got that look."

"Have I?"

He was exciting himself with this talk, and pressing against me, and the fact that I wasn't pushing him away was giving him ideas.

"Let's find out," he proposed. "How about it?"

"Find out what?"

"You know."

"You're some quick worker, Jim," I protested, not too strongly.

"You have to be in this life," he confided. "How about it, Alice?"

"How about what?"

"Come out back with me?"

"Out back where?"

"You know—round the back of the stores?"

"What happens there?"

"You know what happens there. Now don't be—"

"No, I don't. What happens?"

He told me in my ear, in some detail.

"No," I said, "I wouldn't want to do anything like that."

He was disappointed. I had been leading him on, of course, out of mischief and curiosity . . . and what else? In the face of my direct refusal, he went into a vicious sulk. Without being too prissy about it, I sought to dance further away from him, to ease myself gently out of this situation, but he wasn't letting me. I laughed, and said, "Oh, look, don't be silly now, please . . . really. Now look . . ." He had gotten a sort of frozen leer on his face, and an iron grip around me, and I couldn't break away without fighting him and making a scene that would draw attention to me. He had a very concentrated expression and he was saying things in my ear the whole time, and I was forced to be the accomplice of his wishful thinking as he told me all the things he was going to do that I was going to love. Out in the alley. His eyes were half closed and his face was getting to be all screwed up, and it was obvious from his suddenly speeded-up movements (made me think of a dog mounting a bitch, the unstoppable urgency of

214

it) that he intended to get off, whether I cooperated or not. I was held inside his thighs like in a vise, and then the quick movements stopped, I felt him shake, and clasped tight up against him I felt the warm wetness coming through his pants as he wriggled about like the little worm he was. And he even tried to make a date with me after this stand-up rape. The whole thing had happened in seconds (the last part) and I hadn't even had time to work up to a state of outrage, and now, after the event, it was somehow too late. So I just said I had to go to the Powder Room, and since his hold on me had at last slackened, slipped away and ran.

The truth was I panicked—I suddenly had thought: my God, his stuff will be all over me, how am I going to go home? Everyone will know. In my consternation I rushed out of the first door I saw, and it was one of those push-bar fire doors, and it was only when I was outside and the door had slammed locked behind me that I realized my mistake. I was out in the back alley that I had been hearing so much about. Oh, the place was sonorous with love sounds! Blind as a bat, but with my sensors out, I had a pretty good idea of what was going on. I thought: How do I get out of here? I couldn't see a thing, but there were all these forms everywhere. I felt around in the dark, and stumbled against a crate of empties, sending bottles crashing over. My searching hand, nervous of what I might find, found the iron lid of a trash can, and beyond that the corrugated iron of a wall, which I figured must lead somewhere, so I felt my way along this corrugated iron, which was vibrating rhythmically with the passionate movements of all the lovelies being had up against it. Oh boy! Trapped in Love Alley—a comic nightmare. My eyes were just about able to make out forms now, and I tried to go around the deeply enwrapped shadows, bumping into some of them with a muttered "So sorry" and "Oops, pardon me" and "Excuse me please."

Suddenly I remembered my cigarette lighter, and by the light of it I was able to make somewhat better progress. A vestigial sense of decency made me extinguish the lighter as I got right up to the shadowy forms, but I couldn't always do that in time, and I saw one girl, thin-faced—anorectic, almost—with glistening overfull eyes, who seemed to be screaming soundlessly. It reminded me of

215

the little Munch drawing David has. Her posture suggested somebody bandy-legged from too much horse riding. I didn't look down, but my! the corrugated iron was jumping against my direction-seeking hand. So this was what soldier Jim had been promising me, that I had so unsportingly turned down. The girl's expression, though I saw it only for a moment, had etched itself into my mind. This is what it means, I thought, to abandon oneself to sensation: it was like a prognosis for me. I brushed past this enwrapped pair with mumbled apologies, still not able to see (even with my lighter) where this love alley ended and how I could get home. I was on the verge of hysterical tears. I could picture myself here for hours, stumbling and tripping and feeling my way around, and not being able to find my way out. What a Dantean punishment for the offense of prick teasing! And then, at last, I made out ahead of me the clubhouse corner and knew where I was. I was out. Just as I reached a point where there was more light and I could actually see to walk—my luck!—one of those double shadows separated and I found myself face to face with Jones. I looked away quickly, and walked on past him, praying he hadn't recognized me.

But suppose he did recognize me? He will naturally assume, seeing me in Love Alley . . . the alley of the knee-tremblers . . . . It does seem terribly unfair.

October 1

Pam came by and asked if I'd like to come for dinner. She was being nice, because she knows David is still away. But I hated her for asking me, putting me in the position of not very well being able to refuse. What excuse could I give? It also occurred to me that Jonesy might have put her up to asking me, for his own reasons. What am I going to do? It's tomorrow. Just us. I said I'd let her know. The only way I can get out of it is by saying I'm ill. In which case she'll come around immediately and fuss over me, and rub Vicks on my chest, and ask me about my bowels. The disadvantage of living on top of one another.

216

October 3

He let on nothing until dinner was over and Pam was in the kitchen washing up. The children were in bed, their door closed. He went to make sure they were asleep, moving through a dog fight of Messerschmitts and Spitfires suspended from the ceiling; below, battleships cruised, and below them submarines and U-boats fired torpedoes at each other. Tony was half hanging out of the top bunk of the double-decker, one arm stuck out like the wing of a dive bomber. Jonesy moved him gently into a safer position, and tucked him in. Very tenderly, I thought. Sarah, with her lovely long blond tresses spread out over the cushions, looked like Sleeping Beauty. Pretty child. When Jonesy came back into the living room he poured brandies for both of us without asking me if I wanted one and came and sat next to me on the sofa. I thought he sat awfully close. He lifted his glass to mine, and gave me what the British call an old-fashioned look. I kept as cool as I could. Suddenly he said:

"We think we know somebody, and we don't, eh?"

"Is that supposed to mean that you thought you knew me? What a nerve, Jonesy!"

He laughed, and I smiled.

"Mind you," he said with that pleasantly unruffled British manner of his, "mind you, people did speculate."

"About me?"

"The smile. The smile. The theory was that it hid something."

"What was it supposed to have hidden?"

"Ah, well . . . that would be telling." He was backing down a little, perhaps he was not absolutely certain that it was me he had seen in knee-trembler alley. If it wasn't me, then he was barking up the wrong tree. So, better mind his p's and q's. "Hmm?" he murmured vaguely, flirtatiously, trying to get information out of me. But I wasn't giving any.

"I didn't say a thing. I was waiting for you to tell me what the theories about me are. What my smile is supposed to hide."

"A passionate nature," he whispered daringly, then waited to see if he had gone too far. He concluded he evidently hadn't, I

217

was waiting to hear more. So he went on. "On the theory of opposites, you see. Cool smile hides passionate nature."

"Neat. And what do you think, Jonesy?"

"I think it is perhaps a little simplistic. But what a lark if it were true."

"A lark, eh?"

"You're not—uh—offended, Helen?"

"I don't know that it's very nice being speculated about in that way. Not very proper, is it?"

"Well, you know people. Nothing else to do. . . ." His tendency to climb down from every gained position was disconcerting.

"And have you got nothing else to do?"

"I didn't say I speculated about you, Helen. I was just saying . . . other people . . ."

"Oh? Why are we talking about *other people?*"

"Well, as a matter of fact, it has passed through my mind."

"What has?"

"To wonder."

"To wonder about me?"

"Yes, Helen."

"Do tell me what you've wondered, Jonesy."

"Well . . ." He shot a quick glance towards the kitchen door. We could hear the sound of washing up. "Sometimes I've thought, Helen, that despite that rather aloof air you have—forgive me for saying that, it's an impression you sometimes give—actually you are a lovely free-spirited woman, not constrained by, shall we say, the conventions." He looked at me closely to see how I was taking this, and I must have appeared to be taking it well, because he went on. "And that since Bambi can't be at the mill and at the ford, as the Italian peasantry say, and since we all know that he works all the time, with almost superhuman expenditure of energy, one wonders, you see, if that doesn't leave you a bit out in the cold. . . . Now what do you think of that for a speculation? Hmmm? Hmm? Wildly out? Warm? Warmish?"

"Warmish," I said. "So now you know, Jonesy."

"Ah," he said, "I thought so. . . ."

"I'm teasing you," I said.

"Are you, Helen?" he asked, disappointedly.

"Oh, I guess there is some truth in your speculation, about as much as there is in what most palm readers tell you. It's not difficult to see that most of the wives here are, as you put it, left out in the cold."

"I could kick myself," he vowed.

"Why?"

"For not having realized it earlier."

"Why, would you have tried to seduce me?"

"Helen, you're a very lovely and exciting woman. Now that we know each other better"—he put his hand tentatively on mine—"tell me, it was you the other night? In the alley behind the clubhouse?"

I could have denied it, I suppose. He didn't sound that sure.

I said, "Yes, but don't tell anyone. Our secret?"

"Our secret. Oh, absolutely."

"I never pictured *you* going in for such louche adventures, Jonesy."

"Nor I you."

"How was yours?"

"Not at all bad. And yours?"

"Not at all bad."

"Even so," he pointed out, "the heart does crave variety, hmm?"

"I think you've hit the nail on the head."

"Could we perhaps have tea together, Helen?"

"Yes, yes, we could perhaps have tea together. The problem is where."

"Yes, that is indeed a problem."

Pam was calling through the kitchen door, "Coffee, Helen?"

"No thanks, Pam. Can't sleep if I drink coffee at night."

"Tea then?"

"No, nothing for me. I should be going."

"Just a sec, be right out."

"Where, Helen?" Jones insisted with sudden nervous urgency, fearful that the catch might slip through his fingers.

219

"My house is not possible," I said. "People stop by. I don't much care for the clubhouse, or the back alley. Why don't we go for a walk? I'll meet you . . . by the hole in the fence. I know a lovely walk. Tomorrow? 6:30?"

"I'll look forward to it," he said politely.

We took my path up into the mountains, the one I had taken the night of Jake's death, and found a clearing under the trees and sat down on a red *Mauritania* knee rug that he had had the foresight to bring, carrying it nonchalantly under his raincoat. We smoked and talked. We were not anonymous bodies pressed up against each other in a smoky dark dance joint but two people with images to live up to and roles to play. It was not just a matter of bodies. About that part I was by no means certain anyway. Did I want to make love with Jonesy? He was good-looking in a blond bland English sort of way, but I could not claim to have been stirred to great passion by him. Why this, then? Curiosity? Boredom? Another piece of research—to provide me with notes for a novel that may never be written? We smoked several cigarettes and talked. I began to wonder if he was ever going to make the first move. I was beginning to feel ridiculous, sitting here in the dark of the forest, on the red *Mauritania* rug, chatting. Finally, as if suddenly remembering why we were here, he put his hand on my arm and said, "You are a very beautiful creature."

"What kind of creature?" I said, giving him the cue to continue in this more promising vein.

"A wild creature, I should think."

"No," I said with unnecessary truthfulness, "I'm not wild at all, but I have been feeling lonely and left out, and Jake's death upset me a great deal. I've been rather searching for myself. The other night when you saw me, actually nothing much had happened. I had just danced with some soldier and then I went out in the alley by mistake. Wrong door. Silly mistake, really."

I saw this confession disappointed him: he wanted me to be some kind of sexual tigress, since that would absolve him of the normal constraints that people in our sort of circles were expected to exercise towards each other's spouses. He kissed me lightly, wistfully, on the lips—it was like being kissed by Leslie Howard.

220

"I thought," he said, "that wasn't your style—the alley."

"But it seems to be yours."

"Men are different. We have a baser side to our natures. You are truly very lovely, Helen. I think I could easily fall in love with you, you know. Beautiful Helen." He kissed me again, romantically. "I have the most enormous regard for you, you know."

"I don't think you should make any mistake," I cautioned. "I love David."

"I can't quite make you out," he said with a quizzical expression on his face.

"You don't have to make me out," I said. "All you have to do is make love to me. That's what we came here for, isn't it? You don't need to examine my motives, or analyze me."

"I'm going to make love to you, Helen. Oh, I'm going to." He lit another cigarette, however. I waited. What was wrong now?

He said slowly, "You know, I hate to do this to Bambi. I feel truly rotten about that part. Is this the first time you've . . . betrayed him?"

"I haven't done it yet," I pointed out. "So it's a bit early to call me names." To salve his conscience, I added, "No, it's not the first time. O.K.?"

I could see there was a danger he might just be gentlemanly enough—in his perverse way—not to lay hands on me, after having gotten me here, out of some belated sense of its not being done. I thought it high time to put an end to all this Leslie Howard business. I thought, what am I doing here, what am I doing here? What had attracted me to him was his sudden ruthless opportunism while Pam was in the kitchen, and having seen him in knee-trembler alley. Someone who went in for low adventures. That had interested me about him, not the Leslie Howard.

I said angrily, "It's not very flattering to me, your hesitating on the brink like this. In one second I'm going to throw this damned invalid's rug on your cold feet, and pick myself up and get out of here."

"No, no, don't do that," he pleaded, and kissed me. It was a bit more passionate this time, but not much more: mere movie passion. Then came the part you do not see in the movies. He sud-

221

denly stood up and began to take his clothes off. It was done quickly, practically, like a sportsman changing for some sporting event: His body was very narrow naked, narrow shoulders, narrow hips with a covering of flesh as fine and sparse as crinkled tissue paper. I noted the way he took off his pants, with lithe deftness, slipping off pants and underpants in one and the same movement, the way children do it. He did not have an erection but his penis had a good length and a kind of importance against the overall leanness and narrowness of his body. He had put down his cigarette on a tree branch to undress, and now he picked it up again and drew on it with a rather beautiful movement.

"Why don't you take your things off, Helen," he suggested.

"All right," I said, and began to undress. He watched me smilingly, taking me in bit by bit. His expression would not have been inappropriate at a whist drive.

"You have lovely breasts," he said, wistfully. Oh, he was being very Leslie Howardish about the whole thing. But his prick had become hard and upright. It seemed to be on a separate circuit from the rest of him. I waited; he had the decency not to smoke his cigarette to the end, but to put it out and take me into his arms. He kissed my breasts, first one, then the other. He kept up this form of lovemaking for a long time. I still had not been touched anywhere else. We were like two nudes in an 18th-century painting of a forest idyll. Nothing untoward—except for that unwavering erection. There has got to be a storyline, I thought, soon I'll know. In the end, I took the initiative a little, sliding my tongue in and out of his mouth in a way that I hoped would suggest something to him. I looked at him. I could see from the set of his mouth that he was going to see this thing through. His male pride was involved. Even if I was not exactly what he had imagined, he was going to do what was expected of him. But we were still only playing footsie—I pushed his foot with mine, and he pushed mine with his. Although this had the effect of pushing my legs farther apart, the game did not appear to be progressive. I'd had enough of all this cat-and-mouse.

"Jonesy," I said, "you have stimulated me quite enough."
"Yes?"

222

"Yes."

"You are not exactly wild yet, Helen."

"This is about as wild as I get," I said. "It's enough. Believe me."

"Put in a request," he said, laughing, and tickling my neck and chin. "And it will be heeded. One does not care to barge in uninvited."

"This is not exactly uninvited," I said, indicating my position, and making it even more inviting whilst I was about it.

"Still, a chap likes to have a formal invitation," he said with a sheepish schoolboy grin on his face.

"Like 'requests the pleasure of' . . . that sort of thing?"

"That's right. That's right. Only more direct, Helen." He seemed to have become breathless.

I invited him.

At once he swung onto me, and the whole thing went off without a hitch.

"How was that?" he asked when it was over, reaching across me to fish in his trouser pockets for a cigarette.

"Very nice, thank you," I said. "Not at all bad."

"Oh, I'm glad," he said. He seemed genuinely pleased—pleased as Punch that it had gone well.

We both smoked and looked at the stars.

I asked, in order to say something: "Does Pam know—that you go in for this sort of thing?"

"Oh, I expect so. She has the decency not to mention it."

"That is decent of her."

"Yes, she's a decent sort, Pam. And Bambi, does he know about you?"

"Oh my God, no. David would kill me if he knew. Or kill you."

"Would he now? Would he? That's interesting. You find the danger adds spice. . . ?"

"You talk as if I go in for this sort of thing all the time. I don't. Frankly, I had no idea such things went on in our little circle. It shocks me in a way, and astonishes me."

"One has to be a member of the circle to know."

223

"You make it sound like a private club."

"It is, in a way."

"Who belongs to it?"

"Rule No. 1 of the club. No tittle-tattle."

"Does Allison belong to it?"

"Ah-ah—that would be telling."

"I bet she does. I bet Allison plays around."

"You never know about other people," he said vaguely.

"I don't think I could do it," I said.

"What?"

"Lead a double life."

"Oh, it's quite easy, once you get the hang of it."

"Is that so? Are you the expert?"

"Controlled schizophrenia—that's the way to do it," he said with his bland smile.

"Somebody else said that. Yes. Klaus Fuchs. We all lead lives of controlled schizophrenia, he said."

"I wouldn't be surprised. I've been told I don't have a very original mind."

We were silent. More stargazing.

"I think I should be getting back now," I said, reaching for my clothes.

"What about one for the road?"

"I think you're boasting, Jonesy."

"No I'm not."

I saw that he wasn't.

"Oh well," I said, "as they say in your country—in for a penny, in for a pound."

It was better the second time. As he pulled on his pants and underpants, with the same single lithe movement with which he had taken them off, he grinned down at me, and, buttoning himself, said, "Welcome to the club, Helen. Beautiful Helen."

TWELVE

June 28, 1945

The men have nearly all left now. Sometimes as many as ten trucks make the journey. They go at night to avoid the fierce desert heat and also because it is more secure to go at night. David has gone too. They all have gone. There are hardly any men left on our side of the fence. The place they have gone to lies 180 miles to the south, in the middle of a vast uninhabited stretch of desert. David has called the place Trinity.

June 29

I think it will happen in the next two or three weeks. Very hot. No rain. The air is tense with undischarged storms.

Klaus Fuchs saying that time that we live in a condition of controlled schizophrenia. He's right.

July 1

No word from the Jornada del Muerto. It must be soon now. It will be seen even here—nearly two hundred miles away. Before he left, David and the others were talking about it in a jokey way and David was saying that maybe their Big Bang would ignite the atmosphere and destroy the world. It was possible, he thought. They were laying bets on it.

David arrived back from the desert looking like a death's head. He hasn't slept for days. But he was elated that the test had been a success. Elated and, by turn, depressed. He half hoped, I think, that it would not succeed. That would have been a sign from God. And he would have been relieved. But the fact that it has succeeded beyond all expectations means to David that God permits everything, even that, and the cleverer you are the more you are permitted, and I think that terrifies the shit out of David, because he is very clever. His mind is so very lucid, he sees where everything leads. Such lucidity can be a great curse. It is terrible to see everything. A petition has been gotten up by some of the leading scientists who have worked on the bomb. They are demanding that, in the first place, its use should be confined to some kind of demonstration. Feeling is running high. General Brown has slapped a top secret classification on the petition, which means it cannot be circulated without security guards to protect it, and, of course, he cannot spare the security guards. So it has stopped circulating. It circulates by word of mouth. David has rejected it outright. David concurs fully with the military recommendation that the bomb should be used against "a war plant or base adjacent to civilian housing and other buildings most susceptible to damage"; and that it should be used without prior warning. He says, "Letting off a firecracker over Tokyo Bay is not going to impress the Japs." The main argument against David's position is that once we have used this weapon, there will be no limits—everything will be permissible. It's the opening of Pandora's box, and there'll be no going back.

I am outside this debate entirely, as are all the wives. We are not supposed to know what is happening. We are not supposed to know anything of the terrible decisions that our men are in the course of making. For all of us. And not just us—for mankind. Have always thought that the sort of meetings from which women are excluded are usually very sinister. David is steering into the skid, steering into the skid . . . as usual. Showing his control. Showing that even the burden of this dreadful decision does not faze him. Of course, I don't suppose he could really stop it on his own—the dropping of the bomb. But if he were to add his voice to all the others coming out against its use on a populated civilian target, then it would put powerful pressure on Truman, and he might find it unpolitic to override the views of all the leading scientists who have worked on the bomb. But while David and others support him fully, it adds to the momentum to go ahead and do it. David is keen to go ahead and do it now.

July 18

David sits there doing his yoga, taking the pressure. He is calm and controlled. Burdens do not bother David. He is always good with outside, real, visible burdens that his clear rational mind can grapple with according to the laws of logic. It is when there are no such outside problems to engage him that he is most ill at ease. Like the time just after we were married. We were on our honeymoon in Europe, and he was miserable, and worse—deeply depressed. He blamed his depression on the manifestations of Fascism and Nazism that we saw everywhere around us. In Berlin we heard, at first hand, what was happening to the Jews under Hitler; David did not believe, as some Jews did, that it was a phase that would pass—he foresaw the worst. In the violent strident colors of the new order he perceived an image of the future. When people made fatuously cheerful remarks, he replied, "Things are always worse than one imagines—in this case, they are much worse." We went to Vienna, and everywhere David saw ominous signs: in the mood of the people, in their stubborn denial of reality, in their refusal to see what was before their eyes. The Jews in Vienna did not want to abandon their businesses and their homes and their professions and their standard of living, they did not want to go to England or America and start again, and be cooks and gardeners and agricultural workers. David told them, "You are going to die if you stay," and they said he was exaggerating. It was before the Anschluss, Austria was still independent. Hitler was making menacing noises, but he would not dare to do all the things he threatened. "Don't count on that," David kept telling the people we

227

met, "just don't count on it." We went on to Switzerland, and there, too, David saw the signs; it's true, events cast their shadow before them, he kept saying somberly. In Switzerland we hired a car and drove across the Alps, and then on to Venice. It was our honeymoon. There was terrible rain. The roads were flooded, and at one stage our windshield wipers stopped working and David had to lean out and wipe the windshield by hand in order to see anything at all. There were times when we couldn't go on and we had to stop by the side of the road with the rain all around us and the water rising and I thought we were going to be washed away and drowned.

We finally got to Venice and there David became ill—in the Hotel des Bains, on the Lido, the setting of Mann's *Death in Venice*. And to David that, too, was a portent, he was seeing signs in everything, and the fact that he should have fallen sick in the setting of Von Aschenbach's disintegration was for him yet another pointer. He was in bed for three days; the weather improved, but not his spirits; when he finally got up I made him walk a little on the beach, though he seemed still very unwell. I had never seen him like this, so frail and destroyed-looking. He was normally full of vitality and drive. I became very afraid, thinking he must be succumbing to some grave illness. I feared the worst. Our honeymoon was wrecked. He seemed to be in the grip of some secret terror on these calm Lido beaches. He talked of Kierkegaard and of the sickness unto death, and of despair being greatest in the very heart of happiness and hope, and I thought that he, too, was going to die of some mysterious sickness of the soul, like Von Aschenbach. But somehow, after a few days of this destroying malaise, he pulled himself together. Overnight he cured himself. Steered into the skid, and came through.

It was when we came back to New York—after his dark vision in Europe—that he went to see Einstein and got him to write a letter to Roosevelt, explaining the necessity of restricting uranium supplies to Germany.

David is so very relaxed; he is almost overrelaxed, considering what is afoot. He sits on the floor of his den in the Buddha position, doing his breathing exercises or playing the violin. He does some deep breathing, and then he plays, some more deep breathing, followed by some more playing. His playing is actually improving. Anything he sets his mind to, he masters in the end. I think he is steering into the skid again—he has got it almost under control.

The only sign he gives of being under any tension is the way he sometimes acts towards me. He has become remote from me. We have not made love since he has come back from Trinity. He has these phases of asceticism and self-denial. Perhaps he is saving his energy. I have tried once or twice to make some little move towards him, but he does not respond. He says, "Soon we'll declare a little holiday—after the fishing trip." There is to be a fishing trip. It is what all the planning is about.

It is true that David associates sex with holidays (a bit like my mother)—or, at any rate, treats himself a little like an athlete in training, and does not expend himself on extraneous things before a big event. Also, at a time when he is subjecting himself to such rigorous self-controls in one respect, he perhaps feels he cannot abandon himself to pleasure, it might open up some fatal chink in his armor. Not that he is ever very abandoned in lovemaking. His sense of style prevents that. I think it may have been different once, before his first marriage. He sometimes refers fliply to "gals" or "dames" he used to know in the old days. One is meant to gather that he was quite a guy for the gals. I find it hard to imagine. He is so, basically, correct. I cannot picture him going in for pleasure. (He is too serious for that.) Of course, a wife is not the same as a gal. He sometimes calls me Madame Pleasure Principle. At other times I am Madame Chaos, because I lose things and do not always act, as he considers it, reasonably; sometimes I act, according to him, quite chaotically. He thinks it is very immature to be so attached to pleasure. In fact, he subscribes to a theory (dating from his analysis) that maturity can be measured in terms of the ability to postpone pleasure. A child has to have it now; as it develops, it becomes slowly capable of giving up some immediate gratification for a greater future gain—all forms of work and learning depend on that ability; the greater the level of maturity, the further into the future can the gain be deferred. As you reach still higher levels of maturity, so the reward recedes ever further. Genius, says David, is being able to work towards a gain only realizable after one's own lifetime. That is how far he will defer pleasure. It is something I cannot understand at all. He is right: I want it now. I cannot be dismayed or joyous about what history will say of me. But to David it matters. I think he would like to know there will be a statue of him standing here one day. I cannot imagine what difference that makes, since he will not be here to see it, and when you think of all the statues that are only good for pigeons to shit on. . . . But David cares deeply about how history will finally judge him. And he insists that is not living in the future. He says that having a concept of the future is an absolutely essential part of living in the present. That we could not live in a futureless universe. He says our awareness of mortality would be unbearable if we did not have faith in the continuation of the human race. If we did not believe in a future extending far beyond our own lifetime, the immediate present would become utterly nihilistic.

As David becomes more and more relaxed, I become tenser. At times he is so relaxed it drives me mad. I want to scream that I know what his fishing trip is, and does *he* know? How can he be so relaxed about it? But if I did that, it would mean I was being hysterical, not able to take the pressure. And it is very important with David to be able to take the pressure. So I say nothing, since I have been told nothing: am not supposed to know. When he goes away for meetings and does not return at night, I feel better, I feel released from my part in his plans . . . I can think about immature things like pleasure. I do not feel accountable to history. Why should I be, since history is not accountable to me?

July 20

I think that somebody must have said something to him, because suddenly last night at the McHenrys' party, Hepler took an interest in me. Before, he had hardly realized I exist, except as a waitress to wait on him. He is not what you would call handsome—he is small, a couple of inches shorter than me, and chunky in build. He is intense and his eyes bulge a little: They have an extraordinary brilliancy. His hair is thinning in the middle, and flies out at the sides, which makes me think of that pre-Raphaelite painter, what was his name? Dante Gabriel Rossetti. He gives himself Bohemian airs, Hepler. His maroon velvet bow tie was covered in cigarette ash and floppily tied. Sometimes he doesn't shave for days—he evidently hadn't shaved yesterday—and that adds to his rather disreputable appearance. Lights one cigarette from the butt of the other, screwing up his eyes. Then inserts the new cigarette in his little ivory holder and puffs away grandly.

Almost at once, without any beating about the bush (one had heard he is not very subtle in these respects) he started a suggestive conversation with me. He asked me how long David and I had been married, and when I said eight years, he leered—he really leers—and said that, according to Wilhelm Reich, people cease to be sexually interesting to each other after four years, and thereafter all that holds marriages together is habit and the economic factor. Natural instinct was for a diversity of partners. I asked him, "And is that what you found?" and he replied with boyish delight:

"In my case, I have to tell you, I could not even be faithful on our wedding night."

"You are painting yourself worse than you are," I said. "On your *wedding* night?"

"A wedding night is a very long night," he said.

I laughed. "Oh, I don't believe you," I said. "You make these things up to shock people."

"You want that I tell you about it?"

"No," I said with an uncertain laugh.

"I will tell you," he said.

"I would rather you didn't."

231

"But I *want* to shock you," he said, and immediately launched into the story. "You must not think I did not love her. On the contrary, I loved her like crazy, my first wife. She was a very beautiful girl. Nineteen years old. Exquisite. An angel. What a wedding! It was in Vienna, and we had the works. Violins, accordions. Dancing. The lot. It is not often credited me, but I have a romantic nature. Then we left for our honeymoon at Lake Steinbach, a lovely place. We stayed in a Gasthaus where Gustav Mahler lived for a time. We had a beautiful large room with a large wooden bed with gold painted scrollwork on the headrest, and there was a balcony overlooking the lake.

"It was perfect. Much too perfect—I began to feel quite oppressed by the perfection of it all. By the wonderful snow-capped mountains around the lake, matched in spotless whiteness only by the sheets of the marriage bed. While my bride performed her prenuptial toilette, I went downstairs to have a Calvados. It was a small Gasthaus and the girl who served me was also the girl who cleaned the rooms and made the beds, and she knew we were on our honeymoon and so it intrigued her, naturally, that I should sit there drinking Calvados and flirting with her, instead of being upstairs with my lovely young wife, enjoying the pleasures of the wedding night. I could see that this little waitress and chambermaid had a lively imagination in these matters, so I offered her a Calvados and explained to her—since this was after all a house where Mahler had once lived—about harmony and counterpoint. Individual melodic lines, I explained, had to be combined in music—juxtaposed—to bring out the full richness of each melody. Upstairs there was waiting for me my wonderful Sabine, and here before me, as if sent to me by the maestro Mahler himself, was the perfect piece of—counterpoint. She was a musical girl, and understood at once the necessity of juxtaposition. We went upstairs together; I had told her I required extra towels, and in the linen closet, on a pile of soiled sheets, Trudi, that was her name, I think, provided me with some juxtaposition that even the maestro Mahler could not have bettered, and I tell you the main melodic theme was much improved as a consequence. . . ."

232

His story made me laugh, and suddenly I found him charming, in the disgraceful sort of way which he cultivates.

"You are very good at telling stories that redound to your discredit," I told him.

"I am?" he said, pleased. "You mean my self-propaganda reaches even the beautiful unreachable Helen?"

"Don't mock me."

"What makes you think I mock you? I am making a pass at you, it is not mockery."

"I know about you, Leo," I said.

"What do you know about me? My terrible reputation. It is not exaggerated—I assure you." I had to smile. "Don't be afraid, it is all true. I am everything they say. Does it excite you?

"Apropos my reputation, I tell you another story. It happened to me in Paris. I was at a scientific congress when a woman came up to me I had never seen before in my life—you understand, a plain woman. It is always these plain women who make ugly scenes. Suddenly she accused me—I cannot imagine why. I had certainly never touched *her*. Perhaps that was the trouble. Perhaps she was mad. Mad for love—ah, who knows? But, in front of everyone, she turned on me and said, 'Monsieur, you are a libidinous, lecherous, unscrupulous, morally depraved, debauched sensualist and—AND!—erotomaniac.' To which I am reputed to have replied (and I do not deny it): 'But isn't everyone, Madame?' "

Again I had to laugh. He was so boyishly proud of his wickedness. Encouraged by my response, and I suppose by David's absence, he took me by the elbow and steered me to a divan, and sitting very close to me began to make advances. I suppose the advantage to a man of having his sort of reputation is that one cannot be unduly shocked if he lives up to it. It is known that he tries with everyone, and so it would have been almost insulting had he not tried with me at some time. He started by telling me I had put very improper thoughts in his head.

I became a bit flushed, and started to say, "Oh, you shouldn't talk like that . . ."

233

"Shouldn't?" he said. "Shouldn't is a Bambi word. He is full of what people should or shouldn't do. He is sometimes full of shit, Bambi. Forgive me. To me it is not an interesting word, shouldn't. Who is to say? Must and mustn't, that is different. I recognize necessity. But 'shouldn't' is an invention of self-sacrificial liberalism. It is King Canute addressing the tide. Or *anybody* addressing the League of Nations. Shouldn't. Where do you put this shouldn't, what do you do with it? I tell you it is no good for anything except scaring little children."

"There have to be some rules of conduct," I said. "Or where would we all be?"

"Party manners, yes, I agree. They are good for parties. Like the rules of chess are good for when you play chess. But, lovely Helen, I have to tell you I am not playing chess with you, I am trying to seduce you. And in that there are no rules."

"At any rate, you state your intentions honestly—not to say crudely."

"Did you never notice?—life *is* crude."

"It is also subtle."

"I agree. I agree. A matter of counterpoint, if I can put it so. It can be also subtle. That is amusing too."

"It's always amusement with you, you keep using that word."

"Is not the purpose of life to amuse oneself?"

"I did not know that had been scientifically established."

"What else could it be, lovely Helen? Ah, if only we would amuse ourselves better. How I could amuse myself with you, Helen!"

"Amusing oneself is often at other people's expense."

"You must not mind putting other people to some expense. That is what other people are there for. Helen—" his voice became a low purr—"I can see you are a lovely sensual woman and that you are too good for Bambi."

I laughed. "I think he is maybe too good for me."

"It comes to the same thing. He does not appreciate you, does not appreciate, that is, your coarser grain."

"My *what?* That doesn't sound very nice."

"Oh, but it is. Very nice. The way I mean it, which is coarsely, of course."

He was so unabashedly wallowing in his wickedness, turning everything upside down and inside out, that it was difficult to think of any even vaguely deflating remarks to make to him. He simply took as compliments what other people regarded as insults.

"Do you know, lovely Helen," he went on, "that you have been sending out signals all night? You cannot blame me if I read them."

"What do they say, my signals?"

"They say," and he leaned very close to me and spoke in his intense foreign voice, "they say—why doesn't anybody notice?"

"Notice what?" I asked quite provocatively.

He whispered in my ear. I laughed.

"Isn't that what every woman who looks in your eyes is dying to be? According to your wishful thinking."

"Wishes come true," he said with his terribly knowing smile.

He reached in his top pocket and took out a visiting card, which he handed to me with absurd formality. "This," he said, "is my apartment in Santa Fe, it is very discreet. Will you come—tomorrow afternoon? When you go shopping to Santa Fe—you stop by for a little half hour, hmmm?"

"No, of course not," I said, flustered, now that the verbal playing was being made into something more concrete. "I don't have time . . ."

"Five minutes?" he said, wickedly teasing me. "You surely have five minutes. Even five minutes of the lovely Helen I would not sneeze at."

I started to move away from him, but did not give him back his card and I saw that he was smiling smugly.

"I will expect you," he said. "Don't disappoint me."

July 21

I was in any case going to Santa Fe. It was something to do. One cannot stay all the time cooped up behind a fence. And Santa Fe

235

is very pleasing to the eye, and I like to look at the silver and turquoise jewelry that the Indian women sell under the arcades of the Palace of the Governors. I was not going to deny myself that little outing because Hepler's proposition now exposed me to some danger. When I got into the car and drove out by the East Gate, I had decided nothing: I was waiting to see what I would do. Wondering if I was going to amaze myself.

I wore a white blouse and a skirt and a broad-brimmed straw hat. It was very hot in the open plaza, and I quickly went into the shade of the portales, walking slowly, as everyone does here; there is such a sleepy feeling about this town, by contrast with the hive of activity on the hill—in Santa Fe they seem to be dozing on their feet. They appear to have all the time in the world (but there was an urgency beating in me now in opposition to this slowness). In the plaza a painter with a white beard had set up his easel under a green sun umbrella, and on a big canvas was painting the side of the square occupied by the Palace of the Governors. I had previously seen him painting the other sides of the square, where there are stores and cafés. He worked with slow meticulousness, getting every detail right. I found it comforting to see him there, this old man in his wide hat, working slowly. It quelled some of the untoward haste in me. I thought: Shall I go and watch him paint, see him space out the wooden pillars exactly . . . ? I was between impetuosity and lassitude. . . . I yawned nervously. I looked around, playing for time.

If, in this way, I could dawdle away enough time, it would be too late for anything else. It is restorative (and calming) to look at the streets and buildings of an old town, a place that has developed over a period of two or three hundred years. There is something soothing about such a vista of growth and continuity. By contrast, our overnight town on the hill jars the nerves with its ugly immediacy, its dire practicality. I was a bit calmer now, and felt less in danger of amazing myself. This course of action that was intermittently in my mind was completely lacking in believability. But I was thinking about it, nonetheless, as I looked at bracelets and rings, and squash-blossom necklaces, and little carved fetishes

236

made of shell or stone or antler. I asked for prices and for other kinds of jewelry, the kind they did not have: I was difficult to please. I bought nothing from any of these women, and went on to look at some of the Rio Grande blankets with Thunderbird motifs, or with diamond patterns of different colors emanating from a central star. I had no intention of buying blankets. I had enough blankets. Now and then I was beset by a sharp little nagging pain of sensual curiosity. It flared up alarmingly each time a certain image flashed through my head. I looked at my watch every so often as I continued to stroll unhurriedly in the portales. I had, of course, torn up his visiting card, but not before fixing the address firmly in my mind. I knew exactly where his apartment was: in an old iron-balconied Spanish building on one of those crooked back streets just off the square. I was no more than a stone's throw from it. The calle Cordoba. How he would gloat if I turned up at his door. The prospect of that, alone, was almost enough to make me think again. Humiliating to go and ask to be made love to . . . unthinkable. But I was going there, I realized, hurrying now with abrupt decisiveness, my objections all falling away suddenly in an excess of anticipation.

I found the house and went in and climbed the dim stone steps to the first floor. The unswept dinginess of the stairs would at any other time have been off-putting to me, but now I found them Bohemian. Outside his entrance door, I waited. It was a shiny black door, recently repainted. There was a brass bell. I reached towards it and hesitated. Perhaps he was not in. That would get me off the hook of my lasciviousness. Then I could calmly return to my senses and go home. Hesitating on the brink, I was on the point of turning round and going away (I had not yet rung the bell) when the door opened and he stood there in a long flame-red dressing gown, with his ivory cigarette holder in his mouth and his feet bare, and a little dirty. I thought: He must have been looking out for me, must have seen me come into the building, must have waited for me while I climbed the stairs, and then he must have watched me through the spy hole while I hesitated. He had waited for me to ring the bell and then, realizing that I might

237

think better of it, had quickly opened the door to me. I went in without a word. What was there to say? My being there said everything.

The apartment was something of a relief after the bare dinginess of the entrance and stairs, though it was not exactly to my taste. It had the faded plushiness of a passé nightclub. It was very dark, with all the shutters of the windows closed, except for one small wicket, through which came a beam of sunlight in which swarmed motes of dust. My eyes were not yet adjusted. I was reminded of childhood transgressions: creeping into dark sinful movie theaters in broad daylight. As I slowly regained my sight, I saw that the walls were red, of a quilted red satiny material, and the carpets were red too. I had a feeling the place must once have been the upstairs of a restaurant. He drew heavy curtains to exclude that one bit of daylight, and lit candles. One room led into another, separated only by open ironwork gates, and I could see a large low bed in a niche. This niche had been decorated in trompe l'oeil to create the effect of a starry night. The bedsheets were black—my God, black! And the bed headrest was red velvet, stained and faded in places. What I could make out of the furniture seemed to be of Spanish style, with tasseled chairs, and elaborately carved chests. Music was coming from somewhere. I think it was Lully. At any other time this love nest would have made me laugh, but now I was totally in its thrall.

He said nothing to me, just drew me further in, and I followed like a child fascinated by fire. He seemed to be breathing me in. I had put on perfume, and his nose was at my neck sniffing, sniffing. I wanted to laugh, but what came out was an awkwardly cut-off sound, half a cry: I could not understand what was happening. I was not being asked to sit down, nor was I being offered anything to drink—none of the conventional social gestures; instead, I was being turned and moved and pressed, and the purpose of this, I saw, was to bring me face to face with myself in a long pier mirror, and as I stared wonderingly at my dim image he, from behind, without any preliminaries whatsoever, was beginning to draw up my skirt. I could see him in the glass behind me, staring at me with his slightly bulging eyes, which moved from my progressively

238

revealed form to my face and back again. When he had the skirt up to my waist he held it there with one hand while with the other he began to pull at my panties like some nasty destructive child pulling the wings off an insect—he was pulling, pulling all around, until the material was around my thighs. He stared at me down there, in the mirror, and then he reached around with his hand and dipped his fingers into my queasy sex, and then he raised his fingers to his nose and sniffed, as he had sniffed my perfume. I could see his nostrils widen and his eyes become drugged. He did this several times, watching my face intently. I now heard him say, "Stroke yourself, Helen. Let me see it, let me see all your secret pleasures, Helen. Helen! Do it, do it! Go on, go on . . . !" His voice was tensely insistent, softly corrupting. His eyes watching me fiercely, I began to do as he asked. It was the first time I had done such a thing before another person and there was a shamefulness about it that made my sensations almost unbearably strong. He had a gleeful look on his face as he watched me. "Show me everything, Helen," he whispered in my ear. "Don't hide anything from me, let me hear all your expressions, and make the sounds, don't hold them back." I began to moan softly and continuously and occasionally to gasp at an especially strong sensation. "Less delicacy, Helen . . . cruder, cruder," he urged, and hooking his foot around a little velvet footstool he pulled it towards us and then pushed it in front of me. By placing one foot on it, I could open myself more widely to the mirror. I began to move my hips regularly, moving forward against my hand. I rolled and twisted my hips. I let him see all my movements. He kept asking, "Is that good? How does it feel? Are you almost there? Are you almost coming?" I nodded, nodded, closed my eyes, and slowed my movements, trying to break the spell. "No, go on," he was insisting, "go on, Helen, don't stop. . . ." And so I increased the pace, my eyes closing and opening again, and my sounds becoming stronger and cruder all the time. I was astonished by this glistening wanton in the mirror. "I want to see it all in your face," he said, "let me see it, show it to me, don't hide anything, Helen. Come, Helen, come . . . make yourself come, I want to see it." His words drove me. "Oh," I gasped,

239

starting to come, "oh—now . . ." feeling the first ripple of this shameful orgasm; as he saw it begin he placed his hands on my hips to feel all the shudders of my body while his eyes savored my facial expressions. His hands went all over me, feeling how it affected me. He said, "Is it good, is it good in your cunt?" and while I was in mid-orgasm he made me bend forward and hold on to the pier mirror, and I felt myself being spread out from behind, and a moment later hugely filled. The way I had been forced forward I was face to face with myself in the mirror, seeing all my expressions as I was being fucked. I had a long spasm, but when I was finished he was not. He was going to amuse himself with me. He made me put one foot on a chair to make me more open, but this was evidently not open enough; now he wanted me to put one knee flat on a table, while supporting my weight, with my hand, on my other thigh, a difficult awkward position for me but one he relished; he was quite deliberately inflaming himself with the sight of how he was using me. When he had finished he lay sprawled out over me, sated and sleepy.

I said, "How about doing something just for me now?"

But he ignored my demand, and said with a tired laugh, "Later. I like you to remain a little unsatisfied still . . . it is more amusing."

Now he took out a cigarette from a box, a cigarette with a black cork tip, and inserted it in his ivory holder and blew out smug smoke signals of triumph. There was a bottle of Calvados by the bed, and he filled two long-stemmed glasses and offered me one. I drank, feeling wonderfully debauched, and free. It was very hot in the apartment and our bodies were covered with sweat. We glistened all over. I had the impression that the windows had not been opened for weeks. The air was heavy and close and laden with the sickly-sweet redolence of some sexy perfume. His? He uses perfume, I realized. The soft furnishings and linen and cushions and pillows gave off a succession of fleeting female smells.

He said, "*Formidable,*" and kissed his fingertips. I was not able to look him in the face. I was glad the room was so dark. "*Formidable,*" he said again, and I realized this was a high compliment indeed, equating me in bed-worthiness with the chambermaid

240

Trudi whom he had fucked on a pile of soiled linen on his wedding night. To my vague surprise, my finer feelings were not offended—my finer feelings, to be frank, did not come into it. My finer feelings were no more. I realized that all my normal finickiness was suspended. Here I was, lying on (I imagined) none-too-clean sheets, that almost certainly had not been changed since the previous love bout, though their being black helped to prevent one from noticing this, and yet I did not mind. Even the thought that prostitutes may have lain where I was lying gave me no qualms. I wasn't even afraid of disease. When I had worked up the courage to swing around and look at him, I said, "I have never done anything as awful as that." It was said with a guilty little smile of pleasure.

"Then how much you have missed," he said.

"Yes, I agree."

"Promise me something," he said, taking my hand, and I wondered what wicked pact I was going to be forced to make. I was ready for anything.

"Yes, what?"

"To please me."

"Yes."

"Never, never wash yourself between your legs before you come to me. A woman's cunt shouldn't smell of soap, it should smell and taste of lechery and dirty, lustful, secret acts." He raised one of my arms and buried his nose in the damp tangle of hair in my armpit. "Superb, superb," he cried, "at this rate you will soon get me going again."

"I wouldn't say no to that," I said, opening my legs a little as he took to licking my armpit, tasting my sweat. I was getting to feel sexier and sexier as he licked me. I groaned, closed my eyes.

"What are you thinking about?" he asked.

"What do you think I am thinking about?" I said, opening my legs further. But a sideways glance showed that I was being premature: My recent source of pleasure had become a soft shrunken thing, like some insipid little stalkless flower, all head and no body.

"Ah," he said, "you will have to wait, you wild wanton crea-

241

ture, I am no longer seventeen, you know . . . at my age, the heyday of the blood is tamed, it waits upon expediency."

"That was not my impression."

"At any rate, it does not reheat so fast."

I could see he was now bored with physical acts and a little dismayed by my continuing eagerness—what kind of creature had he got on his hands? His mood had changed, darkened, become reflective, and I, his performing animal, was required to jump to this new tune. I accepted one of his cigarettes, took a more circumspect posture on the bed, and said, "People do say you are a very wicked man."

"Do you think I am?"

"Yes. Well, fairly."

"Yet you are here with me, panting for the next round."

"You appeal to the lowest side of my nature," I said, and realized it was quite true. I felt a sense of relief and comfort, like an actor taking off his stage face. Ah, to be myself, instead of this image of perfection that David expected me to be. It was a tiring performance I went in for day in day out. There was nobody in this dusty chamber of sex to call me Madame Chaos or Madame Pleasure Principle. What freedom! So, after all, one could do anything, and the world did not open up under you and snatch you into the flames. I thought, the great appeal of the criminal underworld must lie in the fact that you do not encounter moralists there who criticize you.

Before my marriage I had had occasional adventures of a somewhat disreputable kind. Usually when drunk or in a foreign country, or when both drunk and in a foreign country. In this way I absolved myself of responsibility for such acts. They were not part of my normal life. Such hypocrisy I found very useful. And I had so far not come to any harm. But this, now, was of a different order. Much more dangerous, with a man famous for his indiscretions, his impulsiveness, a man who had close dealings with my husband, and all of us living on top of each other in a tight little cliff-edge community. . . . God, what had I gotten myself into? Yet, though the warning bells were going off in my head, I remained calm and happy in this curtained apartment. I thought, I

don't want to leave, I don't want to go back to the daytime ever—
to those clean white acoustical-tiled rooms where the air is filtered
and people go around in white doctors' coats. . . . I much preferred it here, in this dark love nest, with its red walls and its black
sinful sheets.

In reply to my statement that he appealed to the lowest side of
my nature, he answered cleverly, "And mine, too."

"Oh?" I laughed.

"You think I don't have any other? But I tell you, I am often in
love, crazy in love. You think I do not have higher feelings, so-
called? That I only like to roll in the mud? Oh, I also find some
of this . . . this foolishness, disgusting. One is a different person—" he gave a little short laugh—"when the blood has cooled
down. One sees with different eyes. Ah, what an appallingly un-
dignified arrangement it all is. You think I am making jokes? No,
I mean it. Of course, it does not impress you now because you are
still hot for more. But, believe me, that too becomes boring in the
end. Yes, yes . . ." He gave his Viennese worldly shrug, which
said, What can you do? "Now there's an argument against God
for you. Do you think God would have thought up such a dirty
little act for continuing the human race? Couldn't he have made
it more *intellectual*? But of course, I am sure," he added, "it is all
much more intellectual with the Gentleman Physicist."

"It is not so animalistic," I agreed.

"Ah, bravo for good taste!" he cried. "But be honest, Helen, is
it not also a little dull? Have you not had a better time with me?"

"It's true," I said, "that David is always very conscious of himself and of what is fitting. With you, the more unfitting it is, the
better." I giggled. "Oh, David is not against erotica, mind you.
You know, the friezes on the Indian temples, the ruins of Pom-
peii, the poetry of Aretino."

"Yes, time lends respectability to the worst offenders. In my
school days I remember learning that Aretino was valuable for the
picture he gave of 16th-century life but that all his work was
'tainted by licentiousness,' as was his character, and whole life.
But there it is—now even the Gentleman Physicist approves of
him. How the times change!" He was silent for a while, sipping

243

Calvados and smoking. Suddenly he turned to me and said, "You know, Helen, I could fall in love with you. You laugh. Do not laugh, why is that so funny? You think I am such a disreputable person I cannot fall in love? On the contrary, I am often in love. You think such things as we have done do not go together with love—but you are wrong, you are wrong. To do such things with prostitutes or with crazy nymphomaniacs is not interesting. It is to do them with somebody like you: to bend you against your principles, your inhibitions, your commitments and loyalties and attachments—to pervet you: That is what is wonderful. Think, Helen: the great love stories are about priests unbearably tempted, about loving mothers driven to abandoning their children, about great men brought to ruin, dragged down into disgrace. There are no great love stories without great difficulties. Perhaps that is why one talks of 'falling' in love. There is always a kind of downfall involved. People who can't accept that downfall don't fall in love."

But I was bored with all this talk. I had not come to hear him theorizing about love.

I opened my legs a little further and said, "You know, I am going to make you live up to your dreadful reputation, Leo."

"Alas," he said, "there is a time element."

"Time element! You remember what you said to me in my ear at the McHenry party? You remember? That I was dying to be fucked. I still am, Leo."

"But you have been."

"Not enough, not enough, my licentious friend."

"Alas . . ."

"Don't keep 'alasing' me. You gave yourself a very good time just now. All else failing"—I looked straight into his eyes—"use your fingers, or your tongue. I want to be given pleasure."

"But you are insatiable," he protested, laughing.

"Yes, I am," I said, spreading my legs wider and waiting to be agreeably surprised. He began to play with me a little, touching the insides of my thighs lightly, and the matted wet hairs. He was tormenting me with these teasing touches. And then, bending down lower, he did something that drove me wild. With cool ex-

244

pertise, he used two fingers to spread open my sex at the very top, and then with a neat little downward pressure on the surrounding flesh, he squeezed out the little bloated head. By increasing the downward pressure, he made it stick up more.

"Oh, what a sexy thing you've done to me," I said, wriggling about. I was looking down at myself. My "little man in the boat" was positively puffed up with self-importance. He touched me there with a finger of his other hand and I moaned and my "little man" drowned in the gooey flood, his head going under until the expert fingers fumbling in slippery flesh brought him into prominence again. I was twisting about, quite gone, and saying continually, "Oh, for God's sake fuck me, fuck me, fuck me, oh fuck me." And then, as if in answer to some magical invocation that I had uttered, he suddenly was doing exactly that, with a vengeance.

It is true, the more you get the more you want. When I left, I felt my whole consciousness of myself lay between my legs. I had not washed. I smelled of sex to myself and I suppose to others. There were some little boys playing in the street, and they were grinning, seeing me come down from the apartment (I suppose they had seen others come out in the same kind of sexual daze), and they called after me, "fucky, fucky, fucky, lady have fucky, fucky, fucky," and I turned round and smiled at them, not minding at all.

I sat down in a café to gather myself together, and became conscious of a man at the next table looking at me. He couldn't take his eyes off me. I wondered if he could tell. Could he smell me? I raised my eyes briefly to his. He was sitting with his thighs wide apart, and I saw him run one of his hands lightly, casually, along the inside of his thigh and over the bulge in his pants. When he moved his hand back to just above the knee again, I saw that the swelling inside his trouser leg had gotten a lot bigger. I have seen men do this before, touch themselves in this way, almost absentmindedly, as they look at a girl who excites them, and have always thought it must be tremendously exciting to be the cause of that. Now it had happened to me and I acknowledged the salutation with my eyes, feeling marvelously debauched.

245

Funnily enough, Allison suddenly asked me, "Did you ever find a project for yourself?" and I said, "No, no. I could never find a subject matter, but I have made notes." She said, "Oh, I could give you a subject matter, I could give you a dozen." I said, "You are at the center of things, Allison, you know what goes on, I don't." And she said, "I could tell you things, if you kept it quiet. Oh, I could tell you stories. You'd have to disguise them, of course."

The subject matter: a love affair—a veritable downfall. Very strong, very physical. A married woman, unable to work on Project, falls into a mad affair with a womanizing scientist, who corrupts her. She, very ready to be "corrupted," can't stay away from him. Perhaps she is a bit of a nympho at heart.

Heat. Heat is a factor, and altitude. And New Mexico, a primitive setting. A setting of ancient upheavals.

This woman goes completely off the rails . . . walking past the fence she feels the hot looks of the soldiers, and is stirred. Her husband is busy, her husband is a great man, he is making the most powerful bomb there has ever been. She goes to a dance and picks up a soldier and he touches her between her legs and makes her come. After that, she is lost to sensuality. Her name is Alice.

Their culture. Bishop Lamy (who in 1851 became first Catholic bishop of New Mexico) was concerned about unfavorable reflection on Catholicism and banned practice of self-flagellation, under threat of excommunication. Practice went underground. In 19th century Penitente watching became almost a sport. This was when they first began to carry guns and to take potshots at their watchers.

Descriptive based on own observation. The height of Penitente activity occurs in Holy Week, when most likely that their public processions will be seen. But P are active throughout entire year. Holy Week is climax. La Procesión de Sangre (Procession of Blood) takes place on last three days before Holy Saturday. Banned by church, but still occurs, guards posted along route. P dressed in white cotton shorts only, a considerable mortification of the flesh in itself in cold weather around Easter. The Sangrador (bloodletter) makes three slashes on each side of the spine of Penitentes with a knife or piece of obsidian to allow for free flow of blood during flagellation. Said to prevent welts and bruises and permanent scars. Most controversial aspect, the practice of crucifixion. If this happens, takes place on Good Friday.

What I saw that time: the brother chosen to represent Christ was hooded. Said to be (according to Jones, the expert) so that the supreme penitent, by concealing his identity, will not suffer the sin of pride. To observer the hoods and masks do add additional sinister touch to proceedings already sinister enough. Christ substitute bound to cross with horsehair rope. Ropes cut off circulation. He became unconscious. At this point was cut down and revived.

I did not see nails used, but they are sometimes used.

Sometimes the Christ is not cut down in time, and dies. Then his shoes are placed before doorstep of his home as a sign to his family of what has happened. Flagellants have died from exposure and loss of blood. The Procesión de Sangre has sometimes been conducted in a raging snowstorm—the blood from the self-whipping leaving a trail in the snow.

August 2

I have fallen into this affair—it is a real downfall, as he says all love stories must be. I am drawn to him again and again by his crazy demands and my sensuality. If I am free in the afternoon and know he will be at his apartment waiting for me, I feel the pressure in me mount . . . until I get into the car and go to him. This, despite the risks. The risks are considerable. But the danger appears to play a part in my state of sexual excitement, which becomes a compulsion. I cannot stop myself. His mind has a thousand angles, it is diseased I sometimes think, brilliant and diseased.

He insists, now, that he loves me, in the peculiar sense in which he uses that word. Says there is a necessary polarity between love and vice. Our trysts always follow a certain pattern. First

247

comes the sex—hot and immediate and without any preceding normal conversation. He likes me to arrive unannounced, to present myself at his door, saying, Here I am. Afterwards comes the theorizing. When the blood has cooled. Then he lies on the bed that is never made, chain-smoking cigarettes and drinking Calvados. And if I am free to stay, I stay, and we have dinner somewhere, which leads up to the next . . .

Our lovemaking follows a scenario of his devising. It is important that upon arriving I should have a cool and distant air—I wear my most superior smile. My language, at first anyway, is correct and proper, my dress unprovocative, normal for my position and station in life, he wants me to look unreachable as I stand outside his door. His mise-en-scène involves a startling transition from this wife beyond suspicion to . . . the Queen of the Night. One mise-en-scène is that as soon as I have arrived I lean against the wall and lewdly pull up my clothing. Sometimes his scenario requires that I am naked underneath, but more often—his later improvement on the scene—I am wearing stained panties. I have to choose panties of a material that will best show this sex stain— nylon, for example, is not sufficiently absorbent and so unsuitable, but cotton or silk or satin are all right. I have to contrive to supply this sex stain by the exercise of my imagination, or failing that, by any other means. He does not mind a certain amount of artifice to arrive at the right result—which is that I should be, or appear to be, in a condition of helpless lust when I draw up my dress. The fact is that the presence of this scenario in my mind as I climb the stairs to his apartment is usually quite enough to produce the desired effect. What excites him is the contrast between my upper and lower parts—the upper part smiling and distant and superior, unreachable; the lower, vicious and secret and depraved. He sits between my parted legs looking up at this vision of flesh that I expose to him, dizzying himself with the heat and the smells and the sights, sniffing me like a cocaine addict. He is highly displeased if I have washed, or if my panties are fresh. His hands touch me in a dozen different ways. He sticks his nose in all my business. He wants to taste everything. There is no part of me that his tongue disdains. In this acted-out dream of his, I am always

248

fully clothed, with my outer clothing pulled up and my underclothing half pulled down and awkwardly entangling my thighs, or just pulled aside. He does not care for the aesthetic nude form. He wants to draw aside wet material and to find my cunt hot and shiny and fat with heat and to see my stiff little bud stick out; he wants me to shake helplessly, and for my juices to run down his face, and for me to come so that he can taste and smell my come, he wants me to drench him with it. He is in such a transport it is both funny and touching by turn, as he seeks to bury his insolent nose in my innermost part, and in that position he is like some fierce furry little animal nibbling at my innards.

This mise-en-scène is enormously fragile and one wrong move renders it liable to collapse in ridicule and nausea. But he does not make a false move. He is very sensitive to the grip of the scene, and changes it instantly the moment he feels my playing of it falter. Usually, I am totally in my part . . . he is able to make it convincing to me. That is his skill. Part of the effectiveness of certain scenes, as far as he is concerned, is that they should arise as a result of my wishes, not his. He likes me, for instance, to say to him that I want to be fucked in the bitch dog position—he likes me to use that term for it, and to assume the position of my own accord.

I watch it all in the many mirrors, which are arranged as in a tailor's fitting room so that every angle may be observed.

That is the way it is in the state of heat. Which passes like a dream. And the world is the same, and the reality is that yesterday David finally left on his fishing trip.

August 6

David's fishing trip was to a place called Hiroshima. Now everybody knows.

Leo: his prominent glistening eyes quiver with a kind of sensuous exaltation . . . his hair, long and thick around the ears and at the back, and tending to fly out backwards like a mane, thin in front, making the temples into curving prominences. . . . He seems to be, at certain moments, like the conductor of an orchestra in the tense instant of raising his baton . . . his unflagging baton. His eyes are large and dark and heavy-lidded, almost exotic. He is pale, very pale always. He has enormous—ferocious—powers of concentration. When he concentrates on me, I feel as if I am being sucked into a whirlpool.

August 7

Leo and David, at the university in Germany, often quarreled, even then. They had fundamentally different attitudes. Leo's was that there is no right way. Only the one that we happen to have come to. There are a million ways, some better than others. But we must take the one that we find ourselves on. Chance and necessity interact. Things are the way they are, yet everything *could* be different. We cannot imagine how different. Could we have imagined the sense of smell if we had not possessed it? Or the sexual drive? Think of the thousands of others there could be, as strong, that we know nothing of, because so far we have not invented them. What does it mean? It means that all roads are open in theory, but in practice you can only take the one that you have come to . . . though the others should be borne in mind.

Says we should not look for hidden movers. We are the hidden movers. Conceptual problems largely problems of language. Beginning is a word. End is a word. Words do not exist in the world, only in our minds, which are finite in construction. But do not have to be. Simply are at this moment of our self-invention. Emptiness is another mind-word that nature does not know. We confuse ourselves with words. And frighten ourselves. We frighten ourselves with the word death.

August 8

David returned last night very tired and subdued. I did not know what to say to him. Does one say "Congratulations" after something like that? The stories in the newspapers were full of awe and triumph. The bomb was the equivalent of 20,000 tons of TNT. I said to David, "They say in the papers you have done a tremendous thing." He nodded and said, "That what they say? No kidding!" and I did not know how to take his remark. He said he was going to lie down. He didn't eat anything, didn't undress—slept for ten hours on the sofa. At breakfast, he said he had flown over the city and it was an amazing sight. "We circled low and we saw that the whole central area had become a flat red scar. Nothing was standing. One bomb had done that. One bomb, Helen." He shook his head in a kind of amazement at what he and the others here have done. "Helen, it was like they were all Lilliputians down there and we had come along with our giant's foot and trod on them."

August 10

There are no figures as yet, but it is thought that casualties must be high. The hope is that it will finally end the war.

They say the flash was less blinding than at Alamogordo, because of the bright sunlight. Afterwards, the entire city, except for the outermost ends, was covered with a dark gray dust layer. One of the scientists is quoted in the newspapers as saying, "It gave you a funny feeling of watching from above while the earth was being torn apart by some great natural calamity, and you had to keep reminding yourself that this was not an act of nature but something we had done."

I have to remind myself that it is something *David* has done; it is very difficult to make the connection between David sitting here sprinkling brown sugar over his corn flakes and the crushing of the Lilliputians underfoot.

August 16

The main reaction here among the wives has been pride—tremendous pride in what their men have achieved. Lorna said to me, "Oh, I sometimes used to think, what's Dale frigging around with, some bigger bang? So? But this! This is . . . enormous. It's really something. Isn't it?"

We are getting star treatment in the press. The whole place.

When you read again and again about the amazing world-shaking thing you have done, I suppose you can't help feeling impressed. It gets through to you in the end. I, too, feel proud. It is being said that the casualties at Hiroshima must be around 100,000 killed and the same number badly injured. And in Nagasaki about the same too. What a terrible feat of war David and the others have achieved! At any rate they have brought it to an end, this war in which so many have died in such ghastly ways. Who can say they were not right to do what they did? The war could have gone on another year and a half, when you think how fanatically the Japs fought on Okinawa—they still had six million men under arms. It might have cost us a million American casualties to take the main islands by invasion. At any rate, all the mothers with sons stationed in the Pacific give thanks to God for what David and the others here created, and I think now that they were right to use the bombs on populated cities, David's argument was right; given the fanaticism of the Japanese, a demonstration explosion would not have impressed them one little bit, and when I think of Pearl Harbor and of Bataan, I am proud of David, and was finally able to say this to him. He looked at me with that funny expression in his eyes that he sometimes has when he is saying about something that it's not so simple, and he said, "Ah, yes, the sin of pride," whatever he means by that.

August 28

David is getting a tremendous amount of publicity. All the scientists here are being built up into gigantic figures, but David more so than any of the others. They seem to have chosen him to focus on. They use very lavish language. They talk of the Titans and of the war gods. Of Prometheus unbound, et cetera. Others, with a slight twist, call them the devil gods. At the same time, they are also being hailed as the peacemakers and the saviors. David has cut his hair very short now that he is being photographed so much. The haircut makes him look—military. It is as if he is going out of his way to say to the world not to think of him as a longhair and intellectual. He goes to Washington, and other

252

places—God knows where!—all the time for important governmental conferences, and to give briefings to the brass. He is on familiar terms with all the high-ups. Talks all the time of "George this" and "George that" (Truman calls him General Marshall but to David he's "George"), and sees the President, and tells us what he said to the Prez and what the Prez said to him. If this is what he means by the sin of pride, he appears to be wallowing in it.

August 29

Jones is going to Hiroshima with a group of scientific observers—accompanying the occupying forces.

September 2

Stories beginning to filter back. Impossible to determine exact number of casualties as there were no reliable census records. But it is thought that Hiroshima was formerly a city of around 250,000, possibly 300,000. The Japanese say that three fifths of the city was destroyed.

Amid the piles of rubble message boards have sprung up, it seems there are hundreds of these boards in the ruins, with messages like: Wife, where are you? We are in —. Or: Children, we are safe and living in —. Where are you? Or: Where are you, daughter? I am looking for you. Or: Son, if you are alive . . .

September 4

They have found a macabre form of bas reliefs upon the stonework of some buildings, and in the roads. People burned up by the intense heat at the center of the explosion have left their shadows imprinted upon stone. One such shadow is in the form of a man on a cart in the act of raising his whip to the horse. A charred wall bears the profile of a young girl.

253

September 5

Leo says: One must go along with everything, everything.

He has a very Viennese kind of shrug—a lifting of the left shoulder, accompanied by a spreading movement of the fingers of the left hand while the wrist rotates and the eyebrows rise. The gesture says—But what else do you expect? Violins? The gesture is cynical, worldly, and wry and resigned.

Sometimes he says, "This is the way it is in this world, Helen. Who can you complain to?"

He also says, "I love to watch the face of a woman being fucked—the sexual smile. I love to see your face, Helen, when I make love to you. I love your smile of pleasure. It is not at all superior then."

September 12

It appears that the flash produced strange forms of burning. At some distance from the epicenter of the explosion, women had the patterns of their kimonos branded upon their backs. This occurred because the white stripes or designs, acting as reflectors, remained intact, while the black lines in the patterns absorbed the burning heat and transferred it to the skin. There are many cases of what are being called profile burns, people who have been burned— severely burned—down the side of the face that was turned towards the heat flash, while the other side was left unmarked.

September 13

I shop at lightning speed in the portales of the Governors' Palace so that I will have the maximum amount of time with H. I have bought fetishes carved from shell and antler . . . the most highly prized by the Indians are those that in their naturally occurring form closely resemble some specific animal. The fetishes are thought to protect against various forms of evil . . . I have quite a collection of them now. I have also bought a grotesque kachina doll, a black ogre, it is a marvelously monstrous-looking thing.

'Tis said when the black ogre kachina visits the village, naughty children quickly mend their ways. . . .

September 17

There are four main causes of death and serious injury. The first was the effect of blast, which knocked down acres of city blocks, burying thousands in the rubble. The second was flash burn occurring at some distance from the center of the explosion. Such burns are thought to account for 20–30% of fatal casualties. Then come flame burns—all the people who perished in the flames. And finally there is the effect of radiation. The last is the most insidious and terrible because it strikes people down who believed they had escaped with their lives, and it is often a slow death, and the person knows he is dying. General Brown has said in an interview that he understands radiation death is a very pleasant way of dying. Oh yeah? I saw Jake.

Jones has returned, looks changed. He was taken ill and had to come back ahead of the rest of the team. His blue eyes have become so pale they are almost transparent, curiously empty, like the eyes of a ghost—they make me think of old parchment from which the writing has faded. Light seems to go right through his eyes, as if there is nothing behind them to throw it back.

September 20

Twenty minutes after the explosion there developed a phenomenon known as a fire storm. It is a great wind that blows from all directions upon the burning area and makes it burn more fiercely. This wind is produced by the updraft of the very hot air, which causes the air from all around to be sucked in—on the same principle as in a domestic chimney.

September 21

Bought for David a silver belt buckle, lovely thing, an elongated version of small silver pomegranate once worn by Spanish men as a cape ornament. . . .

I phoned him in Washington when I returned from Santa Fe,

255

but he was not in, I phoned him just before midnight and he was still not in. . . . I did not phone him later, it would have seemed as if I was checking up on him.

September 22

To me the safety crews are somehow ominous . . . every time I see them tearing round in their water-repellent outfits, sometimes wearing their special hoods and filter masks (which completely conceal their faces), I think: Oh my God, what other accident has there been now? Some people feel that way about seeing ambulances. The safety crews, with their long tongs and their special meters for measuring radioactivity, give me the shivers.

Bought a sandcast Naja . . . a crescent-shaped pendant. . . .

Came across something George Orwell wrote at the beginning of the war: ". . . In the space of 10 years we have slid back into the Stone Age. Human types supposedly extinct for centuries, the dancing dervish, the robber chieftain, the Grand Inquisitor, have suddenly reappeared, not as inmates of lunatic asylums, but as the masters of the world."

Allison says that throughout history every weapon that has ever been made has been used in the end . . . once something exists there is an impetus to use it. She thinks that we all were carried by this impetus. She says Truman knew so little about the bomb, had not initiated its development, and so did not dare to reverse all those years of work, all that vast expenditure of money that Roosevelt had embarked upon. To Truman it seemed just too feeble to have done all that and then throw it away. Allison thinks that Roosevelt might have had the courage to reverse the process and not use the bomb, but she thinks that a process once begun is terribly difficult for *anyone* to stop. The momentum builds up and then. . . .

September 24

A young woman was wandering around the ruins for four days with her dead baby in her arms, looking for her husband, a soldier

256

in the anti-aircraft corps. She wanted him to see the child once more. He had been so very proud of his baby son. After the second day the little corpse began to smell very bad, but the mother would not let it be taken from her. She continued to look everywhere for her husband.

When some order began to return to the city, with police from other areas coming to take charge of relief work, the business of disposing of the dead began. Pyres were made at street corners, and bodies were brought from all around for burning. The ashes were put in large brown envelopes. The names of the people whose ashes were inside were marked on the envelopes, if the names were known. Otherwise the envelopes were simply marked "unknown young man," or "unknown elderly man," or "unknown female child." These envelopes then were transported to the district emergency centers, where they piled up in alphabetical mounds against the walls. People swarmed into these offices and could be seen going through the piles of envelopes searching for loved ones.

Long after the thick smoke had cleared and the fires were out, the dying and the maimed could be seen wandering aimlessly through the rubble. This was due to a rule that medical treatment was to be given in the first place to the lightly injured, to those whose lives might still be saved. Those clearly beyond saving were left to their own devices. There was one man who had been impaled upon spiked iron railings. Rescue workers had been unable to remove him, it was quite impossible to do so without elaborate surgical procedures, and in any case he was going to die and surgeons were busy saving those who could be saved. One spike had penetrated his back beneath the shoulder blade and come out of his armpit. Another spike had gone through his waist and come out of his abdomen. Since it had proved impossible to detach him from the railings, workers had cut away the section of railing with him still spiked upon it. Amazingly, he had remained conscious the whole time. None of his vital organs had been pierced, and he was actually able to stand and even totter about. He was given sedation and left. As he staggered around the street, with these

257

iron spikes sticking out of him, he looked like some New Year's drunk wearing a weird form of fancy dress.

I have become a collector of such stories, I don't know why. Perhaps one day, when I come to write my novel, such details will be useful. Who knows? Our scientific teams are in the process of making very precise records of everything, but the story of the spiked man has no statistical or scientific value and thus would remain unrecorded except for some sense of horror that makes people repeat it to each other and makes me write it down.

October 2

I continue to go to calle Cordoba whenever David is away, which is often nowadays. I am irresistibly drawn to the dusty shuttered apartment. H. keeps saying he is in love with me.

The program is much the same as before. On arriving I am always highly charged by the act of having gone there, and what happens is immediate and wild and wonderful. I have no pride left and no inhibitions. But as soon as this part of it is over, there is an abrupt change in him. The "foolishness" past, he becomes philosophical. He talks of the perpetual tug-of-war between the Dionysian and Apollonian spirit in man. Et cetera. Considering what has so recently transpired between us, in heat and sweat and the language of the gutters, this transformation of him into the philosopher is funny. I like him better when he is being lascivious. It is when he starts to philosophize that he makes me fearful. Then he constructs such a terrible system, in which cruelty and bestiality are enshrined as constants of the universe. He is so clever, I cannot follow all his arguments, but something tells me there is a fundamental mistake somewhere at the very heart of his theories, and that it is his great cleverness which prevents him from seeing this mistake.

I like it better when he talks of his past . . . which he does, too, as we lie on the bed with the black sheets, drinking Calvados, smoking cigarettes. He talks a lot about Vienna, evoking a picture of a decadent city, a place of endless masquerades, and lunatic

258

pretensions—even the lunatics used to have their annual ball in this city where every trade or group or society had to have one.

Why was it so awful? I ask. "Because it was all a façade—an endless, beautiful, artificial façade."

He draws a picture of the place where I was born but of which I have virtually no childhood memories. I was seven when I left and I have been back only once—with David, before the war, when we were on our honeymoon.

October 3

Phoned David in Washington . . . he was not in. I phoned again around midnight. This time I decided to risk his annoyance and phoned him again at 1 A.M. and then again at two, and then all night long on the hour. He was not in all night.

About a woman who goes off the rails . . . completely. There are so many things. Nympho tendencies. Loves her husband. But can't . . . In the end she goes mad.

It's a murder story. Yes. It would have to be.

October 5

Flags of four nations were flying over the Palace of the Governors. . . . I walked in narrow crooked streets, I saw the miraculous staircase, the oldest church, in the center of the plaza there is an obelisk to the Heroes.

A form of the patriarchal cross: has two cross members and at its foot the sacred heart of Mary.

I, too, am Viennese, though I do not remember much about the place. Give us the first seven years, as the Jesuits say, and we have got you for life.

He says to me: "Don't you want to know about your inheritance, about what is in your blood, Helen?"

His father was an inventor. Came from Bucharest. Vienna was the principal commercial city of Europe before the First World

259

War and so his father went there to make his fortune. Some of his inventions came close, leading to expectations of riches. But problems arose. There was one invention that was certainly going to make him a millionaire. It was a device for calculating the safe periods in a woman's menstrual cycle. The woman only had to slide an indicator on a calendar to the date of her last period and the little device worked out the answer. Could be carried, conveniently, in the handbag. If temptation arose unexpectedly she could do a quick check. But the invention had to be withdrawn in a flood of lawsuits from pregnant women. Leo says his father's device was sound, the women were just careless in using it, or did not heed the calculations, thought they could cheat "just a little." Such female failings were his father's downfall. He went bankrupt. Spent his life in coffeehouses. Gambled. Occasionally pulled off some deal—but then squandered his money on the horses or at cards. Had charm, though. Women supported him. Amazing how similar to my father—who also was something of a ne'er-do-well, but had the luck to charm a Boston girl of good family on a visit to Vienna.

When we have made love, he sometimes talks of his childhood. I encourage it. I want to picture him as he was. I want to understand him. For my novel that I will one day write.

Because his mother had to go to Berlin to run the family business (buttons), and his father only rarely came home (dividing his time between women and the racetracks), Leo was sent to live with an aunt, one of his father's four sisters. She was married to a prominent Viennese physician. They had a flat in the 1st Bezirk, in one of those fine 19th-century Baroque apartment buildings, with an entrance of elaborate wrought-iron scrollwork over frosted glass. In the apartment heavy curtains could be drawn across the double doors to the doctor's consulting room so as to muffle the sounds of the consultations. Leo remembers those muffled voices, their ominous tone, and then the creak of footsteps coming to the door. It was a large L-shaped apartment with the principal rooms along the main long arm, and a couple of meaner rooms tucked away in the foot of the L. He occupied the foot of the L with a maid called Selma.

In the main section of the apartment the furniture consisted of heavy large oak pieces stained black and limned with white, except for the bedroom pieces which were of amboyna wood veneer. A mottled yellowish red. He remembers ivory handles to drawers, and chair legs of silvered bronze. The furniture in the foot of the L was more rudimentary—white-painted pine, and iron bedsteads. Leo shared an unheated bathroom with Selma the maid. He recalls that she liked to take very hot steamy baths. It was a way of warming up the bathroom. She would come out of the steam wrapped in towels and rush dripping to her bed. She was a plump girl, and sometimes the towels did not completely cover her and he caught glimpses of her opulent body. Her face when she came out of the bath was a steamy rapturous blush.

Although she kept the rest of the apartment shined to the antiseptic standards of cleanliness demanded by the doctor's wife, her own room was always in a mess. There was cotton wool everywhere, and clothing and underwear hanging from hooks and cupboard doors, and endless jars of creams on the dressing table, and lipsticks and eye shadow and mascara and eyebrow pencils . . . she plucked her eyebrows down to thin arcs of seductiveness. And over everything lay a silt of apricot face powder, which gave her room its characteristic powdery and erotic ambience. Sometimes Selma had male visitors. Leo's room was next to hers and he heard everything. Soon he knew it all. He was 13 and precocious. From the few words that he caught and from the sounds of movements he was able to deduce the rest. His mind was vivid, and capable—even then—of constructing a total picture from isolated bits and pieces of information. He says that on the basis of sounds and silences he was able to deduce soixante-neuf, without ever having read about it in a sex manual. He presumed it was done to avoid conception. The sounds were of an exciting nature, and he was excited and had recourse to the obvious remedy.

The other side of this ecstatic picture was presented by the doctor's consulting room . . . which also emitted sounds, but of a more muffled and somber nature. The doctor was a somewhat somber man in his sixties, his wife was in her fifties. Unseemly illnesses were referred to in Latin. That which ye have sown shall ye reap, the doctor was fond of saying. Leo understood this to mean that there were consequences for the ecstatic goings-on in the maid's room, one of which was locomotor ataxia, general paralysis of the insane. He knew there had to be a catch, all that fun could not be had for nothing. He had learned that you pay for everything. Still, from what he gathered, this general paralysis of the insane was a long time coming, you had a good few years first. Selma didn't seem to think the price was too high. He'd heard her crying, Oh it's good, oh it's good, oh it's good, and of course she realized that he heard what went on; she didn't say anything in so many words, but her eyes, when they met Leo's, took him into her confidence. She was very free and easy, and they knew about each other—she knew what he was up to when his bedsprings were going regularly at night. He was beginning to have emissions and since she made his bed she knew exactly. He didn't mind her knowing. He knew about her, and so she could know about him. Sometimes, as a game, in the morning, she'd creep in and pull the sheets off him and catch him writhing about and give him a smack on his bare behind. Sometimes he would get her used drawers out of the linen basket and take them with him into his bed. She'd found them once or twice the next morning with that stiff white stain on them. She'd grin at him and say, "Have nice dreams?" One night when one of her boyfriends had failed to turn up, and hearing the bedsprings going next door, she came into his room and quietly got into bed next to him, hoisted up her nightgown and let him get on top of her. "There," she said when he was bouncing up and down wildly on her ample form, "that's better than the silly old bed sheets." After two weeks of this affair, the boy looked so pale and haggard and had such rings of exhaustion under his eyes (and moreover was getting palpitation attacks) that the doctor soon diagnosed the cause of the trouble; Selma was instantly dismissed and told, in his presence, that she was lucky they were not going to have her prosecuted for corrupting a minor.

After this scandal the boy was all the time closely watched by the doctor and his wife. Leo stood it for a couple of months, to the end of the school term, and then issued an ultimatum to his mother. Henceforth he wished to live at home, even if she was away in Berlin; at 13 he was quite capable of taking care of himself. As long as there was a maid to take care of the cleaning and cooking. He wished to have a say in the choice of a maid. His mother always gave in to his wishes and agreed. Girls came to be interviewed for the position, and he made his choice. Sometimes the maid had to be dismissed and a new one engaged. This seemed to happen rather frequently. If his mother sought to impose her point of view in any matter, he quickly put an end to such nonsense. She must not seek to run his life. It was absurd for her to attempt to do so, he pointed out. He was so much cleverer than her, as his school reports were showing. Not only cleverer than *her*, cleverer than his teachers . . . He got through teachers almost as fast as maids. His grasp of mathematical abstractions was phenomenal—the quickness of his mind. When he had exhausted what a particular teacher was able to teach him he moved on to a higher level. He was a child prodigy, a little Mozart, not only brilliant, but wise and worldly and (which seemed almost normal in the light of his other precocities) crazy about women . . . a veritable little Don Giovanni.

When the fire storm started, people not directly swallowed up in it made their way to the rivers . . . for, even at some distance from the flames, the heat was unendurable, and the only protection against it was to stand in water. They waded into midstream and stood sheltering under a low bridge. Others found shelter in the bamboo groves of Asano Park. It was far enough from the explosion for its bamboo and maples and pines to be alive still, and the green foliage and the exquisitely landscaped rock gardens afforded a sense of refuge. Though the grass was littered with the dead and dying and the monstrously injured, there was hardly a sound. There was no weeping and no wailing, and there were no screams of pain. Nobody complained. There was hardly any speaking, even. The Japanese tradition of politeness prevailed. When somebody came around with water, each person took his share and then lifted himself very slightly, no matter his injury, to give a little bow. When the whirlwind came it brought delicately arched wooden bridges crashing down, uprooted ginkgo trees, tore up flower beds, diverted artificial waterfalls and streams, and filled the air with flying goldfish from the big goldfish tank—in the vortex with the fishes there were hats and small trees and dead birds and scarves and gloves. . . .

Some of the very badly injured who could not walk had been carried to sandpits by the edge of the river and lain there for safety. When the river began to rise abruptly, many in the sandpits, unable to move, were drowned.

October 7

Leo says that there was a brothel in Vienna where, every Thursday night, young women were auctioned. They could be bought for the night. They were not prostitutes and were allowed to wear masks so as to protect their reputations. Young women of good family could sometimes make a small fortune in one night. If the girl was sufficiently desirable the bidding could go very high. The girl had to be prepared to be taken publicly in front of the other clients. This was one of the attractions for which the establishment was famous. There were women as well as men in the audience for these public spectacles. They, too, wore masks (provided by the management) if they wished. Each spectator paid a charge and the ravaged girl got a cut of the takings. The young men who went in for such exhibitions belonged to a group of aristocratic ruffians with very brutal tastes. The girl, once sold, was completely at their mercy and had to submit to the most vicious practices. The fact that the girls were guaranteed respectable was what made it such sport, and the young aristos, having sometimes bid large sums, were determined to get their money's worth. The audience sat on gilt ballroom chairs, as if at a concert. In the summer the ladies had fans and fanned themselves vigorously at the height of the spectacle. No impropriety took place in the audience, and it became quite the thing at one time for a daring young woman to have seen one of these spectacles. After the spectacle, if required, private rooms were available for an extra charge. Also, of course, all the normal services of the brothel.

October 8

At the main Red Cross hospital 10,000 people waited in the road and on the outside steps and under the porte cochère, in the inside corridors, on stairs, in storerooms, in laboratories, in wards, in operating theaters and kitchens. For many hours there appeared to be only one doctor and a handful of nurses to tend to all the thousands of people needing medical attention. Many died while waiting. There was no one to remove their bodies. In the streets cries for help came from the depths of the rubble. People trapped under collapsed beams and fallen roofs called for help in curiously polite and uninsistent voices. Their cries had the dull hopeless singsong tone of prayers that nobody expects to be answered. The passersby did not hear—they had enough trouble saving themselves.

On the whole, people helped those of their own family, and sometimes immediate neighbors, and deafened themselves to the cries of others.

October 9

Leo has become furiously jealous. He demands to know if David and I make love, and I tell him of course we do. Then he wants to know exactly what we do. He wants to know how it is with David. I tell him, Very good. He asks, As good as with me? And I say, Yes, but different. In what way different? I say that Leo acts with the desperate greed of someone who does not know if he will eat tomorrow. David knows he will eat tomorrow, and so is calmer. Ah, Leo says, you mean tepid. No, calmer. This makes him furious, and he tries to prove that what I have with him is utterly different, which, of course, it is, although the basic act is the same. He calls me his fuckbird and his nympho and his whore and his hard-worker in the field of love. He makes me work hard. It is always a sweat with him . . . never easy and gentle. He studies my face while I am having an orgasm as if examining that fleeting phenomenon under a microscope . . . he is like Da Vinci dissecting corpses to lay bare the anatomy of the human form. He

265

wants to discover the orgasmic thread, wants to know, like every curious little boy, what's inside . . . wants to know what it is inside me that gives such racking pleasure. I have never known a man so stirred by women: in their presence he becomes like a quivering animal scenting prey, his nostrils flare, he smells them . . . yes, he sniffs the air around women, his eyes become intense. He has no sense of his own dignity where love is concerned, unlike David, for whom everything, even that, is an exercise of style, has to be done gracefully and graciously, so that he will be able to approve of himself afterwards. He is so anxious to be able to approve of himself. With Leo it is utterly different, he is not at all censorious of himself, or me. I feel like another person with him.

Have always had a secret desire to be someone else. I even used to give myself other names. When I was at school in Switzerland there were those fast O'Donnell twins, one was called Alice, and when I was making forbidden assignations with a man I used to call myself Alice. As Alice I was hot stuff. Not at all the prissy miss I was as Helen. Once I agreed to go on a double date and the other girl didn't show up and so there I was with two eager young men. Mine was called André and the other girl's was a Russian called Vlad. We tried to find a girl for Vlad.

There was a tacit understanding by this time that I was going to bed with André (though we had no more than kissed on our one previous date), and so the only problem was Vlad. I rather enjoyed seeing it from a man's point of view, looking over different girls and speculating about whether they would deliver. We tried approaches to one or two respectable girls, but in each case Vlad said, after a certain amount of chat, that it would take too long. We then looked at prostitutes, but none of them appealed to us. Finally we ended up in André's flat at 2 A.M., just the three of us. I danced with André and he started to kiss me very passionately. Then I danced with Vlad, and sympathized with him teasingly, "Ah, poor Vlad, poor Vlad. No girl. Isn't it sad." Vlad was very hungry for a girl. I danced again with André and we did a lot more kissing. Vlad watched us intently. Every so often I would say, "Ah, poor Vladimir, no girl . . . how sad." We were all three pretty drunk by then. Then André suggested that I get undressed—he thought it was fun to dance with a naked girl. I was still saying "poor Vlad" every so often. Then Vlad danced with me. André did not object when Vlad kissed me, and I didn't either. "We must look after our friend Vlad," André said. "Since he does not have a girl." We all giggled. André took me into the bedroom and started to make love to me. I did not object when Vlad followed us in. He sat on a chair, legs elegantly crossed, smoking a Russian cigarette while André fucked me. I was tremendously excited to be watched by Vlad, and I kept giving little smiles to Vlad. By now it was tacitly understood that Vlad would have me after André. While my first lover was screwing me, I was making eyes at my second lover. After André and I both had come, André wanted to go on, but I said no, that wasn't fair, it was Vlad's turn now. And giving a hot look at his trouser front, I added that I did not think Vlad could wait. Sportingly, André moved off me, and Vlad, who at this point was still fully dressed, took his clothes off. He had a tremendous unwavering erection. I couldn't take my eyes off it. I giggled a bit hysterically. "Poor Vlad," I kept saying, "no girl for such a big strong man." I could see André becoming jealous. Vlad wasn't bashful about enjoying his present, and André could see I was getting even wilder than I had been with him. It was tremendously exciting to me seeing André get more and more jealous. He had an erection again. The moment Vlad had finished, André grabbed me, rolled me over, made me kneel. All of which was not me at all but *Alice*. I never saw either of them again and I never did anything like that again. I never could let myself go enough to do such a thing again, it simply did not happen. I suppressed that side of my nature entirely. Leo has exposed it in me again, has made me once more willing to take great risks for the sake of sensation.

Why do I write these things, with the danger of David, or someone else, finding them, and what would be bound to follow? At times it is almost as if I wish to be found out, as if I am deliberately courting disaster. The fact is that if David were to read such things it would be a form of truth between us that is not possible at present. Our lives steer a tortuous course between unmention-

267

ables. At first when I started writing of such intimate things in this diary I was going to give myself the excuse that they were notes for a novel, and had not really happened. But later that seemed terribly coy to me, as did the various euphemisms for the physical acts and for organs. I wanted to call things by their right names, and it was freeing to me to do so. David is fond of quoting Wittgenstein's maxim "Whereof one may not speak, thereof one should remain silent." But if that is so, one may only speak of banalities. If one cannot speak of love and death, what is left except small talk? It is true, on the other hand, that there is a part of myself that I cannot bring easily into our everyday life, that does not seem to fit in. Perhaps it is only in the unconscious that opposites are capable of being reconciled. In my daily life, I am not able to do it, and so I live—as somebody here said we all do—in a state of controlled schizophrenia. At times it worries me. I feel I am not myself. I have bizarre sensations of being outside my own body. There is certainly a passionate irrational side to my being which frightens David, makes him call me Madame Chaos and Madame Pleasure Principle. David is afraid of this side of me because he feels he cannot control it. He is very afraid of the uncontrollable in himself and others. He feels terribly threatened by anything he cannot control.

Leo, on the other hand, is quite at ease in states of chaos. He is more instinctive than David, less rational, probably more brilliant. He can do things in his head to a far greater degree than David, or any of the others, who slave over their calculations with slide rules and pencil and paper. But Leo can see the answers in his head. That is what makes him so sure of himself. Abstract concepts of infinite complexity are crystal clear to him. He can live in the world of numbers. He says numbers can be amusing or sad or gloriously triumphant; he claims they can even have a kind of sensuality . . . they can pair off in wonderfully satisfying ways. Numbers become something else in his mind, their relationships tell a kind of story in code.

He is now so jealous all the time. Says he loves me, which I say is ridiculous. He says, "You don't love me, because I disgust you. You think love is something pure and noble, à la Bamberger, and

I am a filthy fellow, only good for afternoons of dirty sport. Hmm? Is that it? You think you could not have your cunt so satisfyingly filled if it were love between us. Love you reserve for the Gentleman Physicist Herr von Bamberger, the aristocrat of assholes. Do you know something—when I fuck you, you shine with love. You know that? Look at yourself, the way you glow with my prick inside you. You don't understand that love is also dirty, and evilminded, and foulmouthed, and that I'm terrified of losing you, Helen.

October 11

Leo said to me suddenly, apropos I do not know what: "There is a Persian proverb, Helen: Better to drown with your enemy than for both to survive."

My life is compartmentalized like a spy's. I am one thing with Leo and quite another with David.

Having a secret life makes one nervous. I do not know if I will be able to go on like this, it is becoming very wearing keeping myself so split up. . . .

The safety crews frighten me, frighten me . . . I don't know why.

October 12

It would have to be a murder story, I suppose. That is the only way it can go. I can see no other outcome for it.

October 13

This doctor had escaped serious injury but his glasses had been smashed and without them he could not see a thing. He crawled among the corpses, feeling faces, trying to find an unbroken pair of glasses. The first two that he found were useless, but the third restored to him some degree of eccentric vision. He was able to see general shapes and some details, though only in a rather distorted way. He daubed festering wounds with mercurochrome, sewed and bandaged, sewed and bandaged. When he took one old woman by the arm to draw her gently towards the light, the skin of her arm came away in his hands, and through his peculiar glasses it was like a long white glove coming off.

Leo is one of six scientists who jointly hold a patent in the basic process of the atomic bomb. Most of the other scientists, including David, never thought of filing patents on their ideas. Leo and the others are going to sue the U.S. government for $10,000,000 and have been told they have a cast-iron case. David is furious, says you cannot make money out of something like that, but Hepler merely gives his Viennese shrug and says, "Why not?" He is counting on being very rich. It makes me feel sick.

October 15

In the green refuge in Asano Park a girl with a dead baby in her arms found a group of soldiers huddled under a clump of bamboo trees and asked if any of them had seen her husband, who was also a soldier; they shook their heads and said no. They asked her for water, and she did not understand why they should ask her for water, why didn't they go and get it themselves from one of the little rock pools in the park? And then, peering into the dimness where they were all huddled together, she saw how swollen their faces were and that their mouths were open wounds suppurating pus, and that their eye sockets were dark empty holes; on their cheeks there remained traces of the congealed fluids of their melted eyeballs. Their shoulder tabs told her they were anti-aircraft crews, like her husband, and she thought: They must have been looking up when the flash occurred. She threw away her dead child and went to fetch water for them.

Jones goes around telling these horrible stories—they call him "Horrible" Jones now. He seems to be under a compulsion to talk all the time about what he saw when he was in Hiroshima with the scientific investigation team. It has gotten to be so bad with him that people don't ask the Joneses to dinner anymore because

"Horrible" Jones is quite likely to embark on one of his horrible stories right in the middle of the Chicken à la King. Like the other night at the Weissbergers when, as we were eating our fish, he suddenly started talking about the piles of white bones found in a schoolyard in more or less neat rows, suggesting that the children had been having a physical education class when the bomb exploded. Everywhere throughout the city, he said, enormous numbers of crows were sitting on the crumbling walls of destroyed houses, and would take off suddenly with a great squawking and fluttering of black wings and dive down into the rubble where they had located some rotting flesh. He says these things with a kind of sickly grin on his face, as if he were telling a funny story.

October 20

It is all over between me and Leo. I was ready to accede to all his weird desires, all except the last. He wanted me cold and dripping wet from the bath and that I should lie still as death, and then I realized what he was doing, that he was fucking my drowned dead body, and the horror that swept through me killed all desire in me, killed whatever feeling I ever had for him, awakened me at last to the reality of what I have been doing these past weeks. They are all in love with death. . . .

October 27

David in Washington. He has been gone a week, and I have not once been to Santa Fe. The compulsion is over. I am released.

November 7

Leo sought me out at the Weissbergers' party and kept me in a corner for half an hour, pleading with me. Imploring. Begging. Said he loved me; that he will reform his character for me, give up all his strange and perverted practices. He will marry me even, if I will get a divorce from David. The whole thing is absurd, and I told him so. It was only the glitter of evil in him that interested

271

me in the first place, and having overcome my infatuation with that I am no longer attracted to him. I certainly am not interested in a reformed Hepler, faithful and true. If anything could be worse than Hepler the erotomaniac, it would be Hepler the faithful husband. Not that I believe for one moment he would be capable of being that: I am sure that on our wedding night he would find the immaculate sheets of the marriage bed offensive to his chaotic spirit, and go off in search of chambermaids in linen rooms. Nor would I want him to change. Without his malefic aspect he would be like an eagle with clipped wings, a very sorry thing.

November 9

When I came in, he put down the book he was reading, then put it away in the drawer of his desk and locked the drawer. Did he lock it without thinking, or what? I had the impression he didn't want me to see what he was reading. So when he'd gone out I unlocked the desk drawer and found a Bible. Why was David locking away a Bible? There was nothing else in the drawer except a lab key and some life insurance quotes.

November 10

Not good—dizziness.

November 11

Not good.

November 14

Again some symptoms. Not . . .

November 17

Sudden low point after. Is it? Bad night.

November 22

Couldn't sleep all night long. Anxiety.

November 25

Last night, I think, was the worst night of my life.

November 26

Dr. S says altitude and . . . well, the usual. Nothing organic. My blood pressure is normal. 124/85. I keep thinking that it's low.

November 27

Trying to cut out alcohol. Second day. The vertigo is less.

November 28

No alcohol, better.

December 2

No alcohol till the evening, then several at the Weissbergers. Mistake. The panicky feeling.

December 3

Dr. S made me walk blindfolded to wall and then backwards. My balance O.K., he said.

December 4

Bizarre sensation of being outside my own body.

December 5

Dr. S says—depression. Said the soul not being able to speak expressed itself in bodily ways. I said, Why would I be depressed, and he said: With all our science we find ourselves returning to the rather ancient truth that somewhere in the background of every case of depression there is a lost love. Oh yeah, I said, is that so?

December 6

Dazed. I keep thinking of David sitting there reading the Bible and I'm afraid. Terribly afraid.

December 8

Dr. S wants me to have X-rays of my head, and blood tests. Does not think anything will be found, but as a precaution. Also has delicately suggested that perhaps I should consult a psychiatrist about my "unfounded fears."

December 10

It'll be Christmas in two weeks, the first Christmas of peace. Then it'll be 1946, and in March I'll be thirty-eight. *Thirty-eight*—God! And then it's forty looming up. I can't believe it. What happened to my youth? It all got frittered away, like everybody else's youth, I guess. Where now? The perennial *where now?* I just don't know. My "novel"? Is that a pipe dream? I don't seem to be able to do anything except make notes and write down conversations and describe things—I can't get it together in my mind yet. Not even now that it has happened. I think it was Rilke who said that the mind needs time before events become real to it. None of it is yet real enough for me to be able to make sense of. Perhaps when I am away from here. I want to get out, I want to get out. I can't stand it here any longer, but David is determined to stay—just for a while, he says. He's got something to settle here. He has become very remote from me. Much of the time I feel we are not connecting at all. I don't understand what he's about or what counts for him. All I know is that I am anxious all the time and don't know why.

274

FOUR

DAVID BAMBERGER'S SIDE OF THE STORY—AND THE EVENTS OF EASTER, 1946 (II)

THIRTEEN

The clouds had been heavy for weeks without bringing the relief of rain. Day after day a hot, dry wind swept the mesa, blowing in desert sand by the ton. Bamberger felt the sand in his eyes and throat and nose and saw it pile up against doorjambs. The hot winds withered the grass, dried up leaves on trees, gave the whole place a burnt-desert look. Nights the lightning flickered continuously but came to nothing.

And inside the compound things were getting to be very rundown, he had to admit. There was an after-the-war slothfulness about the way things were done now that there was no urgency. The uniform green paint was peeling on Sundt apartments and McKee duplexes, and on lab buildings and schools, and on all the other sheds and shacks and outhouses. The roads were worse than ever. The green was knee-high in rough scrub; hedges grew wild.

There was a serious water shortage. You sometimes couldn't wash for days. Water had to be brought up by tanker. You washed your teeth in Coca-Cola. People talked about the health hazard— about the dangers of epidemics. Worst of all was the mood, desultory and purposeless, now that the war was over. There were accidents all the time—Hans Weissberger choking to death on a piece of meat, Janie Taylor getting killed by that big truck suddenly rolling down the hill. People said there was a jinx on the place. There was a lot of drinking and a lot of screwing around among those who were left. Many of the scientists had quit, determined to get first crack at the best jobs outside. Others were staying on, but only until the right offer came up.

Bamberger had stayed on, and so had Hepler. The general opinion was that Bamberger didn't want to leave the place to Hepler, and vice versa. So both had stayed, and were getting on each other's nerves more and more. Not that Hepler submitted to any regular work program. He did exactly as he pleased. Sometimes he stayed away from the hill for days at a time—people said he had a love nest in Santa Fe to which he lured a succession of secretaries, lonely wives, and WACs. He sometimes came in at the end of the day, and stayed working in the Technical Area after everybody else had gone. He was working on some project of his own.

Bamberger, too, was often away. He had become a figure in the land and was much in demand as a public speaker and as an expert witness before congressional bodies. His advice was widely sought in Washington. This was the time when, hearing him talk all the time of "George" and "Dean" and "the Prez," people said he was no longer a serious scientist, that he was becoming a politician instead. It was true that he spent a great deal of time politicking, on the highest levels, something at which he had become rather good. He knew how to handle politicians. It was one of those things that he had quickly mastered. He was readily available for interviews by the press and thus had become a well-known public figure. He knew how to dramatize things to get his ideas across. Instead of talking about calorific product and psi at different radii, he told congressmen that if an atom bomb were dropped on Union Station they shouldn't count on there being much left of the Capitol or the people in it. In lectures and briefings he felt obliged to spell out the consequences of atomic warfare. He was strongly opposed to the bomb remaining in military hands. He was also in favor of making a gesture to the Russians; he argued that in return for offering to share existing knowledge with them it might be possible to obtain their agreement to international control of the weapon. This, he said, was the moment to obtain such agreement on control. Once the Russians had the bomb, too, which was only a matter of time, we would have nothing to bargain with.

Having left the cloistered world of the scientific establishment in order to put his case to the politicians, he was exposed to public comment and attacks of various kinds. He was denounced, in some quarters, as "a tool of the Russians," and by others as the "brute arm of Science." In cartoons he sometimes figured as a thin man with a high, bomblike skull, or as Death's angel with a bomb under each wing. Sometimes he was depicted as "the mad doctor" in charge of a hilltop lunatic asylum of crazy foreign scientists. He was also seen, in bomblike form, sticking out of the pocket of a sinisterly grinning Stalin. His features took the form of a mushroom shape rising out of Pandora's box, and poems were written in which he was referred to as "the great Destroyer," "the death dealer," "the man of doom," "the plague bringer." Journalists from all over the world wanted to interview him, and he acceded to many of their requests, and also posed for their cameras. He was not the only physicist to give interviews to the press, but the others were not nearly such good copy; they did not have his star personality, or his capacity for saying startling things in a language completely without scientific cant.

One day an interviewer, an Englishwoman, asked him the usual question about how he felt having created such a monstrous weapon of mass destruction, and in reply he came out with a phrase that was to be widely quoted everywhere: "We physicists have in a very real sense created a new circle of hell." When she asked him if he could live with that, he said with his attractive smile, "I am doing my best." At the end of the interview she told him he was undoubtedly the most intelligent man she had ever met, and the most terrifying.

"Terrifying? I frighten you?"

"Yes, you do."

"Explain that to me."

"You're so calm about it . . . you know what's in the cards, you're always telling people, but you don't seem to *feel* it."

"I'm a servant of the state," he said, "and I guess the state is an unfeeling monster."

"And are *you?*" she asked provocatively.

"No, honey. When a pretty girl flirts with me, I have the ordinary responses."

"I am sure your responses are far from ordinary."

She made it clear she was eager to stay on after the interview was over. He made it clear he had a lot to do, a whole series of appointments. She said she didn't mind waiting. He didn't exactly discourage her (he didn't encourage her either), but gave a little shrug and said it was a free world and anybody could sit and wait in the lobby of the Mayflower Hotel. The thought that she might still be there when he returned was not disagreeable. He could decide then.

It was almost midnight when he got back, and looking around the lobby he was vaguely hopeful she might still be there, but it was really too much to expect. Too bad, he thought. All work and no play, he rebuked himself. As he entered the elevator she slipped in beside him.

"You're a very patient girl."

"My one virtue."

"You must be starving."

"No. I had a sandwich."

In his suite he said, "Look, I'm sorry, there are still some calls I have to make."

"Since I waited this long . . ." She smiled and went into the bedroom. It was after one by the time he got into bed with her.

"God," he said, "I'm so beat I don't think I could raise the flag on the Fourth of July."

"Doesn't matter," she said. "Just hold me." Her naked body was pleasant to hold. She lay against him, very still. He enfolded her, his eyes closing with tiredness, his head on her shoulder. He was half out when he heard her say, "It obviously isn't the Fourth of July today."

"Sheer jingoistic flag-waving," he said. She waited, smiling and looking into his eyes.

"From a tired-out old man," she said, "I am inclined to take that as quite a compliment."

"Oh, you should, you should," he said, lightly kissing her on the lips.

He had found her charming at first; but now, as things developed between them, a note was sounded that he found immediately jarring. She used certain words that he considered offensive on the lips of a woman. Some men found that kind of thing, spoken by women in the sack, highly erotic, but he did not. He did not care for coarseness in women. It became apparent, after a little while, that this girl was quite sick. She was in the grip of some kind of sexual dementia. She wanted to be hurt, hurt "to death"; she demanded, passionately, for him to "kill" her in various weird erotic ways that had no appeal to him whatsoever. When the madness was over, she quieted down and turned her head away.

He asked, after a while, with an effort at lightness, "Well, what was that all about?"

She said, "I love you."

"Oh yes?" He laughed. "Didn't sound like it. Anyway, that's a foolish thing to say."

"I know."

It was amazing how strangers loved him nowadays, or hated him. The ones who hated him he tried to steer clear of, naturally, but this was not always possible, because sometimes the ones who said they loved him turned out to hate him. He did not know about this English journalist. But he knew that there was a great deal of antagonism toward him in the world; it was an antagonism compounded of fascination and horrified awe. Of course, the sensational treatment he and the others were getting in the press, being called "doom doctors" and "death dealers," fostered their dark fame. Some women seemed to find it irresistible. Others who had worked on the bomb had discovered this, too.

Before she left, the Englishwoman, as if to regain some semblance of her self-respect, remembered her professional role and returned to the interview: "Is it true you said to Mr. Truman, 'Mr. President, I've got blood on my hands'?"

"Yes."

"What did he say?"

"I think he thought I was being melodramatic. See, Presidents don't think of having blood on their hands. That's just the normal color for a President's hands. But scientists are not used to that yet."

"What else did Truman say?"

"He thought I shouldn't be upset—after all, he'd dropped the bomb, I had only made it, and since he didn't have sleepless nights, why should I? He told me his philosophy of life." Bamberger smiled.

"What was that?" She was making notes again, writing all this down, professionally alert.

" 'Once something's over and done with, I quit worrying about it,' he told me."

"What did you say?"

"I congratulated him."

She thanked him for the interview, and everything, and said he was a real gentleman. He was not sure how to take that.

―――

When he got back to the hill, there was a message that Captain Richter wanted to see him urgently. Would he stop by the Security Office? He called in at the end of the day.

"What's the urgency, Captain?"

"It's felt you should have more protection."

"Who feels that?"

"It comes from the top."

"I don't see that—"

"Let's get McClure in on this. It's his area."

Greg McClure arrived five minutes later. "I got through the war in one piece. . . ." Bamberger told him.

"I know, I know," McClure said, "but the situation is different now, sir. You're known. You go about. With all the stuff that is being written about you, Doctor—you know, father of the bomb, blood on your hands—it's felt that a mentally ill person might want to harm you or Mrs. Bamberger. We are, I think, required to take some extra precautions."

"I find that a very boring idea."

McClure turned to Richter and said, "I knew the doctor wouldn't like this."

"There is no way to protect oneself against a madman," Bamberger said.

"There is something in what you say, Doctor," McClure conceded. "But still"—he gave an apologetic grin—"it's like the principle of burglary prevention: There's nothing'll keep out a determined burglar, but you can raise the cost to him to the point where he'll choose somebody else's house because it's easier. If there is some crazy who might want to go after you, we want to make it so costly for him he'll choose somebody else instead."

"How do you propose to do that?"

"First of all, we want to install trip wires around your house, to switch on a floodlight system. There are things people will do in the dark they won't do in full glare. Those trip wires will also set off alarms in the Security Office and the Safety Office."

"It's going to be like our late unlamented prowler alarm system, always going off for the wrong reasons—a high wind . . ."

"We've learned since then—I think we can do better now," McClure said.

Bamberger shrugged. "What else?"

"We want you to let us make your hotel reservations, so we can check out rooms. We ask you not to wait around in hotel lobbies. Not to leave your car parked unguarded in the streets. Not to accept unsolicited invitations of any sort . . . no matter how attractive."

"Sounds like you want to make my life a complete misery."

"We want to protect your life," McClure said. "We ask that whenever you are in some public place you take a position with your back to the wall, or if you can't do that, to always stand back to back with one of our people."

"I can't live like that."

"It'll get to be automatic after a while—you won't even notice it, Doctor."

"I think you are being overprotective, Greg. . . . These measures are excessive. This place already has got enough wire fences around it for a prison camp . . . watchtowers, tank at the gate, patrols. . . ."

"The trouble is, sir," McClure said, "if it's some sort of madman, this person might be *inside* the compound, might be somebody you know, or somebody Mrs. Bamberger knows. . . . It could be another scientist whose mind has been affected. He might look and act perfectly okay."

Richter scratched his beard and said a little uncomfortably, "What McClure is saying is the conclusion of a psychiatric study that we had done."

"Seems pretty outlandish to me," Bamberger said.

"We are obliged to make provisions even for outlandish eventualities," Richter said. "The fact is, we have had a lot of accidents here, and also . . ." He hesitated.

"What are you thinking?"

"There have been some heart attack cases where autopsies have shown heart lesions of a kind found when people or animals are subjected to great stress—or fear."

"Well, people here *have* been under great stress."

"Yes, which is why there has been a readiness to accept the most natural explanation. And maybe it is the right one. But we do have a statistically higher rate of such fatalities than comparable groups. Of course, there are no strictly comparable groups . . . because nobody else has been making an atomic bomb."

"Exactly," Bamberger said.

"All I am saying, Doctor, is that we should take certain extra precautions, even if it's being excessively careful. I would appreciate it if you would go along with that. Bear in mind, the danger is not only to yourself. It's also to Mrs. Bamberger."

Bamberger thought for a while, then said, "All right, Richter. As a favor to you and McClure. So you stop acting like a pair of nagging Jewish mamas."

McClure grinned and said, "Thank you, Doctor. I appreciate your cooperation, sir. I'll get the floodlighting installed right away."

284

FOURTEEN

Helen Bamberger kept her diary in a locked blue metal box marked Personal Documents. She usually put the key in her jewelry case.

When she went to get the key that day, she could not find it at first. She finally discovered it under a silver-winged scarab brooch. Looked as if it had been deliberately concealed under the brooch. She did not remember having done that. Usually she just threw it in. Was it guilt that made her think David had been in her file case? She looked carefully at the way the blue steel box was placed at the bottom of the closet. It seemed to be in the position in which she had left it. She opened the box. The loose pages of the diary were kept in a couple of suspension files. Other suspension files contained personal documents, her birth certificate, her marriage certificate, insurance policies, David's will, her own will.

She took out the files containing her diary. Had the pages been touched? Riffling through them, they seemed to be in correct order. But when she took out the insurance policies, she saw that they were in the same file as the wills, whereas she was in the habit of keeping the policies in the file with her birth and marriage certificates.

She left the bedroom and went to the living room. She poured herself a drink, lit a cigarette, began to pace. Had David read her diary? And said nothing—*said nothing*? If so, what did that mean? Or was she just imagining, out of a guilty conscience, that somebody had been going through her private papers? Was it possible that the last time she had been to her personal files and taken out the policy on David's life she had not put it back in the file from which she had taken it? It was possible. But why did she have this strong feeling that somebody had been through her papers—why? It rattled her—the thought that David could have read her diary, with all it contained, and say nothing, act as if he knew nothing. What would that mean? And why did he sit in his study reading the Bible, and put it away guiltily when she came in?

She went into the study, to his desk. All the drawers were unlocked, except one. She knew where he kept the key to the locked drawer: under the cigarettes in his cigarette box. She opened the drawer. It contained a Bible, and some odds and ends. A sheet of paper torn from a school exercise book had been folded into an inch-wide strip to make a book marker. On this strip of paper she read, in David's scrawl, a number of notations. The first was: "Ezekiel 16:25-26." She took out the Bible, turned to Ezekiel, Chapter 16, and then found verses 25-26, and read:

25 Thou hast built thy high place at every head of the way, and hast made thy beauty to be abhorred, and hast opened thy feet to every one that passed by, and multiplied thy whoredoms.

26 Thou hast also committed fornication with the Egyptians, thy neighbours, great of flesh; and hast increased thy whoredoms, to provoke me to anger.

With mounting consternation she looked up the next notation on the marker. This time she read: "And the nakedness of thy whoredoms shall be discovered, both thy lewdness and thy whoredoms. . . ." It went on:

"And the company shall stone them with stones, and dispatch them with their swords. . . ."

"Thus will I cause lewdness to cease out of the land."

The next notation in David's scrawl said "Jeremiah 15:2," and when she had found it she read: "Such as are for death, to death. . . ."

286

She did not look up any more of the verses. Putting the Bible back in the drawer, her hand touched something metallic—a key. She took it out. There was a tag attached to it, on which was written "Y-3 canyon lab."

If David had read her diary, why was he saying nothing? What was he *doing?*

I must go and see Dr. Schneidermann, she thought, I can't stand this any longer. I must get him to give me something so I can calm down.

<hr>

The dark smudge of beard on Hepler's face made his eyes look more brilliant than ever, almost feverish. The sharp, protrusive nose reminded Bamberger of a swordfish.

"How's it coming?" he asked.

"That is the reason for this lunch?" They were alone in the private dining room at the lodge where Bamberger entertained visiting VIPs.

"I like to keep up with what you're doing, Leo."

"Well, if you want to know, I am almost there. I am ready to bet on it. It is a matter of working out a great many cross sections until—"

"How long do you suppose?"

"Impossible to predict. The figures could suddenly jell . . . or, on the other hand, the CUNT may take a while."

"Not something that usually befalls you."

Hepler gave a laugh and declared, "I am working at it."

"I hope you won't feel you've wasted your time."

"I don't waste my time."

"I agree, there is some value in working it through."

"What is this downbeat attitude, Bambi? *Some* value . . . ?"

"You don't have a snowball's chance in hell of getting it acted on."

"I do not? You fix that?"

"Fix? I don't 'fix' anything, Leo. There's no need for me to 'fix' anything—I express my views."

287

"You go on expressing your views, Bambi. Your views make colorful reading. Circles of hell . . . blood on my hands . . . I am become death—and all the rest of it."

"I want to make it quite clear to you, Leo," Bamberger said in his easy, measured way, "that your present line of research is likely to be a dead end."

"I will worry about that when the time comes."

Bamberger paused a second. He put his knife and fork together; he evidently was not going to finish his fish.

"I think the time *has* come," he said.

"What do you mean you *think?*"

"I am in the process of deciding when exactly to terminate this particular line of research."

"You are going to terminate?"

"Yes. I don't think it's the best use of valuable resources— meaning you, Hofmannsthal, Jones, and the others."

"I will take the responsibility," Hepler said.

"You can't, Leo. It's my job."

"I can't? What you want to bet?"

"It's my decision, Leo, while I am the controller."

"Even the controller is subject to controls, Bambi."

"What's that supposed to mean?"

"Oh, only that I also have good friends in Washington, like George and Dean and Jim and Harry."

"The fact is, Leo, your good friends don't make any difference. Whoever you persuaded to let you go ahead, it would cut no ice with me—and see, I am in charge of this establishment."

"You are very opposed to what I am doing. I wonder why."

"Don't act naive, Leo. You know why. It's a piece of research I would not want brought to fruition under my name."

"So now we talk of fruition, not dead ends. Ah! You know, your name does not have to come into it. It is *my* research. It need have nothing to do with you."

"Any work done here is done under my jurisdiction. I take responsibility for it."

"Yes, while you are controller."

"What is that supposed to mean?"

"I was referring to a rumor that you might possibly be leaving. There is no truth in that rumor?"

"None. I heard a rumor that you were leaving. Any truth there?"

"None."

"Maybe you shouldn't be so sure."

"What?"

"About not leaving. Maybe this is the moment for you to leave. Grab yourself a big position somewhere . . . a good moment. Here, you are going to be banging your head against a wall."

"I promise I will not do that. After next week, I will have enough data. The rest I can do in my head. I do not see how you can stop me doing that. I do not need absolutely Hofmannsthal, Jones, and the others. They help to speed things up, but I can do without them, if you are not able to spare them. Then, when it is worked out, I will take a look into the political question. We will see if George and Jim and Harry and Dean really are so ready to throw away . . . !"

Bamberger shook his head. "You're an operator, Leo—oh, you're an operator. But I tell you, you're taking on a battle. I'm going to stop you. Because I do not believe this is what we should be doing. My advice to you is quit while you're ahead. I have always handled you with kid gloves, kiddo. But at this point the going is liable to get rough."

"Why do you want to get rid of me?"

Bamberger considered this question with pursed lips. Hepler watched him closely.

"Let's just say we have come to the end of the road, you and I, Leo."

"There is another solution," Hepler said with an air of helpfulness.

"What's that?"

"*You* quit, Bambi. And I stay."

Bamberger laughed.

"You take this job—run this outfit? You think you could drag yourself out of bed in the morning? This is a fifteen-hour-a-day job."

"If you want to make it that. But I am not so passionate about clerical work as you are. I would hire more secretaries."

"Simple as that, huh? But could you keep your hands off them?"

"Why would I have to? What is this job—pope?"

"The thing is, Leo, though I know you don't consider such things important, there are certain standards that you are required to adhere to when you run a university department or a great research establishment, and one of those standards is that you do not use your position to lay the secretaries."

"It is not my position I use for that."

"You use what comes to hand, Leo. Let's face it, you're a roughneck. A roughneck with a touch of genius, I'll give you that. But a coarse fellow all the same. There are, let me tell you, rules of behavior that I happen to attach some importance to, such as loyalty to friends and colleagues, and just ordinary common decency, and doing things in good faith."

Hepler made a derisive blowing sound with his lips. His face had become flushed.

"You invent the rules and then you want everybody to keep to *your* rules, because that suits you. You are quite right. I do not accept your rules . . . they are not binding on me. I was not consulted when you and your sort worked out your gentlemen's agreements."

"That's because you don't make gentlemen's agreements with people who are not gentlemen, see."

Hepler glared at him. "It is right, I am not a gentleman. But I tell you, not everybody minds that so much."

"All right, Leo," Bamberger said, "let's not get in any deeper before we both regret what we say. Let us say that, the way things are, I don't see us going on together. Now, if you want to do this the classy way, you resign. You'll be one of this town's heroes. We'll name a road after you. Hepler Boulevard. We'll make it a little corner of Old Vienna in your honor. I'll give you a speech of farewell that'll break your rotten heart. You can go and sit in a nice office in Princeton, or somewhere, with lots of cute secretaries and students to chase after, and think up more and better explosions to your heart's content. Okay? Just get out of *my* hair, Leo. Once and for all."

Hepler stared back at Bamberger, and then he said quietly, "You have got the scenario a little bit wrong, Bambi. It is not I who am going to a nice office in Princeton. It is you. I hate to be the one to tell you this, but I have already been offered the job of controller here. Should you resign. It is felt you might feel it appropriate to resign—to, so to speak, disqualify yourself—in view of your past political connections."

"If by my 'political connections' you are referring to my onetime involvement with the Communists, then I should tell you there has never been any secret of that, it was known about when I was given this job."

"Yes, but you see, we were fighting a different enemy then. Your antifascist credentials were always impeccable, I grant you. But now that the enemy has changed, the question arises whether your irrational opposition to my project does not spring from ancient, or not so ancient, loyalties. Since you are a man who finds loyalties so binding."

"Sneaky little asshole, aren't you?" Bamberger said quietly. "That what you been putting around?"

"Oh, believe me, there was no need. Your secret past is rather well known."

"I wouldn't count on the job just yet, Leo."

"As a matter of fact, I don't. As you have rightly guessed, I am not so good at getting up in the morning. And clerical work does bore me. I am more than happy to leave that to you, if you will leave me to *my* work. I continue as before. No interference. I don't get in your hair, you don't get in mine. It would be a very good card for you to play. Nothing could give you better anti-Communist credentials than letting me get on with my work. To the Pentagon you look like a lousy Red, but I am a great American patriot. It is known I detest the Communists. Right? So play your cards right and I get you off the hook."

"Let me tell *you*," Bamberger said, jabbing a finger toward him. His face was tense and white. Little white flecks of dry spittle outlined his mouth. "You have got the idea that whatever you do, people will take it, because of that weirdly wonderful brain of yours, which you have abused as you have abused every other gift you have been given. But you are mistaken, kiddo. You are mistaken. During the war I took a lot of shit from you. For the main objective. But that doesn't apply anymore, and weirdly wonderful as that brain of yours may be, I'm ready to do without it. We'll muddle through somehow. It's something I am going to devote myself to bringing about. Because I tell you, there is a malignancy in you that all your brilliance can't make up for. You're just a rotten human being, Leo. And always have been. And that means, at heart, a rotten scientist, too. Yes, because there is no science in a void. Real science comes from an understanding of the whole equation, the total order that the human being is part of, and you can never understand *that* because you are not part of anything, except the wretched perverted solipsistic universe of your pleasure principle."

Hepler stood up; his face had whitened, and his eyes were flashing with a kind of exultant fury.

"Now," he said, "we see what jealousy does to a so-called gentleman of science. Professional jealousy . . ."

"Sit down, you little squirt," Bamberger threw back at him, "don't walk away from me, I'm not through with you yet. . . ."

"Yes, I see what jealousy does," Hepler continued contemptuously. "I see—reduces him to a foaming-at-the-mouth mass of quivering insufficiency."

Bamberger had also gotten up now. The two men were glaring furiously at each other across the table, both a little breathless. As Hepler, with a contemptuous twist of his mouth, started to turn away, on the point of walking out, Bamberger picked up the ketchup bottle and made a kind of slashing movement in the direction of the fiery theoretician. The meaning behind the movement was: if I were not such a gentleman, you swine, this is what you'd get in the face. Unfortunately, the top of the ketchup bottle had been only loosely replaced, and perhaps Bamberger's symbolic gesture was more violent than he had meant it to be, and a stream of ketchup flew out from the bottle's narrow neck and snaked across the table. Some of the thick sauce hit Hepler on the chin, some got on his shirt and jacket, but most of it landed on his pants. He went rigid, his face looked apoplectic, his eyes bulged, and he gave out a hoarse gasp, as if he had been run through by a sword thrust; you would have thought that the ketchup running down him was blood from the horrified way he touched it. For a second Bamberger held the grim expression on his face, but an uncontrollable laugh pulled at his lips, and he couldn't hold it back. He burst out laughing.

"Sorry about that, Leo," he said, when he had succeeded in controlling himself again. "Couldn't have screwed the cap back on firmly enough. You better go and change, Leo. You're a horrible sight to behold. You look like the murder of Banquo. Buy yourself a new suit and send me the bill, if the stains won't come out."

Hepler's expression had not relented. "You will pay for this, Bambi. You will pay for this insult. This is the end of you and me, I tell you. The end. And that is my final word." And with that he spun round and walked out, dripping ketchup all over the carpet as he went.

———

"There's been an accident," Bamberger told Helen.

"Serious? It *is* serious, I can see from your expression. Any-one—"

"They're all at the hospital now, Hepler and the others. They're having tests. Oh, I think Allison and Jonesy are almost certainly okay. They were outside the room where it happened. They seem to think that Hofmannsthal, Wexler, and Greenson also are going to be all right. They weren't in the direct path of the radiation."

"Who was in the direct path of the radiation?"

"Nobody except Leo."

"Is it bad?"

"It's not good. The medical opinion seems to be that he's in the 'survival possible' category, so there's some hope. His hand slipped. . . . Dangerous stuff he was doing. It could have been a lot more serious, but seems he acted in time to remedy the situation. Brave of him. And damn quick. If he'd panicked and run . . . God knows! But he succeeded in separating the material

293

while it was not yet out of control. Poor old Leo! Poor old Leo! I've known Leo since—since university. Germany. One of my oldest . . . friends."

Helen was staring at him. She had gone very white. He was composed.

"What's the matter, Helen?" he asked sharply. "You don't look well."

"I've had a shock."

"I didn't think you cared for Leo all that much. You used to say you thought him a boor."

"It's a shock to know that such things can happen. It could have been anyone—you."

"That's true."

―――――

The next few days he came back late from the Tech Area and had work to do at home until after midnight. They hardly talked. He read papers while they ate, answered her absentmindedly. She did not know what had gotten into him. Then, on Thursday, when she returned from the movies, she found him by the stone fireplace tearing up pages and tossing the pieces in the grate. He did not turn around as she came in. She felt his tension from the taut line of his back and neck. Coming closer confirmed her initial impression that it was her diary that was being torn up and disposed of.

She stood silent, waiting for him to turn around and say something, but he carried on as if she were not there. Finally she said, "You went through my private papers. I didn't think that was something you would do."

"Evidently," he said, without turning around, still tearing up pages.

"Don't," she said, going over to him. "Tearing this up solves nothing. Can't we talk, David?"

Still without turning round, he said, "People don't know each other—that's what I found out. I don't know you, Helen." He raised a bunch of pages.

"There is an aspect of me that you don't know," she said. "Yes. And I am sure there are aspects of you *I* don't know."

He turned around to face her, and she saw there were tears in his eyes and running down his cheeks. She looked down in consternation. Then she looked up at him.

"David, what can I say? I'm deeply sorry. I don't completely understand it, don't understand myself—I've not been well. . . ." Her voice trailed off in perplexed confusion. Her hands were gripped together with crushing tightness. He stared at her with horrified amazement.

"I don't know you," he said again. "I don't know this . . ." He flourished the pages. ". . . this person."

"You're a perfectionist, David," she said, looking away to avoid the violence in his eyes. "And I am not the perfect object you thought. I think I told you that, or tried to, oh, many times, but you didn't want to hear. You wanted to believe in this paragon who was good enough to be married to you."

He began to speak, cutting her off. His voice had changed, taken on a tone of lamentation. "Gee, Helen," he said, "you were the apple of my eye, that's what you were. I didn't think you were perfect, you're wrong there, I never believed that, exactly. But you were the nearest thing to perfection that I knew on this earth. My love for you, Helen, was something out of a storybook." She was looking up at him, her eyes brimming over with tears, intently examining his face; but he was not returning her look directly, he was looking into the space to the side of her as he went on. "Sometimes when you were asleep I'd sit up looking at you, just looking at you, and saying to myself, 'I love her so much, so much—God, how I love her!' You just had some beauty about you that touched the core of my being and lit me up with happiness. I could just look at you and look at you and be happy." His voice abruptly changed. "I cannot believe that this person, for whom I had such great love, is the same person who is portrayed in these obscene and degenerate episodes described here."

She pressed a fist into her mouth and bit into her knuckles to control the flood of emotion that was threatening to overcome her.

With a great effort she controlled herself sufficiently to be able to speak.

"I broke out, David—that's what it was. I know that women married to great and clever men are supposed to live in their shadow, but I guess that gave me some problems, and I felt compelled to break out of your shadow, David. To be somebody with my own separate being. That was something I could only do in one way—women like me, without going professions, don't have any other way. You see, it's . . . it's . . . I couldn't challenge you in the field of ideas—I'm not on your level there. There's 80 percent of your life I have nothing to do with, am not qualified to participate in. You're a powerful figure, David, and only a very few people are clever enough to answer you back to your face. Your brilliant, logical mind destroys all our puny arguments in a flash. So there it is. David, it was a kind of drunkenness—it's over now, I'm steady now, I'm steady again. . . . I love you, David. As much as—more than—you loved me, even when you loved me most. . . . I love you." She started toward him, to touch him, to make him take her in his arms, and was shocked by the savagery of his response.

"It's too late, you crazy bitch." Enraged, he scattered the remaining diary pages all over the floor; dementedly he began to wipe his feet on them, marking them with the dirt of the road. "You love me, you crazy bitch?" he screamed mockingly at her. "You think acts have no consequences? You stupid whore! You brainless piece of shit! Do you imagine in that ignorant brain of yours that acts can be undone? 'I'm sorry, I didn't mean it, it was a drunkenness. It was delirium. Now I know better.' " He mimicked her viciously. "Don't you know that the world we live in is a world of irreversible events? Our lives are not a cake that can be rebaked if it hasn't come out right. You stupid, goddamned whore, don't you know that in the world we live in there is something called death, and that it is not reversible? . . . I cannot bring back the dead of Hiroshima and Nagasaki by saying sorry, it was a mistake, it was a drunkenness, I made a mistake but I'm sorry now. . . ."

"David, nothing has died for us. What has happened with us *is* repairable, David. Please, David, please. Please say that it is."

"So you think nothing has died . . . ?" he said, his voice rising to a high pitch. "Well, I tell you, my love for you is dead—that's what's dead, Helen. And the genius dwarf Hepler will be dead very soon. Let's hope so. I will put in a little request to the God of chaos and chance to that effect."

Never had she known him like this. A madness had come into him, a rage to punish and condemn. His mind had broken from its anchorage and was being tossed about on a seething sea of anguish and fury. There was a craziness in his eyes. She was frightened, really frightened of him now, of what he might do, or might have done, in this state he was in.

"Let there be a lot of deaths," he prayed quietly. "It might clean things up."

He stooped down and began to gather up fistfuls of her diary pages and threw them wildly into the fireplace. He struck a match, and his hand shook so much that he connected only with a corner of paper before the flame went out. He struck another match, but after flaring briefly it went out, too. He tried another; the same. His hand was shaking as if he had palsy. He was becoming furious with the matches. He threw aside the box, looked around for another.

"Don't," she pleaded. "Don't burn it. . . . I can burn it, but not you—it's *my* life, let me decide. If you try to wipe out that part of my life by burning these pages, you'll be making a mistake, David. . . . It's not to be burned—it's to be heeded, that part of my life. Low as you think I am, and as I sometimes think I am, these things were part of my life, and as you say, cannot be undone. So let me have my experience, don't wipe it out by burning it—that would be a falsity. Let me find my way back to you through this experience, David. Please, David."

But he was oblivious to her words, had found another box of matches, and was kneeling in the fireplace seeking to set fire to the diary. The thick wads of torn pages smoldered, but the flame did not immediately take, and Helen was, as she pleaded with him, dragging him away. He pulled free of her, struck her hands away from him, and in the struggle hit her a glancing blow on the cheekbone, drawing blood. She hung on to him, half to try to embrace him, half to stop him from what he was seeking to do. In despair he said to her that the best thing would be if somebody put a bullet through both their brains, and shortly afterwards Richter had come barging in.

FIFTEEN

Richter, arriving at seven thirty to catch early-rising Bamberger before he went off to work, found him having breakfast with his wife. It looked like a peaceful domestic scene, with coffee and toast and marmalade on the table, empty eggshells in egg cups, and leftover cereal in terra-cotta bowls.

Mrs. Bamberger was in her dressing gown. There was music on the radio, and Bamberger had a freshly shaven, bright-eyed, eager-to-go look. He wore a fresh white shirt.

"Let me pour you some coffee, Captain," Bamberger said, motioning him to sit down at the table.

Mrs. Bamberger was looking composed. "Toast, Captain?"

"No thank you, Mrs. Bamberger. Just coffee."

"You have some questions?" Bamberger asked, and added tolerantly, "That's to be expected." He looked at his wristwatch. "I've got ten minutes, so go ahead. Go ahead."

"Might take a little longer than ten minutes, Doctor."

"Well, let's see where we get in that time, and if there are still one or two things, we can always fit in another session during lunch. Go ahead, Captain."

"The first thing—" Richter began.

Bamberger cut in. "Let me make something clear. The nature of our activity here gives you some kind of right, theoretically, to pry into people's personal lives. As it gives you the right to tap my phone, open my letters. All right, I knew what I was letting myself

299

in for. I have to accept that some invasion of privacy is unavoidable in my position. I will endeavor to be as helpful as I can in elucidating matters that are your legitimate concern. But I will not permit you to probe into matters that are not your concern."

Richter had taken out his pipe and was pressing down the tobacco in the bowl; he looked up slowly.

"This bother you, Doctor?"

"Go ahead, but keep an eye on the time. I have a meeting scheduled for eight."

"Doctor, did it occur to you that some of the things you and the others were discussing could be overheard by your wife?"

"The answer is that there is a difference between the theory of security and the practice. In theory, you seal your lips; in practice, you are a human being, and a human being does not treat his wife as if she might be a German spy. I trusted Helen totally, that goes without saying. I therefore was not concerned about the odd phrase she might overhear. I think that goes for every scientist in this place. That, out of a certain psychological sense of being excluded, she was deliberately listening in and noting things down, I of course did not know. Nonetheless, I am convinced there was no security leak due to my wife. What she did was a personal aberration, that's all. It went no further. I am satisfied of that."

"Anyone who read this material would have known a great deal of what was going on here," Richter said.

"It is pretty obvious, isn't it, that the material was not meant for any eyes other than her own."

"Still, you found it. Somebody else could have found it. How did you come to find it, as a matter of interest?"

"I was looking for my will."

Richter turned to Helen. "Where did you keep the diary, Mrs. Bamberger?"

"I have a small steel file box where I keep some personal papers."

"It has a lock?"

"Yes."

"Where do you keep the key?"

"In my jewelry case."

"Did Dr. Bamberger know you kept the key there?"

"He may have seen me put it there."

"Or perhaps it's a rather obvious place, Mrs. Bamberger. In which case, anyone who came into this house—to clean, for example—could have found it there, and found your diary."

Bamberger cut in. "I knew where the key was because I had once seen Helen put it there. Nobody else knew. It was under a lot of jewelry—nobody else would have found it."

"Were you in the habit, Mrs. Bamberger, of leaving the maid to work here while you went out?" Richter asked.

"No, not in the habit. But it may have happened once or twice."

"You can check out the maids," Bamberger said. "They are locals. Like everybody here, they were security-checked before being given their jobs."

"Did you ever show your diary to anyone, Mrs. Bamberger? Or speak about it?"

"No, I didn't."

"When was it you found it, Doctor?"

"Yesterday, when my wife was at the movie. She kept my will and my life insurance in her file case. I wanted to reread both in the light of the warning you had given me. Since I didn't want to alarm Helen, I thought it best to have a look at these documents while she was out."

"And did you do that? Did you look at these documents?"

"I had gotten out the life insurance, and I was looking for the will. . . . It must have been in another file. That's how I found the diary."

"Let me get a picture of it. You had the life insurance out, but not the will. You had the whole folder out, or just the policy?"

"Just the policy."

"Then, looking for the will, you found the diary instead."

"Right."

"You took out the diary?"

"Yes."

"And put back the life insurance?"

"Yes."

"Right away? Or after you'd read the diary?"

"After I'd begun to read the diary and realized what it was."

"This was yesterday, you say? And as soon as Mrs. Bamberger got back from the movie, you confronted her with what you had discovered, and you had a showdown, on the tail end of which I came in?"

"Yes."

Richter glanced at Mrs. Bamberger. She was looking down. He turned back to Bamberger and found him looking at his wife.

Helen Bamberger appeared to be somewhat paler than before. Richter drew on his pipe, blowing out a lot of strong tobacco smoke.

"Earlier in the day, you'd been to see Dr. Hepler in the hospital." Bamberger nodded gravely. "How did you find him?"

"Worse."

"Did you talk about anything in particular, with Dr. Hepler?"

"The usual things one talks about in those circumstances."

"Then you came back and had the shock of finding your wife's diary. Naturally you must have felt—"

"How I felt is one of those areas that is none of your concern, Captain." He smiled to take the sting out of his remark.

Richter nodded understandingly. "At any rate, bad as you felt about it yesterday, you and your wife appear to have had a reconciliation."

"No comment."

"Or, at any rate, to have come to some understanding."

Bamberger said nothing.

"Why were you trying to burn the diary, Doctor?"

"I would have thought the answer to that is self-evident."

"Did it not occur to you, in the light of the investigations being conducted here, that burning anything—"

"It seemed to me that the contents of the diary only concerned my wife and myself."

Richter smiled, his eyes full of understanding. He had been listening attentively, with an interest that was humanly inspired rather than simply professional. There was something wise and sad

302

in his demeanor; he was not a fanatic of anything, least of all this job, this disagreeable job.

"Yes indeed, a lot of it does only concern your wife and yourself. Quite so. But there are other things in the diary. . . ." He smiled uncomfortably; he was embarrassed to put the controller in a spot. "Other things . . . that—uh—constitute breaches of security. I can't say how grave these breaches would be considered, but breaches certainly."

"You are referring to certain technical data?"

"Yes, yes, and also—"

"Helen, explain to the captain why you were listening in, why you put those things down in your diary."

"Yes, it's the eavesdropping, the quite deliberate eavesdropping that is worrying," Richter said.

Helen Bamberger looked straight at him and said, "I'd like to try to explain that."

"I'd be glad if you would, Mrs. Bamberger."

"The technical aspect was what I knew least about. That was the situation of the other wives, too. I had in my mind the idea of one day writing some kind of account of our life here . . . it was partly for that purpose that I started the diary. Since I was so ignorant about all those sorts of things, I felt I needed to find out— to educate myself. Otherwise how could I hope to reflect anything of what was going on—if I did not understand the central purpose of our being here? I was not aware that I was writing down anything so very secret. It seemed to me that if it was something I could understand, it must be very elementary, and known to everybody else. It was my husband's work, and I was tied down by this work of his, and I surely was no more of a security risk than Allison, who was entitled to know everything. Had I been required to work inside the Tech Area I would certainly have qualified for a white badge. It was merely a technicality that I did not have one."

Mrs. Bamberger was very believable, Richter decided. Her direct, unwavering, and intimate gaze made you want to believe her. She was a beautiful woman, and Richter was not immune to the appeal of beauty—oh, by no means. Through his steel-rimmed glasses he examined her with the same quiet raptness with which he would have regarded a rare orchid unexpectedly found in a field of buttercups. . . . Oh, what a lovely thing, what a lovely rare thing to examine and study and collect in his mind—only in his mind, for he was not one to pick flowers, or to catch butterflies. Or anything else. There was a kindliness in his nature that made him perhaps not the best of interrogators. All he had in his favor in that line was a certain alertness to the unwitting things that people told you about themselves. He had learned about this by his proneness to distraction. While others listened to the main flow, he, distractedly, could not help noticing details: a rigidity of the shoulders, a stiffness of the neck, a raised eyebrow. When somebody told you something, the question to ask yourself was not What is he saying? but Why is he saying it? What is his statement intended to achieve? He asked himself what Mrs. Bamberger was aiming to achieve by being so believable, so composed. Richter hated to entertain mean thoughts about the beautiful Mrs. Bamberger, but the fact was that, after last night, after that terrible row, after having been found out by her husband, she should not now be so composed.

"Mrs. Bamberger," he said, "I'd like to ask you about the conversation you overheard your husband having on the question of the sharing of secrets . . . with the Soviets. Do you recollect the conversation I am referring to?"

"Yes, vaguely."

"You don't say in your diary who the other person was—the person your husband was talking to in the kitchen."

"Oh?"

"Can you remember who it was, Mrs. Bamberger?"

She did not look at her husband. She still had the faint smile on her face.

Richter didn't know where it was coming from—because everybody in the room was so seemingly relaxed—but he could suddenly feel anxiety. He felt it inside himself. Where was it coming from? Somebody was afraid. Was it he? If so, what was he afraid of? What was he afraid of finding out? Or was this anxiety coming

304

from them? They looked perfectly calm—too calm after last night, after having the intimate details of their life spilled out to a stranger.

"Yes," Helen replied after a pause. "It was Jake. Dr. Dubinski."

Richter drew on his pipe awhile and then said, "Okay, well, I'm sure Mrs. Bamberger has things to do. The rest of what I wanted to ask you about, Doctor, you and I could discuss by ourselves. Perhaps we might step across to the Security Office."

"Captain, as I said, I have an eight o'clock appointment."

"I took the liberty of sending a message round to your office that you might be delayed."

Bamberger said, "Let's get this over with here. Helen can go in the next room if you don't want her in here." He gave a smile. "You don't have to worry. You can't hear from the bedroom. Only from the kitchen."

Mrs. Bamberger got up. "If you don't need me anymore I am going to take a bath."

"Go right ahead, Mrs. Bamberger."

Richter had a sense of Bamberger resting between bouts of a strenuous contest; he was breathing deeply but gently, expelling his breath in slow, unjerky expirations. He was perfectly still in every way; it was a forced kind of relaxedness. He had seen the controller in various stressful situations before, and he knew that way he had of taking the pressure.

Richter read out the equation he had copied down from Hepler's blackboard soon after the accident.

"Isn't that," he asked, "Weizsacker's postulation of what makes the stars shine?"

"One tends to forget you are a physicist yourself."

"Not much of one, I'm afraid. I gave up early."

"Wise of you." It was not clear in what sense this was meant—wise because, clearly, he would never have amounted to much in that field, or wise because physics had become a dubious science.

"Yes," Richter mused, "I found physics too . . . too vast. Those enormous concepts of time and space seemed to leave me out, me personally."

"It is an impersonal science," Bamberger agreed.

305

"I got distracted," Richter said, smiling self-deprecatingly. "A weakness of mine. Lack of single-mindedness."

"I wouldn't say that."

"No?"

"I'm referring to the investigation—you seem to be pursuing that very single-mindedly."

"I have a streak of stubbornness in me," Richter agreed. "If there is a word in a crossword puzzle that I can't get, it nags away at me until I have got it. Well, to get back to the stars. What would have been Dr. Hepler's interest there?"

"The equation to which you are referring is a starting-off point for many things."

"In Dr. Hepler's case?"

"I cannot see any purpose in embarking upon a highly technical discussion of research programs."

"Dr. Bamberger, a year ago, the night of the Trinity test, I overheard part of a conversation between yourself and Dr. Hepler. It concerned something that excited him greatly and, if I am right, disturbed you. You said something like, 'Because that could be the match.' You recall what you were talking about?"

"I remember the conversation, vaguely, but I can't recall now what specifically that remark of mine may have referred to."

Richter scratched his beard, shifted his weight about on the chair and drew strongly on his pipe.

"Speaking as a nonexpert," he said, "is of course tricky when you are faced by the expert. I am liable to end up with custard pie on my face. But still, let me put to you very simply what is formulating in my mind, and you can then knock it down if I have got it all wrong. What I have been thinking is that Hepler was coming to you that night with the notion that inside the atomic explosion you had just set off, temperatures would have been reached approaching those at the center of the sun—around twenty million degrees. And that although such temperatures might be attainable for only millionths of a second, the heat would be sufficient to act as a kind of kindling to produce a chain reaction of fusing hydrogen atoms. I think it was in response to some such postulation that you replied, 'Because that might be the

306

match.' By which I think you meant the match that could ignite the atmosphere and burn up the earth."

Bamberger was looking straight at Richter, saying nothing.

"In other words," Richter continued, "Dr. Hepler was outlining the principle that could lead to the making of a superbomb several thousand times more powerful than existing atom bombs. Indeed, if my physics is not too rusty on this point, since the process we are talking about depends on fusion rather than fission, and there is a limitless supply of hydrogen atoms that can fuse together, there is no upper limit to the powerfulness of such a bomb. Am I right in supposing that to have been the subject of your conversation that night?"

"I was told one is always overheard by you people."

"Yes," Richter said apologetically, "that's how we got our name: creeps. Something I have never been too good at—creeping, I mean."

"You seem to have been quite good enough."

"Is my extrapolation correct, Doctor?"

"You know, the principle of such a superbomb is no secret. Hans Thirring describes it in a book that's just been published. It all depends on *if* you can make the hydrogen atoms fuse."

"At very high temperatures, it can be done?"

"In theory. Perhaps. But nobody has been able to achieve such temperatures, or sustain them long enough."

"With an atom bomb to create these temperatures?"

Bamberger laughed. "It isn't as simple as that."

"Is this what Dr. Hepler has been working on lately?"

"He's always been working on it. Leo always likes to make the bangs bigger."

"So the cross-sections he was working out were related to . . ."

"Leo tends to feel that no form of destructiveness is beyond his powers of achievement. It is good news for mankind that this time he is wrong about something. Nature, in her wisdom, has said no to his doomsday yearnings."

"You sound very certain, Doctor. If you are so certain that it cannot be done, why were you permitting him to continue, using valuable resources, manpower . . . ?"

307

"Because in science—and also in defense matters—it is also valuable to prove that something cannot be done."

"And that has been proved?"

"The calculations show the kindling would not light. A self-sustaining fusion cannot be achieved at atom bomb temperatures."

"Then why was Hepler continuing the research?"

"When Leo reaches an insurmountable obstacle he simply pretends it does not exist. He believes in knocking over insurmountable obstacles, at his leisure, once he has found the solution."

"So it is *possible?*"

"It is possible that, given natural selection, men will one day sprout wings and fly. But I see no reason to suppose it is going to happen soon."

"Does Dr. Hepler agree with your assessment?"

Bamberger hesitated before replying; then he said, "I am satisfied it cannot be done. But even if it could be, my entire instinct tells me that this is such a fundamental process of the universe that the Almighty did not mean us to be able to duplicate it, and I would go to very great lengths to prevent its coming about."

"Now that's interesting," Richter said, "that's very interesting. Is that what your quarrel with Dr. Hepler was about, when you threw the ketchup at him?"

"Leo has a capacity for provoking people."

"Even you?"

"After all these years, even me. One's self-control is never a hundred percent, and given enough time and provocation . . ."

"At this point, you say, you did not know of your wife's relationship with Dr. Hepler. Since you had not yet found the diary. Or did you already know from some other source?"

"I did not know."

"So the row was only about his work project?"

"We finally had the falling-out that we have been building up to for the past twenty-odd years."

"Dr. Bamberger, you say you would be ready to go to great lengths to prevent such a superbomb coming into existence. . . ."

"Yes. Since you've deduced this much yourself, I will not conceal from you that the matter is under discussion on high levels, and it is no secret, on those levels, that I have strongly advised against going ahead with the development of such a weapon, even if it were possible. . . ."

"Could you tell me why you have given this advice?"

"I think it's an immoral weapon."

"In what sense is it more immoral than the atomic bomb, whose development you supported wholeheartedly, I believe?"

"This is—would be—of a quite different order of things. Such a superbomb, as Leo envisages it, is, as you correctly infer, limitless in its potential destructiveness. It is thus capable of extinguishing life on earth. It seems to me as a scientist that I have the duty of preventing such means of global self-destruction being put in people's hands."

"You would go to any lengths to prevent it?"

"Anything within my power."

"That poses the question—What does 'anything' include?"

"I have seen the question coming, Captain." Bamberger's mouth stretched in the formality of a smile, but it was more of a conventional token than a true expression of anything he felt. He said, "Those are the perpetual questions, aren't they? What justifies what? Where do you draw the line? How far do you go? Who's entitled to break the rules, and why and when? How long is a piece of string?"

"Well, how long is it?"

"Depends if you want to hang yourself. Speaking for myself, I don't. So what I say to you is, if you want answers to eternal questions, figure them out for yourself, kiddo."

"I've been doing some figuring."

"So I see."

"What is your attitude toward murder, Dr. Bamberger?"

"Now there's a nice breakfast-time question for you. My attitude to murder?"

"Can you imagine circumstances in which you would be in favor of it—speaking theoretically?"

"Speaking theoretically, there are people who say that I am a murderer, a mass-murderer. . . ."

"You yourself said you have blood on your hands."

"What do you conclude from that?"

"I conclude that you are not denying the fact. Which means that your defense is based on justification."

"You got it."

"You can justify the use of the atomic bomb, but not . . ."

"With certain reservations."

"You now have reservations?"

"Some."

"That you did not have at the time?"

"I do see certain things differently now. At the same time, I don't think I, or anyone else in my position, could have acted differently at the time. One was locked in by certain historical imperatives. There was no other way, things being as they were."

"Nagasaki? Was that a historical imperative, too?"

"Nagasaki was a bluff. It was a way of saying to them we have a hundred, a thousand of these bombs, we can take your cities out one by one. When, in fact, we had only two bombs at that time. One, two. It was Nagasaki that ended the war. Yes, it was costly. I am not impervious to the cost, or to the part that is chargeable to me."

"You are a man who accepts the cost of things, and pays the price."

"One of my teachers taught me that—as a matter of fact, it was Hofmannsthal—that a man can, and indeed must, take any action he deems right, provided he is prepared to accept the cost of it."

"Would you consider murder an acceptable action in some circumstances?"

"Clearly it could be inferred, from what I have said, that I would. I'd go so far as to say that, in certain circumstances, murder would become a moral duty. Knowing what we now know of Hitler, would it not have been our moral duty to murder him if, anytime after, say, 'thirty-three, we had been given the chance to do so? Or earlier. Now in case you want to draw Sherlock Holmes conclusions from what I have been saying, let me point out that there would be no point in murdering somebody in order to prevent something that is in any case impossible."

"Good point," Richter agreed. He stopped, drew on his pipe. "I want to turn to something else now. The conversation in the kitchen with Dr. Dubinski. In 1943." Richter paused, working out his approach, and felt the anxious tension swell and fill the hiatus.

"Yes?"

"Would you tell me about that? How did you assess what Dr. Dubinski was saying to you?"

"I have already made several statements about that."

"Oh, I didn't know."

"You mean you guys don't know everything? I'm astonished."

"Perhaps you could fill me in on this."

"Frankly, Captain, I don't have the time right now to go into something yet again that is already amply documented. Look it up, Captain."

"All right, I will. But tell me, if this matter has been so amply documented, why does Colonel Delacy feel you are holding out on something?"

"Who knows what goes on in the minds of you people?"

"Or you people," Richter said with a smile.

"I have told Colonel Delacy everything he needs to know."

"Meaning there are things he doesn't need to know, and you will decide what those things are?"

"That's right."

"I agree—ideally, that should be so. But when you are in a situation where there is a high-level leak, going right back, and someone has been in contact with, at least, possible sources of that leak, then one surely is entitled to expect from you no less than total frankness. Wouldn't you say?"

"I have been frank. I have nothing more to say about it at this point."

"I am going to insist you are a bit more helpful about what exactly is in your mind when you say—"

Bamberger interrupted him brusquely. "Insist?" Bamberger's voice rang like a violently struck tuning fork. He stood up. "Your superiors didn't *insist* with me, kiddo. What gives *you* the temerity to insist?" The whole air was suddenly vibrating with offense, and Bamberger's face was aquiver with resentment. "I know you fellows are obliged to read my letters, listen in on my phone conversations, follow me around, peep through my keyhole to see what I'm doing. I know, I know, it's your job. Okay, I have to put up with that. But I am not obliged to let you guys sit right down inside my skull and take your boots off. My thought processes are my own business. You can pass on that message to Colonel Delacy."

Richter smiled and drew on his pipe. "Look," he said, pained, "I am one of your staunchest admirers, but these are questions that will have to be answered eventually. *They* are not going to let go. They waited until the war was over, and then they waited some more, but eventually there comes a reckoning. They want to know. If I don't get the answer for them, they will hand over this investigation to others. To Tom Borneschaft and the FBI, and Colonel Delacy will bring in the big guns. With all the accidents we're having, and the top-level leak, and now your wife having been in long-term breach of security, there is no way that you are going to be able to retain your right to silence. And believe me, you are better off talking to me rather than any of the others."

"You're saying that to *me*—threatening me? You realize, without me the atomic bomb would not exist?"

"It's possible. You had a lot to do with it. But it may not be necessary for you to take all of the blame upon yourself, Doctor."

"Have you seen the newspapers lately? Haven't you seen me spread my black wings across the future? I *am* the bomb atomic, kiddo. Didn't you know?"

"Yes, I know, I know."

Richter got up and started toward the door. "Think about what I've been saying, Doctor. We'll talk again later in the day." He called good-bye across the room to Mrs. Bamberger, who had come out of the bathroom wrapped in a white bath towel.

" 'Bye, Mrs. Bamberger. Thanks for the coffee." Just before leaving, he turned to Bamberger again and asked, "Do you have a key to the Y-3 canyon lab?"

"There's one in the controller's office."

"Apart from that one? I'm talking about a second key."

"No, I don't."

Richter was watching Mrs. Bamberger closely. "Well, thank you again, Doctor."

When Richter had gone, Bamberger went to the bar and poured himself a Scotch.

Helen said, "Isn't that a little early?" She gave him an awkward laugh.

He said nothing, drank the whisky.

"You all right, David?"

He closed his eyes. His white shirt was no longer crisply fresh on him; it clung to his back and chest, and there were damp patches under the arms. His forehead glistened.

"He's not going to let go," he said, his voice low. He swallowed down the whisky and poured himself another. "He's going to dig it all out, our dumb friend. Not so dumb as he lets you believe. Digging, digging. Bastard of a cunt! Hofmannsthal is right. He says don't let 'em in your laboratories, the politicos desecrate the holy places of science. And he's right. How right he is! Our own fucking fault, for letting them in in the first place. Now they think they own us." He winced and poured more whisky. Helen watched him with wide, apprehensive eyes. She looked at him as if she did not know him. Never had she seen him drink in the morning—never had she felt so unsure of knowing him. His eyes looked feverish.

"Science has gotten to be the whore of government," he spat out, full of black bile. He looked at her sharply, with savage contempt, sweat running down his face. "Science is like a woman," he said, "yes, yes—easily corruptible. Very prone to flattery and attention, and with a blind feminine instinct to find out, find out—at any cost. The lousy bitch gives itself airs of class, but the truth is it opens its legs to anyone who knows what buttons to press." He faced Helen, and yelled at her, his voice rising out of control: "You know what your lover has done? He's found a way. The little skunk has found a way—of finally doing it. Of making a beaut of a Big Bang that can blow up the whole fucking world. That has no upper limit to the power of its destructiveness.

That's what your little sex maniac has done. Aren't you thrilled? Doesn't that give you a great big orgiastic thrill? It's an enormous step. A breakthrough . . ."

"They don't expect him to live more than another day," she said quietly.

"I know. I'm just telling you what he left us in his will."

"How many people know how far he had gotten?"

"Me. Jones. Hofmannsthal, Greenson, Wexler. Allison."

"Couldn't the knowledge stop there? Now that Leo is not going to be around?"

"Once the cat's out of the bag . . ."

"Keep it in the bag, David."

He looked at her closely.

"Trust me, David," she begged. "Please trust me. I'm with you in anything you decide. Anything. Only trust me, love me, David. Please, please. Don't you know I would do anything for you?"

He said nothing.

———

David was in Washington and she was alone in the house.

She felt frightened all the time; she did not know why. There was no lock on the door, and for the first time it occurred to her that anyone could come in. Outside in the unlit streets moon shadows overlapped. The pond was an unbeating heart. She thought, What am I afraid of? She was walking about, wringing her hands. The objects bought in her mad shopping sprees in Santa Fe seemed to accuse her from their various perches in recesses and on shelves and inside display cabinets: petrified spirits ashine with mockery and malevolence. She stood still, shuddering, staring into the cochineal red background of a Navajo blanket on the wall—insect red. The little Munch painting of David's stifled its scream inside her head. Oh my God, she thought, oh my God! She bit her fist.

"I'm not well," she said out loud. "Oh God, I'm not well." She sobbed. I am panicky; what is making me panic? She thought, I can't help it. She thought: a drink. But her heart was already beating in an irregular and violent way, and alcohol would only make it worse.

Be calm, she told herself, be calm. Somebody, she thought, has been interfering with the kachina dolls in the glass cabinet, for she could see they were aglitter with little fragments of broken glass that were embedded in their rag-and-clay bodies. . . . . They were iridescent with these tiny bits of glass, evilly alive with this glitter.

She was trying to stay calm. She went into David's study and looked around. The Stradivarius in the glass case, the guns on the wall racks, the books. Her eyes passed along the rows of books: she never knew what David read. His interior life was a secret from her. She thought: I really don't know him at all. Why had it been necessary for him to lie to Captain Richter? Naturally she had backed him up, since she loved him—that was not the point. She would have done anything for him, as she had said. But why had it been necessary for him to lie? One of the books was a little farther forward than the others on the shelf, and its title caught her eye: *Psychotic Symptoms*.

She took it down, and the thick volume fell open at a heavily marked page.

She began to read the underlined phrases.

. . . according to Holtzer one outcome of this terror is a submission to the tyranny of a bad part of the self which promises to protect one against the terror. In this way the terrorized make an alliance with their terrorizers. A foolish self-divisive pact. This kind of internal arrangement is productive of the classic paranoid condition of not knowing who is an enemy and who is a friend. Because the situation of anxiety can become so intolerable—the symptoms can include feelings of suffocation, of being trapped, and even of being eaten alive—the subject may split up his mind (schizophrenia) in order to not experience the victim's terror. Thus he may be able to identify with his cruel persecutors to the extent of "becoming them," in order not to feel the pain of being terrorized by them. This is one of the mechanisms of the psychotic killer who is said to "feel nothing."

A brilliant white glare, like a photographer's flash but continuous, dazzled her, making her head swivel away, but the window on the other side of the house was just as dazzling; she ran into the living room and all the windows were ablaze with this light, and she thought of the light on the night of Trinity, and of the light that had melted the eyeballs of the Japanese soldiers in the anti-aircraft corps. Moving through this whiteness were many shiny and strangely snouted forms, glistening like fish scales. She saw the front door begin to open, and she screamed and screamed. The huge form that stood in the doorway was tearing at its black rubbery face, and as the black snout came off and the rubber filter mask peeled away, she saw the reassuring bovine features of Greg McClure.

"Oh my God, Greg," she said, "I never was so glad to see anyone in my life."

"Sorry I scared you, Mrs. Bamberger," Greg McClure said. "Safety crew picked up some radioactivity on their meters outside your house. Had to check it. We've found what it was. Some uranium chippings. Very small amounts. Nothing to worry about."

"Oh my God, I'm so relieved."

"Apologize for all the glare. We came in rather fast and activated one of the trip wires. At least it shows it works, if it's ever needed. You all right, Mrs. Bamberger? Anything I can do for you? You look sort of shook up."

"I'll be all right now," she said.

316

SIXTEEN

"Sit down, Greg, sit down," Richter said.

Standing, Greg McClure gave the impression of a caryatid holding up the roof. These low-ceilinged rooms were not designed to accommodate anyone his size.

"You think it could have gotten into the cuffs of his pants?" Richter asked, pulling at the bearded flesh under his chin. "How much was there?"

"Just under a sixth of an ounce. Metal chippings."

"Not enough to make a bomb," Richter said, "but all the same, it's worrying that nobody noticed it was missing. You know how hysterical Washington can get about 'missing uranium.' There'll have to be an inquiry. I don't know if the cuffs theory is going to wash. You check his clothes with a meter?"

"Yeah, we did that, Captain. Nothing. But he could be wearing the pants."

"In that case we should get the controller to go with one of our people to a lab in Washington and have his cuffs checked."

"I didn't want to put the doctor to all that trouble."

"I think we have got to put him to that trouble. If there's no trace of anything in his cuffs, we have to think how else those uranium chippings got there."

"Yeah."

"Any theories, Greg?"

"Well, the stuff is not supposed to be taken out of the lab. Even in small quantities."

"So the doctor was taking it out contrary to regulations, or else it got there by accident. Another of our inexplicable accidents."

"Yeah, Captain."

A silence developed. It was the end of the day, and practically everybody else had left the office. Greg McClure was not the most talkative individual in the world. When he had nothing much to say, he kept quiet. To get anything out of him, you had to dig.

"How about a shot of Old Grand-dad?" Richter suggested, getting the bottle and two glasses out of a desk drawer.

"Wouldn't say no to that, Captain."

Greg was fond of his whiskey. It was said he could put away large quantities of it and not show the effect. After one or two drinks, Greg talked more: about his days in the White House, looking after the Old Man. About other famous people he had protected. Normally, he considered it a rule of his profession not to reveal any personal details about these people, but after a couple of Old Grand-dads he could be induced to relax that rule.

"What d'you make of the controller?" Richter asked him now.

"How d'you mean that, Captain?"

"You must have seen a side of him few others have seen. During the war when you were going everywhere with him."

"That's right."

"On his trips to Washington, and other places, you always used to go with him."

"That's right."

"Even if he took a weekend off, you went with him."

"Right, right. He sort of got used to me handling things for him. Well, he was always so busy. Even if he sometimes took a day out to go skiing, which I think he actually did twice, I went with him."

"What was he like on these occasions, when he was relaxing?"

"Oh, always very correct."

"How d'you mean?"

"Well, you know, Captain, there are some that think a personal

318

bodyguard is there to fix 'em up with women, and maybe it ain't even women."

"You do that sometimes, Greg?"

"Never for the doctor. He was always very correct."

"But for others?"

"Sometimes you have to. If you don't, they're liable to get themselves in dangerous situations. You choose the lesser evil."

"That disillusion you, Greg?"

"You see human nature in the raw, Captain. That you do."

"How does that affect you, in the case of somebody you've admired?"

"You try not to be judgmental in this job. You suspend judgment. You've got to, or you couldn't do the job."

Richter pulled at the coarse hair of his beard in a meditative way, and then said, "Greg, you were with Dr. Bamberger at Trinity. You brought him back here, afterwards. That was a crucial moment in his life. What impression did you get?"

"Impression, Captain? How d'you mean that?"

"How was he affected?"

"Has everything very much under control, Captain. Always."

"He talk at all?"

"You asking me this as part of your inquiries?"

"Yes, Greg. I'm trying to sort things out in my mind. I'm not asking you to be disloyal to anyone, but I'd appreciate your help."

"Oh, sure. Ask anything you want to."

"Coming back, in the car, after the test, he talk about anything?"

"In the car coming back?" McClure thought for a while. "He was in a strange mood, as a matter of fact, that day. Well, naturally, he was very exhausted. I don't think he'd slept for three weeks. He had a little faint as we were leaving base camp, and I gave him a shot of brandy, and I think it must have gone straight to his head because he became sort of talkative, which is unusual for the doctor. While we were driving through the desert he was saying things all the time. Pretty weird things, now I come to think of it."

319

"What sort of things, Greg?"

"Oh, he was quoting from the Bible. And he was saying things like, 'You know, Greg, I may have done a terrible thing today, maybe one of the most terrible things any man has ever done. . . .' "

"Biblical quotations, Greg? Can you remember what they were?"

McClure's big, leathery face screwed up as he tried to remember. "Oh, yeah," he said, "something about he'd seen the beast. That's right. That he'd seen the beast with the seven heads and the ten horns whose name was blasphemy."

"Is that the Apocalypse?"

"That's right . . . the vision of the beast. The doctor was quoting the bit about it being given to the beast to make war with the saints and to overcome them, and to have power over all nations and tongues. Seemed to know his Bible, the doctor."

"So he was identifying with the beast?"

"Right then, yes. Matter of fact, he said at one point that if what he'd done turned out to be a war crime he was quite ready to be put up against a wall and shot. He said that if you did what he had just done, then you had to be ready to be put up against a wall."

"What did you say to that?"

"Me, Captain? I didn't say anything, Captain. You're not required to say anything. Just to listen. They don't expect an answer. If you've done your job right, they're so used to you it's like they're talking to themselves."

"My God, the things you must hear sometimes."

"You sure do."

"It doesn't get you down?"

"You can't let it."

"How d'you manage that?"

"You sort of switch off. I don't mean you're not listening, because you got to listen—if you go blank they know. But you sort of hear and you don't hear, if you know what I mean. You filter things out. If you didn't do that, if you let it all get to you, it'd drive you crazy. Like if you're living next to an airport, you learn

320

to filter out noise. And every minute of the day, your mind is filtering out unnecessary sensations that you don't want. Isn't that so? Well, you as a scientist, Captain, I'm sure you know about that."

"Yes. So, in your job, you filter out anything discreditable? Does it come back, if you think about it hard enough?"

"Yeah, I guess so. If necessary."

"It may be necessary, Greg. I want you to think back, about the doctor. And try to remember anything—anything you may have filtered out—that could cast some light on what's been happening here."

"All right, Captain. I'll do my best for you. What kind of thing are we looking for?"

"Like they say in police reports, acting suspiciously. And anything that might suggest mental aberration."

Greg McClure thought for a while before replying.

"Nothing that comes to mind about the controller," he said. "Is it only him you're interested in?"

"Why? Is there someone else you want to tell me about, Greg?"

"In the light of what you say—mental aberration—Dr. Jones has sometimes acted peculiar."

"You have anything in particular in mind?"

"Yes." McClure looked uncomfortable. "I don't like to be telling tales. . . ."

"I wouldn't ask you to, Greg, if it weren't a matter of serious importance."

"Well, see, once I was driving Dr. Jones. It was the time he came back from Hiroshima. You know, when he was taken sick and had to come back? I fetched him from Albuquerque. He was in a bad way, Captain. I thought he was going off his rocker. He was drunk, of course—but it wasn't just the drink. He was acting real . . . demented. And then suddenly right smack in the middle of the road—he's in the back of the car and I'm driving, see—he tries to kill himself."

"To kill himself!"

"Yeah. Whips out a penknife . . . starts to stick it in his throat. Fortunately, I'd been watching him in my mirror because

321

he was acting so peculiar, and as I saw him go at himself with the knife I slam on the brakes. Throws him forward and the knife falls out of his hand. I was around there in a second, luckily he hadn't hit a vein. He was bleeding, but not badly. I was able to stop it. I have some first-aid equipment in the car. As we drove back, he kept saying to me, 'You fool, Greg. You blithering fool. Why didn't you let me do it? What are you saving me for, the peace prize? I'm better off dead.' And then he said, 'We're all better off dead.' And he said something about the dead babies, all those dead babies. In Hiroshima. And he said, 'We did that, Greg. Clever us. The brainy boys.' I tried to tell him not to take it so bad, it was war. There were times when you had to kill people, I said. He calmed down eventually. I guess I should have reported it at the time, but Mrs. Jones asked me not to. She said that kind of thing went in a man's record, and was always held against him if he was trying to get a job, which I guess is true. So I didn't make an official report about it. He'd only given himself a scratch really, and it might just have been a kind of drunken playacting, you know. You think I did wrong in not reporting it, Captain?"

"I don't know, Greg. Anyway, I understand the thought back of what you did. But I'm glad you've told me now. It's something that has to be known in present circumstances. I'd appreciate it, Greg, if you remember anything else of that nature—about any of the people you've had dealings with here—if you'd come and tell me, in confidence. I would not use any of it, understand, except if it is relevant to the present inquiries."

"I'll try and see what I can remember, Captain."

———

From the night nurse's cubicle at the end of the small isolation ward, Richter watched people come to say good-bye to Hepler. It had been going on all afternoon. It was not expected that he would last out the night. A microphone was concealed in a bowl of flowers by the deathbed. Real creep's work, Richter reflected, but it had been Hepler's own idea.

Hofmannsthal was now by the bed, shaking his head severely, like a tough examiner confronted by an unsatisfactory paper. Hep-

322

ler's eyes were open and staring without focus. But when he spoke his voice came over clearly through Richter's earphones.

"You remember, Professor, when we used to have our long walks, and we used to talk and talk . . . ?"

"Yes, yes."

"You remember we used to talk about death . . . ?"

"Yes, it was a subject we discussed a great deal, I recall."

"And you recall expressing the point of view that to the natural scientist everything was of interest, including his own death."

"I remember that."

"Well, you were wrong, Professor. It is not of interest. It is very boring. Dying is a very boring business. I advise you to have nothing to do with it."

"There are many things that turn out not to be as interesting as one thought they would be," Hofmannsthal reflected.

"It does not matter," Hepler said very tiredly. "One must let everything happen. What else can you do?"

Almost immediately after Hofmannsthal had left, Allison approached the bed. She was looking tense and drawn and fearful Her hands were tightly clenched. It was apparent tò Richter, watching from the cubicle, that this was an ordeal for her. Well, he thought, she has been through it before, with Jake. It must bring back all sorts of memories. He adjusted the microphone level, since she was speaking so softly he could not make out what she was saying. She must have remarked upon his appearance, because Hepler snapped back, "What do you expect? Violins? I must tell you, my dear, that dying is not very aesthetic, contrary to what they show you in the movies, and also it hurts." Hepler turned his head and his words faded, became indistinct to Richter. Then he heard Allison say, "Leo, why don't you tell the truth? Why make trouble?"

"Why not? I am not a good sport. I don't mind my death making trouble for others. Besides, it *is* the truth, what I have said."

"It is not and you know it's not."

"You want me to say I was looking into your beautiful eyes and daydreaming of sinful afternoons we spend together in Santa Fe, and my hand slipped?"

She looked around nervously and said, "Well, you know that's the truth. . . ."

In the night nurse's cubicle Richter frowned and drew more rapidly on his pipe: Well, in the profession of being a creep one was liable to hear what one was not meant to hear. It hurt, all the same.

Hepler said, "I must tell you, Allison, I can keep in my mind your beautiful body and also the matter in hand. The screws had been loosened, or it would not have happened."

Allison looked around again, and said, "Other people are waiting to see you, Leo. So I'm going to say good-bye."

She kissed him on the forehead lightly, and left.

Next came the Bambergers, and Jones. It seemed that Jones did not want to go in alone to see Hepler, and so had tagged on to the Bambergers.

Helen had been warned of what to expect, but even so she was taken aback. This person was barely recognizable as her companion of the calle Cordoba—that lusty spirit. He had lost all of his hair—not only the hair of his head, but also of his eyebrows and eyelashes—making him look inhuman, like a visitor from the sun. He was terribly emaciated, ravaged; his skin was very white and aged looking, like old crinkled parchment, and the skull head showed through. Seeing Helen, the bulging fish eyes in their misty deep suddenly burned with a renewal of energy. They burned so intensely that she looked away.

"Leo," Bamberger said, "for old times' sake, let me ask you to do something. Righten things. You'll feel better for it—clear up! Set the record straight. It's what I would do in your place."

"But you are a gentleman, Bambi, and as you have pointed out to me, I am not." His eyes were vague and knowing by turn. He motioned them both to come closer, and when they were bent over him, waiting for him to speak, he said, "You know it'll work, don't you? My calculations work. I am right. I found the way of doing it, didn't I?" He seemed to faint away, and it was a little while before he was focused on them again. "Is that why you did it, Bambi?" A reedy, whistling laugh shook his frail being. "Is that

324

why you murdered me, Bambi? Naturally, only for the noblest of motives."

"I think he's no longer rational," Bamberger said to his wife.

"What you want to bet? Or was it because of Helen? Hmm?"

"There is no getting through to him," Bamberger said. "It's too late."

"I am not ready to go yet, and I will not go before I am ready—I am a stubborn cuss," Hepler said with surprising force.

Jones had been standing close by, saying nothing, controlling his evident agitation. Abruptly he said, "Good-bye, Leo," turned, and left.

"You go, too," Hepler told Bamberger. "But Helen, you stay. I exercise the privilege of the deathbed."

Bamberger looked at Helen, gave her a faint nod, and with a curt nod of farewell to Hepler, went out.

Once they were alone, Helen said, "Why, Leo? What satisfaction does it give you? To do that, to make such trouble for us all! Why don't you tell Captain Richter the truth? You know David could never do such a thing."

"Ah, the loyal Helen. I do not accuse David, in particular. . . . But don't make any mistake—he could have done it. The father of the bomb! The man with blood on his hands—Oh, yes, he could have done it. To remove an ancient thorn from his flesh. I always thought he was mad, Bambi. Too rational. About things you cannot be rational about. Mad, mad."

"You're crazy, Leo. Why do you hate him so much? You were friends once."

"David never approved of me. . . . I was a little squirt of an upstart to him always. With a freakishly overdeveloped brain. He thinks that is like being born with red hair, no cause to congratulate yourself. He thinks I have no style—and you know, Helen, he is right, I don't have, never have had, was always too greedy, too impatient to have style. Style is a matter of not being in too much of a hurry, and I always was in a hurry. As you know. Ah—to postpone gratification beyond one's own lifetime—what an achievement of the mature mind! Well, I leave that glory to

Bambi. Such self-denial never appealed to me. I could not wait so long. My place in history? I tell you . . ." He made a dismissive sound of the lips. "I would exchange it gladly for another one of our little afternoons in the calle Cordoba."

She leaned down and kissed the dry cold lips. One of his hands went up to her, could not quite reach, and she took it and pressed it to her breast. He fell back and lay very still. For a moment she thought he was dead. But then his eyes opened, bulging fiercely, demandingly, the way they did when he wanted something and had to have it.

"Promise me, Helen, promise me. Make sure they don't put me in the earth. I could not bear to be in the cold earth. Make sure they burn me. . . . I don't trust these bastards. Make sure, Helen. Better hot ashes than cold meat, hmm? Hmm, Helen?"

She gave him a solemn nod.

When the last of them had gone, Richter approached the bed of the dying man.

"Well?" Hepler asked. "Was it of help?"

"There were one or two things," Richter said.

"I try to make them say things," Hepler said. "But . . ." He shrugged.

"Thank you. Now try to get some rest."

"Rest?" Hepler said, "What for do I need rest? I will get nothing else where I am going."

———

Richter was now obliged to consider how Allison fitted into the picture that was emerging. The fact was, she had not told him the truth. Had said nothing about an affair with Hepler. Well, what woman told a man she was involved with the whole truth about her past life? Still, she should have told him, in the circumstances, and it was worrying that she hadn't.

In the light of what he had now learned, he would have to go through her file again, keeping his personal feelings in abeyance.

The secrets-sharing approach to Bamberger had come through Dubinski—Dubinski was married to Allison, and Dubinski had

326

died of radiation. Hepler, too, it now appeared, had been involved with Allison, and he, too, was dying of radiation, probably would be dead by morning.

Allison's first husband had gone to fight in Spain for the Republicans and had been killed in action. Three men involved with Allison. Two dead. One dying.

What did that mean?

He went back through the files—to the prewar period in New York, when Bamberger was a close friend of the Dubinskis, was always coming to their apartment with his latest girl.

The Dubinskis had moved in the best left-wing intellectual circles. The record showed that. They knew the *New Republic* crowd, and the Hollywood crowd, and Malraux's translator Haakon Chevalier, and Lillian Hellman, and a lot of the more left-wing people from the State Department. They also knew less intellectually chic leftists. Richter had a picture of them making the rounds of the Village wine-and-cheese parties, the midtown cocktail parties, the fund-raising dinners, the appeals and benefit performances, the rallies. Jake was a great joiner—a dozen different antifascist groups had secured his support; he signed petitions left and right, gave generously of his money and time, and readily allowed his name to be used on behalf of any antifascist cause. He was a good public speaker and accepted lots of invitations to speak out against the Nazis. He did not bother himself too much about who else was on the platform with him. Like others who had escaped from Germany, he tended to see everything in dramatic life-and-death terms. He thought the world was asleep and must be awakened. To this end, he worked tirelessly and selflessly, using his standing as a scientist to make himself heard in the highest councils. It was Jake who had prevailed upon Bamberger that they go to see Einstein and persuade him to alert the President to the need for an American atomic bomb program. The terrible specter in Jake's mind was that the Nazis would develop such a bomb first. In which case, all was lost. To fight against the ultimate horror of Nazi world domination, he had been prepared to embrace any political ally dedicated to the same cause.

He had been a member of the Communist party. And not only

that; he had known quite a number of people active in the Communist underground.

Allison's background, as it emerged from the files, was that of a girl with a science degree from Columbia University who had got into these sorts of circles as a result of being both clever and attractive, if not exactly on the same intellectual level as some of the men she took up with. At college she had not been specifically committed to the Communists, but had been broadly sympathetic to the left-wing view, and on the whole had hung out with radical leftists and Communists. Those were the sort of men she went for, and she was a girl who when she took a man as her lover tended to go along with his overall view of things. She was loyal to her man; that was one of her traits.

The record showed that as soon as she met the man who became her first husband—the radical Communist who had later gone to fight in Spain—she became an activist, too. She had been on her way to join him in Spain when she received the news of his death. Almost immediately on becoming involved with Jake she changed her approach—Jake thought that it was romantic quixotry for intellectuals to go and fight with rifles in their hands; someone like himself was more valuable making speeches and working behind the scenes to influence and persuade. So she had given up ideas of guns and blood and had become a lobbyist.

After Jake's death a psychiatric assessment had been made of Allison's character, on the basis of general observation and past history. The report was in her file.

The psychiatrists thought that her tendency to commit herself totally to her man might mean that after Jake's death she would have felt compelled to continue his work. Thus, if Jake had been mixed up with the Communist underground, the doctors thought she might have kept up the connection and the work. It was pure speculation. There was no evidence that Jake had worked for the secret Party apparat, or that Allison had followed in his footsteps. But the psychiatrists allowed themselves to say that she might have, on the basis of her personality structure. They also thought that she might be holding the United States government to blame for Jake's death, which would give her an additional motive for

betraying her country. Her actions would be all the more dangerous for being inspired by love. Women acting at the behest of
such a love—one that went beyond the grave—were capable of
great cunning and subterfuge and ruthlessness, the psychiatrists
said.

It was all speculation. Still, Richter could not exclude such
speculation from his thoughts. Indeed, he was obliged to go further, to find out still more.

He went to see Tom Borneschaft in the FBI office.

"I'm glad you came to me about this, Jerry," Borneschaft said.
"I didn't want to have to bring it up first."

"Bring what up first?"

"Certain facts."

"Okay, Tom. Give it to me. I asked for it, let me have it."

The first part of the FBI material corresponded fairly closely
with what Richter already knew—from Mrs. Bamberger's diary
and from other sources.

Two weeks after Jake's death, Allison had begun seeing a laboratory technical assistant called Joe Davidson. It became clear they
were having an affair. He was at that time working in the explosives shop, and involved in making the explosive lenses that triggered the implosion-detonating device of the plutonium bomb. He
had a red badge, which meant he was not supposed to be given
any more information than he needed to do his own job. He was
not supposed to know what the explosive lenses he was working on
were for.

Politically, Davidson was to the left, far to the left. Going by
the company he kept and his FAECT union activities.

Furthermore, he was the man who, according to Bamberger's
statement to Colonel Delacy in 1944, had made an approach to
him through Jake Dubinski, saying he knew somebody in the Soviet legation who could channel information back to the Soviet
Union. All this confirmed what Richter had found out. But now
Borneschaft added some new aspects.

"We didn't do anything about Davidson, because we wanted to
see where he was going to lead us, so we left him free, we didn't
question him even. At first, nothing much emerged. Either he

329

was staying clean or else he had a line through that we couldn't tumble. Then, after Jake's death, he takes up with the widow. Coincidence? Maybe. Of course, if Dubinski had been feeding him secret info and he was passing it on through channels we had not discovered yet, it would be good cover for him to take up with the widow, who could then continue her husband's good work. It was very quickly made clear to Mrs. Dubinski that her relationship with Davidson was worrisome to us—we didn't fill in all the details, but pointed out that any close relationship between a red badge and a white badge was fraught with security risks, and we would prefer for her to find herself some other guy. We finally prevailed upon her, by saying otherwise we would have to post Technical Sergeant Davidson to the Pacific. So she gave him up. Naturally, we continued to watch them both. As far as we know, she didn't see him again, did not make contact with him in any way. This in itself is weird if we were really breaking up true love rather than an affair of convenience. The one time she did see him, as far as we know, ran into him by chance, was at the commissary the day before Hepler's accident. Coincidence again."

"What are you implying, Tom?" Richter said, with a growing unease in his heart.

"She could have given Davidson a key to the Y-3 canyon lab, that's what I am saying. He cannot account for his movements during the lunch hour. Says he took a sandwich and sat in the fields."

"You suggesting that while she was having lunch with me, Davidson was round at the canyon lab fiddling with the screws of the device? I cannot believe that, Tom. She wasn't even nervous. She would have been going back to a situation of great danger. . . . I'd have noticed something."

"She could have had some plan for getting out of the lab, not dependent on Hofmannsthal's suggestion. That may have been a fortuitous accident she made use of, replacing her own plan. Or—another possibility—she didn't know Davidson had interfered with the device; she thought he was copying it, or photographing it—which he may have done too. She may not have known she was in any special danger, because she may not have known he was going to sabotage it. In which case, you see, she would not have had to be too nervous and tense during her lunch with you. And maybe she's good at hiding her feelings, her true feelings. There *are* such dames."

"All of it is speculation," Richter said, full of the most dismal forebodings now. "Let's remember that."

"There's more," Borneschaft said. "More pieces of the puzzle."

"All right, shoot. Let me have it all."

"After the accident, Davidson got compassionate leave—his mother. High blood pressure. We let him go, because we wanted to see what he would do. We put him under discreet surveillance. Under this kind of surveillance we say to our fellows, 'Lose him rather than let him know he's being tailed.' We kept losing him, because he was taking sophisticated evasive action, very professional. Knows all the tricks. But on his third day in New York we got somewhere. Here, have a look at the report yourself."

Borneschaft handed Richter a standard FBI surveillance sheet. Richter proceeded to read:

Surveillance of Joe Davidson by Agents J. Appleby, T. R. Talbot, J. Fieldhouse and R. Westway.

9:06 A.M. Subject left mother's apartment and took downtown bus.

9:15 A.M. Subject descended from bus at Lexington and 62nd. Walked back along Lexington looking in shop windows. Made a left at 65th and walked up crossing Park and Madison. Hesitated at corner of 65th and Fifth. Then crossed over to the park side and started walking towards Plaza. Kept looking around as if for bus or taxi going downtown.

9:38 A.M. On sudden impulse joined crowd going into Zoo. Walking fast. Agent Appleby lost sight of subject for several minutes.

9:45 A.M. Agent Westway spotted subject in cat house, in front of the puma cage. Exchanged remarks with unidentified male next to him. Exchange lasted less than forty seconds.

9:50 A.M. Subject, after a perfunctory look at other animals, left Zoo.

9:55 A.M. Subject having crossed Fifth caught an uptown bus.

10:05 A.M. Subject descended from bus, entered pharmacy and emerged five minutes later with package (medicines?). Subject returned to mother's apartment. Subject remained in mother's apartment until:

7:15 P.M. Subject caught downtown bus.

7:20 P.M. Subject descended from bus at traffic light and immediately picked up cab.

7:35 P.M. Subject left cab at Penn Station. Agent Fieldhouse lost subject in concourse.

7:45 P.M. Subject emerged from Penn Station. Picked up taxi.

8:00 P.M. Subject descended at Madison Square Garden and entered stadium where wrestling match was in progress. Going down aisle to his seat subject encountered individual of his acquaintance with whom he engaged in conversation for two minutes and 35 seconds. Acquaintance identified as Dr. Bamberger.

8:03 P.M. Dr. Bamberger and subject took their respective seats in different parts of stadium.

"Another coincidence," Richter said, unhappily shaking his head. He handed the surveillance sheet back to Borneschaft.

"After that coincidence," Borneschaft said, "I decided to have a word with Davidson myself. Went to see him at his mother's apartment. She *is* sick, that part is true. She had a stroke not long ago. Sat there in a rocking chair, staring. Davidson denied everything. Said the encounter with Bamberger was sheer accident. Said he never asked Dubinski to approach Bamberger for information—either Dubinski made it up, or Bamberger made it up. Denies that he ever obtained any information from Mrs. Dubinski of a secret or restricted nature. Says they never talked about anything like that. We searched the place. Nothing. Except—passport photos. A dozen. A dozen passport photos. I asked him, 'Why d'you need a dozen?' and he said, 'Oh, it's cheaper by the dozen.' "

332

"That's all?"

"For the moment."

"It's not conclusive."

"I know. I have hopes, though. I think we scared him. I told him that I was ready to do a deal with him, if he'll spill the beans we'd let him off light. Get him a ten-, fifteen-year sentence. I told him that if he didn't come clean we'd nail him, and I reminded him that the penalty for espionage in time of war is the electric chair. I had the impression it registered."

"And?"

"I'm waiting to hear from him."

SEVENTEEN

"Leo Hepler passed away five minutes ago," Dr. Schneidermann said on the phone to Richter.

"He say anything before he went? About the accident?"

"No. He just said, 'Who can you complain to?,' gave a shrug, and died."

"Okay. Well, thanks for letting me know."

Richter stared out into the rain. It had been falling steadily since last night and showed no sign of letting up. Could go on like this for days. That was the pattern out here in the southwest: long periods of drought, then continuous rain. The day had become dark. The rain was falling with a regular heavy patter on the asphalt of the overpass linking laboratory buildings on both sides of the drive, and with a tinny drumbeat on the tops of automobiles and on corrugated iron roofs. The main thoroughfare had become a shallow, fast-flowing stream, an incipient river.

So Hepler was dead. That wild outrageous spirit finally had been quelled. Some woman had once described him as "lecherous, libidinous, lustful, venerous, erotomaniacal, aphrodisiac, irreverent, narrow-minded, untruthful, bereft of moral fiber. . . ." Not far wrong as an assessment. But she had left out *genius*.

In his university days Richter had been constantly outshone by the likes of Hepler, and it had hurt. It hurt to be an also-ran. But it was not in Richter's nature to harbor grudges against those who excelled him, and he had come to genuinely admire the dazzling

334

scientists and mathematicians of his generation. These, surely, were going to be the young philosopher-kings. They knew everything. The innermost language of nature had been revealed to them, and they understood. Relativity. The curvature of space. The secret of time. They were able to grasp the ungraspable abstractions: beginning and infinity. The edge of the universe. Others could not conceive of such things, but they were able to. They, with their great knowledge, would lead the way into a true age of enlightenment. And even if he was not to be in the vanguard of that column, he would, in some small way, as a fellow scientist, share in the glory.

But now, as he puzzled over the meaning of Hepler's death, Richter could not rid himself of a profound sense of failure; not just his own—theirs, too. For it was not merely that he had not gone on to become the scientist he had once hoped to be (settling instead for the role of popularizer); but those others, who had lived up to all their great promise and astonished the world with brilliant concepts, also had gone wrong somewhere. It was not possible to live among them, as he had done these past years, and to look into their lives as his job required him to do, without realizing that a pestilence was eating away at the gains of the mind. Some baneful principle of inverse ratio seemed to prevail. There appeared to be a kind of rule that the farther you were able to see, the more terrible your visions became. Hidden penalties were attached to the greatest gifts, and then imposed in the moment of triumph. The great horror was lucidity. They were penalized in their spirit by the extraordinary grasp of their brains. Circumstance and their own cleverness had compelled them to live out a tragic paradox: that it was not barbarians who had made the atom bomb, but poetically minded Jews, civilized Europeans, and the finest, boldest minds of America. Some of these people were poets and philosophers as well as scientists; they believed in a central order, loved life, and felt an affinity between their mathematical calculations and the greatest music. These were the men who had made the atom bombs that wiped out Hiroshima and Nagasaki, and were now, some of them, planning a superbomb a thousand times more destructive still. Enlightened men, not yahoos, were doing this.

335

The concentration camps were the work of dark, mediocre minds, but the atom bomb had been made by men of goodwill and genius.

What did it mean? Did it mean that no matter how artfully you painted over the human spirit, what lay beneath was always the same implacable interaction of chance and necessity that Hepler had postulated, as ultimately impervious to human influence as the jungle to flower arrangements? This Hepler had believed; and he had concluded, therefore, that in the manmade clearing there was only one thing to do: amuse oneself.

Ah, if it were only amusement! But its opposite seemed to exercise a compelling attraction, too. There was also the mysterious lure of pain and suffering, and the ecstasy of destroying. Such a pull had to be contended with, too; Richter had glimpsed it at times in Hepler. And who else? Who else? If he was going to solve the mystery of Hepler's death, he was going to have to understand that dismal attraction, and who was animated by it.

Gloomy thoughts, which Richter felt compelled to pursue for their particular relevance to the problem in hand: namely, Could one of these civilized cultured men have loosened a screw in Hepler's experimental apparatus with the intention of adding some more lives to those already claimed by the bomb—not only Hepler (for such a mishap, if it were wholly successful, could not be relied upon to be so selective), but also Hofmannsthal and Greenson and Wexler and Allison and Jones, not to mention all the others who might have been affected by the radiation before it could be brought under control. Who could have done such an evil thing? And out of what motive? Richter perceived that he had the whole range of human motives to choose from: sexual jealousy; envy; greed—greed for glory/money/power/position; fear; madness; revenge. . . . Which one had loosened the screw and killed Hepler?

Richter tried to put himself in the shoes of such evil. How to understand it? One saw its reflections, its disguises, its masks, and its false smiles; but the dark heart itself was something perceivable only to one who had entered the nightmare.

Richter was conscious of the fact that he had so far been spared

336

such an experience. Others had known it, but not he. He had been lucky. But now, with a sudden stab of profound foreboding, it came to him that only by going right into the nightmare was he going to solve this mystery. It had a feeling about it of not being solvable by gentler means. It was, he was beginning to understand, a mystery with a moral dimension, and one could not simply ask, Who benefits?

Richter crossed to the window. The rain had become almost horizontal. It spattered the gypsum-sided building in strong rhythmic bursts. He looked out, frowning. Either no water or too much. The Indians had been driven off this safe volcanic shelf because of the lack of water. But there were times when it became so plentiful that it washed away buildings. In these parts water formed a subterranean maze into which surface streams suddenly vanished, becoming part of new forest bogs. Water was a very unpredictable element in northern New Mexico.

It was some puzzle that he had on his hands. He drew on his pipe. The more he thought about it, the more ways there seemed to be of putting the puzzle together. Sure the pieces fitted. But only one way could be the right way. He would have to go after Bamberger. Bamberger was at the heart of this mystery. (Or was this merely wishful thinking, because he did not want Allison to be at the heart of it?) The facts were: Bamberger had told of an attempt to get him to "share" secrets with the Russians; Bamberger had spent a night with a Communist girl friend during the height of wartime secrecy and not reported it; Bamberger had received an anonymous note saying, "I will join you on your morning walk, do not approach me"; Bamberger was opposed to the development of a superbomb. And he also had personal reasons for hating Hepler. Bamberger had had access to the canyon lab—and had spilled ketchup on Hepler, which would have delayed his return to the lab on the day of the accident. And on top of all that, Bamberger had run into Davidson at a wrestling match just a few days ago.

Well, he obviously was going to have to see Bamberger and confront him with some of these facts. Suddenly he remembered

337

that there was a wrestling match on the hill that night. The story was that after the last Deanna Durbin movie, Bamberger had said to the entertainments officer, "You should get some wrestlers in."

When Richter got to the meeting hall, normally used for scientific colloquia, the atmosphere was already appropriately smoky and rough-edged. The wrestlers had not yet put in an appearance. Evidently some holdup. The impatient audience was whistling and making catcalls, and the scientists, entering the spirit of the occasion, joined in heartily. Richter spotted Bamberger, next to his wife, catcalling as loud as anyone, and chewing gum.

The fight promoter came into the ring to say that the first bout had had to be canceled because of the indisposition of the Nebraska Pyramid, who had a cold. The audience threw paper cartons, orange peels, and peanut shells at the promoter. He scrambled hastily out of the ring. The audience stamped its feet and chanted, "Shoot him! Shoot him!" and "Exterminate the bug!"

The chanting stopped only when Killer Nakuma and Samson Topolski entered the ring and displayed their muscles. The bout began slowly, with the two large-bellied wrestlers clutching rather tentatively at each other's limbs without getting a hold. The audience began to shout for more action. This went on with mounting impatience and derision until suddenly the clamor was stilled by Killer Nakuma throwing Samson Topolski on the floor, belly down, and getting his left arm twisted up behind his back. He shoved upwards and Samson let out a bloodcurdling scream. In the now silent meeting hall a soldier shouted, "Go on, Killer, kill the bastard! Shove his teeth down his throat!" In the front row, a flushed theoretical metallurgist shouted, "Break his arm, break his arm!" Bamberger shouted, "Bite his nose off, Killer." He bit on a fresh stick of gum.

Richter wondered if the Bambergers knew that Hepler had died. Presumably Dr. Schneidermann would have informed the controller at once. A hard enamel glaze covered Bamberger's eyes. "Come on, you dog," he yelled at Samson Topolski, "get him off your back, you rat-faced moron!"

338

Jaws moving with grinding force, Bamberger turned his head and saw Richter watching him, and gave a sardonic grin.

"Gouge his eyes out, Killer," he shouted and made a thumbs-down sign.

In the interval, Richter went over to the Bambergers.

"I never knew you were such a wrestling fan, Doctor."

"Many things about me you don't know, Captain."

"Yes, I'm sure. You hear that Hepler died?"

"Yes."

"There are a few things I need to talk to you about," Richter said. "You think you could stop by after the fight?"

"Can we make it tomorrow?"

"I'd appreciate it if you could find the time tonight."

"All right, Captain—after the fight."

Richter had been waiting in his office half an hour when there was a tap on the door. He called, "Come in, Doctor." But it was not Bamberger. It was Tom Borneschaft.

Borneschaft said, "You expecting the controller?"

"Yes—said he'd come by after the fight." He looked at his watch. "He's late."

Borneschaft was wearing an oilskin cape, a fisherman's cap, and rubber boots, and glistening with rain.

"I guess the reason he hasn't come is, he's getting up a search party. The Jones children are missing."

"What!"

"Yuh—they were out in the afternoon and didn't come back. A few of us are gonna look for them. They may have taken shelter from the rain, and then it got dark."

"I'll come with you," Richter said.

The assembly point for the search party was one of the new concrete storm shelters near the perimeter fence. Allison was there, trying to cheer up Pam Jones, when Richter arrived.

"I am sure what happened," Allison was saying, "is that the

lightning scared them and they took cover. They're sensible kids, Pam. They'll wait for someone to come look for them."

Greg McClure arrived with a couple of bullhorns.

Bamberger was there with Mrs. Bamberger. "What are we waiting for?" he called out.

"Jones," somebody said. "He's gone back to get an umbrella."

"An umbrella!" Bamberger began incredulously.

Pam Jones cut in and said, "He went back for a drink. He needed it."

Lightning was zigzagging across the sky at regular intervals. Great bolts were followed within a second by violent thunderclaps. Bamberger looked up and shook his head.

"Oh, they'll be so frightened, my babies," Pam Jones said with a sob.

"Now stop that, Pam," Allison said firmly. "They'll be all right, Pam. They're bright children. They won't be so frightened. Oh, sure, they'll be a bit scared, but it'll also be an adventure for them. They'll cope. They know you will keep calm, and that will make them keep calm. Children have more resources than you'd think."

"Oh, I hope so," Pam Jones said. She saw her husband coming toward the shelter under an open umbrella. He was not too steady on his feet; he had a chrome flask in his hand. Pam Jones turned her head away, tears running down her face. Allison squeezed her arm.

"Come on, Pam. Come on. How about that stiff British upper lip?"

"You wouldn't think," Pam said, "that that's the man who climbed to the top of the tower at Trinity and turned all the taps on, would you? That was the man they trusted to have his finger on the emergency stop button. He was so cool and strong always . . . always. In any emergency. Now he's completely . . ."

"You'll have to have the strength for the two of you, won't you?" Allison said.

"Oh, you're a good friend," Pam Jones said. "You're the person I'm going to miss most."

Tom Borneschaft had taken charge of the search.

340

"I think we're ready to go," he called out when there was an interval in the thunder. "Soon as we get beyond the reservoir road we're gonna spread out in a line—everybody keep the person on his left and right in sight, and if you can't do that, maintain contact by calling out periodically. Everybody got flashlights? Good. Then let's go."

The assumption was that if Tony and Sarah had gone out through the hole in the northwestern part of the perimeter fence, they probably would have set off in the first place along the reservoir road. The number of negotiable trails originating from there was not that many, and Pam Jones thought they would have taken some kind of reasonable road through the woods, and would not have gone too far off the beaten track. With luck they would have found a trail shelter and be waiting there. What Richter could not understand was why the children would have set off in such rain. Well, some kids liked the rain. Made it more of an adventure. He hoped that was the explanation.

The search party left in two jeeps, heading out against the rush of water. Every time the lightning flashed the dark landscape was brilliantly lit up all around. Richter had never seen such lightning. These must be the superbolts that some scientists were postulating—the massive accumulation of electricity that occurred during a long period without rain or storms. When the lightning came, you could see the Sangre de Cristo mountains wobble in the watery sky: everything flowing, aqueous and uncertain. It was difficult to drive, because the fast-flowing water had wiped out the defining edges of the dirt roads, and it was an act of faith to assume one was going toward solid ground rather than into a ditch. In some places sections of stone wall had been breached by the water, and there were massive stones all over the trail.

The two jeeps turned a bend, and in the next flash Richter saw down into the valley, where the overflowing arroyos were steaming whirlpools. You had a sense now of the sort of country this had been not so long ago. It was only a few years before the war that the first roads had been made going down into the valley. Before then, the journey to Santa Fe took two days, on foot and by burro-

341

back, over a twisty trail crossing the Rio Grande by means of a plank bridge that was frequently washed away in heavy rain. Not so long ago all this around here had been wilderness.

The lead jeep was coming to a halt and McClure was signaling to the one behind to pull up. He got out and called back: "This is as far as we can risk the jeeps." They all got out, and in the light of the headlamps saw the trail ahead peter out in muddy corkscrews.

Tom Borneschaft placed them all in line and repeated his injunction for everyone to keep the person next to him in sight. "Don't want anyone else getting lost."

Shining their flashlights ahead and calling out the names of the children at regular intervals, the line of searchers made their way steadily forward. Richter, when the next lightning came, had an impression of the narrowness of the swath cut by their little band in these vast, rolling hills, and of how their shouts of "Sarah . . . Tony" were instantly absorbed by the continuously rumbling sky.

They trudged on, McClure and Borneschaft using their bullhorns, but the amplification did not make much difference in this storm. Pam Jones's voice was all the time becoming hoarser and weaker as she called her children's names. After an hour she was speaking in barely more than a strained whisper, and Richter said to her several times, "Save your voice, Mrs. Jones. They can't hear you. The best chance is with the loudhailers after the thunder has died down a bit."

But even when the intervals between thunderclaps became longer and the voices over the bullhorns carried farther—indeed, could be heard echoing through the mountains—there was no responding sound as they all waited, tensely listening.

Shining their flashlights up over the cliffs, whose innumerable cave openings and smaller openings were spouting water, several people said at the same time that children if they were tired could sleep through all hell breaking loose. That must be the explanation.

Allison, next to Pam Jones, was trying to keep her spirits up, which was not easy, as they all saw those sudden falls of water that

342

would have swept away anything in their path, and the way the whole terrain was being remolded by the force of rushing streams that cut muddy new channels out of the soft tuff. This was the way the tooth comb of gorges had come into existence over the centuries.

Richter kept thinking, Why did they go this far? *Would* they have gone this far? Several miles. Was it feasible? Of course, if the weather had changed for the worse after they set out and they found themselves a long way off as the sky prematurely darkened, they could have lost their way and begun to wander farther afield while thinking they were headed home. Landscapes were very uncertain in rain. They may have become confused. For all the fine highways all around, in between these new constructions you were in primitive lands traversed only by intermittent trails that could disappear completely in a bad downpour. This sort of rain softened the soft earth even more, and turned whole tracts of hillside into mud banks. There was a warning cry, and they all pulled up at the edge of a deep, vertical canyon fall.

"I'd swear that wasn't there before," McClure said, "unless we aren't where we think we are."

Pam Jones pushed a fist into her mouth to stifle a sob. Jones was breathing hard and swaying about. The search party changed directions to avoid the canyon.

Tom Borneschaft and Greg McClure carried rifles. From time to time reports came in of a cougar having been seen in these parts, and of course there were coyotes and bears. Once in a while a fatality occurred involving wild animals. It was a wilderness area, rugged and picturesque, and in the daytime, with the proper precautions, delightful to explore by way of the maintained trails that led to the gorges of the Alamo Canyon, the Stone Lions Shrine, the Painted Cave, the pueblo ruins of San Miguel and Yapashi. But it required only a change of weather or sudden nightfall to turn a wonderful excursion into a nightmare. The ease of the organized trails was liable to deceive. It was sometimes forgotten what savage country lay all around. Greg and Tom were right to have come with rifles, Richter decided.

As they continued there was a growing sense of the futility of this search. Their flashlights barely penetrated the thick walls of rain, and the continuing rumble of thunder swallowed up the shouts through the bullhorns. Richter was made to think of that other storm, when Hofmannsthal and Bamberger and Hepler had been walking in the Hain mountains, and Hepler had set out his belief in chaos and chance. Was it chaos and chance that had snatched away the Jones children, or something more cunning and evil? If so, what? He could see the hopelessness and despair in Pam Jones grow. Perhaps they shouldn't have brought her—but she would have refused to stay behind.

"Why? Why them? Why?" she kept asking.

"They're adventurous kids," Allison said. "They've got a lot of pluck."

"No—it's a punishment. It's a punishment on all of us," she said in an unnatural voice, raised to a shout to make itself heard against the rain.

Allison tried to calm her. And Jones added his own unconvincing, bottle-based optimism. At this point Bamberger came up to them and, shouting into the storm, said, "Amazing how dramatic the rain makes everything, Pam. In the morning when it has cleared up you'll see it's gentle countryside that we all know—and they know. I bet they're fast asleep in one of the caves, and they expect us to realize that that's where they are, and not to worry about them. Take my word for it, Pam."

Richter saw that Bamberger had—for a while, at any rate—succeeded in reassuring Pam a little. He had the ability to make others believe what he said. A man with the gift of believability. How well he covered up his feelings! Only a short time ago he had been praying for a lot of deaths to clear the air, including Jones's death. Now he gave no sign of such a vengeful spirit, was a model of quiet, calm leadership.

It was becoming increasingly obvious by the minute that this search was futile, and Tom Borneschaft proposed that it be called off for now and then resumed in the morning, at first light. By then the rain might have stopped and there would be a much better chance of establishing contact with the children, who would be awake and alert for efforts to find them. But Pam Jones said no; however futile the search, she couldn't return home.

"Supposing they woke up and were afraid and started to cry, and there was nobody . . ."

"A couple of us can stay, and the rest return," Allison said.

"We better have a powwow about it then," Tom suggested. "Out of the rain."

He looked around and pointed to a couple of caves that looked accessible. Greg McClure threw a rope around a tree trunk above one cave, and by means of this the members of the search party hauled themselves up. Once in the dry, they shook off the rain and poured coffee from Thermos flasks and passed around the plastic cups; cigarettes were lit. It was a large enough cave for separate groupings to occur. Allison was with Bamberger and the Joneses, trying to work out a plan.

While this was going on, Richter, in another part of the cave, spoke quietly to Greg McClure.

"You think there's any point hanging on here?"

Slowly Greg shook his head. "Not an awful lot, Captain."

"Are you thinking what I'm thinking?"

"What's that?"

"That we've come too far. They would never have gone as far as this. They'd have turned back long before—if they ever came this way."

"What else could it be?"

"I don't know. But this search is based on the flimsiest of suppositions. We have no evidence that they went out by the hole in the fence, and then set off in this direction. The more I think about it, the more unlikely it sounds. Seeing the weather, they'd have turned back."

"What d'you think could have happened to them, then?"

"An accident?"

"Yuh."

"*Another* accident," Richter added. "It's too many, Greg. It's just getting to be too many, even for an accident-prone community like ours."

345

"I know."

Richter walked to the edge of the cave and looked out. The amount of rain coming down made you think of floods covering the earth and ancient prophecies coming to pass. But it was only rain, he told himself. If the Jones children were safely home, nobody would have felt any threat in the rain, and there wouldn't be that queasy sense of dread in his stomach.

They were joined by Allison, who said, "Pam is going to stay here, and I'm staying with her. We think one man should remain with us and the rest go back."

"How about if I stay?" McClure offered.

"I think that's a good idea," Richter said. "What about Dr. Jones?"

"No," Allison said. "Jonesy should return. He's going to be pretty useless here, and maybe worse. He's got a flask with him. We might end up having to carry him back."

"I'll go and see Mrs. Jones about this," McClure said.

When he had gone, Allison turned to Richter with a sudden shiver. "I told you this place was jinxed, didn't I?"

"Allison, come on. You're a scientist, for God's sake! What kind of—?"

"There is something weird going on, Jerry. First Jake, then Leo. Now the Jones children. And all those accidents. Hans Weissberger choking to death on a piece of meat. . . ."

"What are you thinking?"

Allison turned her face up to his. He saw the lines of strain and fear, which she had been concealing while she was trying to keep Pam Jones cheerful.

"Jerry," she said, "somebody around here is saying, 'If you guys can play at being God, so can I. Let's wipe out a few more Lilliputians.' I think we are all meant to die. I think that was what this person intended to achieve when he loosened the screws on the apparatus."

"You believe that now—you no longer think . . . ?"

"Yes, I believe those screws were loosened, Jerry. I am sure they were. And I'm scared. I'm scared. If it's what I'm thinking—my God! *Children*—it has got to be somebody completely crazy,

346

somebody whose mind has been affected, Jerry. Who doesn't know what he's doing. He's playing at being God."

"How do you see Davidson in that role?"

"Davidson?"

"Yes, Joe—'Red'—Davidson. The lab hand. You know him well, Allison."

"Yes," she agreed.

"You didn't tell me."

"No, I didn't."

"You didn't tell me about your connection with Hepler, either."

"No."

"Why not?"

"I assumed you knew."

"Why assume that?"

"I assumed you people know everything. Don't you?"

"No. I don't."

"It's all in my file. I thought you were just being nice and not mentioning it. I thought you knew, Jerry. Jerry, are you doubting me or something?"

"They're after Davidson. They are pretty sure he's involved in the leak here. There's a lot that points to it. He also could have had access to the lab, if you'd given him a key."

"You think that?"

"It's one of the possibilities, Allison. They've offered Davidson a deal. They've told him it's the electric chair, but that he can save his life by naming the others involved with him."

"What are you saying? You offering *me* a deal to save my life?"

"Allison, if you're in any way involved, any form of passing secrets during wartime is espionage, and there is the death penalty for that, and these people are in a tough mood. . . ."

"You think I am involved in that?"

After a little while he said, "No, I don't. The truth is I don't think you are. But I could be wrong. That's why I'm telling you this."

"So it *is* to save my life?"

"Yes. If you think that's what it is, that's what it is."

"Save your own fucking life, Jerry," she said, turning away.

347

"Is that supposed to be a warning?" he demanded, but she did not answer.

Richter went to Pam Jones. "I think those of us going back should start now. The children could have returned. On their own. You go out looking for somebody and meanwhile they've come home." He could see he hadn't convinced her.

Jones said good-bye to his wife. He was tender with her. More tender than he had been with her for some time, Richter suspected.

"Don't worry too much, love," he told her. "I'm sure they're okay. They're bright kids. They can take care of themselves. You'll see. Nothing to be worried about—it's only rain. Just a bit of water. A bit of wet never hurt anybody. A hot chocolate, tuck them up in bed, and they'll be fine."

There was no sign of the children when the search party got back to the compound.

Dispirited, everybody went to get a couple of hours' sleep. Jones had been drinking steadily from the chrome flask, and Richter felt he should walk him back to his apartment. Jones was reeling a bit. Suddenly he stopped in the road and said, "They're dead—they've been killed. . . ."

"Oh, I don't believe that for a moment," Richter began, and then stopped as he realized that Jones was not just giving expression to a foreboding, that there was something more behind his statement. "Why do you say that?"

"I have that feeling," Jones said. "If they were alive they would have found their way back by now. Tony knows the area. He wouldn't have got lost. The lightning has stopped. Tony has done pathfinding in the Scouts. Only the other day he was explaining to me how you can find north and south by which side the moss grows on tree trunks. . . . He'd have found his way back, Richter. They've had an accident. Or . . ."

"Or what?"

"Or something has happened to them."

"What could have happened to them?"

"Something. . . . Something I can't bring myself to say." His voice broke.

"Are you saying that out of your very natural anxiety, or do you have some specific reason for fearing . . . ?"

Jones took something out of his pocket. He opened his umbrella so the scrap of paper he was holding in his hands would not get too wet.

"This came in the post yesterday," he said, handing the paper to Richter.

In bold print on a sheet of paper torn out of a school exercise book was written:

FOR I THE LORD THY GOD AM A JEALOUS GOD, VISITING THE INIQUITY OF THE FATHERS UPON THE CHILDREN.

In the morning, when the rain had stopped, the valley was a steamy cauldron through which the Rio Grande curved bloodred from the red soil of the mesas to the north.

At noon the second search party returned. They had found no trace of the children. Richter telephoned the Los Alamos County Police and asked for a full-scale search to be mounted, using tracker dogs. He said, "We may be looking for bodies."

Now the sun blazed again with its usual intensity in a sky as clear as glass.

At five to one, Bamberger walked into Richter's office.

"Jones has had an accident," he said.

Bamberger was doing his yoga breathing, an ominous sign.

"What sort of accident—bad?"

"He died fifteen minutes ago. I've come from the hospital."

"What happened?"

Bamberger sat down on a chair, crossed his legs, and lit a cigarette. He stared at the wall for several seconds.

"What happened?" Richter asked again.

"A fire in the lab. Jones was working with a small amount of uranium—he must have struck it in some way . . . must have struck it with some heavy metal object to cause it to ignite. I can only suppose it was a futile act of rage. If you bang uranium like

349

that it can catch fire. His coat sleeve caught. None of which would have been too serious. But then he did something totally inexplicable. Tried to put out the flames with a water extinguisher. Well, he knew, of course, that water was the one thing not to use in the case of a uranium fire. What he did was to turn himself into a pillar of fire."

There was a break in Bamberger's voice despite his strenuously exercised self-control.

"One tragedy after another—it's too much."

"Mrs. Jones . . . ?" Richter asked.

"She's been told. She's had a kind of attack of some sort—she is just sitting at home staring. Allison is with her. I take it there is no news of the children or you would have got on to me."

Richter shook his head. "I've informed the county police. They are mounting a full-scale search. Colonel Delacy has been informed, too, and he's coming down here on the next plane."

"No news is not good," Bamberger said, looking at the wall clock. "After this length of time we are bound to entertain the worst possibilities."

"Yes."

"Jones would have entertained those possibilities, too. That may be the explanation of the accident."

"You suggesting it might have been a kind of suicide?"

"It's the only way I can figure it—using water."

"Couldn't it have been a blind, instinctive reaction—fire: water?"

"No—can't have been a big fire in the first place. He had time to think. He would have to have been in a state of panic and fear bordering on dementia to make a mistake like that."

"Perhaps he was . . . did he say anything before he died?"

"Babbling incoherently. Stuff from the Bible. I didn't know he was religious, but I suppose in one's last moments some of that comes back."

"What was he saying?"

"Oh—about 'the sins of the fathers' . . . and something about the father having eaten the sour grape and the children's teeth are set on edge."

350

"It goes on," Richter said, "that every one shall die for his own iniquity, every man that eateth the sour grape, his teeth shall be set on edge."

"I always took that to refer to syphilis," Bamberger said.

"Jones had received a note. It said the iniquity of the fathers shall be visited upon the children. He showed it to me last night. He took it to mean that his children were dead."

Bamberger looked up, startled.

"And now he's dead as well. 'Every man that eateth the sour grape.' Some self-fulfilling prophecy mechanism, you suppose?"

"Yes. Or somebody switched extinguishers, put the water one where the chemical one should have been."

"We're back to Leo's crazy conspiracy theory."

"Hepler is dead, Jake Dubinski is dead, Jones is dead. The Jones children are missing. There have been a lot of accidents around here. Weissberger choking on a piece of meat . . . three fatalities due to drinking ethylene glycol, some drownings, some accidental shootings, falls, a smudge pot explosion . . . a lot of traffic accidents for a small place like this."

"What are you saying, Captain?"

"We have a lousy safety record, that's what I'm saying. The health of this little community is not good, either—we just have more deaths from all sorts of causes. It can't all be the altitude and being the biggest bunch of crackpots."

"What are you getting at?"

"I don't know, that's the trouble. It's a puzzle, and there are a dozen different ways of putting the pieces together. One of our problems is that people are not being frank. We're not getting all the help. Everybody here is hiding something—so it's difficult to figure what the hell is going on. You, Doctor, for one, have been leading us quite a dance . . . withholding information."

"I believe I have answered all your legitimate questions with complete openness."

"With you deciding what's legitimate and what isn't. Look, Doctor, I told you what was going to happen and it's happening. Hepler's death has caused tremendous reaction in Washington. They are out for somebody's blood. Add to that Jones's death, which they don't even know about yet, and the missing Jones children. . . . Colonel Delacy thinks you are holding back on something. He's flying in. He's very determined. Told me to tell you that if you don't cooperate fully he can destroy you."

There was a silence while Bamberger, with lips pursed and eyes narrowed, looked across the small room. "How do I convince you I've been telling you the truth?" he asked.

After some moments' thought he answered himself. "All right. Tell you what I'll do. I'll prove it to you—I'll take a lie detector. How's that? In fact, I formally request it to clear all this up. Just as soon as Colonel Delacy gets here. Tell him I'm ready."

"Tomorrow morning," Richter said, "eleven A.M., this office. I want to settle this, too, Doctor. When children start disappearing it's time to stop playing chess."

EIGHTEEN

Tom Borneschaft had the cozy manner of a family doctor as he strapped Bamberger into the lie detector. He attached a blood pressure cuff to Bamberger's wrist and wound some corrugated rubber tubing around his chest under the jacket, tightening the tubing until it gently hugged the chest. Lastly, Bamberger was given two electrodes to hold in his left palm, and when Borneschaft had made sure they were correctly placed he fastened them tight with a spring clip. These three pieces of equipment were connected by tubes and cords to a desk console on which three pens hung suspended in readiness above a movable belt of graph paper.

Colonel Delacy and Richter were at the desk console behind Bamberger.

"Explain it to the doctor," Delacy said.

"I'm sure you know how this works," Borneschaft said to Bamberger. "We make no mystery about it. The cuff measures your pulse rate and blood pressure. Device across your chest records your breathing rhythms and the thing you're holding in your hand records changes in perspiration, and all these fluctuations in your vital functioning are traced on a moving drum of graph paper behind you."

"I get the idea," Bamberger said drily.

"In that case, let's go," Colonel Delacy said.

Borneschaft squeezed on a rubber bulb, inflating the wrist cuff until Bamberger could feel the regular pumping of the blood through his veins.

"Blood pressure is just dandy, Doctor," Borneschaft said with a grin. "Nothing to worry about there."

Delacy said, "Let me start out by saying this, for the record. This procedure we are adopting was your idea, Doctor. You wanted to get things cleared up, and we welcome that. We also have got a wire recorder fixed up so that everything said here will be on record and we'll have it to refer back to. Now if you're ready, Doctor, I'm going to let Tom Borneschaft start this off, and I would be glad if you would respond as straightforwardly as possible."

Borneschaft, facing Bamberger, began with some routine questions. Full name. Date of birth. Nationality. Mother's maiden name. Mother's nationality. Father's nationality. Parents living or deceased. Cause of father's death. Date. Educational history. Career history. Date of first marriage. Son's date of birth. Date of second marriage.

As he responded matter-of-factly to these questions, Bamberger could hear the steady scratch, scratch of the pens recording his vital functions on the moving belt of graph paper.

From behind him, Colonel Delacy cut in, "Doctor, you say the date of your first marriage was June third, 1926? Is that correct? The record shows June the sixth."

"No, it was June third."

"Are you sure of that?"

"Yes."

"All right, let it pass." He gave a little laugh. "I think you're wrong, but let it pass."

Asked for the date of his second marriage, Bamberger said, after a moment's hesitation, "July seventh, 1937."

"I'm sorry, Doctor," Delacy cut in again, "but you seem to be getting muddled on your dates. I have it here that you were married July third."

"No—the date of my first marriage was *June* third. The date of my second marriage was July the seventh."

354

"Not the sixth?"

"I don't know where you get six from. What you were saying was that it was July third and I am correcting you and saying it wasn't."

"You're sure of that, Doctor?"

"Of course I am sure."

"What is your son's date of birth again?"

"January first, 1928."

"Well, that's an easy date to remember. No chance of getting that wrong. But I do think you've got the other dates muddled . . . but let it go. It's of no importance."

"If it's of no importance, why are you pursuing it?"

"Oh, I didn't think I was *pursuing* it."

"How's my graph doing with this sensational stuff you've been getting out of me?"

"Oh, pretty wild. . . . Doctor, on the twenty-first of October, 1944, you spent the night with a Miss Jenny Latham at her apartment in Washington, D.C. I believe Miss Latham is somebody you have known for quite a few years. Would you know if she is, or was, a member of the Communist party?"

"It's quite possible. Jenny is quite a Red."

"Are you saying that she *was* a member of the Communist party?"

"No, I'm saying it's possible. Her being a member would not be inconsistent with her expressed views, but I have not seen her Party membership card."

"All right. Knowing that she *may* have been a member of the Communist party, do you think it was correct for the head of the Manhattan Project to secretly visit this lady, spend the night with her, without reporting the incident to the Security Office? At a moment when wartime security regulations called for even chance contacts with people outside the Project to be reported?"

"I was responsible for devising some of those regulations, as you know. I think I felt capable of deciding what I need or need not report."

"You decided you need not report this?"

"That's right."

"You took the attitude that the rules applied to everybody except you?"

"If you want to know, I assumed you knew about it. Since you were tapping my phone and having me followed. I didn't feel I needed to come and say to you, Colonel, 'Gee, Dad, I've been with a woman. . . .'"

"I don't see how you could count on us knowing, since you went to some trouble to throw off the tails."

"Not enough, it seems."

"Isn't it true to say that you thought you were not observed visiting this lady, and you decided to keep it secret?"

"Sexual guilt. A legacy of our common puritan heritage, Colonel."

"Isn't Jenny Latham someone you were passionately involved with over a period of a couple of years or more at a time when both of you were also passionately devoted to the Communist cause?"

"Youth, Colonel. Youth."

"Jenny Latham? Or communism?"

"Both."

"You revisit her—for one night of love—almost twenty years later. Was that youth, too?"

"Some people never grow up—haven't you heard? I was in Washington and I knew she was living in Washington, so I gave her a call and she invited me over for old times' sake."

"You didn't make the call from your hotel room. You made it from a phone booth."

"Puritan ethic again."

"Considering you were the head of this country's most secret war project, did it not seem to you unwise—to say the least—to be making a secret rendezvous with someone who had once been a Communist, and who might still be?"

"Yes, it was foolish. The romantic impulse, you may have heard, makes people act stupid sometimes."

"I don't want to be crude, Doctor, but was it worth it . . . ? I don't mean to sound ungallant to the lady, but she must have been in her forties by then . . . an unmarried woman in her forties, and not what one would consider a hot number."

"There was some sentiment involved—harking back to the old days."

"When you both believed in the Communist cause."

"No, when we had had some damn good times together."

"You saw her just that once?"

"Yes."

"Sentiment didn't extend to a second night of nostalgia?"

"Colonel, I admit it was foolish of me, but it was done on a momentary impulse, at a time when I was under a lot of pressure—a visit to an old flame. Nothing more. I didn't know I was going to stay."

"Yet you took all those precautions. The phone call from an outside phone, trying to throw off the tails. . . . You see, what concerns me is which old flame you were visiting that night. Jenny Latham, or Communism."

"The old flame was Jenny."

The questions stopped while Delacy and Richter studied the graph paper, exchanging comments in an undertone. Tom Borneschaft came to join them at the console desk, and for a while the three conferred in low voices.

The questioning was now taken up by Richter.

"Doctor—the superbomb. For the record, I want to ask you to give us your principal arguments against the development of such a weapon."

"Basically, it is this: I think there is in people an impulse toward the edge, and I don't want to make that edge too final. There is a good reason for doctors having the highest suicide rate—they have the means. I don't want to give the human race the means, which no other form of life has, of being able to extinguish itself. That, incidentally, is not just an abstract concern for unborn generations. I believe that it is an essential part of life here and now to be able to feel oneself part of a continuing process rather than just a flash in the cosmic pan."

357

Richter said, "What would you say about the argument that the superbomb in our hands would be a means of safeguarding that process of life?"

"Captain, I don't know if you've noticed that people are not to be trusted. Well, that goes for us, too. There will come a time, if this weapon exists, when somebody somewhere will find an overwhelmingly sound argument to use it. It will be in defense of God and right and mankind, and justice and liberty, and we shall all die for the noblest of reasons. We may scrape by once, twice, a thousand times, and then comes the thousandth-and-one time, when some fateful star is too close to earth, and off we go after the Pied Piper. . . ."

"There is an argument, isn't there, that the next-best thing to such a destructive weapon not existing is to share its secret? There is a theory that if its secret is possessed by both sides, there will be a balance of terror that will ensure that neither side uses its weapon."

"What I have said is this: I have said we should use our temporary advantage, in the case of the atomic weapon, as a means of getting agreement on international control. At the same time we would all agree not to go on to discover even more powerful weapons."

"Supposing they welshed on the deal," Delacy interjected.

"There would be a strong incentive to both sides not to welsh, because once the moratorium is broken by one side, the other will certainly follow suit, and at that stage of things there would be no knowing who could get there first. If at all. It would be starting a race of which the outcome was totally unpredictable. Therefore it would not be an advantage to either side to start. Conversely, if one side has got the weapon, and the other side has not, there is nothing to be lost, to the side that has not got it, in trying to catch up. I have argued this case again and again, and most people see my argument. Hepler didn't. . . ."

"And he had a lot of influence," Richter said.

"That's right."

"So his no longer being around is helpful to your case, Doctor."

"We have to wait and see about that."

358

"In any case, the theoretical breakthrough was Hepler's, and if he's not here to continue . . ."

"What theoretical breakthrough are you referring to, Captain?"

"I am referring to the fact that when he was dying Hepler said to you words to the effect, 'It's going to work, isn't it?' and then he said, 'Is that why you murdered me . . . ?' "

"Oh, you were listening there, too. I will say, you people sure have got your ear to the ground. Where were you, Captain? Under the bed? In that case, you will also know that Hepler was pretty far gone by then. He always had a taste for sinister theories of one sort or another."

"Are you saying that he was mistaken in thinking it is going to work?"

"Let's say that Leo was always oversure of himself."

"At any rate, *he* thought he had found a way, and he thought that you knew this, and thought so too."

"Even if he was on the right track, a solution is still a long way off."

"And one we can choose to pursue or not?"

"Yes."

"You were, for the reasons you've given, against pursuing such a solution."

"Even if we were to do so, we cannot be sure we will find it. What we *can* be sure of is that once we set out on that path the other side will feel compelled to do likewise. And if a solution is to be found, they may find it before us."

"At present we are ahead. They don't have an atomic bomb yet."

"That's only a matter of time. The basic principle is well known."

"I'm not surprised," Tom Borneschaft interjected sourly. "Considering the rate at which secrets are handed out around here."

"The secret wasn't ours exclusively in the first place, you know," Bamberger said.

"Okay, okay," Delacy cut in. "Now, Doctor, would you agree that you have a guilt complex about your role in the development of the bomb?"

"I wouldn't."

"What would you say it was when people talk about having blood on their hands?"

"Might be a simple statement of fact."

Richter said, "You have also spoken of a readiness to be shot, should you be found guilty of a war crime."

"What big ears you've got, Captain. Yes, I think I did say that once. In an emotional moment."

"It is no longer true?" Richter asked.

"I would defend myself against such a charge, while acknowledging that there was a case to be made out against me. If found guilty, I would accept the verdict."

"And let yourself be put against a wall and shot?"

Bamberger laughed. "At that stage, one does not usually have any say in the matter."

Richter persisted. "If you say that you would, in principle, be willing to accept such a verdict and such a sentence, might you be ready, in principle, to impose such a sentence on others?"

"I could see that you were getting to that. It's a big jump. I don't know that I would set myself up as a war crimes tribunal. . . ."

"How about an avenging angel?"

"Not my personality type, Captain."

"Doctor, do you have a key to the Y-3 canyon lab?" Delacy asked.

"There is one in the controller's office."

"I mean a second key, one of your own."

Bamberger was silent for a moment; they all heard the pens moving rapidly across the graph paper.

"Yes, I have a key."

"Could we know why?"

"I found it necessary to visit the laboratory at times, without everybody knowing about it, in order to keep a check on what was being done. Apart from the need to satisfy myself that what they were doing was safe."

"You were a little too easily satisfied on that score, weren't you?" Delacy said.

"I could not foresee all the weird forms that Hepler's flirtations with death would take. But apart from that aspect, I also was going there to see how far he was getting. I went over his calculations. It was preferable to do that calmly and quietly, away from his tendentious personality. On the most practical level, too, it was my job to be fully knowledgeable about work in progress. I am not supposed to waste the taxpayers' money on futile projects."

"How often did you go there?"

"Maybe half a dozen times."

"Did you go there the day of the accident? After your row with Hepler over lunch—when you threw the ketchup at him?"

"No, I didn't go that day. I had made up my mind, by then, that I was going to stop the experiments—for practical reasons, because I didn't think they would be fruitful and were a waste of resources; for safety reasons, because I thought them dangerous; and for moral reasons, because I did not think we should be working on that project for all the reasons I have already stated."

"Of course, you could have gone there without anyone knowing. Since you had a second key. And there is that half hour between two and two thirty that is not accounted for."

"It's my normal practice to take a walk after lunch."

"You could have walked out to the canyon lab, or driven there . . . you agree?"

"I agree it's possible. I didn't know there was going to be an accident and that I might need an alibi, or I would have thought of providing myself with one. Actually, I did not have the key with me that day. It was at my house. In my desk."

"In a drawer?"

"Yes."

"Locked?"

"Yes."

"But of course, as we now know, Mrs. Bamberger sometimes went to your desk drawer, so she must have known where the key was."

"So you say."

"She could have got the key and gone to the lab."

"So could Santa Claus, if he'd come down the chimney at that moment."

"Let's be serious about this, Dr. Bamberger," Delacy said. "Your wife could have gone to the canyon lab."

"It is notoriously difficult to prove a negative. Therefore, yes, she could have. . . . For what earthly reasons . . ."

"People set fire to old people's homes because they don't like old people . . . people who do these things do not always have motives that seem adequate to the rest of us," Tom Borneschaft said.

"Okay, I'm not going to fight with you about that."

"Let's summarize where we have got so far," Delacy said. "One: You had your own key to the canyon lab and you had some time that is not accounted for, between two and two thirty. You had just had a furious row with Hepler, ending with you throwing ketchup all over him. As a result he went off to change his pants, which meant you could be reasonably sure of getting to the lab ahead of him. Two: This was something you had done at least half a dozen times before . . . you went there all alone to check up. So you could have gone out there that day. Right, you had the opportunity. You also had the motive. You are a man of principle, and you considered what Hepler was doing a crime against life. . . . Add to that, he was a man who was having an affair with your wife. Your mood was uncontrolled, uncharacteristically uncontrolled. Throwing ketchup at people is not your usual style. You go out to the canyon lab—maybe just for another final check, maybe with no definite plan. Maybe because out of a sense of high principle you are sharing this secret with our former allies, the Soviet Union, and so you have to keep up with what progress has been made. There, before you, is this evil brainchild of the man you hate most. At one stroke you can destroy it and him, and others, too, who had lent themselves to the war crime. . . ."

"You make out such a good case for it, Colonel, I am almost ashamed I didn't do it."

"You didn't?"

"Colonel, you leave out of consideration that Allison was there, of whom I am, as you must know, very fond, and Hofmannsthal," who is more than a second father to me, he's a little like God to me. . . ."

"People do destroy their God," Richter said. "You might have been ready to sacrifice us all, yourself included . . . for your beliefs. Perhaps you thought this whole place, and all the people who had a part in what it brought about, deserved to go up. . . . 'I am become Death, the destroyer of worlds.' It's your own quotation from the *Bhagavad-Gita*."

"Pretty crazy behavior you are postulating. And Jones, too? And the Jones children—are you postulating I may have been responsible for that as well? Are you suggesting I am some kind of madman?"

"Perhaps the Jones accident was a tragic outcome of all the other things. Maybe the children *have* had an accident. Or perhaps somebody has got a list and they are ticking off names: Dubinski, Hepler, Jones. . . . Who's going to be next to pay for the sins of the father, the father of the bomb? Doctor, why did you have a Bible in your locked drawer with a marker on which were notations of half a dozen biblical quotations?"

"Because, Captain, I had been getting those chapter and verse numbers in the post. I looked them up to see what somebody was saying to me."

"Why didn't you report this?"

"I didn't take it that seriously. I was getting lots of hate mail, and there was nothing new to me about being condemned from the pulpit. I presumed this was some religious nut. . . . In the light of Jones receiving those notes, too, and Hepler, of course I see I should have taken them more seriously, but I didn't."

Colonel Delacy resumed the questioning.

"Dr. Bamberger, in August 1943 you came into my office and said there was a man in the laboratory who would bear watching, a Technical Sergeant Davidson, who worked in E Building under Professor Kistiakowsky, and you thought asked too many questions."

"Yes."

"I had a lot of trouble getting you to be more explicit as to why you wanted us to watch Davidson, but finally the story came out that somebody—whom you refused to name at that time—had spoken to you in your kitchen one evening when you were getting ice, saying that Davidson had approached him on the subject of, quote, 'sharing scientific information with the Russians.' Although, according to you, you straightaway told this someone that such a thing sounded terribly wrong to you, you didn't report the conversation to us for seven months, on the grounds that it had not seemed important until later, when you noticed that Davidson kept asking a lot of questions. Now your wife's diary casts a very different light on this event. According to the diary, you had earlier expressed yourself as being quite sympathetic to the idea of sharing our secrets with the Russians. . . ."

"I said I would perhaps support a policy decision to share scientific information with our allies. But I certainly was not in favor of treason or espionage."

"Seems," Colonel Delacy said, "you were not the only one sympathetic to such an idea. It had been widely discussed among you, and others had also considered it desirable."

"It was discussed in theory, as many things were. That didn't mean anything. . . . If everything we theorized about . . ."

"Considering that there was some sympathy for such an idea, even if only in theory, it is amazing that you could be so sure Davidson's approach had obtained no results. This was the reason you gave for not reporting the matter for seven months—you thought it was so unimportant."

"With hindsight, I agree, I should have reported it sooner."

"It took a further four months, four months of continuous pressure from me, culminating in a direct order to you from General Brown, before you would tell us the name of the person who had approached you in your kitchen—that it was Jake Dubinski. You said you didn't want to get somebody involved who was 'wholly innocent' and had merely been reporting a conversation to you . . . not trying to recruit you. That was what you said."

"Because I knew you'd tear him apart. He had a lot of Communist connections in his background, and though I was a hundred percent sure of his loyalty, I was not so sure that he had never been indiscreet in his past associations, and he was a good friend, and I did not fancy throwing him to the wolves. About which I was right, as it turned out. Once you got your teeth in you didn't let go, and even though you couldn't find anything against him you harassed him so much and so long that he finally made the slip-up that cost him his life."

"Of course, if you had reported the conversation as soon as it happened, and if you had not then refused to give his name, maybe the whole thing would not have looked so suspicious, and we would have been satisfied with a more perfunctory check."

"Maybe. But at the time I took it upon myself, as controller, to decide that there was nothing I needed to report to you. When I changed my mind, I reported to you straightaway."

"You often 'take it upon yourself' to do this, or not do that?"

"That's what being a leader is about—may sound arrogant to you, Colonel, but that is the way I work, and I did get results, you remember."

"For example, you have taken it upon yourself to employ people that we consider questionable."

"I thought they were good people, and I needed them."

"How would you now evaluate your taking it upon yourself not to report the 'kitchen conversation' for seven months and the identity of the intermediary for a further four months?"

"The former was a mistake on my part. I should have reported it straightaway. As for the latter, I regret profoundly ever having given you Jake Dubinski's name—he might be alive now. I know for a fact that he was wholly and completely innocent in that whole business."

"Davidson, of course, is not innocent. Not at all innocent. We are agreed there, are we not? The way it finally came out, Davidson had mentioned to Dubinski knowing somebody in the Soviet legation who knew all about microfilm and that sort of thing and through whom this information about the atomic bomb could be channeled. Right?"

"Yes."

"Now, however we interpret Dubinski mentioning that to you in your kitchen, there is no question that *Davidson* was *not* wholly innocent and was *not* theorizing. *He* was quite specifically seeking

365

to get people like yourself to hand over secrets that would be put on microfilm and conveyed to the Soviet Union. That was his objective, whether he succeeded or not."

"That would seem to have been his objective; that was why I came to you and said he would bear watching."

"Seven months after the event. And let us bear in mind that by this time we had gotten on to Davidson of our own accord, which you must have realized. Okay. Now for various reasons, partly because we never had any specific evidence of his involvement in espionage acts, and partly because we wanted to watch him, we allowed Davidson to continue here—of course kept away, after that date, from anything secret. But you were left in no doubt that he was a very questionable person, almost certainly a Soviet spy. You agree?"

"Yes."

"Nevertheless, Doctor, you have been having secret meetings with Davidson, haven't you?"

"I don't think so."

"Come now. Don't deny it. We have the evidence."

Bamberger laughed. "I wouldn't call running into somebody in the aisle at Madison Square Garden a secret meeting, Colonel. That is the only recent encounter I have had with Davidson that I can think of. I think it lasted about thirty seconds."

"Two minutes and thirty seconds. What did you talk about in that time?"

"We discussed Nakuma's chances of beating the Russian Sphinx."

"I never knew you were such a wrestling fan."

"It's a new interest of mine . . . lets off some tension. I kind of got to like it."

"Doctor, Davidson has been questioned. We've offered him a deal. We said we'd get him off the death penalty if he'd talk. He's talked. He's told us everything. Now why don't you tell it from your side?"

"Colonel, I am familiar with that technique—two people being questioned, you tell each that the other has confessed . . . therefore you might as well come clean, help save yourself. Et cetera.

However, that only works when you have got two guilty parties. In this case you don't, so it doesn't work."

"Who was the person who wrote to you, 'Don't get in touch with me, I will join you on your walk'?"

"My, my. You do creep around, don't you? Another indiscretion of mine . . . a lady with a husband, a foolish little flirtation, but she took it rather more seriously than I meant her to."

"Her name?"

"I am not going to give you her name, Colonel."

Colonel Delacy was silent, studying the movements of the pens over the graph paper.

"All right," he said at last, "I won't press you about that, at this moment." Again he was silent for some seconds, following the movements of the pens. "I want to turn to something you said before, Doctor. You said something like, 'You think I'm a madman?' This was said, you will recall, apropos the possibility that you could have gone to the Y-3 canyon lab and initiated a malfunction that might have killed your colleagues—and a whole lot of other people here. Now the underlying meaning of that remark—'You think I'm a madman?'—was to deride the possibility that a man of your evident rationality could be so insane as to commit mass murder, right? You're with me, Doctor?"

"I'm with you, Colonel, but I don't know where you're going."

"That will emerge in due course. Just bear with me, please."

"I'll try."

Colonel Delacy allowed another silence to ensue, during which he studied the movement of the pens over the graph paper and consulted in mumbled undertones with his two colleagues. He opened his briefcase and withdrew from a thin folder two sheets of paper covered with doublespaced typewriting.

"I have here," he said, "a copy of a letter you wrote, in December 1944, to your former psychiatrist, Dr. Arnold Hillier."

"Can I ask you how you got this letter, Colonel?"

"I think that's irrelevant."

"I don't think it's irrelevant. One's communications with one's medical and spiritual advisers are supposed to be protected from the agents of government."

367

"Be that as it may . . ."

"Just answer one question for me, Colonel. . . ."

"You are here to answer the questions, Doctor."

"I insist on this . . . if you want to go on."

"Yes, what is your question?"

"Did this letter come into your possession with Dr. Hillier's knowledge?"

Colonel Delacy was studying the graph paper before replying.

"In case you can't tell from my graph," Bamberger said, "I'm good and angry, and nervous about your answer. All right?"

"It was not with Dr. Hillier's knowledge," Colonel Delacy said.

"You will now be able to see," Bamberger said, "that I am relieved, if not one hundred percent convinced you are telling me the truth. But let's go on, since you've decided to embark on this unseemly course."

"I'm going to read to you some relevant parts of the letter. The original is in your handwriting, so I take it you won't dispute the authenticity of the material."

"That remains to be seen."

Colonel Delacy mumbled through some preliminary remarks and then read out in a clear voice:

" '. . . I suppose you would put these things in the category of auditory hallucinations, these alarming sounds in my head, which are like warning bells, though I ought to tell you we have a somewhat erratic prowler alarm system that is always going off for no reason, so maybe it's no more than a kind of phantom alarm in my brain. You know how people can be woken by the ringing of the alarm clock before it has rung. I have a tendency to that.

" 'But you know I would not be writing to you and breaking our 1936 concordat that I soldier on alone if this were not something more serious than alarm clocks in the head, if I did not feel in profound need of help. The truth is I fear I may be in the course of committing a great crime, perhaps the greatest crime that any man has ever committed. I cannot tell you about it, which is part of the problem. I cannot discuss it with anyone outside. That is usually the case when one is committing a crime.

" 'You know my stability has always been a fragile thing, a mat-

368

ter of the most delicate weights and counterweights, and that what appears to the rest of the world as my great self-possession is the outcome of a perpetual balancing act, at which, after all these years, I have acquired enough expertise to make people think I walk on solid ground. I can only tell you that I am very fearful at the moment of losing my balance. All the tricks of the trade gleaned from four years in your care, plus all my yoga training, are barely enough to keep me on a level course. It is touch and go—but then it *always* is, as you once said.

" 'Only this time, more so!

" 'To tell you the truth, I fear I may be about to blow up the world. I am aware that such a fear is symptomatic of dementia praecox, and that I have always had some schizophrenic tendencies. And, yes, I fear for my sanity when I hear the bells going off in my head, and I try to keep calm. The truth, is, I also fear, in another part of myself—yes, I am very split, of course—that it is *not hearing the bells* which is the insanity, and that everybody else here is insane. I know; another symptom of dementia praecox. I have applied to my fears the appropriate test to determine if they are delusional. Are the fears shared by others? The answer is the others seem to me unafraid. But then so do I to them. I cannot help thinking we may have contrived a delusional system for ourselves which, by its nature, is of course self-proving.

" 'There are great pressures on me. These pressures push me toward a great catastrophe. But the alternative is catastrophe too. I cannot stand far enough back to see which of the alternative catastrophes is the greater. Sometimes I think that the course I am embarked on is the greater catastrophe by far, and yet I am helpless to stop it . . . there is a momentum that I cannot halt.

" 'I can only tell you that my mind feels as if it has been split a thousand ways. I feel I am in fragments, that I am smashed to bits—yes, I know, another symptom—and in this smashed condition, I feel murderous. I am sometimes in a state of watching myself from a great distance, as if I were God dispersing souls, with thousands of millions of souls at my disposal, and I wonder why, with all those souls, I have given myself the one I am stuck with. The Bamberger soul seems inadequate: I want one that is stronger, finer, purer. I detest the soul I have been given. I am aghast. I am aghast about everything I have done in my life. I am aghast about Science, which in the past I felt I needed more than friends but which now appears to have betrayed me. This may sound utterly mad to you but I have sometimes thought that Science is the greatest delusional system of all, self-proving and self-deceiving in the same stroke. Science, which I loved, it now seems to me has no light to throw on the fundamental issue of the human equation, which remains essentially irrational and illogical, and, contrary to the definition of a scientific test, unrepeatable.

" 'You can see that I am in deep trouble and that I need help.' "

Colonel Delacy had reached the end. He busied himself studying the graph of Bamberger's reactions during the reading of the letter. Bamberger did not speak.

"Well, you see, Doctor, that would seem to be the tip of the iceberg, so to speak, and given that, can we entirely exclude the possibility of your having acted in some irrational way?"

"It is obvious, Colonel," Bamberger said, "that you have never undergone psychoanalysis, or you would know that discussion of delusions, hallucinations, murderous feelings, and sensations of being split are the commonplace argot of the couch. They refer to the inner world, not to external reality."

"Is not the one sometimes transferred to the other?"

"That's called acting out, and greatly frowned upon."

"Would you say it never happens?"

"Oh, mad people act out . . . yes."

"Exactly, Doctor."

Bamberger laughed.

There was a further consultation behind his back. He could see Tom Borneschaft exchange eye signals with the others. The steel pen nibs continued to squeak and scratch in their regular rhythms.

"All right, Dr. Bamberger, we can wind it up there," Borneschaft said. "Thank you, sir. Let's get you out of this contraption." He went to the chair and proceeded to detach the handpiece and deflate the wrist cuff; Bamberger felt the pressure ease on his wrist, and he lost awareness of his pulse. He could hear low, monosyllabic exchanges between Delacy and Richter without being able to catch the words. He heard the rustle of the graph paper being examined. Borneschaft was unfastening the chest band, easing the rubber tubing. Bamberger took a deep breath and let it out slowly, steadily.

"Well, how'd I do?" he asked Richter, who had come round to the front, holding wads of graph paper.

"Very well," Richter said. "Very well indeed." He saw the exultant flash in Bamberger's eyes, and let the graph paper unfold until it reached to the floor. Shaking his head, he followed the gentle rise and fall of the pens' markings, unfolding more and more of the graph paper, until it formed a substantial heap at his feet.

"You did very well indeed," he said again thoughtfully, and then looked straight into Bamberger's eyes. "Much too well, in fact."

"What the hell is that supposed to mean?" Bamberger snapped back.

"You haven't been telling us the truth, Doctor," Richter said. "That's what it means."

"You don't trust your own damned machine?"

"I never saw such an impressive demonstration of yoga technique. The way you controlled your heartbeat and blood pressure—it's really impressive. The trouble is it shows up. You controlled all your reactions. Even when we said about you getting your marriage dates wrong—you hadn't, of course—you didn't have a flicker of annoyance. That's unnatural. Even when we were saying about Jenny Latham not being a very attractive woman, there wasn't any reaction from you. You are too gallant not to have resented a gratuitous insult to a woman who, quite recently, you found attractive enough to go to bed with. But you didn't react at all. You had yourself pretty much under control—until right at the end. When you thought you were unhooked, and I said you'd done very well. Tom loosened the chest band and detached the handpiece, and he loosened the wrist cuff a little, but it was still functioning, Doctor. And when I said you had done okay, that's when the pens practically went off the paper. You'd beaten the machine. Triumph. Up went your pulse rate, up went your blood pressure. Proves that all your reactions up till then had been faked. So now let's start all over again without any of these contraptions, and let's have the truth this time. If you wouldn't mind, Doctor."

━━━━

Richter said, "Let's go back to the 'kitchen conversation,' when you learned that Davidson had a contact in the Soviet legation who was an expert on microfilm 'and that sort of thing,' and that he, Davidson, was trying to get people from here in the research establishment to pass on secret information. Why didn't you go straight to the Security Office then, instead of waiting seven months?"

"Because I was an idiot."

"Yes? Could you elaborate on that, please?"

"Trying to retrace a mistaken course of action in order to explain how you got started on it is not easy."

"Will you try, please?"

Bamberger got up. There was no necessity for him to remain seated in the chair now that all the wiring had been taken off him, and he was not by nature someone who could easily stay still. He went to the window and pushed down a slat of the green Venetian blinds and looked out. The afternoon sunlight was strong. There was some wind, and it blew down on the surface of the pond, breaking up the solid sunlight into minute, rippling light points. Each time the wind struck, the water glittered, and then immediately after became mat again. Bamberger watched this happen three times, smiling.

"Well, Dr. Bamberger?" Richter prompted. "Will you try, please."

"The reason I did not report Davidson straightaway was because I naturally anticipated the question how did I know about Davidson's overtures, and that meant, since I had not been directly approached by him myself, I would be asked to give the name of the intermediary."

"Which you didn't want to do—because he was a close friend of yours and you thought you might get him into trouble?"

372

"Yes."

"And that outweighed all other considerations?"

"Well, not entirely." Bamberger turned around to face Richter. "Because, you see, in the end—belatedly, I admit—I did go to Security and tell about Davidson and the approach. You have to understand, in retrospect it would seem he clearly was trying to get people to spy, but at the time the tone of the way it was presented was more like a piece of bravado—bucking Security. A way of asserting the independence of science from laws and restrictions. And since I made it clear I was having nothing to do with anything like that, and I assumed others had done the same, I was able to persuade myself that the entire episode was a nonevent."

"What changed your mind about that?"

"Well, discovering that there really was a leak at Los Alamos, that stuff was getting out. And when I asked around, what I heard about Davidson's always asking questions about how everything worked—that seemed to me very disquieting."

"So then you came forward and told your story. But it was still only half the story. You still were making out that the 'kitchen conversation' was wholly innocent and for that reason you refused to give the name of the intermediary. Finally, you did. Four months later, in response to General Brown's order, you gave Dubinski's name. Army Intelligence and the FBI went over him with a fine-tooth comb and found nothing. They questioned him repeatedly and not a thing emerged. His phone was tapped. His past was probed, and though a lot of parlor pinks and fellow travelers were dug out of the woodwork, no underground connections were found—no murky secrets at all. Dr. Dubinski, as you had insisted, was in the clear. What I cannot understand," Richter went on, "is why, if you knew that, you waited so long to give his name—thereby making it look as though you had been protecting somebody who had something to hide. Your action made it much, much worse for your friend, instead of helping him."

"As I say, I was an idiot. . . ."

"That doesn't explain it sufficiently, to say that. What was your rationale?"

"My rationale was, as you say, to protect someone. I gave you

373

Jake's name, knowing that you would turn up nothing . . . so I thought he wouldn't be too badly harmed. He was sort of a pinko, he was kind of in favor of sharing secrets with the Russians—none of that was any secret—and since I was sure he was not a spy, I didn't see what harm it could do him to be investigated in depth. . . . I underestimated your people's techniques of harassment and intimidation."

"What you have just said is precisely the argument for giving his name straightaway, instead of—"

"Yes, I know. But the point is, I only thought of it later."

"Thought of what later?"

"Giving you Jake's name."

"I cannot see what the thought processes were that took that length of time."

"Figuring out that my saying it was Jake wouldn't harm him— about which I turned out to be wrong—and that it would get me off the hook, about which I was also wrong, as it turns out."

"I still don't see why you needed eleven months to get to the point of giving Jake Dubinski's name."

Colonel Delacy's tycoon's cigar had gone out; the dead butt was stuck wetly in the corner of his mouth. There was a twitchiness about his eyebrows. Richter could see he was holding himself back. Bamberger rubbed his face and shook his head several times, smiling wryly.

"You can't see, you can't see what took me so long, Richter? You're not as intuitive as usual. What took me so long was my hesitation about embarking upon a course of deception."

Colonel Delacy took the dead cigar-end out of his mouth and tossed it on the floor. He nodded to Richter to continue.

"Tell us about this deception, Doctor."

He seemed to be hesitating again. Again he turned to look out of the window.

"I had never noticed it before," he said, "the way gusts of wind make the pond glitter. Beautiful effect . . ."

"The deception," Richter said.

"Ah, yes. How slow you are today, Richter."

"I am waiting for you to explain—I hope it's not going to take eleven months this time. Are you saying to us that the statement you finally gave to Colonel Delacy was the deception?"

"Bright of you to tumble to it, Richter."

"It was a false statement?"

"In one respect only."

"What was that one respect?"

"About the so-called 'kitchen conversation'—I didn't give Colonel Delacy the right name."

"It was not Jake Dubinski?"

"No, it wasn't."

"Will you tell us now who it was?"

There was a silence. The three security men exchanged looks. Richter felt his heart beating painfully and the apprehension well up through his chest and fill his throat.

"It was Professor Hofmannsthal," Bamberger said.

The only thing Richter felt at first was relief that it was not Allison. Then the ramifications of what Bamberger had said became clearer.

"So it is Hofmannsthal you've been protecting?"

"Yes."

"Because you felt that, unlike Dubinski, Hofmannsthal might not bear deep investigation—is that it?"

"No. Let me make something clear. I realize that my having invented a cock-and-bull story about Jake is not conducive to your putting a lot of trust in my truthfulness, but this is the truth now. There was nothing underhanded about Hofmannsthal's approach to me. It was not a proposal that I should engage in espionage. He was simply—and quite correctly—reporting to me a conversation with Davidson that he thought I should know about."

"In that case, why did you so determinedly withhold his name, and in the end give somebody else's name?"

"Because, Richter, a shadow of doubt passed across my mind."

"A shadow of doubt about your God . . . Hofmannsthal?"

"That's right."

"Tell us about this shadow of doubt, Doctor."

He gave a sigh and lit a cigarette.

375

"As you have put it, Richter, Hofmannsthal was a kind of God to me. . . ."

Colonel Delacy cut in. "Dr. Bamberger, just to make this all official, I want to say that the recorder is on and that a transcript will be made of what you say, and that you will be asked to sign your statement. Is that acceptable?"

Bamberger nodded.

"All right, then. Please go ahead, Doctor."

"The way Hofmannsthal put it to me was like this," Bamberger said, speaking slowly and carefully. "He said that one had to be prepared, as an individual, to take action oneself—not to leave it to governments. He said that governments were impelled by forces acting on them, and sometimes these forces were both irresistible and catastrophic, and then it required some action by an individual with the courage and vision to arrest the calamitous onrush. He then said how dangerous it was going to be if we alone had the atomic bomb—he seemed to be quite sure that the Germans were nowhere near having such a weapon. 'It will drive America mad if it has such power,' he said. Then he said, 'There were a dozen of us who could have stopped this thing from coming into existence; we didn't—history will say, "Why did these men allow such a thing to be brought into existence?" How will we answer?'

"All this was very theoretical. We had all debated in this way countless times. Nearly everyone here had misgivings, but we overcame them, believing that what we were doing was in the end necessary. At this stage, Hofmannsthal, correctly sensing my sympathy with his general theme, said I ought to know that there was a man in Los Alamos, Davidson, who was in touch with the Soviet legation, and that he was trying to get people here to take the step of sharing their information, which was the next best thing . . . et cetera. It was still being said on the level of debate, and I said, 'That sounds terribly wrong to me,' et cetera. He at once said, 'I agree, I told Davidson he would draw a blank with you and everybody else here. I sent him packing.'

"Whether it was wishful thinking on my part, or whatever, I at first truly did not attach too much importance to that conversation. You must understand, we were used to talking of very large concepts—the end of the universe—the existence or otherwise of moral laws—and so it was no big deal to *discuss* the sharing of secrets with an ally, whatever the strict legal aspects of that were.

"For a while I tried putting the conversation out of my mind. But there was a nagging doubt that persisted. It was a matter of interpreting a tone of voice—maybe we had gotten our signals crossed in some way, but I could not put out of my mind the thought that Hofmannsthal may have been trying to get me to join him in some idealistic gesture.

"I tried a few times to draw him out again on the same topic, but each time he said I had been absolutely right, one must not do things by the back door. However commendable the objective, one was not entitled to employ dubious and dishonest means. It was this statement of his that alarmed me most, because it ran counter to something he had once said to me. For the first time I had a feeling with the old man that maybe he was lying.

"What I was thinking about was something that had happened early in the war, in 1941. It was a time when he was still in good standing with the Nazis, and had gone to attend a scientific congress in Bâle, and there I met him. After a morning's scientific discussion, we walked around and talked, and I said to him that a lot of his friends around the world were deeply disturbed by the fact that he had not made a public break with the Nazis. His silence appeared to give support to them.

"I remember clearly his words to me: 'Ah, of course,' he said, 'you would wish me to speak out against all these monstrous things that are happening. But do you suppose that if I did, it would take them long to silence one voice like mine?'

"Then he went on to say, 'David, you must surely know that I would soon disappear. If not under the ground, then into some ignominious banishment, or some jail or camp, from which my voice would reach no one. It is naive heroics to suppose that one individual can pit himself openly against the great power of the tyrannical state. The only weapon that the individual has against the tyrannical state is—secrecy and cunning, David.' He gave me a wink, a most extraordinary thing in that austere face. It was like the pope winking and saying, 'You don't have to tell the truth.'

377

Then he added to me, 'Don't worry, David, our cause is the same.'

"All right—to get back to my thought process in 1943. It occurred to me that if he could use secrecy and cunning in retarding the development of the German atom bomb—which he and Heisenberg undoubtedly had done, giving us a lead that we might not otherwise have had—if he had been willing to act in this way against his own country, would he hesitate to follow the dictates of his conscience now, if his conscience told him that he had stopped one country from coming into possession of such monstrous power only to hand it over to another? Even if he thought Germany totally wrong, he did not therefore believe that America was totally right. He had gone to some lengths in risking his life in order to prevent Germany from having possession of the bomb; it seemed to me not inconceivable that he might now be using secrecy and cunning against another 'monstrous state.'

"These were the thoughts that went repeatedly through my mind. I had no proof . . . I did not feel justified, on the basis of my vague suspicion, in going to you and delivering Hofmannsthal to your tender mercies. I was probably wrong in that, but there you are. I tried to withhold his name as long as I could, and when I couldn't any longer I gave you Jake's name, to put you off the trail, thinking that since Jake was innocent no one would be harmed.

"Meanwhile I began to conduct my own investigation in my own way. You'll say I took it upon myself. Sure I did: I had the arrogance to believe I could get to the bottom of this whole business better than you people, and cause less harm to the innocent. I began to make discreet inquiries. As you have found out, I have excellent Communist party connections. . . . I proceeded to make use of them. I called up Jenny Latham when I was in Washington, I spent the night with her, and I talked to her about my disillusionment with governments, all governments. . . . I knew what hints to drop to make myself seem approachable. And as I had anticipated, I was approached. 'Don't contact me, I will join you on your walk. . . .' The message you intercepted. I needed to find out if Hofmannsthal was in with them in fact as well as in

378

spirit. If he was, of course he would have to be stopped. I had been instrumental in getting him accepted for the Project, had vouched for him, staked my standing and career on his loyalty and trustworthiness. If he had betrayed us, I felt responsible, and I wanted to find out.

"My plan was to let them think that I might be available, too. My admiration for Hofmannsthal was well known. I had various meetings with various people at which I equivocated and hesitated on the edge. . . . I made it seem that I would need only one little extra inducement to throw in my lot with them, and I made it clear that if Hofmannsthal was with them it would be for me a decisive factor. For their part, they hinted too, without providing proof, but I did not respond to the hints.

"Finally I think I was making clear to them that they would have to play their trump card to get me—namely, Hofmannsthal. The meeting with Davidson in New York was for the purpose of his delivering that trump card. Of course, I had to compromise myself in order to make it look genuine to them that I was ready to come over. And I *was* compromising myself with these secret meetings—and with other things that you people were picking up on. I knew the risk, but I felt I was nearly there. The night of the wrestling match, I had been promised something that I would consider an overwhelming argument. Unfortunately, Davidson cottoned to his being followed, and sheered off. So I am exactly where I was before. I know nothing for certain. The whole thing could be a figment of my imagination. . . ."

FIVE

THE THREAD OF
UNREASON

NINETEEN

Next day, round-the-clock surveillance of Hofmannsthal began. Like other scientists on the hill, he had previously been subjected to routine checks of various sorts. His movements, his mail, and his telephone calls had been monitored from time to time. But never on a continuous basis as now. Now everything he did was put under a magnifying glass.

The first days of this intensive surveillance served to confirm his known life-style. During the week he rose each morning with the work siren at seven and quickly showered and dressed and shaved—using an old-fashioned cutthroat razor. He prepared a light breakfast for himself (coffee and toast) and made sandwiches for his lunch and filled his Thermos with coffee. Then he slipped on bicycle clips, put his sandwiches, wrapped in wax paper, into his saddlebag, and set off on his cycle for work, arriving at the Y-3 building at eight sharp. On the third day of intensive surveillance he also took with him a white linen bag, and during the lunch hour he went with it to the Peewee PX and handed it in at the laundry distribution station. At the same time he collected a package of developed film from the film-developing collection point, and bought cigarettes. Later, while Hofmannsthal was at a long meeting, these photographs were removed from his desk and taken to Richter in the Security Office. They were all nature studies. Richter was able to identify most of the plants, and made a list. Apache plume, white puccoon, wild rose, rose locust, Arizona valerian, white prairie clover, narrowleaf sunflower, red-flowered prickly pear, firewheel, kinnikinnick, red columbine, mock orange, thimbleberry, white clematis, and a beautiful little wild orchid that he was fairly sure was a fairy slipper. He envied Hofmannsthal that find.

The list of plant names was sent to Albuquerque for cryptanalysis, and the photos returned to Hofmannsthal's room before he had come back from his meeting.

The surveillance reports showed that at the end of work Hofmannsthal usually went directly home, showered, changed into another suit, and then went to dinner. He dined early, around six-thirty, usually in the handsome main dining room of the lodge, where he had a table reserved for him left of the big stone fireplace. Colleagues would say hello to him but did not stop to chat. They knew he liked to be left to himself. His grave and distant demeanor was not encouraging of social contact. During his meal—that is, between courses—he read the newspapers, a Swiss paper in German that he received by post, and a local paper, the Santa Fe *New Mexican*, and sometimes a scientific journal. He was usually finished eating and back at his apartment before half past seven.

There he normally spent a couple of hours dealing with his considerable correspondence. While he had little personal contact with people on the hill, lived almost like a hermit, he kept in touch by letter with many of the outstanding figures of the day. He was in correspondence with Einstein, with Werner Heisenberg, Otto Hahn, Wolfgang Pauli, Linus Pauling, Bernard Shaw, Martin Heidegger, Max Born, Max Planck, the Joliot-Curies, Frédéric and Irène, Bertrand Russell, Julian Huxley, Albert Schweitzer, Konrad Adenauer, and others. He wrote on airmail paper in a small, neat hand, sitting at a small table by the window. Night after night he could be seen sitting there writing.

These letters to Einstein and others were carefully tested for invisible ink writing, and their contents analyzed for possible coded messages, but nothing was found.

His apartment was searched while he was at work. It contained little except for the standard-issue government furniture and a few examples of local arts and crafts, rather less than were to be found in other apartments on the hill. He had two Yei masks of deer buckskin of the war gods Born-of-Water and Monster-Slayer. He had a polychrome wood Our Lady of the Seven Sorrows, and one or two interesting Indian paintings. Little else in the way of decoration. On the strip wood floor there were Altillo and Chimayo blankets. There was also, sitting on his bookshelves, a grotesque black ogre kachina doll.

A meticulous search produced nothing.

During the week Hofmannsthal kept to his routine. After his letter writing he read or listened to music on his gramophone or on the radio. He listened only to classical music. Shortly after ten he retired for the night.

The first Sunday of the intensive surveillance he went for a hike in the mountains. He put on hiking boots, took his steel-spiked stick and a knapsack. While going on bicycle to fetch cigarettes, he left his knapsack in the unlocked apartment, and security men came in and took a look at what he was taking on his excursion. They discovered an apple; a bar of Swiss chocolate; a Thermos of coffee; sandwiches (cheese and egg); a mariner's compass; a large-scale map of the area; a folding Kodak camera; and reading matter: Kierkegaard (*Fear and Trembling, The Sickness Unto Death, Either/Or*).

The course of his hike that day was monitored from a dozen observation points by FBI and MED agents with field glasses and telescopes. The cave in which he sat down to eat his sandwiches and apple was later examined from top to bottom for any signs of erased messages on the ground or the walls. Nothing was found.

As far as could be ascertained he did not speak to another human soul all day long. (But he did take many photos with his Kodak camera, and these turned out to be of plants again. When handed in for developing on his return, everybody who handled the film was checked—the person in the film-developing service at the PX; the people in the photography shop in Santa Fe who did the developing and printing; the firm that handled transportation back to the hill; the driver of the van. Nothing was found.)

Hofmannsthal on returning from his hike took a hot shower and went to bed.

The following week went exactly like the first. Then on Friday Hofmannsthal told Greg McClure that he would like to go into Santa Fe on the following day.

Richter called in McClure.

"Yeah," he explained, "I usually drive the professor into Santa Fe when he wants to go, since he doesn't drive himself. It's a little favor. He doesn't need a bodyguard now, but he got used to me during the war. He likes me to drive him, and if I can I do."

"Where does he go?"

"Oh, he has a little walk around. Does his errands. Some shopping. Then usually to Le Baron for dinner."

"I don't think I know it—Le Baron?"

"In the Camino del Monte Sol. Little place. Swanky, though. White tablecloths, and all that flambéing going on. French. Said to be good. Should be, the prices they charge. He has himself a real blowout there—one of those six-course meals. A nice bottle of French wine. Brandy. Fancy French cheeses . . ."

"He eats alone?"

"That's right. At any rate, I've never seen anyone with him, and the table is set for one."

"So, no lady friend?"

"Not as far as I know. The table is by the window and he comes out as soon as he sees me. He's always finished and settled the bill by the time I arrive."

"You drive him straight back here?"

"That's right. Except sometimes I don't do that the same day. Sometimes he stays the night. At Le Baron. They have a few rooms. He sleeps late on Sunday, and I fetch him after lunch."

"Sounds civilized," Richter said.

That afternoon Hofmannsthal made three phone calls, one from the administration building, one from the commissary, and one from the lodge. (He had no telephone in his apartment.) The first phone call was to a book shop in Santa Fe asking if a book he had ordered (*The Passionists of the Southwest, or The Holy Broth-*

erhood, a revelation of the Penitentes) was in. It was, and he said he would stop by on Saturday between five and six to collect it. His second phone call was to a watchmaker, asking if his watch was repaired. The watchmaker said it was, and Hofmannsthal said he would stop by between five and six. The third phone call was to Le Baron, making a dinner reservation.

A conference between Tom Borneschaft and Richter was held that afternoon in the Security Office. They went over the possible area where Hofmannsthal could be making contact with someone outside. There were the long walks. Prearranged meetings could have been set up at particular spots on particular dates. There were the photographs of plants, which might embody some sort of code. But Richter doubted this. How many spies were botanists and would know the names of the plants? Finally, there were the regular visits to Santa Fe. On these he would have ample opportunity to meet someone and pass on material or messages. On the other hand, it could be quite innocent—a man of normally abstemious tastes indulging himself in a fine meal once a week. Why not? He had few pleasures in his austere and solitary life.

Borneschaft reported that his boys were leaning heavily on Davidson in New York to get him to come up with some better names. "So far all he's given us are crumbs. I got the message to him that he don't get off frying for telling us things we already know. We tried lists of names on him, including Hofmannsthal's. No reaction. But he could be faking. My feeling is, if we can crack Hofy, Davidson'll crack, or vice versa, and then it'll all come pouring out like hot molasses."

He was going to have ten men around Santa Fe on Saturday and Sunday, watching every step that Hofmannsthal took.

Richter said, "Tom, this is my show, remember. I want you to lay off Hofmannsthal."

"It's your show here," Borneschaft agreed. "The hill, yeah. But Santa Fe is an open market."

"Tell you what, Tom," Richter compromised. "You have your men there, okay. But whatever happens they're to be told not to make a move without my authorization, okay? They can keep him

387

under close observation, fine. But if it *is* him, I want to handle it. He's a very special fish, Tom, and he is going to need very careful reeling-in."

"It's a deal, Captain."

———

The Packard was going down State 4 in the direction of Santa Fe. Richter was following in a Pontiac from the car pool, keeping well behind. Even at this distance the back of Hofmannsthal's head was unmistakable. He had the stiff-necked erectness of a generation that was taught to sit up straight. And to keep its shoulders back, and its head up.

McClure was driving. A peculiar calling—bodyguard. Requiring some very special abilities and character traits. A presidential bodyguard had to be prepared to put his body between the President and an assailant's bullets. Richter had asked him about that once, and Greg had said, without any expression in his pale blue eyes, "It's discipline. In that situation you're an instrument, an arm of government. You don't have any ego. You follow instructions. That's all. You've learned to do it without thinking and you do it."

Well, there were clearly advantages to being able to act without thinking. No time for issues to get too complicated; you did what you had to do. There were people like that—they followed instructions, and no arguments. Something to be said for it. By contrast, what an argumentative lot all these scientists were. Endlessly debating everything. No idea was too outrageous to pass their lips. They would stand the world on its head for the sake of argument. But arguments rarely became actions with them; their ingenious minds would usually find a suitable counterargument. Was Hofmannsthal the exception—someone who took action? A mystery with a moral dimension: what a thing to have to solve!

Richter followed the Packard over the narrow Otowi bridge, and presently the landscape opened up into a treeless plain, sand red and empty and vast, dotted with clumps of brush and sage and

388

other low-growing shrub—an agoraphobic vision. He spotted a vulture circling, a grim reminder that the Jones children had not been found, despite the most extensive searches by police and National Guard with tracker dogs. Over two weeks they'd been missing. The possibility had to be faced that some wild animal had attacked the children and devoured them completely—without leaving enough of a trace even for the dogs. Or else Tony and Sarah had drowned, and their bodies had been sucked down into an underground stream. Or something else had happened to them. . . . He stopped this train of speculations; it was too gruesome and depressing.

Stick to the facts, he told himself. Okay. The Jones children were missing. Jones was dead, dead because he had attempted to put out a uranium fire with water. Leo Hepler was dead of radiation disease. Jake Dubinski was dead of radiation disease. Weissberger was dead of choking on a piece of meat. Some two dozen others were dead of a variety of accidents, some of them bizarre. A religious nut was sending out biblical maledictions to some of the most prominent atomic scientists. A man called Davidson had tried to get people in the research establishment to pass secrets to the Russians. And in October 1943 Hofmannsthal had said something to Bamberger that had led Bamberger to think that the old man, whom he loved and revered, might be engaged in espionage. Were these unconnected events, or was there some link between them? Were they separate segments of a macabre and tortuously twisting plot—or was this plot something present only in the mind attempting to make some sense of these events?

Richter's thoughts vacillated wildly between competing improbabilities. He did not know what to think. Nothing was clear. While it was possible to imagine Hofmannsthal giving away secrets as a matter of principle, it was hard to see him as a mass murderer picking off his fellow scientists.

In Santa Fe the Packard had to slow down in the narrow streets clogged with summer holidaymakers. It drew up before the La Fonda Hotel and Hofmannsthal stepped out. He did not look around; as soon as the car had driven off he began to walk toward the plaza. With his high head and his erect posture he stood out

389

in the crowd and was easy to follow. He did not walk fast. People stepped out of his way—there was something about him that made them do that, something impressive and daunting. Some turned to look at him.

The Indian market was on, and there was a feeling of festiveness in the narrow crowded streets converging on the plaza. With his cane and his white linen suit, Hofmannsthal looked like the frequenter of some nineteenth-century spa as he walked in the shade of the market awnings. The plaza had become a maze of bazaars. Looking at this and that, sometimes with a slight smile on his face, examining, touching, Hofmannsthal's pace was unhurried. Once he paused, took out his pocket watch, clicked open the lid, regarded the time solemnly, musingly. He emerged from under the roofing of sun umbrellas in the central green to cross the hot, open street to the *portales* of the Palace of the Governors, and here he continued his strolling examination of the wares. One or two things made him smile, but he did not buy—he was obviously a difficult man to please, a person of the most exacting standards.

Having come to the end of the arcade, he appeared to be deciding what to do next. His air was casual. As if suddenly remembering something, he turned round and crossed the plaza to the east side and went into the book shop there. Richter did not approach too close, so as not to be spotted. He saw that one of Tom Borneschaft's men was just going into the shop; it could be left to him to observe what went on inside. The agent was someone Hofmannsthal did not know, and would be able to get up close to him. Ten minutes later Hofmannsthal came out carrying a wrapped book. He paused to take out his pocket watch. He clicked open the lid and looked at the time with a solemn gaze, then put the watch back and, with the book under his arm, walked quickly round the corner, followed by the agent. At the corner the agent from the book shop went straight on, and another agent crossed his path to follow Hofmannsthal. Richter came some distance behind. This time the professor went into a watchmaker's. Coming out five minutes later, he paused at the entrance to examine the watch he had collected. He held it to his ear, then wound it and, pulling out the stem-winder, set the time by his other watch.

Now he continued to walk at a leisurely pace to the plaza. He made his way through a dense cluster of holidaymakers around a soda pop stand and returned to the central green with its many bazaars and its atmosphere of lively salesmanship and bargaining. A stall selling Indian masks attracted his attention. He stopped to examine examples of this work. For a moment he held up to his face a Yaqui Pascola mask, with long beard, an iron cross symbol on the chin, huge red lips, a black face with heavy lines running from the nose downwards, a white-painted nose, and white-rimmed eyes with white triangles underneath. For an instant the linen-suited professor was horrifyingly transformed . . . and then he handed back the mask, shook his head. He was not going to buy it.

The next stall that attracted his interest was selling silver hammer-work jewelry, decorated with incised or stamped designs. He picked up a phoenix of silver and semiprecious stones, a tiepin in the form of a serpent. But again he did not buy. All the time the aloof smile was firmly fixed on his face. He was not someone to make rash purchases.

The next stall appeared to come closer to earning his considered approval. It had a number of rugs and blankets suspended from hanging poles, and Hofmannsthal examined these with a knowledgeable eye. The faint, reserved smile appeared to indicate real interest. The stall holder was engaged in conversation. Richter looked around to see if there was a way of getting closer without being seen. The bazaar adjacent? Yes—the tarpaulin flaps would hide him effectively enough, and he could listen. Quickly he slipped into this booth.

"And this yellow green, how is that obtained?"

"Peach leaves."

"The reddish black?"

"Apple bark."

"And this extraordinary black?"

"Ah, the black. The black we get from iron nails soaked in urine."

"It's a fine rug," Hofmannsthal said, stepping back from it to get the full effect of its pattern and colors.

"Very fine rug," the stall holder agreed. "Very fine, certainly. You see the culebrías—the diagonal zigzag lines, very fine. And look, the five lozenge figures that make thunderbird . . ."

"Very fine," Hofmannsthal agreed. "I am going to look at some others, but I shall be back. Almost certainly. Don't sell this one— keep it for me. For half an hour?"

"I will."

Richter remained in his concealed place until Hofmannsthal had passed, decided not to follow him. If the professor turned around abruptly it would bring them face to face. Let Tom Borne-schaft's boys follow him—yes. Richter came out of the booth and took up a position by the hot-dog stand immediately opposite the stall selling the Chimayo blankets. Unfolding a newspaper, he hid his face in the prescribed manner. After ten minutes of this his arms were beginning to ache, and he was about to fold up his paper and call an end to the afternoon's shadowing when Tom Borneschaft, spotting him easily through the newspaper, came up and said, "What is it you are so immersed in behind there, Captain?"

"I am disguising myself," Richter said with dignity.

"Ah—is that what you're doing?" The FBI man chuckled. "You mustn't hold the newspaper upside down, in that case."

Richter lowered the paper in disgust. "Well?" he asked.

"Only place where he talked to anyone for any time was in the book shop. He chatted there to one of the assistants. He was searching for a book on the shelves and the young man was helping him. Our man couldn't get close enough to hear what they were saying."

"And the watchmaker?"

"The conversation was confined to what the cost of the repair was, the nature of the trouble, and what a beautiful old watch it was. Hofy said it had belonged to his father. Both men admired the workmanship of the incised gold."

"So—all on the level?"

"No positive indication to the contrary, let's say."

Borneschaft suddenly grabbed Richter's lowered newspaper and

392

raised it, spread out upside down, in front of both their faces. "Here he comes back."

Hofmannsthal did not waste a sideways glance on them as he passed. He never looked anywhere except where he was going, and he was going back to the stall with the exquisitely patterned and colored Chimayo blanket. Again he examined it. It clearly pleased him. But now he caught sight of another spread out on the ground, one that he hadn't noticed before. He stepped back from it, head nodding with approval, and then stooped to examine it more closely. As he was doing this somebody came alongside and began to speak to him. He was a slender young man with intense, nervous eyes, darkly ringed. He wore a seersucker suit, no tie. The conversation that ensued seemed both intimate and casual. It was difficult to gather what the subject matter might be, because Hofmannsthal had his head down. There was, however, a discernible tension between the two men. Hofmannsthal looked up from the blanket; he seemed to be formulating a reply to something that he had been asked. The young man was waiting with a kind of sullen nervousness for the answer. Hofmannsthal took out a mechanical pencil and wrote something on a card. The young man took the card, without looking at what was written on it, and went off.

"I'm gonna go get him," Tom Borneschaft said. "You stick with the prof, Captain."

"Okay."

Again Hofmannsthal took out his pocket watch, clicked open the lid. After a moment's deliberation, his mind made up, and all thought of buying the beautiful blanket abandoned, he strode away from the bazaar and, fighting his way through the throng, walked with decisive urgency toward Palace Avenue. Richter followed. The professor continued for a short distance on the avenue, then took a right turn toward the Paseo de Peralta. A few minutes later Richter saw him go into an ice cream parlor called Tomaso's.

———

"I had a message that you wished to see me," Hofmannsthal said, coming into the Security Office. "At the gate they said to-

393

night. Such exigence! Well, Captain, you see I am here. What is it that could not wait?"

"I appreciate your stopping by. Sit down, Professor. Cigarette?"

"No thank you," Hofmannsthal said, seating himself and carefully crossing his long legs in the white linen trousers.

Richter took out his pipe and lit it. "I'd like to preface this by saying that in this job you sometimes have to ask silly questions . . . and you get silly answers. If all this is just silliness, I hope you'll excuse it."

"Don't apologize, Captain. I have become quite used to silly questions. Go ahead."

"Silly question number one." Richter smiled. "When you went to Santa Fe today, may I ask: Did you talk to anyone, meet anyone?"

"No."

"You didn't talk to anyone at all?"

"Apart from the people in the restaurant where I ate dinner— Le Baron—and in the bookstore, of course, and in the Indian market, stall holders—apart from these, I don't believe I talked to anyone. Oh, there was the watchmaker, when I collected my watch. I talked to him briefly."

"What about the young man who came up to you in the market, while you were looking at some Chimayo blankets?"

"Ah yes, there was that young man."

"What did he want?"

"He was asking me for directions—to a hotel."

"It seemed to take you rather long to give him directions."

"He was also looking at the rug. He became interested in it."

In the course of the next two days, as the questioning passed through successive stages, Hofmannsthal kept cool. His tone was tolerant, ironic, superior. Even though his answers became increasingly unconvincing, he did not lose one jot of his imperturbability. It was like a great game to him, it seemed: the whole of that formidable intellect devoting itself to evading the implications of a steadily accumulating mass of facts. Individually, these facts did not amount to anything conclusive; but together they pointed to a whole substructure of secrecy and cunning in his life.

When confronted with evidence of his secrecy, he neatly side-stepped it.

"Professor, your secret meeting with Davidson late at night in a downtown Washington bar in September 1943 . . ."

"Not secret, Captain. Private."

"Why so private?"

"Since evidently I was observed, it was not so private."

"How about the meetings you had that were not observed?"

"If they were not observed, how can you presume I had other meetings with Davidson?"

"Davidson says so."

"You know Davidson. He was always getting up petitions, and he did tend to go about obtaining signatures in a somewhat conspiratorial way."

"Did it occur to you that he might be a spy?"

"I thought he wore his colors rather too openly for that. He never exactly disguised his sympathies."

"Were they also your sympathies?"

"Do you really think, Richter, that Sergeant Davidson and I have much in common?"

"Enough, evidently, for him to have confided to you about his contact in the Soviet legation."

"Confided! Good God, he boasted about it to everyone."

"But he did say to you certain things that he didn't tell everyone. For example, that this contact of his could be instrumental in channeling information to the Soviet Union."

"Yes, I thought it was unwise of him to go around saying things like that, which is why I reported the conversation to the controller."

"You didn't report to the Security Office."

"I intend no slur upon you, Richter—you were not even here at the time—but I did think that the security people were liable to get very hysterical about something like that, and that I could leave it to the controller to deal with the matter as he saw fit. Again I cast no aspersions, but—perhaps because of my experience with the Gestapo—I have never been entirely at ease with internal security offices."

395

The questioning continued, and Hofmannsthal remained unshakable. If anything, his manner became more superior and subtly contemptuous as his credibility diminished.

"Professor," Richter said several hours later, "what was the name of the hotel to which the young man wished to be directed—the young man you met in the Indian market?"

"The Sands."

"Why do you suppose he was heading toward the Paseo de Peralta when he was picked up? Since the Sands is in the other direction."

"I have no idea. Perhaps he decided to go to a different hotel."

"Or to have an ice cream at Tomaso's? Like you?"

"That would be too much of a coincidence, I suspect."

"As much of a coincidence as the fact that the man who asked you for directions to the Sands Hotel is the same man who served you in the bookstore."

"Yes, I thought I had seen his face before. He must have followed me. What do you suppose he could have wanted?"

"Perhaps you could tell me that."

"I find it difficult to imagine—human motivation being as impenetrable as it frequently is."

"Let me make a guess. Supposing whatever business you had with him could not be conducted in the bookstore, for one reason or another. There were too many people around, perhaps. You arrange to meet him by one of the bazaars. He meets you there, but it is still too crowded, and perhaps you sense you are being watched. You suggest he meets you at Tomaso's."

"An imaginative series of suppositions, but incorrect."

"The young man has confirmed them."

"People get confused—and frightened—when questioned by the police. It is natural enough. If they have anything to hide—and who hasn't?—they start to tell lies."

"Is that what you are doing, Professor?"

"But *I* have nothing to hide."

This sparring went on until midnight, at which point Richter decided to halt.

396

When the questioning resumed on the following day, Hofmannsthal said, "I have heard you people go to great lengths in pursuing your hunches. I have heard that Colonel Delacy once had an express train stopped, believing that somebody he wanted to talk to was on it. It turned out he wasn't. Very embarrassing for the colonel. It seems he had got the wrong train. Or perhaps it was the right train but the wrong man—the precise details of the gaffe have become blurred in the retelling. You must be careful, Captain, not to go chasing after the wrong train."

Every question was firmly parried by the professor.

In the afternoon Richter continued going over the same ground again and again.

As the hours went by, Hofmannsthal's steady smile became more and more fatigued, his patience tautly stretched. Finally, at around six, he said, "Isaac Newton once counseled a friend embarking upon a long journey to humor the natives, since the purpose of travel is to learn, not to teach. I am trying to adhere to that wise advice. But I must tell you that I have set a limit to my patience. As part of my policy of humoring this kind of absurdity, I am ready to go on with this up to a point—seven o'clock. I am then going to have dinner, and I do not intend to return after dinner. I do not wish to be rude, Captain, it is nothing personal. I am sure you are doing what you consider your duty and I believe in being cooperative—within reason. But this has gone beyond reason now. I have already been questioned for two days. So at seven sharp I propose to pick myself up and get out of here."

At five to seven, Hofmannsthal took out his pocket watch, clicked open the lid, and said, "In five minutes I am leaving, Captain."

"I wish you would give this a little more time, Professor," Richter said. "Look—this questioning, it's like a scientific experiment. It has to run a certain course to be of any value. Believe me, I am as impartial in this as any scientist. One has no desires, no preconceived notions . . . one conducts the test, and draws conclusions. But the test has to be a valid one. If you cut it short, without certain things being resolved, the test will have to be gone over again by others."

"I am sorry, Captain. I have made my decision." Hofmannsthal stood up. "I am leaving."

"Sit down, Professor," Richter said. "Please."

"It is seven o'clock, and I made it clear—"

"Sit down, please. Professor, Tim Harvey, the guy you talked to in the square and who served you in the bookstore—he says he knows you well." Richter shrugged uncomfortably. "He's been questioned as long as you have, and his mental stamina is not as great as yours. He broke soon after lunch. Came out with everything."

Hofmannsthal remained standing stiffly upright. His smile was like something painted on a mask.

"I have told you, I know these secret police techniques. It is unworthy of you to try and trap me by such tricks."

"I am not using any tricks."

Richter looked down at his folded hands. He was puffing at his pipe rather rapidly, putting a lot of tobacco smoke around himself. He spoke without looking up.

"Professor, Harvey claims that you have met him at least a dozen times, that you go together to a room that he has in the Camino del Monte Sol, or else to your room at Le Baron, and that acts . . . of a sexual nature take place between you. That is what he says."

Richter looked up through all the tobacco smoke. Hofmannsthal was still standing. He seemed to be wavering slightly on his feet. His face was very white.

"Why don't you sit down a moment, Professor," Richter said kindly.

Hofmannsthal did so. "What an incredible invention—" he began.

Richter cut in gently. "Please, please. Harvey says that from time to time he arranged for other young men to participate in these things. He has named four. He says they can all identify you. The FBI have found one so far, and he confirms Harvey's story. They are looking for the others."

"What could be the purpose of such an elaborate conspiracy?"

398

Hofmannsthal asked himself, but his words lacked vigor, were spoken without conviction.

"Why go on with this pretense of not knowing Harvey?" Richter said. And he added with a sudden surge of toughness, "Oh, for God's sake, Professor, they've gone over the room . . . they've got fingerprints. People across the road have seen you go in. They've identified you from photographs. Look . . . I am not interested in this aspect of your life. Your tastes in this respect are none of my business. But the problem is that the one thing does not exclude the other. Tim Harvey. He's had a strange life, not to say bizarre. He's been many things. Among other things, he has been a member of the Communist party. He's run messages for them. This is why I am, unfortunately, compelled to go into this whole area of your life. There is a possibility that these secret meetings with Harvey had a double purpose. We have even to entertain the possibility that the story of homosexual practices is a blind, a cover for the real purpose. You understand, we have to consider it."

"I understand." Hofmannsthal's breathing had become heavy and noisy. His skin had taken on the grayness of dim alleyways and dark corridors. His expression was one of nausea.

"Perhaps there is something wrong with us," he said after a while, ". . . some genetic defect in the way we are made . . . some gene left out or wrongly placed. . . . What a sordid little secret it is, the secret of the human condition." His hand described a vague circle of disgust. "You understand, I am not a religious man in the conventional sense, but if there was something in the central order that was capable of making us, of forming us as we are, there must be a capability that recognizes the mistake, the bad design, the missing element, and gives out the order to abort . . . to end the nasty little experiment and start again. And if so—who knows?—we here may be the chosen instrument of that self-correcting purpose."

"Is that what you think?"

"When a mistake has been made, it must be corrected."

"You take any steps towards correcting the mistake?"

"Is *that* what you think? Dubinski, Hepler, Jones, the children

. . . one would have to be mad. . . . You think I am mad, Captain?" He shook his head several times, bitterly. "What I have to tell you, Richter, is that this unfortunate aberration of mine that you have so cleverly uncovered is, after all, the wrong train. All your questioning of these young men will not produce one jot of evidence of the kind you are looking for. It will merely drag me through the mud. I know what it means . . . a full-scale security investigation. No stone left unturned. I saw what happened in the case of Dubinski. You will show me up before my colleagues as this depraver of youth. . . ." His voice was bitter and full of dark anger.

"There's nothing I can do about that, Professor."

"I tell you—these young men, they have nothing to do with the passing on of secrets . . . they catered to my weakness, nothing else. There is no spy channel there . . . take my word for it." He stopped and gave a sardonic little smile. "But you can't, of course. Of course. I quite see."

"I'm not able to, am I?"

"No, no—of course." There was a silence lasting several seconds. Then Hofmannsthal said, "If you had what you wanted . . . a full statement . . . would there be any need to question these young men?" As Richter hesitated before replying, Hofmannsthal continued, "I am held in some esteem by certain people. By Dr. Bamberger, for example. He always imposes such high standards of conduct on everyone, impossibly high. It would, I'm afraid, be shattering to him to learn that I do not live up to his high opinion of me. He is a man continually shattered by the failure of others to live up to his expectations."

"What is it you want me to do, Professor?"

"If I give you a complete statement, a statement that will satisfy you, can you keep the young man of the Camino del Monte Sol out of this?"

"I will do my best."

"I have to take your word for that."

"I'm afraid that's all I can give you."

"It is enough, Richter. I have always regarded you, though we are, so to speak, opposed in the roles allocated to us, an honorable man. I will trust you to do your best for me. Very well." He took a deep breath and became quite businesslike with resolution. "Now if you will take a sheet of paper and write this down . . . I will go at dictation speed."

"I'm ready, Professor."

"My name is Hans Friedrich Hofmannsthal. I am sixty-six years old. I was born . . . But you have all that. Let us get on to the essence of the matter."

He paused only for a moment. "My father taught me when I was a child that one must always act in accordance with one's beliefs, no matter the cost to oneself, and I have treated this as a kind of holy commandment. My father was a most exceptional man . . ." Hofmannsthal's face lit up briefly, then became dimmed again as he continued. "I have not been able to live up to his high standards, but I have tried to do so in certain respects."

His voice became matter-of-fact now, and rapid and flat, like someone running through a mere form of words. "In accordance with my beliefs that exclusive possession of the atomic bomb by any one power constitutes an overwhelming inducement to national self-aggrandizement, and to aggression, and therefore is a threat to the whole world, I have felt it to be my moral duty to impart information about the atomic bomb, and also about the principles of a so-called superbomb, to representatives of Great Britain and the Soviet Union. I decline to reveal the names of the people I have dealt with, but I am willing to answer all further questions about my own acts in this regard."

TWENTY

Richter sat in the Security Office looking out on faded-green laboratory buildings lit by late sunlight.

He puffed concentratedly on his pipe. Yes, this could be the truth at long last: Bamberger's and Hofmannsthal's statements bore each other out. It could be; it could be. It was in keeping with Bamberger's character to go to such lengths out of a sense of loyalty. He was a man who attached a great deal of importance to personal loyalty. Delacy and Borneschaft could not see why an innocent man would not go straight to the cops; but Richter could understand that it would have had the meaning of a betrayal. Yes, he had to say, Bamberger's story seemed to check out.

Yet something was not right. There were things that Hofmannsthal's confession did not explain.

Allison. Well, Allison was cleared, and that was a relief. Yes, both Bamberger and Hofmannsthal had been categorical in stating that Allison was in no way involved in any of this. From which it would have to be assumed that her relationship with Davidson had had no political angles on her side. It was plausible, Richter thought. From Davidson's point of view, okay, he was someone who was always trying, a dedicated operator—he tries with Hofmannsthal, he tries with Allison and with others. No evidence that Allison had responded to him, except sexually. Okay, so he's an operator and she is a lonely unhappy widow, and he finds the right line through to her. Yes; no reason to think that Allison was not

402

in the clear. Even Delacy and Borneschaft agreed on that. But a lot of things were still not explained. Jake's death, Hepler's death, Jones's death . . . the disappearance of the Jones children . . . some of those other accidents . . . the biblical quotations in the mail. Hofmannsthal had said, "Do you think I am mad?" The question made derisory echoes in Richter's head. Hofmannsthal mad! That great intellect.

Impossible to see Hofmannsthal, logical and rational and high-minded—yes, and kingly, too—being responsible for all those dreadful and bizarre things that had been happening.

Could it then mean that his confession was, after all, not true? Under continuous questioning, in a situation of high stress, even the strongest mind could become suggestible. The fear that his shameful secret life was going to be discovered must have put the old man in a state of blind terror. Under the pressure of such fear, paradoxical modes of behavior could ensue. The desire to give the questioner what he wants becomes paramount. The person questioned can begin to believe the opposite of the truth. Utter absurdities can come to seem reasonable. This was one of the basic mechanisms of false confessions. He might have chosen to confess to the nobler crime, the crime of principle, rather than let the sordid secrets of the Camino del Monte Sol be exposed.

It had to be considered. Was it a false confession Hofmannsthal had signed? If so, Richter was back to square one. But no, it could not be. There was corroboration. Bamberger had been forced, in the end, after much pain, after endless attempts at evasion and deception, to point the accusing finger—however shakily—at Hofmannsthal. Davidson, offered a deal to spare his life, had finally admitted that Hofmannsthal was in with them. But most convincing of all for Richter was the way in which Hofmannsthal had suddenly collapsed. For much of the questioning he had been totally on top of the situation, unintimidated, unquestionably superior—only with the sordid evidence of the Camino del Monte Sol had he cracked. After that, the rest had followed: the sudden slowness, the flatness of speech, the heaviness of movement, the dimming of his entire being, as if all the light had gone out in him suddenly—closing time.

The confession coming out of that—though so far lacking in verifiable details—was surely genuine. It had not been extracted by third degree. It had been offered . . . volunteered almost. No, Richter could not believe that this confession was false.

But then, how to explain all the other things that had been happening? They smacked of the irrational, whereas Hofmannsthal's treachery was distinguished by a supremely arrogant kind of logicality—a crime of reason! The other was the very essence of unreason. If he had also done these other things, there would have to be a mad part of him alongside the supremely rational.

And then, all at once, it struck Richter why, perhaps, there were so many bits of puzzle left over when the picture would appear to have been completed. Supposing there were two puzzles, not one. Like the two sides of a coin . . . head and tail, reason and unreason, science and madness.

Supposing somebody had taken it into his head that if the scientists could play at being God, then so could he: a punishing God, a God of vengeance and terror. A jealous God. A God who with some turns of a screw could visit destruction upon an entire community. *"And I will make this city desolate, and a hissing; everyone that passeth thereby shall be astonished and hiss, because of all the plagues thereof."*

If there were two separate threads in the tangled skein he had been unraveling, and if he had picked out the thread of reason, that left . . .

He remembered suddenly that he was going to Allison's for dinner, and it was already eight. As he walked to her apartment he was deep in thought, working out the ramifications of the theory of two threads, two plots, two puzzles. If he had the solution to one . . .

Allison's front door was as usual unlocked; he pushed it open and called out, announcing himself, but immediately had a sense of the place being empty, and his heart did a little premonitory flip-flop. There was no answer to his call. He went inside. He felt, perhaps because of the line of thought he had been pursuing, a sense of chill. The apartment was in considerable disorder. The beds were not made; the lunch and breakfast things were cluttering the sink, unwashed. There was no sign of any meal in the course of preparation. And no sign of Allison, or of Benjie.

On the kitchen table he found an envelope against a bottle of ketchup. Across the back flap was written in Allison's hand:

Benjie's late so I've popped out to get him. I know, I know. The overprotective Ma that's me. Sorry, darling. Back in five minutes. Sorry about the mess. The maid didn't come, darn her. She used to be so reliable.

He felt real fear now. This note (judging from the fact that Allison had not even started cooking) must have been written more than an hour ago, because dinner was usually not later than eight (so Benjie wouldn't be too late going to bed). It was now ten past eight. He looked in the ice box. Maybe she was planning a cold meal. He found meat wrapped in wax paper, chilies, tomatoes . . . but no cold cuts. Allison was not someone who forgot the time. She was a punctual person. Something was wrong, something was wrong. She must have gone out to look for Benjie before starting to prepare the meal, which meant she must have gone out at least an hour ago. Since she was not back, it meant that she hadn't found him, was still looking for him. He told himself to hold tight, not to jump to conclusions. What could have happened? He thought about the theory of two threads . . . reason and unreason.

He turned over the envelope he was holding; it was addressed to Allison in a large, impersonal print. He recognized the anonymous hand at once. He had by now seen enough messages in that hand. Extracting the by-now-familiar sheet of exercise-book paper, he read with a new intimate sense of personal dread:

AND I WILL CAUSE THEM TO EAT THE FLESH OF THEIR SONS AND THE FLESH OF THEIR DAUGHTERS, AND THEY EACH SHALL EAT THE FLESH OF HIS FRIEND

Jeremiah 19:9

He looked at the postmark on the envelope—mailed Friday in Santa Fe. The day Hofmannsthal went to Santa Fe to meet his friend in the Indian market.

What could have happened to Benjie? Nobody could enter or leave the compound without passing through one of the gates. The gates were guarded. There was a high wire all around. Had Benjie also slipped out through the hole in the fence? That was not like him; he was a cautious child. He would surely not have done that, especially in view of his mother's stern warnings not to go too far. All the mothers were very conscious that the Jones children were still missing. Children were not allowed to roam around outside the compound now. But he had heard that they sometimes showed adults where the hole in the fence was . . . it was a kind of game, and there was some silly kudos in being able to say "I know the secret way out." If some adult Benjie knew and trusted had challenged him . . .

Pieces of the second puzzle were suddenly fitting together in his mind in a most alarming way. He left Allison's apartment and ran all the way to the Security Office. In the file section he went to the cabinet where the personnel Security clearances were kept. He got out Allison's file. On the first page, giving basic details of status and position and her work assignment, he found the note: "Entitlement to domestic maid service—see clearance on L. Gonzales." He wrenched open the GON drawer and pulled out the file on Gonzales. It consisted of a single sheet of flimsy, giving her date of birth, marital status, ethnic status, and other such basic details. Under *Observations* there was written, "Nothing known," and below there was a rubber-stamped approval, "Cleared Grade 3 Red Badge Category." To which was added, in the clearance officer's handwriting, "permission granted to work in the following households. . . ." Altogether she had been allowed to work for four different families, and Richter saw that she had been the Joneses' maid too. His eyes went to the top of the sheet of flimsy for her address, and he read: Xoaté Pueblo.

Something flowed into consciousness, like a suddenly remembered dream . . . a piece of the second puzzle. Xoaté.

He phoned Tom Borneschaft at his apartment. His wife, Daisy, said he was out. He put the phone down fast and called Colonel Delacy. He, too, was out. Back to Daisy.

"Daisy, listen, this is important. Go and find Tom. If he's had a few, pour some black coffee down him. I need him sober. Tell him to get in touch with Colonel Delacy. There's been another disappearance—a child, Benjie Dubinski. Tell him I've got a hunch about something that may be the explanation. Say I've gone out to Xoaté, because if my hunch is right I can't afford to wait. For him to get out there with Delacy, double fast. I'm going to need help if what I'm thinking is right. And see that somebody takes care of Allison, will you? Have you got all that, Daisy?"

"Yes, Jerry."

After that, Richter went to the armory and selected a revolver from the firearms rack and a couple of boxes of ammo. He had learned to handle firearms at FBI training school in Washington, but he had often wondered: Could I shoot to kill? Now he knew. He felt about Benjie as he would have felt about a son of his own.

As he jumped into the driver's seat of his open Ford coupe, Richter felt something soft and slimy wet under him, and without knowing what it was he felt his skin crawl with a reaction of revulsion. He got up and saw that he had sat on a dead toad; its abdomen had been slit open and its guts were spilling out. He was on the point of shifting the mess from the seat with a folded newspaper when he realized what this was: a message. Part of the second puzzle. He bent over the dead thing and examined it closely. On either side of the slit-open belly small fragments of glass were embedded in the warty skin. He picked the toad up by one leg and tossed it out, then found a rag to wipe the seat clean. He found he was brushing away white seeds—chili seeds.

He felt as he drove off fast the strong pull of unreason. There had been chili seeds and broken glass between the pages of Jones's spiral notebook when it was examined after his accident. Absurd to suppose that a man of science could be affected by such primitive forms of magic . . . but the fact remained that he had somehow started a uranium fire and, contrary to what his scientific knowledge should have told him, had attempted to put it out with water. Richter once had gone into the whole phenomenon of voodoo spells and self-fulfilling prophecies—what had he not gone into for the popularization of science, and to make a buck? The victim of a voodoo spell took into his psyche what the psyche perceived as an all-powerful destroying force . . . Richter remembered that from one of his "Would You Believe It?" pieces. Self-fulfilling prophecy. Had something—some form of despairing unreason—told Jones to die, and he had simply done as instructed? In which case, what was this dead toad supposed to be telling Richter? To die also . . . to be damned? He slowed the car slightly; all these signs and messages were meant to make him lose his head. No reason to be so obliging to whoever was playing this ghastly death game.

He had been to Xoaté—the part that could be visited—once before and knew the way. It was a curious road that seemed to descend into the cracks of the earth. A bone-jolting ride down. He wondered if the Ford's suspension would take it . . . if the next bump might not throw him clear out of the open car.

In a while he came to a dark-red stream that threw up along its erratically twisting and leaping course a reddish vapor. There was a red sinking sun hugely present on the edge of the horizon. Going down fast. He was in a dim chasm. At this level the sun penetrated only intermittently, dependent on the lie of the land. Sometimes it was there, sometimes not.

———

Xoaté.

It was really very near the scientific research establishment—only a few miles of twisting dirt road below the hill, but completely hidden from sight. . . .

Xoaté. Where the Spanish friars had fought their centuries-long battle to suppress the pagan spirit. The Church fought with torture and executions, and the other side with magic, broken glass, rag dolls, and the seeds of wheat and corn and chili. Continuing to follow the red stream, he began to catch glimpses of the tumble-down old pueblo ahead. As he came closer he was able to make out the half-moon shape—one crescent arm was roughly parallel with the road he was on. The entrance to the still-inhabited part was further on, but Richter decided on a roundabout approach. Leaving his car, he made his way along an overgrown path, past the ruined extremities and toward the central plaza. He clambered over mounds of earth and felled trees. These trees appeared to have been blown over by a strong wind—it was really very surprising. It looked almost like the effect of a whirlwind. The trees on their down sides were still rooted and gaining nourishment from the earth, and as he climbed over them he saw that their bark had become a fertile breeding ground for beetles. The trees were being slowly devoured by beetles. He looked about him. The vegetation all around was mat gray, lifeless.

Where was everybody? Not a soul to be seen. Must all be inside. As he walked on, he saw that the whole place was crumbling away—the mud building-blocks were literally dissolving, becoming part of the earth again. . . . To the east, the Sangre de Cristo mountains were red-rimmed; the red trees looked unnatural. In the valley, the leaves of the trees were lusterless yellows and browns and grays, and shriveled. As he went further in, he saw the sun go down, and as it descended it seemed to take with it the last hopes of his sinking heart. Pray God, he said to himself. Pray God.

He made his way into the dead village. Like most of the pueblos the Spanish missions converted, it had a church in the center of the plaza. It was uneasily placed there, where no such building was ever intended to be—standing out, with its Folk Gothic belfry, like something displaced from the Middle Ages.

He glanced around, looking for movements, signs of life, but the sprawling pueblo with its dark window openings was still as the grave. The rooms, piled one on top of the other, in places reached a height of four or five storeys, but the haphazard growth of the pile made it hard to see on which level of the structure any particular room was situated. He saw that the usual round kiva was missing from its customary place in the plaza. These ancient ceremonial chambers had disappeared from a number of pueblos—as a result of the friars. He knew that in the case of Xoaté the friars had emptied the kiva of its ceremonial objects and publicly burned them, and that the kiva itself had been destroyed, since this pagan edifice seemed to stand in blasphemous contradiction to the fine new church. As in other pueblos where this had happened, the kiva would no doubt have disappeared into the labyrinthine interior.

Richter walked slowly, hoping that somebody might come out to demand what he wanted. But nobody came. He did not know where to start looking. As he advanced deeper into the U of the crescent, he saw large pools of stagnant water, black and noxious and thick with beetles, too—they formed large raftlike clusters—and, looking up, he saw another dense swarm of them in the sky.

He went into the church. It was dim and cool inside. Behind the altar there was a large wood crucifix with an anguished Christ dripping gouts of blood from his nailed hands and feet. This Christ was not serene and accepting; a scream of mortal pain came from him—and just then a small western window to the left of the altar (obviously placed for just this purpose) let through the last red rays of the sun, which made the Christ's wounds seem to bleed anew.

Having ascertained that there was nobody in the church, Richter went out again. He stood in the cruciform shadow of the spire.

Where to begin?

The pueblo rose in set-back terraces, with many long ladders reaching to the upper storeys. The ground-floor doors were all blocked up: probably used only for storage. The villagers traditionally lived on the upper floors, hauling their ladders after them as a defensive measure. The usual way into one of these places was by way of the smoke hole in the roof. He did not fancy the idea of going down some narrow hole into a dark interior. He was squinting against the last sunlight, trying to catch sight of any movement beyond the window openings. He called out. No answer. The inhabitants of Xoaté, those who remained, were known for their dislike of visitors . . . a closed little society. A throwback to a bygone age. Less than a century ago two men had been executed here for

410

alleged child eating; they were said to have been seen with the bones of little children coming out of their mouths and ears and noses. A woman, the concubine of a married man, had been ritually stoned to death. Subsequently the village had become depopulated by mysterious waves of illnesses, which were followed by waves of vengeance against the witches. . . .

"Benjie! . . . Benjie! . . . Tony! . . . Sarah!" Richter called several times, stopping to listen between shouts. Nothing . . . not a murmur. He began to think that his hunch was one of those crackpot notions to which people on the hill were sometimes prone. And then there came a flash of light from somewhere inside. The windows were without glass—they had wooden grilles, or shutters, but no glass. Another flash of light. Somebody moving his head to catch the last sunlight on his glasses. Both Benjie and Sarah wore glasses. A third flash. The sun was almost gone. He was trying to determine the precise source of the flash . . . so far he had only established the general area. He prayed there might be another few rays of sun to give him one last signal. And this time it came quite definitely: two quick flashes and then a pause, another two flashes and a pause, and another two flashes. . . . The sunlight faded from the adobe façade, leaving it dull and blank. But he had succeeded with these last flashes in pinpointing their exact source, and had fixed this in his mind.

He made his way to the access point nearest to the source of the flashes and climbed one of the ladders to a first-floor terrace. Many former windows here were walled up; those that remained open were narrowed with adobe and rags to the size of loopholes. No way to get in at this level. He leaned his ladder against the next terrace and climbed up to the higher level. Here there were some window openings large enough to squeeze through, but they gave only into small enclosed chambers without doors. He knew there would be a level on which the rooms intercommunicated, and in theory one should have been able to make one's way from one end of the pueblo to the other; but to do this without knowing the layout of the maze was going to be tough. Its construction could not be deduced by means of reasoning, since there was no logical plan to the arrangement of the rooms; they had been strung

411

on as and when required, often shutting off access and light to existing rooms, for which other sources of access and light then had to be found, either through the flat roofs or else by means of twisting tunnels from the terraces.

Richter decided on the roof, and climbed one more storey. Here he found a number of horizontal openings, hatchways, surrounded by stone rims to keep rainwater out. Some of these holes served the triple purpose of letting out the smoke of fires, letting in air and light, and affording a means of entry. The ones not in use were covered up by heavy stone slabs. He decided to go in at one of the unused entry points, and shifted aside the slab. The ladder had been removed, but there were several on the terrace, and he selected one that seemed to be the right height and width and lowered it carefully into the hole. When it touched ground it was protruding several feet above the top of the roof. He shone his flashlight into the darkness below. The room seemed to be empty. But, all the same, he took out the revolver, a Smith & Wesson, cocked it, and slipped off the safety catch. Then he went down. Gingerly—oh, very gingerly.

It was a small chamber with a blocked-up window—the only light came from the smoke hole through which he had just descended. There was a crude archway formed by a low lintel. He stepped under it, the blob of light from his flashlight searching out the space ahead. He took a good strong grip on the revolver.

Each of the narrow chambers he entered led to another. Every so often he stopped to listen. He was making his way in the direction from which he had seen the light flashes. He had worked out that they came from a room on the level below the roof. But he was discovering that there was no certitude about levels here; levels changed within what was roughly the same storey. He was all the time going up and down short ladders. The way the rooms were strung out, like a twisting string of beads, imposed a certain direction on him. There was only one way to go—on. No turnings in corridors. One way only. It was difficult to tell if he was in fact going in the direction in which he wanted to go.

He came to a room with windows and looked out to orient himself in relation to the church; he judged that he must now be quite close to the point from which he had seen the light flashes coming. He took a firmer grip on the gun. Whoever was in there would be ready for him. Since getting to Xoaté Richter had not exactly concealed himself. If his understanding of the second puzzle was correct, the person in there would not hesitate to kill. Richter considered whether it was a mistake to go in alone, instead of waiting for the others. But there was no knowing how long the others might be, and the overriding consideration was that every moment that went by was an extra moment of dreadful danger for the children. He could not afford to wait.

There was a primitive door ahead of him. It had stenciled on it a large red cross of Calvary, with a stepped base. This he knew was the kind of marking that was usually put on the entrance to a *morada*. He tugged on a leather door pull, and the door swung open, pivoting on pintles. He stepped over a sill, gun ready.

The room he entered was much larger than any of those he had been through so far; it obviously consisted of several normal-size rooms knocked together. It was big enough to hold forty or fifty people, and there were wooden benches for them to sit on. A *morada*. He went to the window and looked out. He measured the angle to the church and compared the line with the reverse angle he had drawn earlier in his mind, from the square. Yes, he was fairly sure this was the room from which the flashes had come. Now it was empty. So the children had been taken somewhere else. . . .

He was becoming more and more fearful as he looked around. . . . He saw yucca whips, wooden crosses, hoods. A red cross of Calvary on the wall. A Woodstock typewriter, an Edison cylinder Dictaphone, a wire recording machine. The sun had gone down now, and the room was dim and shadowy; shining his flashlight around, he saw that the walls were covered with writing—biblical quotations mostly, as far as he could make out, and much in the same vein as the maledictions sent through the post:

ALL THEY THAT TAKE THE SWORD SHALL PERISH
WITH THE SWORD

Matthew 26: 52

THEN IT SHALL COME TO PASS THAT THE SWORD
WHICH YOU FEARED SHALL OVERTAKE YOU
                                        Jeremiah 42:16

THEY SHALL SLAY THEIR SONS AND THEIR
DAUGHTERS AND BURN UP THEIR HOUSES WITH
FIRE
THUS WILL I CAUSE LEWDNESS TO CEASE OUT OF
THE LAND
                                        Ezekiel 23: 47–48

FOR THIS IS THE DAY OF THE LORD GOD—A DAY
OF VENGEANCE

He was about to turn away from these by now all too familiar
biblical threats when another quotation, from a different and surprising source—the *Bhagavad-Gita*—caught his eye:

I AM BECOME DEATH, THE DESTROYER OF
WORLDS

He feared the worst now. Going to the table with all the machines, he pressed the "play" button of the recorder, and the room
became filled with wailing and screaming and piercing laments
and wild chanting and the rattle of maracas: the celebration of
darkness, confusion, ignorance. . . .

He switched off the recorder. The tumult must have been heard
throughout the entire village. It was loud enough to raise the dead.
But going to the narrow window and looking out, he saw that the
plaza was still deserted: dominated by the church, no movements
anywhere. It was difficult to see all around, because the window
was barred by a wooden grille. He went to the next window and it
was the same there.

Something standing in a corner attracted his attention; it looked
like a telescope but for the bifocal eyepiece on the barrel. He went
and picked it up. It was a Japanese army periscope. Kind of thing

414

used in dugouts. He'd heard of private eyes using them after the war to spy on illicit couples through hotel-room transoms. Richter opened the periscope to its full length—about five feet— and pushed it through the grille of the window and then manipulated the eyepiece until he had the church in focus. By turning the barrel it was possible to sweep the whole plaza: a way of keeping an eye on people. With a sudden prickly sense of being watched, he raised the revolver and shone the flashlight around. The light climbed the pitted walls with their bloodthirsty writings and described a series of zigzags; any one of these cracks and holes could contain a watching eye. He swung and aimed at his own shadow. But there was nothing in the room.

He would have to go on now; he thought he knew what he would find, and the thought froze his blood. He shone the flashlight ahead. As far as it reached he could see a series of irregularly shaped openings, and right at the end a rough wooden door. He went toward it. He was again going through rooms the windows of which had been blocked up. The air was humid and stale, cellar air. The adobe roofs and walls were not very effective in throwing off rain; they soaked it up and then got rid of it by evaporation, which made the walls seem to breathe. He kept grimly on, revolver pointing ahead like a diviner's rod. Before the wooden door he paused, his heart beating with a heavy beat. There was a steady sound coming from inside that he could not at first place—a buzzing like a buzzing in the ear that will not stop, swelling and falling. He pushed open the door and stepped into the nightmare. The moving light picked out flies . . . the flies buzzed in the bloody mess, bluish-green, fat, feeding things, buzzing and plopping against the walls. He was for some moments unwilling to direct his light downward into the pit from which the stench came, but it had to be done. The next step must always be taken, and then the next, and the next: There was no other way. The beam showed up the blood on the walls—vast amounts of it, and more on the ground, and more, and more; it was like an abattoir. And then the light fell on a small headless body, and after more searching, on another; then on a pair of glasses, then on a child's head, and further on, on another. He forced himself to search for a third.

He did not find a third head.

To proceed he had to pass through the death pit. He went down a short ladder and across the earth floor to a door on the same level. He placed his weight gently against it; it did not give. He stood back and examined the door, and listened. He heard not a sound. The door was made of rough-hewn wood planks, and these had separated in places. He put his eye to one of the wider cracks.

There was an oil lamp on the floor, and by its light he saw Benjie in a corner. His hands were tied under his knees, from between which extended a spiked stick that would be driven up into his throat with the movement of trying to rise. He had a gag in his mouth. His glasses lay smashed on the ground. Richter shifted his position to another crack, and the change in his angle of vision revealed a large, hooded figure standing against the wall. On the ground by his feet was a broadsword, its double-edged blade dulled and tarnished and stained.

Richter tried to see if the barrel of his revolver could be insinuated into one of the cracks in the door to enable him to get a shot in, but it was not possible to do so and still aim the gun accurately. He felt panic begin to press in on him. What to do? It would take too long to break down the door . . . give that madman in there ample time to . . . He exhaled slowly, steadily, and fought back panic. Think clearly, sequentially, he told himself. To rush in alone would be a mistake. No; he must wait, wait for help. Like the other rooms, this one would have a smoke hole in the roof. Blocked up, judging from the absence of moonlight. The way to do it would be for one person to drop through the smoke hole while others broke down the door. And so there was nothing to do but wait, and keep calm. When help arrived he ought to have a plan ready.

He retraced his steps through the death pit and the series of small rooms opening one into the other, until he was back in the *morada*. He made use of the Japanese periscope to survey the plaza; it was still empty. Could he get aid from some of the villagers? There was no one around; they'd all vanished into their holes. Besides, he had a feeling he would not get much help from them. If he was right, they were part of the puzzle, the second puzzle, the one that did not have a logical solution. He reminded himself that the executions in this place in the nineteenth century had been carried out on behalf of the entire village. A madness repeating itself . . . it was too incredible. And then he remembered a line of Joseph Conrad's, about the essence of dreams being the sense one had of being "captured by the incredible." That was how it felt to him as he struggled to stay calm and to retain a clear and methodical approach to the nightmare he was in, which was not a dream. He thought, I have to wait. So: use the time to make a plan. Get maximum information.

He turned again to the wire recorder. The great uproar he had heard before was the chaos of *Las Tinieblas*. A ceremonial wildness. What had preceded it? He thought he knew. There would have been an address by the lay priest or the headman. He pressed the "start" button on the machine and then the "rewind." From time to time he stopped the unspooling wire and switched to "play." It was all chaos and wailing. Back further, further. Finally he came to a silence, and then a voice, a voice that was infinitely strange—drugged-sounding in its fanaticism—but also at the same time uncannily familiar. A voice that, he was sure, he knew well, but distorted by a kind of dark exaltation. The voice said: (in English)

"Lies will be told about me, terrible lies—the world is ignorant and will never understand. But you here, my brothers, my brother Passionists and Penitents, know that I have never shirked the brutal truth. I prophesied to you the blight that would fall upon your village from the contaminated clouds and the contaminated rain and snow, and the agonizing deaths from the poisoned water of our mountains. All this I told you would be, and so it is. I tell you now that the force of corruption must be excised. When a limb has become gangrenous, the surgeon must not hesitate to use the knife. These children, though innocent, are the inheritors of that evil about which—"

Richter switched off. He had heard enough.

He went back the way he had come and climbed the ladder to

417

the roof. He was seized by a fit of shivering. He made himself remember something his father had once told him: "Don't you ever forget that no matter how hopeless some problem might appear to you, a human problem is something made by another human being, and therefore capable of human solution. Only problems of God's making are insoluble."

He waited in the clammy moonlight with his thoughts and his fears, holding on to his father's belief in human solutions. But how long could he wait? Supposing Daisy had not been able to find her husband . . . supposing Tom Borneschaft was too drunk . . . supposing Colonel Delacy had gone to Albuquerque. But Daisy would find somebody. If not, Allison would find somebody. She must be running around crazy with anxiety—she'd be bound to find out, through Daisy, where he, Richter, had gone. Then she would organize something, get hold of somebody. Greg McClure and a bunch of security guards. They would come. They must come. Give it half an hour, he thought, and if nobody has come by then I'll go in alone and do what I can. Try to talk to the hooded madman in there, or else . . .

Five minutes went by . . . ten . . . fifteen. He stayed on the roof; from there he would see the lights of the vehicles as they approached. He didn't want anyone rushing in unbriefed and maybe triggering something. Another five minutes went by. It was agony to stay still and do nothing, just wait.

Then he saw them come; he counted one, two, three, four jeeps making their roller-coaster approach over the unlevel ground and pulling up in thick smudges of earth dust. The security guards spilled out, but stayed back.

As he scrambled down the ladders from terrace to terrace, looking over his shoulder now and then, he caught sight of Tom Borneschaft and Colonel Delacy coming out of the dust of the dirt road. The colonel wore battle dress and had a submachine gun dangling from his shoulder; Tom followed, revolver drawn, instantly recognizable even at this distance by the glare of his Miami Beach tie and by his slouch hat. Allison had stayed in the jeep. He was glad of that. In her presence he would not have been able to say what he had to say. As he reached the two men he saw that

Colonel Delacy was geared up to go—he had that twitchiness about him—and Richter thought, I am going to have to hold him back.

"Well," the colonel called gruffly, when Richter was still some few yards away, "your hunch right?" Richter made a *pianissimo* sign and slowed his pace to a walk. It would not do to be too itchy for quick action in the present situation. He had worked something out in his head. Speaking in a low voice, he said, "I suggest nobody reacts to what I say." He paused. Now that he was going to have to say it in words, the horror was that much more concrete, and he needed to make sure his voice would be steady and firm as he spoke.

"The Jones children are dead," he said quietly. "They're in there. I saw their bodies. They've been . . . beheaded. Benjie is alive. I've seen him. He's being held by . . . a madman, wearing a hood—a Penitent. There's a whole *morada*. . . ."

Keeping his voice at a low conversational pitch, Colonel Delacy said, "Let's go get the motherfucker."

"We're going to have to work out something," Richter said.

He proceeded to give a detailed description of the situation as he had appraised it.

Delacy had lit a cigar and was pacing three yards to the left, then three to the right, as Richter talked. Now he spoke decisively. "Choose our moment. One man drops through the smoke hole. Same time two others break down the door. I'll go through the smoke hole." He tapped his submachine gun like someone touching a good talisman. "My pleasure."

"Trouble is," Richter said, "there's a heavy slab covering the smoke hole. Removing it gives him a warning we're coming in. Even if it's only a couple of seconds, that could be too much."

"He has a gun?"

"I didn't see one. I just saw the broadsword. But that doesn't mean he couldn't have a revolver in his jacket pocket."

"What's the alternative you propose, Captain?"

"Not much of one, I'm afraid. But I think it's worth trying. It's hot and airless in there—no windows—and there are a lot of flies, and there's the smell. The smell is bad, Colonel. It's a small room—eight by five. I think sooner or later he'll need air. He may remove the slab himself, and put his head out. That would be the moment. He'd be up on the ladder, and Benjie would be below."

"And suppose he doesn't come up for air?"

"We wait until he does. At some moment he has got to come out, and that means the ladder."

"Suppose he kills the kid first."

"Yes, it's a risk. But I have a theory. . . ."

"Another theory?" Delacy said with a touch of contempt.

"What's the theory?" Tom Borneschaft asked.

Richter made sure that Allison was not coming toward them—she had remained in the first jeep, pale and still, scarcely moving, as if by her immobility she was maintaining the delicate balance upon which her child's life depended. Richter, his back to the jeeps, spoke softly, looking toward the room where Benjie was.

"My theory is . . . about the madman. Okay, he's mad, yes. But it's a highly systematic form of madness. It's not arbitrary. There's a ritual to it. It's part of a whole worked-out scheme of things. Sin, punishment, vengeance. *Scapegoats.* It's a sect, with ceremonies and rules that they keep to. I think one of the insane rules is—sunrise. I don't know why I think that. It's something I read somewhere." He smiled a little bashfully. "It's one of those useless bits of knowledge I have floating in my head. But I am sure, from what I know about them, they do these things at dawn. In front of the whole damned place. The whole lot. An execution, you see. Like the execution of the witches. Otherwise why is he *waiting* in there? Otherwise what is he waiting *for?*"

"Could be, could be," Delacy agreed. He shook his head several times, looked at Borneschaft, and then at Richter again.

"I don't like waiting," he said. "Anything could happen. It just goes against my grain to wait."

"I know, Colonel, I know. But I really think I've got the picture: There'll be a dawn mass, all of them, and then . . . 'Vengeance is mine, saith the Lord.' "

"Vengeance? Who d'you think it is? You have an idea?"

"I think I know his voice," Richter said cautiously.

"Yeah?"

420

"Colonel, it doesn't help going into that now. Why don't you consider the alternatives while I go and talk to Mrs. Dubinski? She has got to be told something."

"Okay. But don't be long."

Richter walked back to where the Army vehicles were drawn up. Allison saw him come and got out of the jeep and started toward him. He took her hand and gave her a firm smile that was meant to be encouraging without being too encouraging. He could not help thinking of one of the biblical quotations that had come through the mail: "That which you fear most shall come to pass." Most of all she had feared that some harm might befall her child, had felt the unspeakable danger, had wanted to leave. And he had not let her; he had made her stay on, because it might have looked suspicious for her to have left then. If only she had left. He felt the weight of having persuaded her to stay, with his talk of love. She had stayed for him in the end, no other reason. She had swallowed her fears for his sake. And now this had happened: that which she feared most.

He said, "We're going to get Benjie out."

"Is there a chance?" she asked.

"Yes, I think so," he said carefully.

"And the Jones kids?"

"I don't know about them," he said, not looking at her. "I've only seen Benjie."

"You've seen him? How . . . ?" She stopped herself, knowing she must not ask too much, that it was a mistake to press him to say more than he was choosing to say. She had to trust him to say as much as she should know, and no more.

"He's . . . okay," Richter said, not going beyond that despite her desperately appealing eyes.

"Should I come with you?" she asked.

"No, no—I don't think so. It may be a long wait. Stay here. Wait. It's all you can do. I know that's tough, it's the toughest . . . but . . ."

"I can do whatever's necessary," she said. Her voice broke and then recovered. "And so can Benjie, remember that, Jerry . . . whatever you need him to do, he can do. And so can I." She let out a sob but quickly caught it. "Benjie knows I won't break up," she said, "and I know he won't break up. I can stand whatever has to be stood, Jerry, and so can he. So take the time you need, Jerry—but get him out, get him out alive, Jerry."

"We're going to," Richter vowed. She was a valorous lady, this woman he loved, and he hoped he was not doing her a disservice in encouraging her to have hope. To a human predicament there had to be a solution—according to his father the optimist.

He said, "Take care of yourself, Alli," and kissed her lightly on the side of the mouth, not wanting to make too much of a drama of this kiss.

"You take care of yourself, Jerry. I love you. Next to Benjie—" She stopped.

"I know, I know."

He left her, and rejoined Borneschaft and Colonel Delacy. "Well?" he asked unhappily.

"We'll try your way first. I just wish to God we had some way of seeing into that room. I hate to be in the position of not knowing what's going on in there while we're outside biting our nails."

"There's a way," Richter said, and he explained about the Japanese army periscope he had discovered in the *morada*. The extendable glass eye could be placed in position at one of the air vents, where it would not be easy to spot from inside, and if necessary could be retracted instantly.

"Who's going to take the watches?"

Richter hesitated. That was going to be the worst part—to be looking in, seeing everything, and not able to do anything.

"I'll do it," he said, "with Tom. We'll share the watches."

Colonel Delacy nodded. "Now I want you to take me up there, Richter. I want to be by the smoke hole myself when he comes up. I'm going to take two of my best shots with me on the roof, and let's pray he puts his head out for air. Can he see us?"

"By standing on tiptoe he can just about get his eye to one of the air vents, but it's a narrow, limited view. He can only look straight out. Can't see to the sides, or on the roof."

"So we should keep our people in front of him, so he can see we're not making any moves."

"Exactly."

Returning to the jeeps, Delacy selected four men, two to go with him onto the roof, two to break down the door at the appointed time, and a system of signals was arranged in case anything happened inside that would necessitate forgoing the plan and rushing in. If Richter raised his open hand, it was the alert; if he clenched his fist once, it meant get ready to go in; if he clenched it twice, it meant go in. Ammunition magazines were checked and weapons cocked.

"You have a revolver, Captain Richter?" Colonel Delacy asked.

"Yes."

"Know how to use it?"

"I had some training in that, yes."

"But you never actually shot a gun *at* anybody?"

"No—only targets."

"Well, aim to leave that to us, Captain. You give the signals. Right?"

Colonel Delacy gave a nod to the first security guard, who, covered by the others and the vehicles, quickly and silently slipped away through the moon shadows and made his way behind the church, where he waited. Delacy nodded to the second man, who followed suit. Then the third man, and the fourth. When all were assembled behind the church, Richter led them to the right side of the pueblo crescent, and there they climbed from terrace to terrace to the rooftop.

Taking his orientation from the church, Richter brought them to the point where he had made his first entry. He took two of the security guards down through the succession of rooms, through the *morada*—where he picked up the periscope—and then left them at the entrance of the death pit, pointing out the door they would have to break down when they got the signal. Since, from where they were, they would not be able to see him signaling with his hands, a complementary light signal had been agreed upon. Someone at the jeeps would watch Richter and Borneschaft all the time through binoculars, and as soon as a signal was given would translate it into flashes of the car headlights. These lights would be seen by the guards on the wall opposite the air vents. Richter left the men in place and went back up to the roof. He led Delacy and the two marksmen to the smoke hole. After taking in the layout and where Richter and Borneschaft would be on the terrace below, Delacy placed his men so they would be able to see the signals, and himself took up a position right at the smoke hole. Nobody spoke.

Richter and Borneschaft climbed down the ladder and made their way along the outside wall, stopping when they had come to the room beyond the death pit. Richter extended the telescopic periscope until it reached one of the high air vents, and placed it. He put his eye to the eyepiece and adjusted the focus ring. At first all he saw was an expanse of cracked wall, but by tilting the lens he was able to alter the angle of vision until the viewfinder was filled by a hooded head. The hood was wet with sweat. From the eye slits came no shine or flicker of any sort of light. He revolved the periscope until he found Benjie. He was in the same position as before, tied and gagged and with the sharpened stick at his throat. His throat muscles were in spasm as he choked against his tight gag. Maybe Delacy's way was the best, Richter thought. Theories, he thought, theories! A notion, based on God only knew what, that the madman would wait until sunrise. It meant another seven hours of not knowing, of being captive to the incredible.

"I'll take the first watch," he told Tom Borneschaft softly.

Inside the room nothing moved. The child was immobilized by the ropes, the madman by catatonia. Only the heavy, painful rise and fall of his chest indicated a living being. An hour passed and nothing had happened. He handed over the watch to Borneschaft and sat on the ground and lit his pipe. The steady, rhythmic sucking helped to keep the panic at bay. He thought: He must be choking in there from the heat and the stench. But he doesn't budge. He just stands there against the wall, like a statue. Why didn't he put his head out for air? Did he suspect that there were three people on the roof waiting for that moment to blow his head off? Was the madman smart enough to have figured that? He had seemed barely conscious, but the voice on the wire recorder indicated that he was capable of coming out of the stupor, and that then he went the other way—toward frenzy.

At the end of Borneschaft's hour Richter took over again. The madman was in the same position as before, didn't seem to have moved an inch. This watching was like taking a photograph with an enormously slow exposure. Now Richter noted that the breathing was faster; his chest was rising and falling more rapidly. Not getting enough air. The tilt of the hooded head had changed, too, very slightly. Were the unshining eyes looking toward the smoke hole? Let him be thinking about air, Richter prayed fervently. Let him climb up the ladder, lift off the slab, and take a good, deep, last breath of air . . . please, God. But the madman did not budge.

There was no change throughout Borneschaft's next watch, and Richter began to have a disquieting picture of Colonel Delacy pacing and moving the cigar wetly from one side of his mouth to the other. How long would the colonel be able to hold his turbulent horses? He'd be looking at the stone slab, working out the length of time it would take for two men to lift it off and for a third to drop down into the hole with a blazing submachine gun in his arms. Two seconds, three? Would a catatonic madman be able to react in that time? All that was holding the colonel back was Richter's theory. Perhaps I should go up to the roof and change the plan of action, he thought. He would assess it during his next watch.

At first it was the same as before, and Richter began to think that rushing in might be the way to do it after all. But just as he was beginning to be persuaded of this, a change occurred. The madman was suddenly gasping for air—having a choking fit. He was staggering toward the ladder, his hand at his throat, tearing. He's going up, Richter thought, and he raised his open hand to give the alert signal. He saw the jeep lights flash once. The madman was clawing at the ladder. Richter closed his hand into a fist: once. . . . He pictured the colonel leveling his submachine gun, the marksmen with their rifles aimed. One little gulp of air and it would all be over.

But he wasn't going up the ladder; Richter let his hand drop again, canceling the alert, and watched the madman tear at his hood. The material was sticking to his forehead and neck, and he

425

seemed not able to stand anymore the enclosing, coarse, dark dampness. With a sudden movement he tore off the hood and stood there breathing violently.

The big face was seamed with the effort of the muscles to hold everything together. But it was coming apart. It was all coming apart.

Greg McClure.

The face was in bits, nothing tying the bits to a center. There was no center. The center had fragmented. There were only bits and pieces.

Greg McClure.

He said to Tom Borneschaft, "You won't believe this."

Borneschaft came to the eyepiece and looked into the room. He said, "Makes no sense."

Richter thought it made a certain sense. McClure, with the safety crews, had had access to the Y-3 canyon lab. He could have gone in to check the equipment. In the course of that he could easily have loosened two screws. People talked freely to him, confided in him. Any number of them could have mentioned the dangerous experiment in Y-3 and what would happen if the screws were loosened too much. . . . Also, McClure could easily have replaced the chemical extinguisher by Jones's workbench with a water extinguisher. The last Bible quote—the one sent to Allison—was postmarked Santa Fe, Friday. Greg had been in Santa Fe that day. He had driven Hofmannsthal there.

The fact was—no one was in a better position to arrange accidents than the head of the safety crews. From the point of view of physical opportunity it made sense . . . but from no other. Greg McClure! Who never had a grouse against anyone, who did what he was told, was the perfect bodyguard. That Greg, whose job was protecting others against threats and dangers, should be the danger and the threat, was a sort of turning of everything inside out.

Through the viewfinder he saw Greg sit down on the ground, very agitated still, though seemingly recovered from the choking fit, and almost casually reach behind him—his hand went out of view, and Richter frantically swiveled the periscope; he'd lost the hand, lost it. He saw Benjie's terrified face fill the turning view-

426

finder, then nothing, nothing but earth floor and cracked adobe. And then he had the hand again . . . and it was holding the broadsword. Up shot Richter's arm for the alarm, his fist clenched once, then opening; fingers spread wide, he hesitated on the point of giving the signal to go in. He waited like that, with the headlights full on behind him, while Greg kept turning the tarnished blade over, like a thought in the mind. As casually as he had picked it up, he put the sword down again, took out a pack of cards, and, squatting on the ground, began a game of solitaire. The fat flies buzzed around him, and he kept swatting them with his big hands; but they kept coming back, and some of them settled on his face, leaving there a faint tracery of blood.

Richter did not move from the periscope when his hour was up, and Borneschaft, whose eyes were strained, was glad to be relieved of his watch.

About three quarters of an hour had gone by when McClure got up and went to the corner and started to untie Benjie. He removed the pointed stick from his throat, took the gag out of his mouth, and Richter's hand rose again and closed at once into a fist. But McClure wasn't going for the sword—not for the moment; he was motioning Benjie to sit down opposite him on the. ground. He dealt him cards. McClure needed somebody to play cards with him, having evidently tired of solitaire.

There was a half-empty bourbon bottle on the ground and from time to time McClure filled his glass and drank, or pointed to Benjie to fill it. Richter saw many faces in that demented face, one flowing into another like waves on a shore. He was totally absorbed in the card game. The headless bodies in the next room did not exist for him; nor did the many others he had killed to appease his vengeful God. All that was in some other part of his mind—a mind full of secret compartments, in which the ghastliest things could be hidden away, and who would know?

The sweat was pouring off him, gathering in the gulleys above his eyebrows until it overflowed down his face and neck. From time to time he tapped his glass and Benjie refilled it; sometimes he refilled it even when not beckoned to do so, filled it to the rim. Good boy, Richter thought. Good boy! He is terrified but steady.

427

holding back his panic. Allison was right—you could count on him. He hadn't broken up. He was holding on, confident that there were things being done to save him. He was looking up to the smoke hole from time to time, imagining that someone might come in that way. His eyes also went to the broadsword at McClure's side, estimating his chances of kicking it away when something happened, to gain seconds.

The level in the bourbon bottle was falling steadily. Once or twice McClure's eyes closed. If only the whiskey would make him drop off. But the opposite was happening—the alcohol was arousing him, agitating him. Driving him in the direction of frenzy. Seeing this, Benjie was not pouring out any more whiskey. This made McClure wild. Violently, he grabbed the bottle and filled up his glass to the rim, then smashed the empty bottle against the wall.

In his great agitation, which was like a minor epileptic seizure, McClure began to scratch himself. His nails raked his face and neck and inside his shirt, drawing blood. But it was not enough. The flow of blood was too sparse. The fat flies were tormenting him, and his God was tormenting him, and he couldn't escape. His eyes kept going up to the blocked smoke hole, and then round and round the narrow room in continuous circles, looking for some opening, some way out of his terrible confinement within the envelope of his body. His eyes kept sliding over the glass lens just under the ceiling.

And now, through one of the high loopholes, came a shaft of light, coloring the opposite wall red. The first ray of sun. A bell rang out, a wild, fast, fearful ringing that made Richter spin round. He could see the big bell in the latticed belfry swinging from side to side with such force that it seemed as if it might burst out of its housing. A line of Penitentes were making their way into the church, beating their bare backs with yucca whips. McClure, in response to the ringing, had stood up on tiptoe to look out of the air vent. Quickly Richter pulled the periscope lens clear and snatched at his revolver, and as he brought the point of it to the air vent he saw the eye at the hole moving from side to side, looking for the sun. Richter positioned himself for the shot. But

428

now the eye was gone again. Replacing the periscope at the hole, he saw McClure crawling on the floor, like a blind man looking for something. He found the broadsword.

Benjie screamed.

Richter's fist shot up, once . . . and the headlights flashed behind him. And at this moment McClure spotted the little hooded lens spying on him under the ceiling, and instead of going for Benjie he turned his fury on the all-seeing eye. The broadsword smashed into the soft adobe in a succession of blows, one of which found the delicate arrangement of lenses and mirrors, and Richter had lost his eye. His hand closed into a second fist, and at the same time he heard Benjie scream again.

He heard the security guards battering down the door while with heart in mouth he scrambled up to the roof. Colonel Delacy and his sharpshooters were around the smoke hole, but holding their fire.

Two more steps and he saw McClure. He was coming up the ladder, using Benjie as a shield.

As he rose level with the rooftop and saw the aimed weapons, he put down the broadsword and, holding Benjie before him with both hands, came carefully out of the hole, protecting himself with the child. Richter called, "Let go of the kid, Greg," and McClure swiveled toward him. He shot a look down the ladder; below, the security guards were on the point of breaking through. Richter saw a ghastly grin spread across the moon-white face.

"But he's my bodyguard, Captain."

Richter held the revolver out before him with extended arms, gripped in two hands for maximum steadiness. He was aiming over Benjie's head; but, as Benjie struggled desperately to break free, his head kept bobbing into the gun sights. Richter was seeking an opening, gunpoint moving. Slowly, carefully, McClure bent his knees to pick up the broadsword—he was feeling around for it, knowing it was somewhere by his feet, all the time keeping his eye on the gun, and the child clamped to him. There was no line of fire that was safe while Benjie, terrified, was struggling with all his might within the arm's iron circle.

Richter saw McClure's searching hand find the broadsword. He

429

knew how fast Greg could move; there was no choice. He yelled, "Freeze, Benjie," and Benjie froze; and Richter, sighting over the child's still head, fired once and saw a sizable hole open in Greg's forehead just below the hairline. With the slackening of the iron grip, Benjie was just able to get clear of the large body as it toppled over into a muddled heap, like some huge, clumsy beast brought down.

TWENTY-ONE

There was tremendous relief on the hill that the mystery had been solved, the killer found and eliminated. Everybody could breathe again. The threat was over. The fact that it was a madman who had committed the murders, someone whose mind worked without rhyme or reason, made it easier to live with what had happened, to see the atrocities as vicious strokes of chance for which no one could be blamed.

But even after the case had been formally closed (which was done with dispatch—nobody wanted the inquiries to drag on) Richter kept it open in his own mind, and continued to ask questions. Being a man incorrigibly drawn by life's byways, he had conceived the need to pursue the thread of unreason—to see where it led. What had brought Greg McClure to his dreadful abyss? Tom Borneschaft was impatient with all such speculation—there was no figuring crazies; why, there were nuts who burned down old people's homes because they didn't like old people. No point asking why. Greg McClure had gone crazy, and that was all there was to it.

A predisposition to schizophrenic breakdown must have been present in McClure, the psychiatrists said; it must have been latent in him for many years, and something had brought it to fruition. You could never know what would do that. There was also a clear indication of religious mania. These two psychotic strands had interwoven with tragic consequences. That was their extrapolation,

431

and it was generally found acceptable. Richter did not disagree with it. But it seemed to him to leave questions unanswered, and in his stubborn way he continued to search the records. Security clearances. Psychological tests. Lie tests. Medical examinations. Questionnaires. Biogs. Reports. Testimonials. In none of it was there any hint of psychosis. He appeared to have led a blameless life before coming to the hill. The sort of investigations conducted when a man was recruited for the Secret Service—and being considered as a potential presidential bodyguard—were extensive and deep. Nothing had been found against him.

Yet this was the man who set up the accident that killed Jake Dubinski—in the light of later events that had now become clear to Richter. This was the man who, with some turns of a screw, sent Leo Hepler to his death, and intended to kill a lot of others at the same time. This was the man who had murdered the Jones children by ritual decapitation; had murdered their father by replacing a chemical extinguisher with a water extinguisher and turned him into a pillar of fire; had intended to kill Benjie; and was probably (though this had not yet been proved) responsible for at least a half-dozen other fatal accidents on the hill. The murders had all been coldly and cunningly planned and ruthlessly executed.

(Benjie's story was that the maid—one of the Xoaté Penitentes—had asked him to show her the hole in the fence, and he had taken her to it—the kids were all very proud of knowing the secret way out. As they got there McClure drove by in one of the Safety jeeps and offered to give them a lift. This, it turned out, was also the way the Jones children had been lured away.)

Even before he had personally spilled any blood (as far as anyone knew) Greg McClure had joined that weird sect of Penitentes at Xoaté, a village gone mad—a classic case of mass psychosis—and been present at a mock crucifixion in which the Christ figure was not cut down in time and died. The headman had proclaimed that to be a Sign. It was Easter, '43. A year later Jake died.

The village had been taken over in this way before, and the fact was that it had so declined over the years, for one reason or another, that the only people left there by then were the human

432

flotsam and jetsam. They were superstitious, uneducated, primitive, and they'd seen the fireball in the sky, and could be persuaded that all their misfortunes came from that.

Richter continued to dig, and bit by bit he was able to fill in more of Greg's past. Relatives, neighbors, friends, schoolmates of long ago were tracked down and asked to cast their minds back. It all went to confirm the general picture. He had been a good child, almost too good, some said. Weren't normal for a boy not to have no deviltry in him, one old-timer said. A big, strapping lad he was—tremendously strong; but always perfectly behaved, respectful, and courteous. It was remembered that unlike other boys he never complained, never sulked or moped. Did his work, and if he was told off for any reason he accepted the scolding without demur. He was not the brightest boy, but he tried. One of his teachers said you sometimes had the impression he wasn't entirely there, wasn't really listening to what was said to him—that he was daydreaming. But if challenged to repeat what the teacher had been saying, he usually knew—as if his mind was recording these things even when it was somewhere else. Just like a little saint he looked, somebody recalled. Somebody else remembered that he had oddly empty eyes, in which "nothing seemed to be going on." Always did what he was told, though—not one to be cheeky or a rebel.

His parents were good, simple people—his father worked as a janitor at an apartment building, his mother took in sewing. He was an only child. There was something that had happened when he was eight. A car accident. He'd stepped off the curb sideways, looking the wrong way, and been hit by a speeding car, a hit-and-run driver who was never found. Greg was in a coma for several days. They thought he was going to die. His Ma and Pa sat by his bedside night and day, talking to him. The doctors said that sometimes in such cases the voice of a loved person could reach into the dim half-world of unconsciousness and bring the unconscious person back out of his limbo. So they sat there talking to him all the time. When they were not doing that, they were on their knees praying to God to spare their little boy. They told God to take them instead, or to give them any task, no matter how arduous, if only He'd spare their baby. They told God that if He would spare Greg, Greg would live to revere and hallow His name all the days of his life. They promised it. After five days the boy came out of the coma. He told his parents that God had been watching over him the whole time and had heard their prayers.

Greg made a good recovery, and the doctors were satisfied that he had suffered no permanent brain damage. He was fine, it seemed; felt fine; and remembered his time of being suspended between life and death without a shudder. It was as if he'd been on a trip, and now he was back. "If God had of wanted to have took me, He would have, but He didn't," he'd say philosophically.

From that time on, there was definitely a sense of having a personal tie with God. It was just a private, deep-down feeling, and he wasn't mystical or cranky about it, and never tried to use this special connection. He was a very reticent boy. One thing it did, though, was to make him conscious of being in God's eye; and so he'd help others by, say, breaking up fights—and he had the size and strength to do it—or protecting smaller kids who were being bullied.

If character is destiny, Richter thought, then Greg seemed to have had the earlier part of his life all mapped out for him: law enforcement agencies, the Secret Service, White House protection detail, presidential bodyguard. But of the other part of his destiny there appeared to have been no forewarning. Unless . . . unless his exemplary goodness as a child was the forewarning. What child was so entirely good—didn't have some deviltry in him?

Richter was beginning to get a glimmering of how it must have come about. Those years of blameless clean living would have depended on an ability to keep his devils locked away—locked up in the deepest, darkest dungeons of his being. Where even God couldn't see them. He'd have had to make sure of that, since God was going to keep an eye on him always. That would have been the beginning of the split.

Yes, that was how Greg came to create all those secret compartments in his mind, in which, in the end, the ghastliest things could be hidden away. So that he could truthfully say that he had no knowledge of evildoing. It was always others who did those bad

434

things. The sadistic Spanish priests. The headmen. The fiscals and the constables. The witch-men who ate little children. The biggest bunch of crackpots, the generals. The controller. The Army. The government. America. It was all their doing. Sometimes it would be the gang of witches, practicing the evil crafts of their trade with chili seeds and broken glass and eye of toad, et cetera; and sometimes it would be the other side, God's gang of avenging angels, visiting the sins of the fathers upon the children. Greg must have been like an empty stage taken over first by one side and then the other.

Anyway, something like that must have been going on in him, Richter conjectured; it was not the final, definitive unraveling, but it was a working hypothesis, a way of looking at Greg McClure and what he had done.

But what did it add up to? Richter asked himself. Even if he had a glimmering of the steps and stages, as he now thought he had, in the end what it all amounted to was that Greg was mad. Greg's was a terrible world apart, not governed by the laws of reason. You could not relate it to the world in which the rest of them lived. So for all my searching, Richter thought, I have ended up at Tom Borneschaft's position, that you can't make sense out of craziness. Well, so be it. Now it was time to stop thinking about Greg; Greg was beginning to be an obsession. I must think about my future, Richter told himself, and stop running down every sidetrack I see.

It was a week or so after having made this resolve that a new batch of material about Greg arrived, relating to his school days. He was not going to get involved in all that again, Richter decided, and he put the bundle of papers aside. It was only months later, when he was clearing out his desk prior to leaving the hill, that he came upon some of Greg's old school reports. Not quite knowing what to do with them, he flicked quickly through the pages. He had been an average sort of pupil. Quite good in arithmetic and geography and physics . . . bad at French. The teachers' comments on his character and performance were in keeping with what others had said about him.

And then Richter came upon a comment that gave him pause,

written when Greg was eleven. It said: "McClure has had a fair year. He has made some slight progress in several subjects. It is surprising that he has not done better, because he is hardworking and conscientious. But he is inclined to be a bit of a chameleon. He is too readily influenced, with the result that his performance tends to be a reflection of whoever he's been involved with. He would need to develop more of a mind of his own."

By the time he had cleared up all that remained to be cleared up, made his final report, and handed it over to Colonel Delacy, Richter knew that the career of counterintelligence, for which he had revealed a certain surprising aptitude, was not for him. New byways beckoned.

Allison had already left with Benjie. He would join her in New York as soon as his successor arrived.

The doctor, too, had given his notice, having finally decided to accept an appointment at Yale. He was going to be a theoretician again. There was something in his nature that vacillated between the ivory tower and the tumult. Perhaps he had a premonition of tumult enough to come, and hoped to enjoy some peaceful years while he could.

Richter went down to the east gate to see him off.

As they were standing alone by the gate (Helen had gone back with the car to fetch something she had forgotten), Bamberger suddenly said, "I wanted to ask you, Richter. In that place—the place you found him with the children's bodies—I was told he'd written on the walls, 'I am become Death, the destroyer of worlds.' Is that right?"

"Yes."

Bamberger breathed deeply and slowly.

"Remember that time in the Security Office when he said about the danger I was in from some madman because of the things I was going around saying—that I might be giving somebody ideas?"

"Yes, I remember."

"You suppose there was a part of him that was trying to warn us?"

436

"Could be, Doctor."

"Did you ever figure it all out?"

"Not really. But he was someone without much sense of himself, so he took from what there was around him. That was part of it, I suspect."

"And what was around him was us."

"Yes."

Bamberger looked at the ugly sprawl of buildings that he was leaving, and up at the cloudless sky, and at the mountains, where the aspens were a gently quaking mass of dark gold.

"What a beautiful place in which to have done such an ugly thing," he said, drawing in the dry, sparkling air with finality. "I guess it had to be done. It's what I tell myself. I wish I could say it with more conviction."

Richter said nothing, and Bamberger looked at his watch with his old hurried air; though he was going to have plenty of time now, the habit of being in a hurry was not an easy one for him to break. "What the hell is Helen doing. Always mislaying things. Always having second thoughts. Chaotic woman . . ." He smiled, shook his head. "Anyway, Richter, I want to say to you, now that I'm going—there are no hard feelings on my part."

"I'm glad. I always admired you tremendously." He hesitated. "What made the job so difficult for me was—you were kind of a hero of science to me, like Galileo, or Louis Pasteur."

"I wish you wouldn't mock me, Richter."

"I am not mocking you, Doctor."

Helen returned in the car, and Bamberger got in beside her. He was looking very tired, Richter thought, but she was radiant—there was some continual exchange of energy between those two. Evidently she was going to drive. These days he sometimes let others drive. The pleasures of steering into the skid seemed to have diminished for him, and he was no longer seeking out such tests of his prowess. He was looking older, too, and quieter and less commanding.

Richter did not know what he was going to do next with his own life, but there was one project that rather interested him. A group of scientists who had worked on the bomb wanted to look

437

into the mystery of what had caused the dinosaurs to die out after 130 million years of world dominance. Richter could never resist a mystery—especially an insoluble one. An atomic scientist had conceived the idea that an asteroid could have struck the earth sixty-five million years ago and produced a cloud of dust so dense as to cast a total pall over the globe, preventing sunlight from getting through and thus halting the photosynthesis on which life depended. If this had continued for several years, following upon the elimination of chlorophyll in plant life, one after another creature in the chain of terrestrial interdependence would have become extinct (except for such sea creatures as could adapt to the new circumstances), and finally the dinosaur, too, would have died out. As their food supplies came to an end, some of them would have gone on a while longer by devouring each other.

It was, Richter thought, an interesting theory—if some evidence could be found. A quest for the pieces of a sixty-five-million-year-old puzzle was just the sort of thing to lure Richter. He could write some articles about the perennially interesting subject of dinosaurs and their extinction. The fact that a group of atomic bomb scientists were embarking upon this project gave it newsworthiness. So he was game to go. The first step was to take preliminary surveys in areas of the world where geological formations were such as to indicate that asteroids might have struck around the time they were postulating. The search could start next summer.